Ken Hughes was born in 1957 in Bethnal Green, East London, England. He married at 28 and has two sons, aged 33 and 36. He attended Morpeth Street School and John Scurr Primary. He enjoys sports, especially football, gold, and tennis, and did a lot of martial arts work in school.

This book has been dedicated to the following people:

My two sons, Marc and Scott,

My late wife Joan.

And my new daughter-in-law and granddaughter.

Also, to the Jack the Ripper Museum in London.

Ken Hughes

Jack the Ripper and the Whitechapel Murders

Austin Macauley Publishers™

LONDON * CAMBRIDGE * NEW YORK * SHARJAH

Copyright © Ken Hughes 2024

The right of Ken Hughes to be identified as author of this work has been asserted by the author in accordance with sections 77 and 78 of the Copyright, Designs and Patents Act 1988.

All rights reserved. No part of this publication may be reproduced, stored in a retrieval system, or transmitted in any form or by any means, electronic, mechanical, photocopying, recording, or otherwise, without the prior permission of the publishers.

Any person who commits any unauthorised act in relation to this publication may be liable to criminal prosecution and civil claims for damages.

This is a work of fiction. Names, characters, businesses, places, events, locales, and incidents are either the products of the author's imagination or used in a fictitious manner. Any resemblance to actual persons, living or dead, or actual events is purely coincidental.

A CIP catalogue record for this title is available from the British Library.

ISBN 9781398472075 (Paperback)
ISBN 9781398472082 (ePub e-book)

www.austinmacauley.com

First Published 2024
Austin Macauley Publishers Ltd®
1 Canada Square
Canary Wharf
London
E14 5AA

I would like to acknowledge Scott and Marc Hughes for their input in writing the book in the first place.

Table of Contents

Introduction   11
    Jack the Ripper   *11*
Chapter One: The Victims   13
    Victim 1-Mary Ann Nichols   *13*
    Victim 2-Annie Chapman   *18*
    Victim 3-Elizabeth Stride   *20*
    Victim 4-Catherine Eddowes   *22*
    Victim 5-Mary Jane Kelly   *24*
    Alleged Victims-Emma Elizabeth Smith   *27*
Chapter Two: The Whitechapel Murders   37
Chapter Three: The Contemporaneous Police Opinion   45
Chapter Four: Contemporaneous Press and Public Opinion   57
    Photos   *64*
    The Letters   *73*
Chapter Five: Suspects Proposed by Later Authors   74
Chapter Six: Officials Involved in the Murders   92
Chapter Seven: The Mary Ann Nichols Inquest   101
Chapter Eight: The Annie Chapman Inquest   111
Chapter Nine: The Elizabeth Stride Inquest   150
Chapter Ten: The Mary Jane Kelly Inquest   197
Chapter Eleven: The Martha Tabram Inquest   210
Chapter Twelve: The Alice McKenzie Inquest   216
Chapter Thirteen: The Catherine Eddowes Inquest   230
Chapter Fourteen: The Emma Smith Inquest   254
The Conclusion   258

Introduction

This book is not about saying who I think Jack the Ripper was, it is about finding what went on during the Whitechapel Murders, how did the police conduct their enquires, what were the witness views on what happened to the victims, were the witnesses telling the truth or just speaking for the sake of being involved in the cases. All the witnesses were just character witnesses telling what they thought of the victims and how they lived their lives before being murdered.

I hope it will give the reader some insight to the way people of the East End of London went about their daily lives in 1888, whether they were employed by a business or whether they were unfortunate to be on the wrong side of the law. Will I say who I think the killer is at the end of this book? Perhaps but hopefully after reading this book, reading the witness reports from the inquests and who other authors say was the Ripper, you will come to your own conclusions as to who Jack the Ripper was.

In 1888 in the East End of London, a place that was rife with violence and theft, it was also one of the poorest places in England. The East End was full of thugs, drunks and gangs; it was not a nice place to live in the 1800s. In April 1888, the first of 11 murders was to take place, these were to become known as the Whitechapel Murders and later become the Ripper murders, one of the unsolved murder mysteries for crime writers and sleuths to try and detect and name the one person, whom for over a century, has become a household name and a person to be known as:

Jack the Ripper

Jack the Ripper was a mysterious serial killer who roamed the streets of the Whitechapel area of the East End in London, England. Never to be caught, he outwitted the police from August to November 1888 before mysteriously disappearing, never to kill again.

The Ripper murders were committed by someone with exceptional knowledge of the human anatomy, who may have been suffering from schizophrenic tendencies. There are many theories about who he was and there were many suspects from lawyers to doctors to princes. The Whitechapel murders started in the early hours of 4 April 1888 with the murder of prostitute Emma Elizabeth Smith.

Five of the eleven Whitechapel murders were down to one person as the murders were committed in the same manner; of the other six murders, three were committed by gang violence or domestic violence and three are inclusive as to whether they were committed by Jack the Ripper as these killings were similar but not exact to the Ripper killings.

Chapter One
The Victims

Victim 1-Mary Ann Nichols

Born Mary Ann Walker on 26 August 1845 in Dawes Court, Shoe Lane, off Fleet Street. She was christened some years before 1851. At the time of her death, the East London Observer guessed her age at 30-35. At the inquest, her father said:

"She was nearly 44 years of age but it must be owned that she looked ten years younger. She was 5'2" tall, brown eyes, dark complexion, brown hair turning grey, five front teeth missing (Rumbelow), two bottom-one top front (Fido), her teeth were slightly discoloured. She was described as having small, delicate features with high cheekbones and grey eyes.

"She had a small scar on her forehead from a childhood injury. She was described by Emily Holland as 'a very clean woman who always seemed to keep to herself.' The doctor at the post mortem remarked on the cleanliness of her thighs. She was also an alcoholic."

Father: Edward Walker (Blacksmith, formerly a locksmith). He had grey hair and beard and as a smithy, was probably powerfully built. At the time of Polly's death, he was living at 16, Maidswood Rd, Camberwell.

Mother: Caroline. Polly married William Nichols on 16 January 1864. She would have been about 22 years old. The marriage was performed by Charles Marshall, Vicar of Saint Bride's Parish Church and witnessed by Seth George Havelly and Sarah Good. William Nichols was in the employ of Messrs. Perkins, Bacon & Co, Whitefriars Rd and living at Cogburg Rd off Old Kent Road at the time of his wife's death.

The couple had five children. Edward John, born 1866; Percy George, 1868; Alice Esther, 1870; Eliza Sarah, 1877 and Henry Alfred, born in 1879. The oldest, 21 in 1888, was living with his grandfather (Polly's father) at the time of her death. He had left home in 1880, according to his father, on his own accord.

The other children continued to live with Nichols. William and Polly briefly lodged in Bouverie Street then moved in with her father at 131, Trafalgar Street for about ten years. They spent six years (no dates) at No. 6, D block, Peabody Buildings, Stamford Street and Blackfriars Rd. There they were paying a rent of 5 shillings, 6 pence per week.

If Peabody Buildings was their last address, then they would have lived there from 1875-1881, with her father from 1865 to 1875. Polly separated from Nichols for the final time in 1881. It was the last of many separations during 24 years of marriage. In 1882, William found out that his wife was living as a prostitute and discontinued support payments to her. (Sugden: she is living with another man, probably Thomas Dew).

Parish authorities tried to collect maintenance money from him. He countered that she had deserted him, leaving him with the children. He won his case after establishing that she was living as a common prostitute. At the time of her death, he had not seen his wife in three years. Polly's father spread the story that the separation had come about due to William having an affair with the nurse who took care of Polly during her last confinement. William does not deny that he had an affair but states that it was not the cause of her leaving.

"The woman left me four or five times, if not six." He claims that the affair took place after Polly left. There is obvious disharmony in the family as the eldest son would have nothing to do with his father at his mother's funeral. After the separation, Polly begins a sad litany of moving from workhouse to workhouse. 24 April 1882 to 18 January 1883, she was at the Lambeth Workhouse, 18 January 1883 to 20 January 1883, then she stayed at the Lambeth Infirmary, and then on 20 January 1883 to 24 March 1883, she went back to the Lambeth Workhouse.

From 24 March 1883 to 21 May 1883, she was living with her father in Camberwell. He testifies at the inquest into her death that she was 'a dissolute character and drunkard whom he knew would come to a bad end.' He found her not a sober person but not in the habit of staying out late at night. Her drinking caused friction and they argued. He claims that he had not thrown her out but she left the next morning.

21 May 1883 to 2 June 1883, she went back to the Lambeth Workhouse. Then, on the 2 June 1883 to 26 October 1887, she is said to have been living with a man named Thomas Dew, a blacksmith with a shop in York Mews, 15 York St Walworth. In June 1886, she had attended the funeral of her brother who had

been burned to death by the explosion of a paraffin lamp. It was remarked by the family that she was respectably dressed.

25 October 1887, she spent one day in St Giles Workhouse, Endell Street. 26 October 1887 to 2 December 1887, she stayed at the Strand Workhouse, Edmonton; then from 2 December 1887 to 19 December 1887, back to the Lambeth Workhouse. On 2 December 1887, it is said that she was caught 'sleeping rough (in the open)' in Trafalgar Square. She was found to be destitute and with no means of sustenance and was sent on to Lambeth Workhouse.

19 November 1887 to 29 December 1887, again at the Lambeth Workhouse. 29 December 1887 to 1 April 1888, no record. Until 1 April 1888 to 16 April 1888, she stayed at the Mitcham Workhouse, Holborn and Holborn Infirmary. 16 April 1888-5 December 1888, a much longer period at the Lambeth Workhouse. It is in Lambeth Workhouse that she meets Mary Ann Monk, who eventually identified Polly's body for the police.

Monk was described as a young woman with a 'haughty air and flushed face.' Polly had another friend in the Lambeth Workhouse, a Mrs Scorer. She had been separated from her husband James Scorer, an assistant salesman in Spitalfields Market, for eleven years. He claimed that he knew Polly by sight but was unable to identify the body at the mortuary.

On 12th May, she left Lambeth to take a position as a domestic servant in the home of Samuel and Sarah Cowdry. This was common practice at the time for Workhouses to find domestic employment for female inmates. The Cowdry's lived at 'Ingleside', Rose Hill Rd, Wandsworth. Samuel, born in 1827, was the Clerk of Works in the Police Department. Sarah was one year younger than her husband, they were described as upright people. Both were religious and teetotallers. Polly writes her father:

"I just write to say you will be glad to know that I am settled in my new place and doing all right up to now. My people went out yesterday and have not returned, so I am left in charge. It is a grand place inside, with trees and gardens back and front. All has been newly done up. They are teetotallers and religious, so I ought to get on. They are very nice people and I have not too much to do. I hope you are all right and the boy has work. So, good bye for the present.

From yours truly,

Polly.

Answer soon, please and let me know how you are."

Walker replied to the letter but did not hear back. She worked for two months and then left while stealing clothing worth three pounds, ten shillings. 1 August 1888 to 2 August 1888, she was at the Gray's Inn Temporary Workhouse. Her last address was at Wilmotts Lodging House at 18 Thrawl Street, Spitalfields. There, she shared a room with four women including Emily Holland. The room was described as being surprisingly neat. The price of the room was 4d per night.

On 24 August 1888, Polly moved to a lodging house known as the White House at 56 Flower and Dean Street. In this doss-house, men are allowed to share a bed with a woman. Thursday, August 30th through Friday, 31 August 1888. Heavy rains have ushered out one of the coldest and wettest summers on record. On the night of August 30th, the rain was sharp and frequent and was accompanied by peals of thunder and flashes of lightning.

The sky on that night was turned red by the occasion of two dock fires. 11:00pm, Polly was seen walking down Whitechapel Road, she was probably soliciting trade. 12:30am, she was seen leaving the Frying Pan Public House at the corner of Brick Lane and Thrawl Street. She returned to the lodging house at 18 Thrawl Street, 1:20 or 1:40am. She is told by the deputy to leave the kitchen of the lodging house because she could not produce her doss money. Polly, on leaving, asks him to save a bed for her.

"Never mind!" She says, "I'll soon get my doss money. See what a jolly bonnet I've got now." She indicates a little black bonnet, which no one had seen before. 2:30am, she met Emily Holland, who was returning from watching the Shadwell Dry Dock fire, outside of a grocer's shop on the corner of Whitechapel Road and Osborn Street. Polly had come down Osborn Street. Holland describes her as 'very drunk and staggered against the wall.'

Holland called attention to the church clock striking 2:30. Polly told Emily that she had had her doss money three times that day and had drunk it away. She said she would return to Flower and Dean Street where she could share a bed with a man after one more attempt to find trade.

"I've had my doss money three times today and spent it." She says, "It won't be long before I'm back." The two women talk for seven or eight minutes. Polly left, walking east down Whitechapel Road.

PC Neil discovered Nichols' body in Buck's Row, from *Famous Crimes Past and Present*, 1903. With all of her faults, Nichols seems to have been well-liked by all who knew her. At the inquest her father said:
"I don't think she had any enemies, she was too good for that."
Death Certificate: No. 370, registered 25 September 1888.

Victim 2-Annie Chapman

Annie Chapman (born Eliza Ann Smith, 1841–8 September 1888) was a victim of the notorious unidentified serial killer Jack the Ripper, who killed and mutilated several women in the Whitechapel area of London from late August to early November 1888.

Annie Chapman was born Eliza Ann Smith. She was the daughter of George Smith of the 2nd Regiment Life Guards and Ruth Chapman. Her parents married after her birth, on 22 February 1842, in Paddington. Smith was a soldier at the time of his marriage, later becoming a domestic servant. On 1 May 1869, Annie married her maternal relative John Chapman, a coachman at All Saints Church in the Knightsbridge district of London. For some years, the couple lived at addresses in West London and they had three children.

Emily Ruth Chapman, born on 25 June 1870, Annie Georgina Chapman, born on 5 June 1873, John Alfred Chapman, born on 21 November 1880. In 1881, the family moved to Windsor, Berkshire where John Chapman took a job as coachman to a farm bailiff. But young John had been born disabled, while their firstborn, Emily Ruth, died of meningitis shortly after at the age of 12.

Following this, both Chapman and her husband took to heavy drinking and separated in 1884. By the time of her death, young John was said to be in the care of a charitable school and the surviving daughter Annie Georgina, then an adolescent, was travelling with a circus in the French Third Republic.

Annie Chapman eventually moved to Whitechapel, where in 1886 she was living with a man who made wire sieves; because of this, she was often known as Annie 'Sievey' or 'Siffey'. After she and her husband separated, she had received an allowance of 10 shillings a week from him but at the end of 1886, the payments stopped abruptly. On inquiring why they had stopped, she found her husband had died of alcohol related causes. The sieve maker left her soon after, possibly due to the cessation of her income.

One of her friends later testified that Chapman became very depressed after this and seemed to give up on life. Her friends called her 'Dark Annie', for her dark brown hair. By 1888, Chapman was living in common lodging houses in Whitechapel, occasionally in the company of Edward 'the Pensioner' Stanley, a bricklayer's labourer. She earned some income from crochet work, making antimacassars and selling flowers, supplemented by casual prostitution.

An acquaintance described her as 'very civil and industrious when sober' but noted 'I have often seen her, the worse for drink.' In the week before her death, she was feeling ill after being bruised in a fight with Eliza Cooper, a fellow resident in Crossingham's lodging house at 35 Dorset Street, Spitalfields. The two were reportedly rivals for the affections of a local hawker called Harry but Eliza claimed the fight was over a borrowed bar of soap that Annie had not returned.

Victim 3-Elizabeth Stride

Elizabeth 'Long Liz' Stride (née Gustafsdotter; 27 November 1843 to 30 September 1888) is believed to have been a victim of the notorious unidentified serial killer called Jack the Ripper, who killed and mutilated several women in the Whitechapel area of London from late August to early November 1888.

She was nicknamed 'Long Liz'. Several explanations have been given for this pseudonym; some believe it came from her married surname 'Stride' because a stride is a long step, while others believe it was either because of her height or the shape of her face. At the time of her death, she was living in a common lodging-house at 32 Flower and Dean Street, Spitalfields, within what was then a notorious criminal rookery.

Elizabeth Stride was born Elisabeth Gustafsdotter in the parish of Torslanda, west of Gothenburg, Sweden on 27 November 1843. She was the daughter of a Swedish farmer, Gustaf Ericsson and his wife, Beata Carlsdotter. In 1860, she took work as a domestic in the Gothenburg parish of Carl Johan, moving again in the next few years to other Gothenburg districts.

Unlike most other victims of the Whitechapel murders, who fell into prostitution due to poverty after a failed marriage, Stride took it up earlier. By March 1865, she was registered by the Gothenburg police as a prostitute, was treated twice for a sexually transmitted disease and gave birth to a stillborn girl on 21 April 1865.

The following year she moved to London, possibly in domestic service with a family. On 7 March 1869, she married John Thomas Stride, a ship's carpenter from Sheerness who was 13 years her senior and the couple for a time kept a coffee room in Poplar, East London. In March 1877, Liz Stride was admitted to the Poplar Workhouse, suggesting that the couple had separated. They had apparently reunited by 1881 but separated permanently by the end of that year.

She told acquaintances that her husband and two of her nine children had drowned in the sinking of the Princess Alice in the River Thames in 1878. In the accident according to her story, she had supposedly been kicked in the mouth by another of the victims as they both swam to safety, which had caused her to stutter ever since. In fact, John Stride died of tuberculosis in Poplar and Stepney Sick Asylum on 24 October 1884, more than five years after the Princess Alice disaster and they had no children.

After separating from her husband, Stride lived in a common lodging house in Whitechapel, with charitable assistance once or twice from the Church of Sweden in London and from 1885 until her death, lived much of the time with a local dock labourer, Michael Kidney in Devonshire Street. She earned some income from sewing and housecleaning work. An acquaintance described her as having a calm temperament, though she appeared at Thames Magistrates Court numerous times for being drunk and disorderly, giving her name as Anne Fitzgerald.

She learned to speak Yiddish in addition to English and Swedish. Her relationship with Kidney continued in an on and off fashion. In April 1887, she laid an assault charge against him but failed to pursue it in court. She left Kidney again a few days before her death. Dr Thomas Barnardo, a leading social reformer, claimed to have met Stride at the lodging house at 32 Flower and Dean Street on Wednesday, 26th September.

Victim 4-Catherine Eddowes

Catherine 'Kate' Eddowes (14 April 1842 to 30 September 1888) was one of the victims in the Whitechapel murders. She was the second person killed in the early hours of Sunday, 30 September 1888, a night which already had seen the murder of Elizabeth Stride less than an hour earlier. These two murders are commonly referred to as the 'double event' and have been attributed to the mysterious serial killer known as Jack the Ripper.

Eddowes, also known as 'Kate Conway' and 'Kate Kelly' after her two successive common-law husbands, was born in Graisley Green, Wolverhampton on 14 April 1842. Her parents, tinplate worker George Eddowes and his wife, Catherine (née Evans), had 10 other children. The family moved to London a year after her birth but she later returned to Wolverhampton to work as a tinplate stamper.

On losing this job, she took up with ex-soldier Thomas Conway in Birmingham; she moved to London with him and they had a daughter and two sons. She took to drinking and left her family in 1880; the following year she was living with new partner John Kelly at Cooney's common lodging house at 55 Flower and Dean Street, Spitalfields at the centre of London's most notorious criminal rookery. Here she took to casual prostitution to pay the rent.

To avoid contact with his former partner, Conway drew his army pension under the assumed name of Quinn and kept their sons' addresses secret from her. At the time of her death, she was described as being five feet tall, with dark auburn hair, hazel eyes and a tattoo that read 'TC', for Tom Conway, in blue ink on her left forearm. Friends of Eddowes described her as 'intelligent and scholarly but possessed of a fierce temper' and 'a very jolly woman, always singing.'

In the summer of 1888, Eddowes, Kelly and their friend Emily Birrell took casual work hop-picking in Kent. At harvest's end, they returned to London and quickly went through their pay. Eddowes and Kelly split their last sixpence between them; he took four pence to pay for a bed in the common lodging house and she took two pence, just enough for her to stay a night at Mile End Casual Ward in the neighbouring parish.

They met up the following morning, 29th September and in the early afternoon, Eddowes told Kelly she would go to Bermondsey to try to get some money from her daughter, Annie Phillips, who was married to a gun maker in Southwark. With money from pawning his boots, a bare-footed Kelly took a bed at the lodging house just after 8:00 pm and according to the deputy keeper, remained there all night.

Victim 5-Mary Jane Kelly

Mary Jane Kelly, 1863–9 November 1888, also known as Marie Jeanette Kelly, Fair Emma, Ginger and Black Mary, is widely believed to be the final victim of the notorious unidentified serial killer Jack the Ripper, who killed and mutilated several women in the Whitechapel area of London from late August to early November 1888. She was about 25 years old and living in poverty at the time of her death.

Compared with other Ripper victims, Kelly's origins are obscure and undocumented and much of it is possibly embellished. Kelly may have herself fabricated many details of her early life as there is no corroborating documentary evidence but there is no evidence to the contrary either. According to Joseph Barnett, the man she had most recently lived with prior to her murder, Kelly had told him she was born in Limerick, Ireland, in around 1863 although whether she referred to the city or the county is not known and that her family moved to Wales when she was young.

Barnett reported that Kelly had told him her father was named John Kelly and that he worked in an iron works in either Caernarfonshire or Carmarthenshire. Barnett also recalled Kelly mentioning having seven brothers and at least one sister. One brother, named Henry, supposedly served in the 2nd Battalion Scots Guards. She once stated to her friend Lizzie Albrook that a family member was employed at the London theatrical stage.

Her landlord, John McCarthy, claimed that Kelly received infrequent correspondence from Ireland. Both Barnett and a reported former roommate named Mrs Carthy claimed that Kelly came from a family of 'well-to-do people'. Carthy reported Kelly being 'an excellent scholar and an artist of no mean degree' but at the inquest, Barnett informed the coroner that she often asked him to read the newspaper reports of the murders to her, suggesting that she was illiterate.

Around 1879, Kelly was reportedly married to a coal miner named Davies, who was killed two or three years later in a mine explosion. She claimed to have stayed for eight months in an infirmary in Cardiff, before moving in with a cousin. Although there are no contemporary records of Kelly's presence in Cardiff, it is at this stage in her life that Kelly is considered to have begun her career as a prostitute.

In 1884, Kelly apparently left Cardiff for London and found work in a brothel in the more affluent West End of London. Reportedly, she was invited by a client to France but returned to England within two weeks, having disliked her life there. Nonetheless, it is believed to be at this stage in her life that Kelly chose to adopt the French name 'Marie Jeanette'.

Kelly had been variously reported as being a blonde or redhead, whereas her nickname, 'Black Mary', suggests a dark brunette. Her reported eye colour was blue. Reports of the time estimated her height at 5 feet and 7 inches (1.70 metres). Detective Walter Dew, in his autobiography, claimed to have known Kelly well by sight and described her as 'quite attractive' and 'a pretty, buxom girl'. He said she always wore a clean white apron but never a hat.

Sir Melville Macnaghten of the Metropolitan Police Force, who never saw her in the flesh, reported that she was known to have 'considerable personal attractions' by the standards of the time. The Daily Telegraph of 10 November 1888 described her as 'tall, slim, fair, of fresh complexion and of attractive appearance'. By some, Kelly had been known as 'Fair Emma', although it is unclear whether this reference applied to her hair colour, her skin colour, her beauty or whatever other qualities that she possessed.

Some newspaper reports claim she was nicknamed 'Ginger' after her allegedly ginger-coloured hair (though sources disagree even on this point, thus leaving a large range from ash blonde to dark chestnut). Another paper claimed she was known as 'Mary McCarthy', which may have been a mix up with the surname of her landlord at the time of her death. Gravitating towards the poorer East End of London, she reportedly lived with a man named Morganstone near the Commercial Gas Works in Stepney and later with a mason's plasterer named Joe Flemming.

When drunk, Kelly would be heard singing Irish songs; in this state, she would often become quarrelsome and even abusive to those around her, which earned her the nickname 'Dark Mary'. McCarthy said:

"She was a very quiet woman when sober but noisy when in drink." Barnett first met Kelly in April 1887. They agreed to live together on their second meeting the following day. In early 1888, they both moved into 13 Miller's Court, a furnished single room at the back of 26 Dorset Street, Spitalfields. It was a single twelve foot square room, with a bed, three tables and a chair. Above the fireplace hung a print of 'The Fisherman's Widow'.

Kelly's door key was lost, so she bolted and unbolted the door from outside by putting a hand through a broken window beside the door. A German neighbour, Julia Venturney, claimed Kelly had broken the window when drunk. Barnett worked as a fish porter at Billingsgate Fish Market but when he fell out of regular employment and tried to earn money as a market porter, Kelly turned to prostitution again.

A quarrel ensued over Kelly's sharing of the room with another prostitute whom Barnett knew only as 'Julia' and he left on 30th October, more than a week before her death, while continuing to visit Kelly.

Alleged Victims-Emma Elizabeth Smith

Although 45 years of age, a mother or two, a widower and a prostitute, Emma Smith is generally looked upon as something of a mystery. Her acquaintances gave her a much higher standing than others of her kind would have received and the events which were to lead to her death must still cause the casual reader to wonder at the absolute strength of this woman.

Emma claimed to have both a son and a daughter living somewhere in the area of Finsbury Park and was often heard to say that they should do something to help her situation. She had been a prostitute for some time now, at least since she last saw her husband (she claimed to have been a widow but also claimed she left her husband in 1877). Emma was also somewhat of a belligerent woman, often seen with a black eye and other various cuts and bruises as a result of many a drunken brawl.

She had been living at 18 George Street for about a year and a half, with a routine practically set in stone; she'd leave her lodgings between six and seven in the evening, practice her trade for the night and return in the small hours of the next morning. And so it went on Bank Holiday night, Easter Monday (3 April 1888) that she left around 6:00pm searching for trade. She was next seen by Margaret Hayes at around 12:15am talking to a man dressed in dark clothes and a white scarf in Fairance Street, Limehouse.

The next time she was seen was about four hours later, when she staggered into her lodgings at George Street, her face bloodied and her ear cut, with her woollen shoulder wrap pressed between her thighs to clog the injury, which would later lead to her death.

As she would later report, she was returning home that night, probably the worse for drink, when at least three, maybe four youths followed her from Whitechapel Church. They stopped her on the corner of Brick Lane and Wentworth Street, where they beat, raped and viciously jabbed a blunt object into her vagina, tearing the perineum.

The boys emptied her purse before leaving her to die on the street. Here is where the story becomes incredible. Having just been beaten and raped and having sustained a sizeable (and no doubt excruciatingly painful) injury, Emma Smith stood up and walked back to her lodgings at 18 George Street. She had apparently removed her shoulder wrap and placed it between her thighs to soak up the blood, which had undoubtedly been flowing from her ripped perineum.

The lodging house deputy, Mary Russell and lodger Annie Lee, amazed that she could even have made it this far, rushed her to the London Hospital on Whitechapel Road, apparently against Emma's will. Once there, she was seen by George Haslip, the house surgeon and she fought unconsciousness long enough to describe her assailants and the details of her assault. Finally, Emma could no longer stave off the severity of her injuries and succumbed to a coma, in which she would die four days later.

It is believed by most that it was one of the many Whitechapel gangs which killed Emma Smith and not the Ripper. 'High rip' gangs were known to patrol the area in which the incident occurred, extorting money from prostitutes and other downtrodden women in return for their protection. In fact, it wasn't until September of 1888 that she was first attributed as a Ripper victim by the press. Emma's death is also important in that many believe it may have been a contributing factor in the creation of the mythical 'Fairy Fay' murder (if indeed, it is taken to have been a mythical murder).

Some authors note that 'Fairy Fay' was said to have been killed by a stake jabbed into her abdomen much like Emma was killed by a blunt object stabbed into her vagina. Therefore, many claim it was the means of Emma's murder combined with the date of Rose Mylett's death which led to the creation of the 'Fairy Fay' murder.

Whether or not Emma's death should be attributed to the Ripper is a question responded to in the negative by almost all Ripperologists. There is no reason to doubt her story that she was attacked by three (or four) men and no other Ripper victim (except for the possibility of Stride, according to Israel Schwartz's account) was believed to have been killed by more than one man. Also, the fact that she was raped is not consistent with the other Ripper victims.

In fact, to accept Emma as a veritable victim, one must accept that the Ripper was either part of a group at one time or even part of a gang. Unfortunately, there is little evidence to back this theory.

Martha Tabram

A.k.a. Martha Tabran, Emma Turner.

Born: Martha White, 10 May 1849, at 17 Marshall Street, London Rd, Southwark.

Father: Charles Samuel White, a warehouseman.

Mother: Elisabeth (Dowsett).

Brothers: Henry (twelve years older than Martha), Stephen (8 years older).

Sisters: Esther (10 years older), Mary Ann (3 years older).

Martha's parents separated and in May of 1865, Charles was lodging alone in the house of Mrs Rebecca Glover. The house was located at 31 Pitt Street, St George's Row. His health was questionable, he suffered severe diarrhoea in October and a surgeon was called to examine him. The surgeon found him troubled by his familiar situation and complaining of bad circulation and cold.

According to his daughter Mary Ann, he also stated that he had a weak back and was unable to work. On October 11th his estranged wife, Elisabeth, visited him for the first time since their separation. Over the next few days, she visited often and on the evening of November 15th, both she and her daughter Mary Ann had supper at his lodging. The meal consisted of bread butter and beer. According to his landlady, Mrs Grover, he was cheerful that evening.

At approximately 10:00pm, he rose to go to bed and while removing his waistcoat, he fell to the floor and died. As there was no evidence of anything suspicious, the death was ruled as coming from natural causes. He was 59 years old. On Christmas Day, 1869, Martha married Henry Samuel Tabram at Trinity Church in St Mary's Parish, Newington. He was a foreman furniture packer. A short well-dressed man with iron grey hair, moustache and imperial. They had already been living together in Pleasant Place and moved to 20 Marshall Street in February 1871. The new house was very near by the house in which Martha was born.

Martha had two sons by the marriage, Frederick John, born in February 1871 and Charles Henry, born in December of 1872. The marriage ended in 1875. Henry left due to Martha's heavy drinking. He gave her an allowance of twelve shillings per week for three years but reduced it to 2s 6d due to her pestering him in the streets for money. She had a warrant taken out against him and had him locked up. He had also learned that she was living with another man.

At this time, he refused to support her any further. Henry Turner was a carpenter with whom Martha lived, off and on, for twelve years. He is described as a short, dirty man who dressed in a slovenly manner. He was young and had a pale face, light moustache and imperial. Their relationship also appears to have been greatly affected by Martha's drinking. Turner stated at the inquest into her death:

"Since she has been living with me, her character for sobriety was not good. If I give her money, she generally spent it in drink." Martha was in the habit of staying out late at night, usually not returning before 11:00pm and occasionally staying out all night. Her excuse was usually that she had been taken with hysterical fits and had been taken to the police station. Turner had witnessed these fits and stated that they usually came about due to drunkenness.

In 1888, Turner was out of regular employment and making his living hawking cheap trinkets, menthol cones and needles and pins. The couple lodged in the house of Mrs Mary Bousfield at 4 Star Place, Commercial Road. Bousfield described Martha as a person who would 'rather have a glass of ale than a cup of tea.' She also said, however, that she was not a perpetual drunk.

The couple left their lodgings without notice and behind in the rent, approximately 4 to 6 weeks prior to the murder. Perhaps out of guilt, Martha secretly returned one night and left the key to the lodging without seeing the landlady. Turner left Martha for the last time in July of 1888. At the time of her death, he was living at the Victoria working man's home on Commercial Street.

She tried to carry on earning a living through selling trinkets and prostitution. It is very likely that whatever small amount of money she made was spent on drink. Indeed, Turner is quoted as saying:

"If I gave her money, she generally spent it on drink. In fact it was always drink. When she took to drink, however, I usually left her to her own resources, and I can't answer to her conduct then."

Her last known address was 19 George Street, Spitalfields (known as Satchell's Lodging House). Turner saw a destitute Martha for the last time on Leadenhall Street, near Aldgate pump on 4 August 1888. He gave her 1s 6d to buy trinkets for trade with which she might earn some sort of living.

On Bank Holiday Monday, August 6th, Martha went out with Mary Ann Connelly, who was known as 'Pearly Poll'. They were seen throughout the evening in pubs in the company of a soldier or soldiers. According to Pearly Poll, she and Martha picked up two guardsmen, a Corporal and a Private in the Two Brewers public house and drank with them in several pubs including the White

Swan on Whitechapel High Street. Discovery of the body of Martha Tabram, from Famous Crimes Past and Present, 1903.

Sometime around 11:45pm, Martha and Pearly Poll went separate ways. Martha with the Private into George Yard and Pearly Poll and the Corporal into Angel Alley. Both, obviously, for the purpose of having sex. 1:50am, Elizabeth Mahoney returned to her home in George Yard Buildings. At the time that she ascended the stairs to her flat, she saw no one or anything unusual in the building.

2:00am, PC Thomas Barrett saw a young Grenadier Guardsman in Wentworth Street, the north end of George Yard. Barrett questioned his reason for being there and was told by the Guardsman that he was waiting for a 'chum who went off with a girl'.

3:30am, Alfred Crow returned to his lodging in George Yard Buildings and noticed what he thought was a homeless person sleeping on the first floor landing. As this was not an uncommon occurrence, he continued on to bed. John Reeves left his lodgings in the George Yard Buildings at 4:45am. By this time, the light was improving inside the stairwell. Reeves also noticed the body on the first floor landing but he was also aware that it was lying in a pool of blood. Reeves went off to find a policeman.

He returned with PC Barrett. Although not yet identified, the body was that of Martha Tabram. The body was supine with the arms and hands by the side. The fingers were tightly clenched and the legs open in a manner to suggest that intercourse had taken place. Others who testified at the inquest include Francis Hewitt, the Superintendent of George Yard Buildings and Mrs Mary Bousfield (also known as Luckhurst) and Martha's former landlady at 4 Star Street.

The Post-Mortem: The post-mortem examination of Martha Tabram was held by Dr Timothy Killeen (also spelled Keeling or Keleene) at 5:30am on the morning of August 7th. Tabram was described as a plump middle-aged woman, about 5'3" tall, dark hair and complexion. The time of death was estimated at about three hours before the examination (around 2:30-2:45am). In all, there were thirty-nine stab wounds including.

Alice McKenzie
a.k.a. 'Clay Pipe' Alice, Alice Bryant

Little is known of Alice McKenzie's early years and upbringing, except that she was born sometime around 1849 and was said to have been raised in Peterborough. She was later to move into the East End of London sometime before 1874 and began living sporadically with a John McCormack (also Bryant) around 9 years later in 1883. According to a press article:

McCormack told an interviewer on Thursday that he first knew the deceased woman in London about seven years ago. She had not a friend in this city but he believed she had a son, probably in America. Before he became acquainted with her, she lived with a blind man who played a concertina in the streets for a living. McCormack 'took up' with her because she was homeless and appeared to be a hardworking woman.

He had often heard her say she was the last of her family and had heard her speak of her father, who was a postman in Liverpool. McCormack never saw any of her relations. For several years, he served in the army and took part in the Crimean war, after which he was invalided and received a pension for eighteen months.

McCormack, an Irishman, was in the employ of some Jewish tailors in Hanbury Street as a porter. He shared lodgings in various doss-houses with his common-law wife for around six years and their last cohabitation was at Mr Tenpenny's Lodging House, Gun Street, and Spitalfields. They moved there around April of 1888.

The lodging house on Gun Street was managed by a Mrs Elizabeth Ryder, wife of Richard John Ryder. While there, McKenzie was said to have worked for her Jewish neighbours as a washerwoman and charwoman but the police considered her a common prostitute and she was known to have frequented the streets on occasion. At this time, Alice was around 40 years of age, described as a freckle-faced woman with a penchant for both smoke and drink, engaging more in the former than the latter.

She preferred the smoke of a pipe, which was soon to grant her the name 'Clay Pipe' Alice by her friends and acquaintances. Her left thumb was also injured in what was no doubt some sort of industrial accident.

Tuesday, 16 July 1889, 4:00pm. McCormack returns from his morning shift at work somewhat drunk and sets himself down in bed. He hands Alice 1s.8d to pay Mrs Ryder for the rent and a shilling to spend for other necessities. Alice left the room with the money but did not pay the rent.

7:10pm; according to the Pall Mall Gazette, Alice took a blind boy named George Dixon or Discon, another resident at Mr Tenpenny's, to the Royal Cambridge Music Hall. Dixon would later testify that he had heard Alice speaking to a strange man, asking him to buy her a drink, to which the man replied:

"Yes."

Alice then saw Dixon home to Gun Street. 8:30pm; Elizabeth Ryder sees Alice at the house, 'more or less drunk' and watches her leave Gun Street after having had some sort of argument with McCormack (this would negate his statement that the last time he saw Alice alive would have been 4:00pm).

11:00pm; McCormack emerges from the room and precedes downstairs, passing Mrs Ryder who informs him that Alice had indeed not paid their rent. 11:40pm; a friend of Alice's named Margaret Franklin was sitting with two acquaintances (Catherine Hughes and Sarah Mahoney or Marney) on the step of either a barber's shop (Sugden) or a lodging house (Begg et alia) on Flower and Dean Street at the side connecting with Brick Lane.

Alice passed the three ladies 'walking hurriedly' towards Whitechapel. Margaret asked Alice how she was doing and she replied in the same hurried manner:

"All right. I can't stop now." According to the three ladies, Alice was not wearing a bonnet but rather a 'light coloured shawl' around her shoulders. 12:15pm; P.C. Joseph Allen (423H) takes a break under a street lamp in Castle Alley, just off Whitechapel High Street, for a bite to eat. According to Allen, the alley was completely deserted. After about five minutes, Allen notices another constable entering the alley.

12:20am, Walter Andrews (PC 272H) enters Castle Alley just as Allen is leaving. Andrews remains in the alley for about three minutes and again he sees nothing of a suspicious nature. 12:25am around about this time, Sarah Smith, deputy of the Whitechapel Baths and Washhouses (which lined Castle Alley) retires to her room. She begins reading in bed, the closed window of her room overlooking the entire alley. Sarah later testifies she heard nothing suspicious until she heard the blow of Andrews' whistle at 12:45am. It begins to rain in Whitechapel.

12:50 am, Andrews returns to Castle Alley on his regular beat, about 27 minutes having passed since he left the area. This time, however, he discovers the body of a woman lying on the pavement, her head angled towards the curb and her feet towards the wall. Blood flowed from two stabs in the left side of her neck and her skirts had been lifted, revealing blood across her abdomen, which had been mutilated.

The pavement beneath the body of Alice McKenzie was still dry, placing her death sometime after 12:25am and before 12:45am when it began to rain. In her possession were found a clay pipe often referred to as a 'nose warmer' and a bronze farthing. She was noticed to have been wearing some 'odd stockings.' P.C. Andrews heard someone approaching the alley soon after and ordered the man (Lewis Jacobs) to stay with the body while he went to fetch help.

1:10am, Inspector Edmund Reid arrives only moments before Dr George Bagster Phillips. Reid notices that blood continues to flow from the throat into the gutter (about 1:09am) but it begins to clot upon the arrival of Phillips (about 1:12am). On a side note, a fellow prostitute and companion of McKenzie's named Margaret Cheeks, was also thought to have been killed along with Alice because she was not to be found for two days following the discovery of McKenzie's body.

Actually, she had been staying with her sister at the time. Cause of her death was from severance of the left carotid artery. Two stabs in the left side of the neck 'carried forward in the same skin wound'. Some bruising on her chest. Five bruises or marks on left side of abdomen. Cut was made from left to right, apparently while McKenzie was on the ground. A long (seven-inch 'but not unduly deep' wound from the bottom of the left breast to the navel.)

Seven or eight scratches beginning at the naval and pointing towards the genitalia. Small cut across the mons veneris, Dr Phillips believed there was a degree of anatomical knowledge necessary to have committed the atrocities to McKenzie. The severing of the left carotid artery is consistent with previous Ripper murders, although the canonical five were murdered with much deeper and longer injuries, which cut down to the spinal column.

McKenzie suffered only two jagged wounds on the left side which were no longer than four inches a piece and had left the air passages untouched. The bruises on the chest region suggested the killer probably held her down to the ground with one hand while inflicting the wounds with the other.

The mutilations committed upon McKenzie were mostly superficial in manner, the deepest of which opened neither the abdominal cavity nor the muscular structure. The wounds also suggested that the killer was left-handed (as opposed to the Ripper being right-handed). Phillips suggested the five marks on the left side of her body were an imprint of the killer's right hand, which left only his left hand to facilitate the injuries.

Dr Bond disagreed, claiming there was no evidence to support the theory that those marks were made through such processes (admittedly, Bond saw the body the day after the post mortem and it had already begun to decompose). The weapon involved was agreed upon to have been a 'sharp-pointed weapon,' although it could be smaller than the one used by the Ripper. Phillips ultimately claimed that McKenzie's death was not attributable to the Ripper.

After careful and long deliberation, I cannot satisfy myself, on purely anatomical and professional grounds that the perpetrator of all the 'Whitechapel murders' is our man. I am on the contrary impelled to a contrary conclusion in this noting the mode of procedure and the character of the mutilations and judging of motive in connection with the latter.

I do not here enter into the comparison of the cases neither do I take into account what I admit may be almost conclusive evidence in favour of the one man theory if all the surrounding circumstances and other evidence are considered, holding it as my duty to report on the P.M. appearances and express an opinion only on professional grounds, based upon my own observation.

Dr Thomas Bond chose the opposite conclusion, telling Sir Robert Anderson he believed it was indeed a Ripper killing: I see in this murder evidence of similar design to the former Whitechapel murders, viz. sudden onslaught on the prostrate woman, the throat skilfully and resolutely cut with subsequent mutilation, each mutilation indicating sexual thoughts and a desire to mutilate the abdomen and sexual organs. I am of opinion that the murder was performed by the same person who committed the former series of Whitechapel murders.

Anderson himself disagreed, writing: I am here assuming that the murder of Alice McKenzie on 17 July 1889, was by another hand. I was absent from London when it occurred but the Chief Commissioner investigated the case on the spot and decided it was an ordinary murder and not the work of a sexual maniac. Monro, who was on duty during the investigation since Anderson was on leave at the time, disagreed.

I need not say that every effort will be made by the police to discover the murderer, who I am inclined to believe is identical with the notorious Jack the Ripper of last year. In fact, on the day of the murder, Monro deployed 3 sergeants and 39 constables on duty in Whitechapel, increasing the force with 22 extra men. The inquest was held on July 17th and 19th and later adjourned to August 14th, the conclusion was the all too familiar 'murder by a person or persons unknown.'

The Scotland Yard Files pertaining to the McKenzie murder detail, an interesting sidebar concerning an individual named William Wallace Brodie, who confessed to murdering the woman. It was earlier printed in the Kimberley Advertiser of 29 June 1889 that Brodie had confessed to all the Whitechapel murders while in a drunken stupor. His statement was forwarded by Inspector Moore but Inspector Arnold gave instructions to dismiss Brodie as of unsound mind.

Scotland Yard gave the same prognosis: "Let him be charged as a lunatic." It was soon discovered that Brodie had a conviction for larceny and just to be sure, enquiries were made into his character and location during the Whitechapel Murders. It was found that he was in South Africa between 6 September 1888 and 15 July 1889. Ultimately, Brodie was released from custody but was almost immediately rearrested for fraud.

Chapter Two
The Whitechapel Murders

On 4 April 1888 following the Easter bank holiday on Monday, prostitute Emma Elizabeth Smith was assaulted and robbed at the junction of Osborne Street and Brick Lane in the Whitechapel area of the East End of London in the early hours of the morning. Although she was seriously injured, she survived the attack and managed to walk back to her lodging house in George Street.

There she told the deputy keeper Mary Russell that she had been attacked by two or three men, one of which was a youth. During her assault, she was beaten and raped, after which a blunt object was violently inserted into her vagina. Mary Russell took Emma to the London Hospital Whitechapel, where she had an examination which revealed that a blunt object had been inserted into her vagina rupturing her peritoneum.

It was then she developed a peritonitis injury which would take her life the following day. Local Metropolitan Police Inspector Edmund Reid of H division Whitechapel would lead the investigation into the attack but the culprits were never caught. Prostitutes were often managed by gangs and it was the thought of Detective Constable Walter Dew also stationed at H division that Emma Smith may have been the victim of her pimp as a punishment for disobeying him.

This would seem unlikely as to cause serious harm to a prostitute in their command would lose them money. It may have been the attack of an opposing gang, as gangs were rife in Whitechapel at the time and violence was a regular occurrence. Or it was just an assault by random thugs looking for easy money and prostitutes were easy prey.

On 7 August 1888 again following a Monday bank holiday, another murder took place, this time it was another prostitute by the name of Martha Tabram, aged 39 who also lived at lodgings in George Street. Tabram was murdered around 2.30am. Her body was found at George Yard Buildings, George Yard Whitechapel, she had been stabbed 39 times with a short blade.

Tabram and another unfortunate acquaintance of Tabram were out drinking with two soldiers at a public house near George Yard shortly before midnight on the 6th August. Tabram and her friend paired off with their clients, Tabram headed through an archway into George Yard onto Wentworth Street. Tabram's body was first seen around 3.30am by cart man George Crow, he had been returning home from work and because it was so dark on the stairwell, he mistook her body as that of a drunken woman passed out on the landing.

At around 5.30am, her body was again discovered by another resident but the light was much better this time and it was enough to reveal her ghastly wounds. The wounds focused on her throat abdomen and chest, her wounds seem to have been created by a pocket knife with the exception of one violent stab wound through her chest, this looked to be inflicted by a larger knife like a dagger or a bayonet. From statements of other prostitutes and a Police Constable Thomas Barrett who was patrolling nearby, Inspector Reid put soldiers at the Tower of London and at the Wellington Barracks on an identification parade which proved to be a negative result.

The Police did not connect the deaths of Tabram and Smith but they did connect them with later murders. Today, these two murders were ruled out as Ripper murders due to the fact that Tabram and Smith were stabbed, whereas the Ripper victims were slashed not stabbed. However in 1888, the term serial killer had not been coined yet, even though crime was always around in Whitechapel, where most murders were carried out by gangs or domestic violence, crimes referring to ripping consisted of robberies, revenge killings or just random violence to keep the public fearing them.

Police were very limited to investigative techniques as forensic investigation was almost non-existent, relying mostly on medical investigations to determine the cause of death. Even results from autopsies were cause for disagreement between medical professionals and coroners; at the time, coroners were elected officials who sometimes had no medical background at all. Fingerprinting technology was not even invented then. Fingerprinting techniques was not invented until the 20th century.

Police could only catch perpetrators by eliciting confessions from murderers or to catch them in the act. Failure to catch criminals, especially ones like Jack the Ripper, led to intense criticism from the tabloids competing in London at the time, scathing articles were released on a daily basis to mock the futile efforts of the London Police.

The main target for the press was Police Commissioner Sir Charles Warren, who was maligned in the press for his role in the Bloody Sunday in 1887 a year before the Whitechapel murders started. Warren made several unpopular decisions in the handling of the Ripper case. The Police had already loaded the streets with plain clothes officers and more beat constables but were still unable to catch any killers or robbers in the act of committing crimes.

During the Ripper murders, there were around eighty suspects. But narrowed down to twenty nine. Suspect number one was Montague John Druitt Born in August 1857; at the time of the murders, he would have been 31 years old. Druitt was born in Wimbourne Minster, Dorset. He came from a middle class English background and studied at Winchester College and the University of Oxford. While at Winchester College, he won a scholarship at the age of thirteen years old.

He was excellent at sport and Cricket being his favoured sport. Druitt was active in the schools debating society, an interest that may have inspired him to become a barrister. Druitt spoke in debates and in favour of compulsory military service and the resignation of Disraeli, he also condemned the execution of King Charles 1, according to Druitt this was a most dastardly murder. In his final year at Winchester 1875-1876, he became prefect of Chapel treasurer of the debating society, he was the school fives champion and opening bowler for the cricket team.

Druitt was awarded a Winchester Scholarship to new college Oxford. While at Oxford, he became popular with his peers and was elected steward to the Junior Common room. Druitt gained a second class in Classical Moderations in 1878 and graduated with a third class Bachelor of Arts degree in Classics in 1880. In May 1882, two years after graduating Druitt was admitted to the Inner Temple, this is one of the qualifying bodies for the English Barristers. Druitt was promised a legacy of £500 from his father.

This allowed Druitt to pay for his fees with a loan from his father secured against his inheritance. He was called to the baron on 29 April 1885 and set up a practice as a barrister and special pleader. Druitt never lived in the East End, he lived in Blackheath, south of the river Thames. Also, Druitt never entered into the world of medicine even though his father was a practicing doctor as well as a lawyer.

To help pay for his training and to supplement his income, Druitt worked as an assistant schoolmaster at George Valentine's boarding school at 9 Eliot Place

Blackheath. Druitt was found dead, his body floating in the river Thames on 30 November 1888; this would dismiss Druitt as one of the Ripper suspects.

John Pizer or Piser was another suspect as being the Ripper, he lived in Mulberry Street. He was a Jewish boot finisher and better known as a Leather Apron due to his line of work as a boot finisher, it was reported after the Mary Ann Nichols murder that the police were looking for a Leather Apron who had been ill-treating prostitutes in the area.

According to a star reporter, at least fifty women described the man mistreating them as five feet four inches tall and wears a dark close fitting cap, he is thick set with an unusually thick neck, his hair is black and closely clipped, he is aged between 30-40 with a small black moustache, he is said to have an expression as sinister, his eyes were small and glittering, his lips were usually parted in a grin, he always carried a knife.

Sergeant William Thick had known Pizer for 18 years and knew people speaking of Leather Apron, it was Pizer they were talking about. Thick went to Mulberry Street shortly after 8am on 10 September 1888, to fetch Pizer. Pizer had been laying low in Mulberry Street after advice from his brother. Pizer believed that he would be grabbed by angry mobs searching for Leather Apron. Sergeant Thick took Pizer to Leman Street Police Station for questioning about the murder of Mary Ann Nichols; his alibi was confirmed by his brother and other relatives.

It is understood that Pizer never knew he was known as Leather Apron as he had recently been out of work. Pizer was soon cleared of the murder of Mary Ann Nichols after witness statements confirmed that on the night of her murder, Pizer was in fact in North London staying at the Crossman's Lodging House in Holloway Road. At 1.30am, Pizer had spoken to a policeman about the London docks fire which he went to see, the fire had broken out at 8.30 at one of the warehouses, the fire could be seen for miles around, it was around 11 o'clock before it was under control but not fully extinguished until several hours later.

Pizer returned to Crossman's Lodging about 2.15am, he paid his 4d for his bed and sat in the kitchen smoking a clay pipe. Pizer died of gastroenteritis at the London hospital in July 1897. Now, two suspects who were thought to be the Ripper are dead leaving the Police to think again about who was doing the murders in Whitechapel.

Rose Mylett was murdered on 20 December 1888, Mylett also went under the names of Catherine Millett and Lizzie Davis, aged just 29 years old. She was strangled in Clarkes Yard off Poplar High Street, Mylett would lodge at 18 George Street as did Emma Smith. Four doctors who examined Mylett's body believed she had been murdered but Robert Anderson thought she had accidently hanged herself on the collar of her dress while in a drunken stupor, at the request of Robert Anderson, Dr Bond was asked to examine the body and he agreed with Anderson.

Commissioner Munro also suspected it was suicide or natural causes as there was no sign of a struggle. The Coroner, Wynne Baxter told the Inquest Jury that there is no evidence to show that the death was the result of violence. Nevertheless, the Jury's verdict was wilful murder against a person or persons unknown. As a result of this, the case was added to the Whitechapel files.

With the verdict being returned like this, it made the police's job more harder into finding the murderer in Whitechapel, to return a verdict of wilful murder when the evidence was easy to see that there was no sign of violence or a struggle it would suggest that Mylett could have killed herself either accidently or suicide. For sure, Mylett was not a Ripper victim. The Ripper murders took place between August and November 1888. Mylett died after the last Ripper murder.

Mary Nichols' murder was on 31 August 1888. Again, the Police were helpless as to who committed the crime, no clues were left, no witnesses to see the murder and plenty of people falsely accused of the murder and many witness testimonies were fabricated, leading the police to many a false leads and plenty of man hours wasted following these false leads. Local folk were blaming the police for not being able to catch the killer, yet it was the local people, who by giving the police extra work to do by following false leads and folk, wasting police time it was no wonder they were getting nowhere.

Because of the area, a deprived place in the East End of London, villains would gather there to commit all sorts of crimes; this was mainly violence on prostitutes performed by rival gangs and prostitute's pimps, to keep prostitutes in fear of them and to do as they were told. Women in the 1880s led an awful life mostly in squalor for the underprivileged.

Later on in this book, you will see how prostitute's lived their lives. It is said that the Ripper was a man of intelligence and good upbringing. This would be because of his knowledge of the human anatomy. Seeking most theorists to believe he was a doctor, if he was of a good education and upbringing then the letters that were sent to the police were false as there are plenty of signs that they were written by an non educated person or an educated person writing the letters in a way the police would believe he was an uneducated person.

On 8 September 1888, another murder would take place. Annie Chapman was found dead in Hanbury Street, Spitalfields. Chapman was once married to John Chapman, an ex-soldier had three children, two girls and a boy. Life became hard for Chapman after the death of her daughter aged only 12 years old of meningitis and her son being born disabled, both John and Ann took to drinking heavily and separated in 1884.

Chapman moved to Whitechapel in 1886 and lived with a wire sieve maker. Chapman received 10 shillings a week from her husband but the payments stopped in 1886, when inquired as to why the payments stopped, she found out that her husband died of alcohol related causes. By 1888, Chapman was selling flowers and doing the casual bit of prostitution.

On 30 September 1888, Catherine Eddowes and Elizabeth Stride were both attacked and murdered, both believed to be the victims of The Ripper, as to why he would commit two murders in one night is still a mystery, it is believed he was disturbed before he could finish his ghastly deeds on Elizabeth Stride, the attack took place at Dutfields Yard, off Berner Street, Catherine Eddowes was found about an half a mile away in Mitre Square.

In one of the Ripper letters, it is said that the next victim would lose part of an ear which was the case, so it may have been planned to murder two women on the same night. It would have taken The Ripper around 7-10 minutes to walk half a mile, if he ran it would have taken around 5-7 minutes depending how old he was, how fit he was and if he was carry a bag or blade in his pockets as he would have to keep them from dropping onto the ground.

During this time, he would have also had to keep out of the light and away from other people in fear of someone seeing him; if he was able to run that far without being seen, I would imagine that he would have been out of breath as jogging and keeping fit in 1888 was a thing of the future, not only that someone running in the early hours of the morning being seen would arouse suspicion amongst other people around the area.

So from this, I dismiss he ran the half mile to Mitre Square but walked and well-hidden keeping mostly in the dark and away from people, was it just a coincidence that he met Catherine Eddowes and was it frustration from being interrupted after killing Elizabeth Stride only half a mile away that he took his anguish out on Eddowes. I believe it was a case of wrong place wrong time for Catherine and that she was taken by surprise by the killer.

He would have worn soft soled shoes as not to make too much noise while walking on the cobbled roads and pavement. This is one of the reasons the police were badgering about wearing boots and walking in them would alert criminals of their presence. Entering into Mitre Square took Jack into the precinct of the City Police, so now there are two police forces looking for him, the City Police and the Metropolitan Police.

Now, what was needed to know was the Ripper interrupted while he murdered Elizabeth Stride or did he go out intent on killing two women on the same night edging his chances of not getting caught, whichever the reason for killing two women in one night, it certainly got the locals riled and demanding results from the police in bringing in the killer. It was another three weeks before the killer would strike again.

Question is why did this person wait another three weeks to kill again and why did he kill Chapman only a week after the Nichols murder, three weeks after Nichols murder, Stride and Eddowes were murdered. What was the reason behind the delay in murders, was it because this person was a sailor or was he someone who lived outside the area and only came into the East end to work, did he wait until the murder investigations died down a little before striking again?

These are a few questions that have not been thought of by many or they have not written about these questions. I believe that this person did not live in the area, he may have lived in the area once before but moved way. The thinking of this is that all the Ripper murders were performed at the weekend. Nichols Friday evening, Chapman on a Saturday and Stride and Eddowes on a Sunday and Mary Jane Kelly on a Friday evening.

So, this would assume that this person was working during the week and only had time to his self at weekends. So all the victims were prostitutes; was there a grudge against these types of women, was he only after these women because they had no families or were not well educated? Did educated women turn him down for romance, was he someone who may have caught a disease off a woman and wanted to pay women back?

As of the questions as to whether this person was mad or not it is without question, he was a person with schizophrenic tendencies. His way of murder would suggest that he did have some sort of medical knowledge, whether a fully qualified doctor or a student doctor who never finished or passed their qualifications as a doctor or surgeon.

Chapter Three
The Contemporaneous Police Opinion

Let's look at some of the suspects in the Ripper case. We have read about Druitt, and Pizer or Piser, now to look at a few more. Carl Feigenbaum, Feigenbaum was a sailor of German decent possibly in Karlsruhe near the French border, according to writer Marriott; this is hearsay though, as Feigenbaum was not his real name, apparently his real name was Anton Lahn or sometimes known as Karl Zahn.

With no evidence to provide a date of birth, his real name is not really known. It is believed that he was born in 1840, making him in his 30s when the Ripper murders were committed and 54 when he was executed in prison on 27 April 1896 for the murder of Juliana Hoffman. In 1894, Feigenbaum on his admission form to prison had described him as 54 years of age and 5feet 4 inches tall, which would correspond to the year he was born but no actual day or month, his height is smaller than what some witnesses have described the killer to be.

According to witnesses, the killer was around 5'7" tall. Feigenbaum, as we will call him, was put to the chair at 11.10am, present at his execution were two Reverend Fathers, Father Creeden I Penitentiary resident priest with whom he spent his last night alive praying. And the other was Father Bruder, of the Poughkeepsie Catholic Church where he was to be buried.

Feigenbaum was given his last rites just before breakfast. He then made out his will in which he directed that his property in Cincinnati, reportedly a house and lot, were sold and the money including money held in a German bank in New York be given to his widowed sister Magdalena Strohband, who was living in Ganbickelheim, Alzel in Hesse-Darmstadt, Germany.

With an exception of $90 that would be held back for his funeral expenses, Warden Omar Van Leuven Sage was made his Executor. Feigenbaum before sitting on the wooden chair kissed the crucifix he was carrying and then handed it to father Bruder. He took of his glasses and handed them to Bruder asking that they be buried with him. Feigenbaum shook the hands of the two Fathers and also the hand of his executioner, State Electrician Davis.

The electrodes were attached to the base of his head and the calf of his right leg; after Dr R.T. Irvine, the prison physician, gave the okay the warden signalled to Davis to turn the current on. The first shock of 1,820 volts was given at 11:16 and lasted for thirty seconds before being gradually reduced to 300 volts, a level that was held for 40 seconds.

Then the current was turned off for a few seconds before a second shock of 1,820 volts was administered at 11:17:45 and held till 11:18. Drs Irvine and John Wilson Gibbs, who had held the watch timing the length at which the voltage was applied, examined the body and pronounced Feigenbaum dead at 11:18:30.

It was reported in one newspaper that Irvine and Gibbs invited other physicians who were observing the execution to come forward and examine the body, this was to obtain consensual medical opinion that the prisoner was indeed dead, this is after what was considered to be some horrifically botched executions using the still fairly new method of electrocution.

After several minutes of examination, the paper stated one or two doctors expressed the thought that although the man was not alive, perhaps he was not quite dead. So to satisfy this punctilious minority, the current was switched on again at 21.25pm on full voltage for three seconds. After which it was announced that Feigenbaum was dead.

If this story in the paper was true, what were the two physicians thinking off, if a person is not breathing nor do they have a heart beat after having 1800 volts shot through their body twice, I would imagine that person would be dead, so to say that he was not alive but may not be dead is a mystery to me; if you are not alive, you are dead, if you are not dead, you are alive, there cannot be an in-between.

To put a man who is pronounced dead at 11:18am back in the chair and electrocute him again at 21.25pm, surely that amount of time of 10 hours, did he come back to life because if he did that would have been the one and only miracle, so to put this man, no matter what he did, back on the chair for three seconds was the most disgusting thing ever achieved by man, this would have been very degrading for those involved in electrocuting a dead body.

After the death of Feigenbaum, you would think that would be the end of his story and he would be found in the history archive's one day but as his body was being taken to the Sin I death house's autopsy room, his lawyer William Sanford

Lawton gave an interview to a reporter from the New York Advertiser, stating that in his belief his ex-client was in fact the notorious murderer from London, Jack the Ripper.

This announcement caused a brief sensation in newspapers all over North America, however the world moved on and the story quickly died and was forgotten about. Until Trevor Marriott wrote a book called Jack the Ripper the 21st Century Investigation. The problem with this book is that Marriott made plenty of speculations on his theories as to who the Ripper was and in fact for that matter who Carl Feigenbaum was.

Lawton stated that Feigenbaum ceased to follow the sea about six years previous, around 1890, so in fact Feigenbaum was not a sailor in 1888, so how did he stay in London, if he was in London that is, how did he manage with lodgings and food, what job did he do,' it was stated he was a florist on his admission form in I and was said to have worked as a Gardener in the states. So where did he work during the day in London?

I believe that Feigenbaum was in fact in Germany staying with his widowed sister and in 1891, he set sail to the States on board one of the passenger ships leaving Bremen. It is claimed that he left his sister a lot of money from the sale of his house and lot in Cincinnati and money he had in a New York bank.

It seems he had plenty of money and able to look after himself well without the aid of full employment; thinking about it, Feigenbaum whatever his real name was used aliases Strohband, Feigenbaum, Lahn or Lahm, so no one really knew his real name, neither did anyone know the real person named Feigenbaum, for his lawyer claimed that his client was a cunning sort of fellow.

So I believe that Feigenbaum was not his real name, neither was Lahn, as this was the name of one of the Bremen Atlantic liners he would have worked on. I also believe Strohband was his real name and that his widowed sister living in Germany was in fact his wife and that he came from Ganbickelheim, Alzel in Hesse-Darmstadt, Germany.

Another suspect was Frederick Bailey Deeming. Deeming born on 30 July 1853, in Ashby-De-La-Zouch, Leicestershire, it was said had an unnaturally strong relationship with his mother; when she died in 1873, Deeming became emotionally distraught, it is said he stayed that way for some time afterwards. At 16, Deeming ran away and became a seaman, one day he fell prey to a 'brain fever' attack while on a voyage and many contend that he never quite got over the trauma.

Deeming's movements from 1888-89 are not easy to find, there is not much about where he was and when between the beginning of 1888 and the end of 1889. Trying to find his movements for this time is proving impossible as his next movement traced was in 1891, it seems that Deeming was keeping out of the limelight in fear of being caught over crimes he has supposed to have done while in Australia and south Africa.

It is believed that Deeming served a nine month prison sentence for obtaining goods under false pretences; he was released in July 1891, so was in prison from November 1890. This does not account for the missing steps of him from 1888-89. He was said to have been involved in a Transvaal diamond mine swindle in 1889 in the South African Republic. This means he was not in England sometime during 1888. But what date did he return.

Deeming's brother did hear that Deeming was returning to England in 1888, the exact date is not known. So, he was in England and able to commit the Ripper murders but we know that he arrived in Birkenhead, Liverpool because he bought a home there, did he travel down to London just to commit murder on five prostitutes? I very much doubt that.

Deeming was hiding from authorities from other countries, so travelling around would let others know of his whereabouts. Deeming after being caught for the murders of his wife and child boasting that he was indeed the Ripper, all murderers caught around that time would boast that they were the Ripper. So therefore, I believe that Deeming was not and did not travel to London on his return to England but stayed in Liverpool until he had buried his wife and children under the floor of their family home and just fled back to Australia or South Africa.

Another suspect in the Ripper case was to be, HRH Prince Edward Victor, grandson to Queen Victoria and son to Prince Albert Edward and Princess Alexandra. Albert later to become King Edward. 7th Prince Edward was born on 8 January 1864, Albert was born two months premature, this would lead into later life about his mental state of health and rumours about his sexuality were also put into question, some reports suggesting that he was gay.

If he was gay, he would not have any need to pester prostitutes, this report was and is total madness from the speculators. During his upbringing, Albert was educated with his younger brother; at the Queen's request, they were educated by John Neal Dalton, the two princes were given strict programme to study, the two young Princes were very close to each other due to the 17-month gap between them.

The Programme set by Dalton included, games, military drills as well as academic subjects. Dalton complained that Albert Victor's mind was abnormally dormant, though he did learn to speak Danish. Yet progress in other languages and subjects was slow. Sir Henry Ponsonby, the Queen's private secretary thought that the young prince may have inherited his mother's deafness. Prince Albert and his young brother, Prince George were sent on a world tour for three years on board HMS Bacchante.

Albert Victor was rated midshipman on his 16th birthday. The brothers were parted in 1883, George continued in the navy, Albert attended Trinity college, Cambridge. One of Albert's instructors, he learned by listening rather that reading and writing and had no difficulty remembering information. 'The London Cleveland Street Scandal' was a male brothel under interrogation of the Metropolitan Police and implicated that Prince Albert was involved, due to one of the Prince of Wales Equerry being named as one of the clients attending this brothel.

Homosexuality between males was against the law and carried a prison sentence of two years hard labour. None of the prostitutes named Prince Albert as a client. The dates of the Ripper murders and Prince Albert's movements are as follows:

31st August, Mary Nichols was murdered. Between 29 August and 7 September 1888, Prince Albert was staying with Viscount Downe, at Danby Lodge, Grosmont Yorkshire. All the movements of the Prince can be seen by Royal Appointment, on 7 September 1888, Albert was staying at the Cavalry Barracks in York, for three days until the 10th September; Annie Chapman was murdered on the 8th September.

From the 27th September till 30th September, the prince was at Abergeldie, Scotland, where Queen Victoria recorded in her journal that he lunched with her on the 30th. Stride and Eddowes were both murdered on the 30th September at 1 and 2am. On 1 November 1888, Albert arrived in London from York, from the 2nd-12th November.

He was staying at Sandringham. On 9th November, the body of Mary Jane Kelly was found in her lodgings, 13, Millers Court. I have no reason to dismiss the dates of Prince Albert's movements, purely because he would not have been walking around London in the middle of the night without an escort nor without anyone knowing he was missing. He would have had to bypass many a guard on duty on them nights, I also have no reason to disbelieve the reigning monarch at the time Queen Victoria, the stories about Prince Albert were solely to sell newspapers or books.

People may have thought that Prince Albert was a bit of a lazy person or not very academically gifted but I believe that the lack of his learning from reading and writing may just stem from what we call dyslexia and he had trouble reading words and writing words.

Another suspect on the list was Frances Tumblety; Tumblety was born in Ireland and his family moved to the states sometime in the late 1840s or early 1850s. Exact date not known, they lived in Rochester, New York, a few years after his birth, Tumblety had ten brothers and sisters, at the age of 17 he was selling books, some may suggest that they may have been pornographic but not proven, he was selling them along the Erie Canal between Rochester and Buffalo.

He did not return home for another ten years, he was briefly employed as a cleaner in Lispenards Hospital in Rochester. Tumblety set himself up in business initially in Detroit, he claimed to be a great physician but was commonly perceived as a quack. He started his practice as an Indian herb doctor. This must have been a lucrative amount of money, as of 1854, he always appeared as if he was considerably wealthy.

He sold patent medicines such as Tumblety pimple destroyer and Dr Morse's Indian Root pills. He also gained a reputation for eccentric, ostentatious clothes, which were frequently of military nature, according to Tumblety. In 1857, he was practicing medicine in Canada, before moving to New York and Washington DC. Tumblety's medicinal approach was based on herbal remedies, rather than mineral poisons (Mercury) or surgical techniques.

He was connected to one of his patient's death in Boston but managed to escape prosecution. Federal tax records show he was in Maryland in 1863 but he soon moved to St Louise, Missouri, living at 30, Olive Street. Again setting up his 'medical' practice and again promenading himself around the city with his arrogant splendour. He was arrested in St Louis for wearing military garb and medals he did not deserve.

After many fiascos in the USA, Tumblety left and headed back to England. In the late 1860s soon after travelling to Berlin, then to Liverpool in 1874, it was here that he was to meet the not yet famous Sir Henry Hall Caine, (then 21), who was bisexual and almost certainly carried an homosexual affair with Tumblety. The two carried on their romance until 1876 when Tumblety returned to New York, Tumblety aroused suspicion through his seeming mania for the company for young men and grown up youths.

In the years that followed, Tumblety would travel across America and Europe, in October 1885 his brother Patrick was killed in Rochester when a crumbled chimney fell onto him, Tumblety returned to Liverpool in June 1888 and once again found himself in trouble with the police, he was charged with gross indecency and assault with force and arms against four men between July 27th and November 7th.

The eight charges were euphemisms for homosexual activities, for some reason Tumblety was then charged on suspicion for the Whitechapel murders on the 12th, suggested that he was free to kill Kelly between the 7th and 12th of November. Tumblety was bailed on November 16th, a hearing was held on the 20th at the Old Bailey, the trial was postponed until December 10th, Tumblety while on bail fled to France under the alias Frank Townsend on the 24th November, from there he took the steamer La Bretagne to New York City.

Tumblety was charged by the police for crimes against four men between July and November; if this was the case, he would not have murdered any women because he was only interested in men at that time. So what others are saying is that Tumblety would tout for homosexual activities and in between, he would murder prostitutes.

I do not think that would have been the case killing prostitutes would serve no purpose in his liking for younger men. James Thomas Sadler, 2.15am Friday 13 February 1891, Constable Ernest Thompson was patrolling the area of Chambers Street and Rosemary Lane, he was just entering Swallow gardens when he heard footsteps running away from him, heading in the direction of Rosemary Lane, as he turned into Swallow Gardens he saw the body of a woman laying on her back, her throat had been cut and blood was still flowing out of the wound.

Her black hat lay near her, Thompson moving closer to the body noticed that one eyes was flickered open, she was still alive, the woman was identified as Frances Coles, a 25-year-old prostitute; Coles unfortunately died on her way to the London Hospital. Dr Bagster Phillips examined the body and found that her throat had been cut with a sawing motion, there was no other wounds about her body just her throat, her clothing had not been altered either, Dr Phillips detected no surgical skill and that the instrument used was not sharp, as far as he was concerned this was not the work of the perpetrator who carried out the murders of prostitutes in Whitechapel 1888.

Apparently there was a witness named William Friday known to his friends as Jumbo, came forward to say that he saw a man and woman standing in a doorway around 1.45am on the night of the murder. He identified the hat as the same one worn by the woman standing in the doorway. He continued to describe the man as stocky and looking like a ships fireman, the police checked the docks and discovered that Coles spent a couple of days with James Thomas Sadler, 53-year-old ships fireman, on the Fez.

This was moored at the London Dock. The police discovered that Sadler had a violent temper and returned to his lodgings covered in blood. They also found that he had sold his knife for a shilling and a piece of tobacco, the police arrested him for the murder. Police inspector Swanson believed that not only had they caught Coles murderer but also Jack the Ripper. Sadler was represented by the seaman's union and the case soon fell apart as two witnesses came forward, Thomas Fowles and Kate McCarthy told that they were the ones seen by William Friday aka (Jumbo) in the doorway the night Coles was murdered.

The knife Sadler sold also turned out to be a blunt knife and was in no way the weapon that killed Coles. Sadler had a credible alibi on the night of the murder, when he left the Fez he had money in his wallet of £8.7shillings, value of today around £200.

In the Prince Alice public house, Sadler saw Coles and greeted her like old friends as Sadler and Coles had met about 18 months earlier, Coles sensing Christmas had come early, Sadler and Coles set off to sample every pub in the East End, in today's terms a pub crawl.

As the drunken pair passed through Thrawl Street, Sadler was suddenly and violently hit about the head by a woman in a red shawl, falling to the ground he was set upon by several men, when he regained consciousness he had found that he had been robbed of his wallet and watch, feeling he had been set up he turned his anger on Coles who made no attempt to help him, he made his way to the London Hospital where his wounds were seen too.

The bloodstains found on him were from his troubles that night, as for the other murders Sadler provided an alibi for the murders he was at sea from 17th August to 1st October, on board the Winestead. Despite being cleared of the Coles murder, the police watched him for quite a while afterwards, they believed that Sadler did murder Coles, in January 1893 Sadler told the police that he was wisely leaving the area.

This was again with evidence in his favour, the police still believed that they had caught the Ripper and Coles' murderer, Sadler may well have murdered Coles but how he was beaten to unconsciousness I very much doubt that he had the energy and strength to attack Coles and his knife was extremely blunt and not the murder weapon.

On to another police suspect, this time it was Severin Klosowski, known as George Chapman, no relation to Annie Chapman, was born in Poland and immigrated to England sometime either 1887-88, Klosowski became an apprentice to a senior surgeon in Moshko, Rappaport, in Zwolen. Try not to get Zwolen, Poland and Zvolen in Slovakia, like some authors have done.

He assisted in procedures such as the application of leeches for blood-testing; he then enrolled in a course in practical surgery at the Warsaw Praga hospital. Depending on your sources, he either enrolled or finished his studies at the Warsaw Praga Hospital; when he emigrated to London, he entered in the career as an hairdressers assistant, in either late 1887 or early 1888, working for a Abraham Radin, at 70 West India dock Road, the job lasted for five months only, Klosowski was soon running a barber shop on his won at 126 Cable Street, St Georges-in-the-East.

The Post office Directory of 1889, lists this as his address. So it is likely this was his address during the Ripper murders, in 1890 he took up a similar job in a barber shop in Whitechapel high street and George yard. Why people think because he moved to George yard barber shop, he murdered Martha Tabram in 1888. During his stay in the East End, he married a young polish girl Lucie Badewski in 1889 and had two children by her.

The problem was that Klosowski was already married. Klosowski left his wife back in Poland. She had got wind of his marriage and children and travelled to London to confront her husband and oust Badewski. His wife's attempt to oust Badewski failed so she left, maybe because of the birth of Klosowski and Badewski's first child in September 1890.

They moved around quite a bit, living in Cable Street, Commercial Street and Greenfield Street, before they finally immigrated to New Jersey later that year, the exact date is not quite known. Klosowski took four mistresses he used poison to kill three of them, it is said that a serial killer does not change the way they kill their victims and this would be the case for Klosowski.

He only lived in Cable street and Georges Yard in 1889 not 1888, it was very unlikely that he knew the Whitechapel area as good as The Ripper did and he was much younger than that of the witnesses description of who the Ripper was. Klosowski is not Jack the Ripper and it is proven in his movements from 1888-89 that he was not living in the Whitechapel area at that time.

Now for the next police suspect, this was one Aaron Kosminski. Kosminski was born in Klodawa, Poland on 11 September 1865, at the time of the Whitechapel murders he was only 23 years old, younger than that the witnesses gave when describing the assailant murdering prostitutes in Whitechapel. The ages were given from 28 years old or older.

Kosminski emigrated in 1880-1881, probably with his sisters families, the family initially lived in Germany for a time before the family emigrated to London around 1881-1882, his mother who was listed as a widow did not travel with the family, she joined them in 1894 alone as his father did not emigrate because it is not known whether he had died or abandoned the family.

It is known that a death certificate in 1887 indicates that an Abraham Kosminski died in the town of Kolo five miles from Grzegorzew where he was born. In London, Kosminski embarked on a career as a barber in Whitechapel, like many a refugee from Eastern Europe escaping the hardships and pogroms (persecution) in Tsarist Russia. However he may have only work now and then, it was reported that he had not attempted to work for years by 1891, he probably relied upon his sisters for money and probably lived with them.

20 July 1890, Kosminski was placed in Mile End old town workhouse because of his insane behaviour, his brother Woolf certifying his entry. He was released three days later, on 4 February 1891, he was returned to the workhouse possibly by the police and on the 7th he was transferred to the Colney Hatch Lunatic Asylum. A witness of the certification of entry stated that a Jacob Cohen was recorded, Kosminski stayed at Colney Hatch for three years before being transferred to Leavesdon Asylum in Abbots Langley in 1894.

Kosminski was of mental health issues and committed to an insane asylum in 1891, there is no proof that Kosminski was around any of the areas that the Ripper was seen, all evidence collected by the police was just made up any reports were fake to please the locals that they had caught the Ripper and ease tension in the vicinity of Whitechapel.

He had no medical training and he was ill from the year 1885 according to doctors, he suffered from Auditory Hallucinations. Kosminski died on 24 March 1919, weighing only 44kg due to his poor diet.

The last Contemporaneous police opinion was Michael Ostrog. Ostrog was born in 1833, not a lot is recorded about Ostrog because of the many aliases he used during his life of crime, Ostrog was a con-man and thief from Russia believed to a Russian Jew, who claimed to has surgical training and served in the Russian Navy, Ostrog committed the following crimes none of which were violent.

In 1863, he was arrested for theft at Oxford College using the alias Max Grief (Kaife), was sentenced to ten months in prison, in 1864 convicted at Cambridge he was sent to prison again for three months. In July, he appeared at Tunbridge wells under the name of Count Sobierski, served 8 months in prison from December 1864. January 1866, acquitted on fraud charges, March 19th stole a gold watch and other items from a woman in Maidstone, committed similar thefts in April.

Arrested in August and sentenced to seven years in prison. He was released from prison in May 1873, committed numerous thefts and arrested by Superintendent Oswell in Burton-on-Trent, produced a revolver and nearly shot his captors. Convicted in January 1874 and sentenced to ten years in prison, released in August 1883, in 1887 sentenced to six months hard labour in September for the theft of a metal tankard in July, on September 30th he was listed as suffering from Mania.

On 10 March1888, he was released as cured, in the police Gazette October 1888 he was described as a dangerous man who failed to report. 18 November 1888, he was sentenced to two years in prison for theft in Paris. In 1891, he was committed to the Surrey Lunatic Asylum. In 1894, charged for theft in Eton in 1889. He was again charged in Woolwich for the theft of books in 1898.

More charges came in 1900, imprisoned again for theft of a microscope at the London Hospital Whitechapel, known to be partially paralysed by this time. The last time Ostrog was heard of was in 1904 when he was released from prison and entered St Giles Christian Mission in Holborn. Ostrog was a serial thief not a serial killer, why Macnaghten had Ostrog as the Whitechapel murderer shows that he had no idea who this person was, suggesting a serial thief was a serial killer must leave serious questions about the police's investigations going on at the time, apart from being a serial thief not once was violence involved in his history of theft.

Neither was there any question that Ostrog would have been in his 50s at the time of the murders. This would again have questions about witnesses who testified about the age of the Ripper. Ostrog was not Jack the Ripper, he was not a violent person, he was a thief and he did not live in the Whitechapel area of London.

Chapter Four
Contemporaneous Press and Public Opinion

Firstly, we have spoken about two of the press and public opinions, which were Carl Faigenbaum and Frederick Bailey Deeming; we can now discuss the next four suspects, to start we will question whether not Robert Donston Stephenson is Jack the Ripper. Stephenson was born on 20 April 1841, in Sculcoates, Hull. At the time of the murders, he would have been 47 years old.

Stephenson was a writer and journalist, he had been staying at the London Hospital since 26th July until December 7th, his profession and his interest in the occult sciences made him take a more than average interest in the forthcoming murders. At the London Hospital, the murders were as with everywhere else the major topic of conversation, after witnessing a Dr Morgan Davies demonstrating how the murderer may have been subduing and killing victims, he found his behaviour suspicious and brought the story to a George Marsh, an ironmongery salesman claiming to be an amateur detective.

George Marsh found that Stephenson was the more suspicious person and went to Scotland Yard, one of the officers an Inspector Roots, who immediately recognised the person as someone he has known for twenty years. Robert Donald Stephenson, a travelled man of education and ability, from Roots reported it seems that Stephenson was cleared of suspicion straight away, it seems that Stephenson's cultured manner and eagerness to assist the police with arcane knowledge evoked admiration from the police rather than suspicion.

Stephenson's interest in the crimes eventually led to an article in the Pall Mall Gazette, presenting his own theory on the motivation and identity of the murderer. According to Stephenson, the murderer would have to be practicing Black Magic, as the parts removed from the victims would be used for ritual purposes, the problem with Stephenson being a suspect was that he was in the London Hospital as a patient and was not allowed to leave the ward and no non-patients were allowed to enter the Hospital. With this knowledge Stephenson could not have been the Ripper no matter what his interest in the occult sciences were.

William Henry Bury, another suspect in the Whitechapel murders. Born 25 May 1859 making him 31 years old, born in Stourbridge, Worcestershire, he became a suspect because he murdered his wife. He was the youngest of four children. Bury was orphaned in infancy; his father worked for a local fishmonger died in a horse and cart accident in Halesowen on 10 April 1860, Bury was 11 months old, while on an incline he fell beneath his cart wheels and the horse bolted and pulled the cart over him.

Burys mother may have been suffering from post-natal depression at the time of her husband's death and was committed to the Worcester County Pauper and Lunatic Asylum on 7 May 1860. She remained there until her death aged just 33 years old. She died on 30 March 1864. In October 1887, Bury arrived in bow and got a job selling sawdust for one James Martin, Martin seems to have run a brothel at 80 Quickett Street, Bow.

Bury would sleep in the stable with the horse but later he moved into the house. There he met Ellen Elliot, Martin employed her as a servant probably a prostitute, Ellen was born in October 1856 in Walworth London, at the Bricklayers Arms public house run by her father George Elliot, in adult life she worked as a needlewoman and in a Jute processing factory. In March 1888, Ellen and William left Martin's employ and moved into a furnished place at 3 Swaton Road, Bow.

This is where they lived up to their marriage on Easter Monday, 2 April 1888 at Bromley Parish Church. Martin later disclosed that he dismissed Bury for unpaid debts, Martin and Elizabeth Haynes the landlady of 3 Swaton Road, both described Bury as a violent drunk. On 7th April, Haynes claims she saw Bury kneeling over his wife of five days, threatening to cut her throat with a knife.

Haynes evicted them from her lodgings, if this was a true event and one that is not made up, why did Haynes not contact the police and tell them what she saw and have Bury arrested for assault and threatening behaviour, with the Whitechapel murders going on at that time notifying the Police about what she saw could have prevented another murder and Bury would have been a promising suspect for the Whitechapel murders.

Ellen sold one of her six £100 railway shares she inherited from a maiden aunt, to pay Bury's debt to Martin. Bury was re-employed by Martin and the couple moved to 11 Blackthorn Street, Bow, close to Swaton Road. According to Martin, Bury was suffering from venereal disease; how Martin knew about Burys venereal disease I don't know, I would have thought that it would not be something to broadcast about even in the 1800s.

Ellen sold the remainder of her shares in June and in August, the couple moved to 3 Spanby Road adjacent to where Bury stabled his horse. With the money from the shares, the couple had a week's holiday in Wolverhampton with a drinking friend of Bury's. Ellen bought new jewellery. Bury continued to assault his wife in the latter half of 1888, by the first week in December, Ellen's windfall was almost spent so Bury sold his horse and cart.

In January 1889, Bury told his landlord of 3 Spanby Road that he was thinking of immigrating to Australia. Bury ask the landlord to make two crates for the journey for him but instead the couple moved to Dundee in Scotland, Ellen was not keen on the idea but only went when Bury told her he had obtained a position in a Jute factory. They arrived in Dundee on the evening of 20th January having travelled on the steamer Cumbria as second class passengers, the next morning they rented a room in a bar at 43 Union Street.

They only stayed for 8 days before moving on to squat at 113 Prince's Street on the 29th January, it was a basement flat under a shop. Bury obtained that by pretending to the lettings agent that he was interesting in renting the flat, Ellen found a job in a local mill but quit after just one day, Bury continued to drink heavily with David Walker, a decorator who was re-painting the public house frequented by Bury.

On 4th February, Bury bought some rope from the grocer shop and spent the rest of the day observing cases at the sheriff court from the public gallery. He attended the court again on the 7th and on the 10th he visited Walker, who lent him a newspaper that featured a woman's suicide by hanging, Walker is said to have asked Bury to look up news of Jack the Ripper, at which Bury threw the paper down in fright.

That very night, Bury walked into Dundee central police station on Bell Street and reported his wife's suicide to Lieutenant James Parr. Bury explained to Parr that they had been drinking heavily the night before and in the morning when he woke up, found his wife's body on the floor with a rope around her neck, Bury did not summon a doctor instead he cut up the body and put it in one of the crates they brought with them from London.

Bury said his actions were playing on his mind but in truth, he was a man desperate to get out of a murder charge, as well as be accused of being Jack the

Ripper, Parr took Bury to see a Lieutenant David Lamb, head of the detective department, Bury re-told his story to lamb but omitted Jack the Ripper and said he stabbed his wife once. Bury was searched and a small knife bankbook and his wife's jewellery were confiscated pending enquiries.

Lamb and detective constable Peter Campbell went to Bury's dwellings and found Ellen's mutilated body stuffed in the wooden crate, Lamb returned to the police station and arrested Bury for his wife's murder. On 18 March 1889, Bury was arraigned of the murder of his wife Ellen, he entered a plea of not guilty. On 24th April, Bury was hanged for the murder of his wife.

Bury was not Jack the Ripper as some people would like to think, Jack the Ripper cut his victims throats and then slashed their abdomen, Bury strangled his wife then cut her and stuffed her body in a crate, why would the Ripper have the need to visit a sheriff court to observe trials then read papers about suicides, this would not be of his character; serial killers do not change the way they kill their victims (Fact). Also, Bury spent most of his time with his wife drinking at night and working during the day.

New suspect for the press and public is Thomas Neill Cream. Cream was born on 27 May 1850 making him 38 years old at the time of the murders, he was also known as the Lambeth Poisoner. He was a Scottish Canadian, born in Glasgow and raised in Quebec City after his family moved there in 1854; he attended Gill University in Montreal and graduated with an MDCM Degree in 1876.

His thesis was chloroform, he went for post-graduate training at St Thomas's hospital medical school in London, in 1876 Cream married Flora Brooks after she became pregnant and almost killed while aborting the pregnancy. Flora died in 1877 apparently of consumption, her death would be blamed on Cream later, in 1878 he obtained additional qualifications as a physician and surgeon in Edinburgh. He returned to Canada to practise in London, Ontario.

In August 1879, Kate Gardener a woman Cream was alleged to have an affair with was found dead in an alleyway behind Cream's office, pregnant and poisoned by chloroform. Cream claimed that she became pregnant by a prominent local businessman but after being accused of both murder and blackmail, Cream fled to the United States. Cream opened a medical practice not far from the red light district of Chicago offering illegal abortions to prostitutes.

In August 1880, he was investigated after the death of Mary Anne Faulkner a woman he had allegedly operated on but managed to escape prosecution due to lack of evidence. In 1880, a Miss Stack died after treatment by Cream, it is said he tried to blackmail the pharmacist who filed the actual prescription. In April 1881, Alice Montgomery died following an abortion in a rooming house half a block from Creams office.

The case was ruled a murder but never solved, Cream was the likely suspect due to three methods location time and period. 14th July, Daniel Stott died of strychnine poisoning at his home in Boone County, Illinois, after Cream supplied him with an alleged remedy for epilepsy. Daniel Stott death was attributed to natural causes but Cream wrote to the coroner blaming the pharmacist for the death again attempting to blackmail.

Cream was arrested with Mrs Julia Stott, who became Cream's mistress and procured poison from him to kill her husband. To avoid jail, she turned State's evidence against Cream, this left Cream to face a murder conviction on his own; he received a life imprisonment penalty in Joliet prison. Cream was not released until July 1891 Governor Joseph W Fifer had commuted his sentence after Cream's brother pleaded for leniency and allegedly bribing the authorities.

Cream using money inherited from his father who died in 1887 sailed back to England arriving at Liverpool on 1 October 1891. He returned to London and took lodgings at 103 Lambeth Palace Road, at that time Lambeth was ridden with poverty petty crime and prostitution. Cream started his poisoning spree, his first victim was Ellen Nellie Donworth a 19 year old prostitute, she accepted a drink from Cream and next day became seriously ill, the next day she died on 16th October from strychnine poisoning.

During her inquest, Cream wrote to the coroner offering to name the murderer in return for a £300,000 reward. He also tried to blackmail W F D Smith, owner of W H Smith bookstall accusing him of murder. Cream tried to blackmail others as well after killing more prostitutes but after trying to blackmail Dr William Broadbent, the letter was sent to Scotland Yard. Through his accusatory letters, Cream brought significant attention to himself, the police realised the innocence of the accused and realised that the accusations made by the anonymous letter writer he had referred to the Matilda Glover death but this had been registered under natural causes.

The police knew that the letters were written by the serial killer the newspapers were calling the Lambeth poisoner, not long afterwards Cream met a new York policeman visiting London who had heard about the Lambeth poison, Cream gave him a brief tour of where the victims lived, the American happen to mention this to a British policeman who found Cream's detailed knowledge of the case suspicious, Cream was out on surveillance and soon discovered his habit of visiting prostitutes.

They also contacted the States and learned of their suspect's conviction for murder by poison in 1881. 3rd of June, Cream was arrested for the murder of Matilda Glover. 13th July, he was formally charged for the murders of Glover, Donworth, Marsh and Shrivel, the attempted murder of Harvey and extortion, at the trial which lasted from 17 to 21 October 1892.

The jury only took 12 minutes to find him guilty on all charges; justice Henry Hawkins sentenced him to death. On 15th November, Cream was hanged on the gallows at Newgate prison by James Billington. The body was buried the same day in an unmarked grave. Cream was not Jack the Ripper, he poisoned his victims, he did not attack them and he was serving a life imprisonment in the United States from 1881-1891, Ripper killings stopped in 1891, it would be impossible to name him as Jack the Ripper.

Thomas Hayne Cutbush is the last on the list, born in Kennington 1866 depending on history searches. He would have been 22 years old around the time of the murders. Far too young for the Ripper who told by witnesses was older between 28-40 years old. Not a lot is known about Cutbush but he was named by the Sun newspaper on 13 February 1894 as Jack the Ripper and then again in later additions.

Out to disprove the newspapers, Commissioner Melville Macnaghten penned his memoranda. And not only did he dispute Cutbush as the Ripper, he named three other suspects, Ostrog, Druitt and Kosminski, some say that Macnaghten disputed this to protect Cutbush's uncle who was a fellow police officer but Macnaghten claimed that Cutbush was not the Ripper because the knife used by Cutbush was different to the one used by the Ripper and also it was not purchased by Cutbush until February 1891, over two years after the Ripper attacks and it was unlikely that the Ripper would stay dormant for over two years and then re-emerge and be content with just stabbing his victims in the backside, his father died when he was young, Cutbush was said to be a spoilt child he lived with his mother and aunt at 14 Albert Street, Kennington.

It is said that they were both of a nervous and rather excitable disposition. Cutbush was at one time employed as a clerk and traveller in the tea trade at the Minories and subsequently a canvasser for the directory. He seemed to me to have been an intelligent young man so whatever tuned him to give up his job and lead an idle and useless life is a bit of a mystery, why would he give it all up, was it too much for him staying with his mother and aunt or did the effects of not having a man around in his childhood catch up with him, whatever the reason he became interested in medical books during the day and street wandering during the night.

He would often return home in muddy and allegedly, sometimes bloody clothes, the term allegedly is used as it is not clear if the bloody clothes story is true, on 5 March 1891 Cutbush was arrested charged with malicious wounding and sent to Broadmoor prison, Cutbush died in 1903 while still in Broadmoor, he died of a severe kidney condition. Cutbush not only too young to be the Ripper, his behaviour towards women was that of the London monster from the 18th century.

Cutbush also lived in Kennington far away from Whitechapel. Cutbush uncle, Superintendent Charles Henry Cutbush shot himself in front of his daughter in 1896, it is claimed that he knew his nephew was the murderer but he had been suffering from depression and paranoid illusions for some time and his nephew was never convicted of murder neither was he Jack the Ripper.

The story of Cutbush only stabbing women in the buttocks and shouting obscenities at them proves that he was not the Ripper as it is never mentioned that the Ripper stabbed women and shouted at them. For the Ripper to do those types of crimes, he would have been caught and stories about him and his identity would not be out into question like they are today.

On the next few pages, you will see photos of the victims and scenes and how accommodation was in 1888.

Photos

Mortuary photograph of Alice McKenzie.

Catherine Eddowes

Mary Jane Kelly

Police clearing Mitre Square

Photo of how the Ripper may have lived

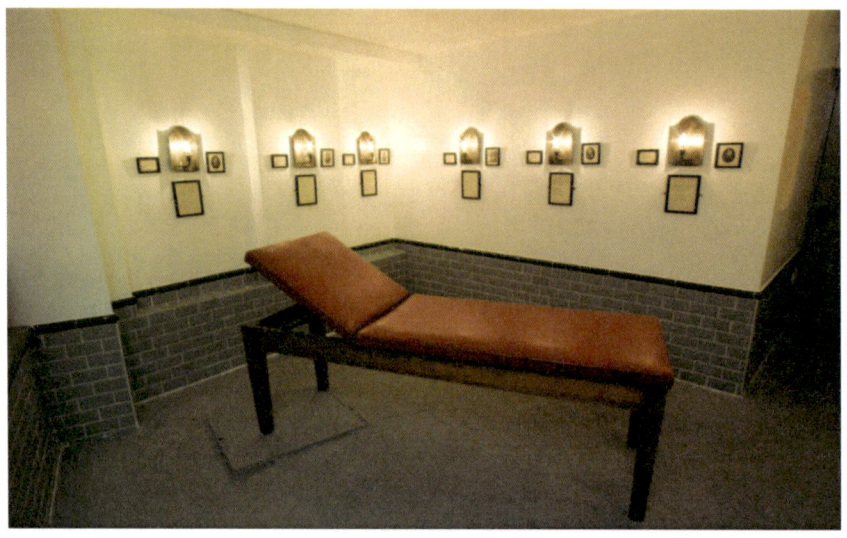

How the Morgue may have looked on the wall are snippets of the victims.

An 1888 Bedsit where prostitutes would have stayed, on the wall details of victims

Inspector Abberline at his office desk

Catherine Eddowes lay on the ground with a policeman on scene

The supposed Death mask of Frederick Bailey Deeming

George Lusk chairman of the vigilante committee

George Lusk home today

Entrance to George Yard 1888

George Yard Building where Martha Tabram was murdered

The Letters

During the autumn of terror, hundreds of letters were sent to the police and local newspapers purporting to be written by Jack the Ripper. Most of them were deemed to be fakes, written by either newspapers trying to start a story or fools trying to incite terror. Many Ripperologists believe them all to be hoaxes, other experts believe some ,specifically the Dear Boss letter, saucy Jacky postcard and the from Hell letter are genuine.

Dear Boss letter was received on 27 September 1888, by the Central News Agency; this is originally believed to be just another hoax. Three days later, the double murder of Stride and Eddowes made them reconsider. Especially once they learned a portion of the latter's earlobe was cut off from the body, reminiscent of a promise made within the letter. The police deemed the 'Dear Boss' letter important enough to reproduce it in newspapers and on post-bills of the time; hoping someone would recognise the handwriting.

A postcard received at the Central News Agency on 1st October making direct reference to both the murders and the 'Dear Boss' letter, is believed to have been written by the same hand. Whether or not the letter is a hoax, it is the first written reference which uses the name 'Jack the Ripper' in reference to the Whitechapel murderer.

If you look closely, you will notice that the small letter is written differently to the one in the log, so which one is false or are they both force letters, the writing on the envelope is also written by a different person.

Chapter Five
Suspects Proposed by Later Authors

There are many suspects written by authors of Ripper books, let's look at these suspects to see if authors are better at detecting murderers than the police. Suspect one, Joseph Barnett, born 25 May 1858, at 4 Hairbrain Court, Whitechapel. He was one of five children and the third son to be born to John and Catherine Barnett, John was a dock labourer in Ireland when they left to settle in London, in 1861 the couple moved from Hairbrain Court to nearby Cartwright Street, they were still living there in 1864 when John Barnett (Senior) who was now a Billingsgate Fish Porter died of Pleurisy in July.

His widow was his informant on the death certificate, However, this is the last known whereabouts of Catherine Barnett, she never appeared on any official records, what became of her is unclear, she may have abandoned her children and went back to Ireland or she may have changed her name and turned to prostitution, it would therefore been left to the eldest son Denis to look after the rest of the family, although he married in 1869 and lived in Bermondsey.

By the time of the 1871 Census, with no parents and Denis starting his own family elsewhere, the four remaining Barnett children were living at 241-2 Great Pearl Street Spitalfields, (a notorious slum district) and Daniel listed as the head. Later that year, Catherine married a Joseph Beer and eventually relocated to Poplar. Denis Daniel Joseph and John all received their Billingsgate fish porter's licence on 1 July 1878.

Although dates are uncertain, Joseph is listed on his licence as living at 4 Osborn Street, St Thomas Chambers, a lodging house at Heneage Street and North End Passage, Wellclose Square. He is described as 5'7" tall with a fair complexion. Joseph Barnett met Mary Jane Kelly on Good Friday, 8 April 1887 in Commercial Street, that night they had a drink together and arranged to meet the next day.

This was when they decided to remain together and Barnett took up lodgings in George Street for them both, apparently Barnett was known here; from there they took up lodgings in Little Patemoster Row, Dorset Street. They got evicted from there for non-payment of rent and being drunk, they lived in Brick Lane for a while then moved and settled in 13 Millers Court Dorset Street, March 1888.

During this time, it is said that Kelly gave Barnett details of her past life, this would help furnish the authorities with some biographical details of her life. During his initial police statement taken on 9 November 1888, Barnett stated that he was a Billingsgate market porter but has been out of work for three to four months and he had been living with Kelly at 13 Millers Court and they have been together for about 18 months, when in consequence he was not earning enough money to give her and she went back to prostitution he resolved on leaving with her, he said that they were still on friendly terms.

He visited her on 8th November between 7pm and 8pm, he said that there was another woman there when he left and that was the last time he saw her alive. He later changed this too, he had seen her about 7.30pm and 7.45pm and she was still alive, he had left her because she had a prostitute staying with her and he had objected to this, so he left and not because he was out of work. She was sober and when with him, she was only drunk a few times in their 18 month relationship.

It was claimed that Maria Harvey was the woman with Kelly but it is believed that it was actually Lizzie Albrook who would confirm Barnett's statement in press interviews. It is not quite clear why Barnett lost his post at Billingsgate market. Barnett was a named suspect by former private detective Bruce Paley.

Barnett matched the description of the Ripper and so would plenty of other men aged between 28-30, other men also would have known Kelly from her prostitution times and may have used her flat to take men home, the trouble is Barnett may have fitted the description of the Ripper but he was with Kelly for 18 months from 1887-1888, she would have been with him all the time day and night until she went back to prostitution, after Barnett lost his job and could not afford to give her money.

There is no evidence that Barnett was not the last person to see Kelly that night and he has broken off their time together not the other way round. If Barnett was not on friendly terms with Kelly after leaving her, why would he spend an hour with her and another woman in her lodging if he wanted to kill her, especially as there was a witness who could testify against him, I believe that the night of her death Kelly did in fact meet up with the Ripper and took him back to her place, a copycat killing would not match a serial killer there would only be similarities in them.

Kelly was murdered by the same person who murdered the other four women. Barnett's life after Kelly is a bit of a mystery until 1906 when he was given a new porters licence at Billingsgate market and living at 18 New Gravel Lane Shadwell, with his brother Daniel, the following year his licence recorded him living at 60 Red Lion Street Shadwell and in 1908 Tench Street Wapping, in 1919 he is recorded on the electrical register as living at 106 Red Lion street Shadwell with a Louisa Barnett his wife but there is no documentation to confirm this or if they had children.

The couple stayed at this address until their deaths. Louisa died on 3 November 1926 and Barnett on 29th November the same year. Barnett was 68 and died of edema of the lungs and bronchitis.

William Witney Gull is another suspect brought up by an author. Gull, born 31 December 1816 would have been 77 years old, Gull was born in Colchester, Essex and his father John Gull was a barge owner Wharfinger, Gull was born on his barge the Dove then moored at St Osyth mill in the parish of St Leonards. When William was four, the family moved to Thorpe le Soken, Essex.

His father died of cholera in 1827 when William was ten years old. After the death of his father, his mother devoted herself to her children's upbringing on very slender means. William Gull often said that his real education came from his mother. She was a woman of character instilling in her children the proverb 'Whatever is worth doing, it's worth doing well.'

As a young boy, William attended a local school with his elder sisters, later he attended another school in the same parish kept by the local clergyman. William was a day boy until he was 15 at which age he became a boarder for two years. It was here he first began to study Latin but the clergyman was of limited knowledge so William at 17 said that he would not be going any longer.

William became a pupil-teacher in a school kept by a Mr Abbot in Lewes Sussex. He lived with the schoolmaster and his family, studying and teaching Latin and Greek, it was at this time that he met the botanist Joseph Woods and formed an interest in looking for unusual plant life that would remain a lifelong pastime. After two years at Lewes, he became restless and started to think about other careers including working at sea.

The local rector took an interest in William and told him he should resume his classical and other studies on alternate days at the rectory, William did this for around a year, on his day at home he would join his sisters on the estuary by the sea and watch the fisherman and collect wildlife specimens from the nets of coastal dredgers. He would study them using any book he could find, this seems to have given him an interest in biological research that would help him in his career in medicine.

Medicine now became his true goal in life. It was around this time that the rector's uncle, Benjamin Harrison, the treasurer at Guy's Hospital was introduced to Gull and was impressed with his ability. He invited him to Guy's Hospital under his patronage. In September 1837, the autumn before he was 21, Gull left home and started on his life's work. Encouraged by Harrison and determined to make the most of the opportunity, he would try for every prize he could compete for in the course of that year.

He succeeded in gaining every one. During the first year of his residence at Guy's hospital together with other studies, he carried on learning Latin and Greek. In late Victorian Britain, women were not encouraged to enter the medical profession, Sir William Gull spoke out against this bias and led efforts to improve the prospects for women who wished to pursue a career in medicine.

In February 1886, he chaired a meeting at the medical society in Cavendish square to establish a medical scholarship to be awarded to women. This was the Helen Prideaux memorial fund named after Frances Helen Prideaux M.B and M.S. She was a gifted university of London medical student who had died a year before from diphtheria having previously won the exhibition and gold medal in anatomy and gained a first class degree.

Sir William Gull suffered the first of several strokes at his Scottish home Urrard house, Killcrankie. The attack of hemiplegia and aphasia was caused by cerebral haemorrhage. He recovered a few weeks later and returned to his London home; he knew the danger of his health. Over the next two years, he stayed at his London, Reigate and Brighton suffering several more strokes, the fatal attack came at his London home 74 Brook Street on 27 January 1890, he died two days later.

Gull featured in a number of theories and fictional works in connection with the Whitechapel 'Jack the Ripper' murders of 1888. These are usually though not always associated with variants of conspiracy theories involving the Royal Family and the Freemasons.

George Hutchinson was another name thrown into the hat as Jack the Ripper by authors, Hutchinson an out-of-work labourer and former groom described as being of military appearance and living at the Victorian working men's home, Commercial Street. On 12 November 1888 at 6 pm, he went to commercial street police station and gave the following statement to Sgt Edward Bagham 31H.

About 2am on the 9th I was coming by Thrawl Street, Commercial Street and just before I got to Flower and Dean Street, I saw the murdered woman Kelly. And she asked if I would lend her sixpence, I told her I spent all my money going to Romford; she said, good morning, I must find some money. She walked towards Thrawl street and a man heading in the other direction tapped her on the shoulder and spoke to her, they both started to laugh, I heard her say 'alright', to him, the man said, 'you will be alright for what I have told you', he then placed his right hand around her shoulders.

He was carrying a small parcel with a strap of some sort around it. He claims that he was standing against a lamp post outside the queens head public house and they both walked past him as he was watching them, he said that the man looked down and he stooped down to look at his face and the man looked at him with a stern look. He said that they went down Dorset Street and he followed them, he claims that they stood on the corner of court for a couple of minutes then he said something to her, she replied, 'alright my dear come along, you will be comfortable'.

He then placed his arm on her shoulder and gave her a kiss, she said she had lost her handkerchief. He then pulled out a red handkerchief of his own and gave it to her. They moved on up the court together. Hutchinson said he went up court to see them but could not, so he hung around for about 45 minutes then moved off, after they did not appear. Hutchinson's detailed description of the man is unbelievably accurate.

It was November, dark, poor light and he stooped down to look at the man with Kelly, why was he so interested in what Kelly did as she was a prostitute after all, why follow them, was it to rob the man he had no money which means no bed for the night but if that was the case why leave, was he Kelly's pimp or was he just lying to get his story in the paper for cash, Inspector Abberline thinks he was telling the truth but I don't think Abberline was the smartest Inspector on the police force and if you had seen someone with a prostitute and she ended up murdered and you saw who you think was the murderer the next day, would you not alert the police straight away.

Hutchinson gave a detailed description of the man as, 5'6" tall, age around 34-35. Well-dressed man with a horseshoe tiepin and gold watch chain hanging from his waistcoat, he was of dark complexion with a dark moustache curled up at the ends. He was wearing an Astrakhan coat, white collar and black tie. His watch chain had a big seal with a red stone hanging from it. He wore a pair of dark spats with light buttons over button boots, he looked like a foreigner, in his right hand he had a pair of kid's gloves and he walked very softly.

Now, it was November 1888 early hours in the morning, the lighting at the time was not very good, only on major roads was there was good lighting and the back streets were almost dark with no lighting. So George Hutchinson who described the man with Kelly in great detail in poor lighting was making his story up, it would have been impossible for Hutchinson to describe anybody from a distance or if he was that close to describe someone like he did he would have had to be with the man for a good couple of minutes, not as they walked by, I very much think that his story of events actually happened.

Very little is known about Hutchinson, where he was born, his age, what he did for a living height, where he lived, was he married, did he have children and why did he leave after watching Kelly for almost an hour, if he had feelings for Kelly then he would have either knocked on the door to her lodgings and interrupted what was going on or stopped her going with the man she was with by making some kind of excuse to be with her.

And how was he able to hear their conversation from a distance, were they shouting, I doubt it but Hutchinson did elaborate on his story to the press by stating he thought the man suspicious because of the way he was dressed, so every man who was well dressed was a murderer. Hutchinson reported what he had seen to the police on the Sunday morning.

There is nothing known about Hutchinson after the murder of Kelly. Hutchinson was paid the equivalent to two months wages and he also got paid from the press so selling a story that everyone would believe was easy. I do not believe Hutchinson was the Ripper, because if his story is to be believed then he did not murder Kelly so therefore he was not the Ripper.

Next on the list of suspects by authors is Charles Allen Lechmere AKA Charles Cross. Lechmere or Cross was a suspect because he lived in the area his mother lived in the area as well and on his way to work, he would pass the streets the murders took place, he was a meat cart driver for the Pickford's company.

Do not get confused with cart man and car man, these are two different things; cart men deliver goods, car men are taxi drivers.

Lechmere was a cart man delivering meat around London but he did not cut up the meat that would have been a butcher's job, not a job for a cart man. Lechmere found Nichols in Bucks Row, he claimed he was only there a few minutes but it is suggested by some he was there longer and had time to murder Nichols, this is not the case and nor can it be, he was seen by Robert Paul at the time and between them they saw a policeman and notified him of what they saw.

On the arrival of Paul, Lechmere would not have had time to hide any weapon there were no drains nearby, the police searched the area thoroughly and found no weapon, Lechmere would have been taken to the police station to give a statement and he would have been searched by the police. There was no blood at the scene either. Being a cart man, Lechmere would not need to carry a knife while he was delivering his goods.

Lechmere was a delivery man for the Pickford Company. Lechmere was born in 1849 in St Anne's, Soho, his mother and father divorced and his mother remarried to a Thomas Cross a policeman in 1858 Lechmere took his surname, in 1871 Cross married Elizabeth Bostock and was living at 22 Doveton Street.

Cross took the same route to work for 25 years according to reports, he would have taken the shortest route possible and I do not see why he would change route and why now after so long he would start to murder prostitutes, there is no logic behind this reasoning. I believe that Cross did arrive when he said and that he and Paul did meet at the time Cross said.

James Kelly, another suspect by authors, Kelly was born on 20 April 1860. Kelly was born in Preston, Lancashire; his mother Sarah Kelly was only fifteen years old, after his birth his mother returned to Liverpool leaving Kelly with his Sarah's mother Teresa. In 1870 at the age of 25, Sarah Kelly marries master mariner John Allen.

In 1873, Kelly leaves school and starts an apprenticeship as an upholsterer. Allen dies in Peru on 16 May 1874 leaving Kelly with a house and a share in a cargo ship, Sarah falls to pieces after Allen's death and her health starts to decline, Sarah dies two months after Allen on 29 July 1874, Kelly was never to meet his mother. Sarah leaves Kelly a small fortune in her will, a sum of twenty five thousand pounds to be held in trust until his 25th birthday.

In today's money, he would be worth over 1.7 million pounds. In 1875, Teresa tells Kelly of his history and his inheritance. This is the first time that

Kelly learns that the woman he knew as his mother was in fact his Grandmother. He is withdrawn from his apprenticeship as an upholsterer and sent to Dr Robert Hurworth's commercial academy in New Brighton to lean bookkeeping and clerical skills.

In 1876 Teresa dies, in 1877 Kelly finishes his education and takes a job in Liverpool with Isaac H Jones pawnbrokers. Then Kelly begins to act irrationally and experience mood swings. In late 1878, Kelly decides to quit his job and return to his previous trade, an upholsterer, he also decides to move to London. Kelly has to apply to the administrators of his trust fund to agree the move which they do.

On arriving in London, Kelly applies to the East London upholsterer's trade society in Shoreditch for work. They agree to help him find work but suggest he does casual work while waiting, early 1879 Kelly takes lodgings at 37 Collingwood street, Bethnal Green, with a fellow upholster Walter Lamb and another friend John Merritt, a cab driver.

From 1879-81, there is little known about Kelly's movements, for some of the time he was living in Brighton and also serving on board an American Man-o-War. Mid 1881 he returns to London and renews his acquaintance with Lamb and Merritt. He has several casual jobs and also serves on continental cargo ships, his drinking becomes heavier than ever and he spends his night in Whitechapel and Spitalfields.

In December of that year a few weeks before Christmas, he meets Sarah Brider and quickly becomes enamoured of her. Sarah takes him to meet her parents and the pair became an item, Sarah thinks he is a serious and religious young man with good prospects. In March 1882, Kelly moves into the Brider home at 22 Cottage Lane, just of city road between Shoreditch and Islington as a lodger.

He has to share with another man and he cuts down on his drinking and spends most evenings in the house with Sarah and her parents. In February 1883, he proposes to Sarah, after some delay she accepts, Meanwhile Kelly finds out that he has a venereal disease and fearful of doctors, he treated the complaint himself. On 1st April Kelly lands a permanent upholstery job with John Hiron 4 Orchid building, Acton Street, Haggerston. And Sarah's family pressures him to set a date for the wedding.

Reluctant to name a date because of his disease, they set a date for 4 June 1883, Kelly's erratic behaviour continues and he begins experiencing serious headaches and discharging from his ears, on 1st June, he is dismissed from his job, all this is because he is not medically trained and treating himself for his disease. Kelly and Sarah are married at St Luke's Parish Old Street EC1, on the same day, he gets a new upholster job with Cornelius Vincent Smith, at Marshall's Yard, 4 Henry Street, close to Regents Park, a two mile walk from Cottage Lane.

It is believed that because of Kelly's disease, the marriage was never consummated, on 9th June, Kelly demands Sarah sees a doctor about her deformity, Sarah consults her parents and her father question Kelly, he pours out his supposed abuse from his uncle and their sexual problems, Sarah's father agrees that Sarah should see a doctor. On 11th June, Kelly travels to Liverpool to ask the fund trustees for money so he and Sarah can set up home together, he is successful and returns to London that same day.

17th June Mrs Brider finds a syringe and drugs Kelly had been using to treat himself. When confronted by Sarah and her mother, he denies that they are his; then he flies into a rage and accuses Sarah of being a prostitute and infecting him and accuses both of them into tricking him into marriage to get his inheritance. 18th June is Sarah's birthday, filled with remorse from the previous night he resolves to take Sarah out when they return from work but Sarah turns up late around 9pm.

She ignores Kelly and goes straight to her mother and tells her she is not feeling well, Kelly after waiting so long flies into a rage and drags Sarah into the kitchen screaming abuse at her and threatens her with a knife unless she tells him where she has been, she claims to have got some Quinine to help with his problem. Kelly immediately drops onto a chair and starts crying.

On 21st June, Sarah arrives home from work and says she is going to meet Kelly then leaves, an hour later Kelly arrives home without Sarah, when asked where Sarah was, he snaps that he saw her but did not go to her he then shouts that no woman will master him and he goes back out.

20 minutes later, they both return home Sarah pulls away from Kelly and locks herself in her room, Kelly breaks the door down, Mrs Brider arrives and Kelly is calling Sarah a whore, she tells him she no longer wants anything to do with him, Kelly again breaks down and begs for forgiveness but Sarah is not interested, Kelly flies into a rage again throws Sarah to the floor and stabs her in the neck with a penknife.

Mrs Brider tries to pull him off but he throws her across the room, he runs off and locks himself in his room. 22nd June, Kelly is charged with attempted murder at Clerkenwell police station, 23rd June Kelly is taken to the hospital by Inspector Maynard where Sarah gave her statement in his presence. 24th June, Kelly writes to Sarah begging for forgiveness, at 10.30 pm Sarah dies from her injuries, 25th June Kelly is charged with murder.

28th June Kelly is formerly charged and pleads insanity. 1st August Kelly is found guilty and is sentenced to death by hanging. On the 2nd his lawyer lodges a petition for clemency, 3rd August the home secretary refuses clemency and the date is set for the hanging on 20 August, 7th August Kelly is examined by Dr W Orange, Superintendent at Broadmoor and declares that Kelly is of defective mental capacity.

17th August, Kelly is certified insane, his sentence is commuted and he is to be held at Broadmoor for life, Kelly arrives on 24 August 1883. Sometime in 1884, Kelly obtains a violin and plays in the Broadmoor band; he is also put to work in the garden at the asylum. In 1886, Kelly and his cell mate George Stratton begin to plan their escape, they fashion keys from metal found in the asylum garden.

On 23 January 1888, Kelly escapes Broadmoor and his escape is not noticed until inmates are called for bed at 7.30pm. Kelly heads for London which takes him four days, he ends up in a lodging house in the docks where he hides out for a week or more, February 1888 head of the metropolitan police takes interest in the case, February–June receiving money from friends, Kelly heads to Liverpool, so not to be caught, he walks the whole way.

After being looked after by friends and obtaining more money, Kelly heads for the continent. He starts his walk to Harwich, after his escape Kelly's movements are based on his own statement. July–December Kelly provides no details of his movements until late that year, November or December, he walks to Dover and boards a streamer to Dieppe; he stays in France for three years.

On 10 November 1888, the day after Mary Kelly killing detectives raid Cottage Lane and question Mrs Brider of Kelly's whereabouts. 1892, Kelly returns to England obtains £3.10s for a ticket to New York via Rotterdam, in 1896 he walks into the British consulate in New Orleans and gives himself up. On 18 March 1896, Kelly returns to England on board the SS Capella, the foreign office make arrangements to meet him when he arrives in Liverpool. The Capella arrives a day early, the authorities have not checked this out, Kelly waits for some time to be arrested but no one shows, so Kelly decides to head off into Liverpool.

When the officials do turn up, Kelly is nowhere to be seen, he stays for another two to three years, working as a coach trimmer in Guilford, then heads off to Vancouver on the steamer SS Beechdale. In 1901, he gives himself up, he tells his story to the British Consulate in Vancouver but when the message is relayed back, no one is interested.

After three months, Kelly returns to England under his own steam, when he arrives he does not give himself up, it is not known how long he stayed but he worked as a coach trimmer in Godalming and at one point spotted working as an upholsterer in North London, at some point he returns to America and crosses the Atlantic several times, then in 1927 he does give himself up.

In April 1907, Broadmoor had officially discharged Kelly after the police failed to re-capture him. 11th February, Kelly arrives at the gates of Broadmoor and asks to be let in. He is profoundly death and of poor physical health, he is readmitted and remains there for the rest of his life. Kelly died on 17 September 1929.

The reason Kelly was a suspect was he stabbed his wife in the neck killing her and he was living around the East End and hanging around prostitutes who had given him VD, I do not know why he blamed his wife when they never had sex but maybe because of the treatment he was giving himself to try and cure his complaint affected his mind as he never saw a doctor he would treat the ailment probably with the wrong drugs.

I do not believe he was insane but he would have probably been a drug addict, he travelled to the continent on his own there were no Ripper type murders where he stayed in France and also in America and Canada; if he was a serial killer then he would continue his killing spree wherever he went.

The next suspect on the list of authors was to be Jacob Levy. Levy was born in Aldgate 1856, the son of Joseph and Caroline, the former having a butchers shop at 111 Middlesex Street, Spitalfields. Levy became a suspect for two reasons, first he was a butcher so knew how to cut open animals which meant he knew the human anatomy, two he contracted syphilis from a prostitute.

The 1881 census list Jacob as a butcher by trade and living with his wife and two children at 11 Fieldgate Street, Whitechapel. There is not a lot of history for Jacob Levy but in 1890 Jacob Levy was delivered to the City of London lunatic asylum, Stone, in Kent, as an insane person. Under the heading of 'address of friends', as recorded in his case notes, the cause of his illness was mania, which had a duration of 'some time'.

His hereditary predisposition was that his elder brother was insane and that his expression countenance was 'restless'. In description his bodily health was good and stood 5'3" tall and weighed 9st 3lbs. His previous history was that he was sentenced to twelve months in prison back in 1886 but was instead sent to the Essex County asylum. The calendar for the central criminal court, have an entry for Joseph Levy having been arrested on 10th March for stealing a weight of meat from his master Hyman Sampson, who had a business at 58 Goulston Street.

During his time at Stones, it is said his wife complained that he almost cost her the business and he himself stated that if he was not restrained, he will do some violence to someone and that he hears strange noises, his wife claims he was once a shrewd businessman. Levy never actually committed any violent crime against anybody but was classed dangerous and insane but he died in the asylum on the evening of 27 July 1891.

He was not the Ripper, he may have been a butcher by trade but that does not qualify him as someone who knows the anatomy of the human body as well as he knows the anatomy of animals. He may have been with prostitutes and caught syphilis but that would be his own fault, if he wanted sex he had a wife at home. To blame a prostitute for his problems was the fact that he was not right in a mental capacity.

The next suspect on the list was James Maybrick. James Maybrick was born on 24 October 1838, in Liverpool, Merseyside, Maybrick was a well-known cotton merchant, Maybrick was almost 50 years old at the time of the Ripper murders, this would make him too old to be the Ripper as witnesses say that the man the police were looking for was between 28-35 years old, the second and most important reason that Maybrick is not the Ripper is because in early March he and his family moved into the palatial Battlecrease house in Aigburth Liverpool.

Maybrick died on 11 May 1889, the events leading to his death and clearing him of being the Ripper are as follows. The Maybrick family had been established in Liverpool for several generations when James was born in 1838 to William and Susannah, James was one of seven boys. While his marriage to Florence is well documented, it is said that James had another wife, even though no marriage certificate can be found.

In 1891, Scottish lawyer William Macdougal alleged that Maybrick had been married before, one Sarah Ann Robertson but in one legal document, a will from her uncle he has called her Sarah Ann Maybrick. Maybrick had several mistresses, he travelled to and from the states quite a lot on business, he was also addicted to Arsenic and Strychnine after Quinine failed to cure him of his Malaria, he contracted Malaria while in Norfolk Virginia after three years there.

The health of Maybrick has never been put into question but it is clear that he was addicted to Arsenic and Strychnine which would have serious consequences on his health, he had been taking it for at least 5 years prior to the Ripper murders, his health would not be good he was almost fifty years old and lived in Liverpool from March 1888, his travels to London would be far less frequent than normal he would not have the stamina to maintain the effort needed to carry out such gruesome murders.

On 12 March 1880, Maybrick boarded the SS Baltic travelling from New York to Liverpool. During the six day voyage, he was introduced to 18-year-old Florence Chandler and her mother Baroness Caroline Von Roques. Although there was 24 years difference in age, a whirlwind romance began and on arrival at Liverpool, they planned their wedding which took place on 27 July 1881 at St James Church, Piccadilly and London.

Their marriage would not be a happy marriage and 8 months after the wedding in 1882, Florie gave birth to their first son James Chandler; he was born two months premature. The Maybricks returned to America; for the next two years they spent in Norfolk, Virginia and Liverpool, Maybrick declining business opportunities returned to England in March 1884 and on 24th August he formerly resigned from the Norfolk cotton exchange.

The family settled in a suburb of Liverpool called Grassendale, however an economic slump occurred that same year, Maybrick became increasingly distressed with health and financial worries. He continued with his addiction to Arsenic and other powders. On 20 July 1886, Florie gave birth to a little girl Gladys Evelyn, the birth of Gladys did nothing for their troubled marriage, it was rapidly deteriorating and James has been showing signs of substance abuse for several years.

In 1887, Florie discovered that James had another woman, it may well have been Sarah Ann Robertson the original Mrs Maybrick. And later that same year, Florie had an affair with cotton broker Alfred Brierly, around early March 1888 the Maybricks moved to Aigburth, Liverpool into the palatial Battlecrease house less than a mile away from Greendale. The estate consisted of several acres of well tendered gardens and trees with a pond full of fish and a small natural stream.

Despite their new home, their marriage was still rocky; James maintained his gloomy disposition of hypochondria and hot temper. On 29 March 1889, Florie suffered a black eye after violence erupted. In April that year, Florie bought a dozen fly papers and James received another prescription as his health continued to fail. More medicine arrived by package on the 26th, James Maybrick became seriously ill the following day apparently from an overdose of substances.

From here James Maybrick never regained his health after seeing his doctor on 3rd May, he visited his office for the last time and it would be the last entry in his diary that day, this is assuming that the diary is authentic and on 11 May 1889 fearing the worst, James' brother Michael travelled from London to visit him and on that same day at 8.40 pm, James Maybrick died. James Maybrick was an Arsenic addict as well as other substances, when he died through substance abuse, his wife Florie was convicted of murder.

The evidence pointed to her because she had bought a dozen fly papers which contained Arsenic, she had a very poor defence lawyer who failed to produce valuable evidence that Maybrick was an Arsenic addict. And the judge was a Mr Justice Fitzjames Stephen, the father of S.K. Stephen, a Ripper suspect himself. Judge Stephen who was biased at the trial would die in an insane asylum in 1894 in Ipswich.

The next suspect made by authors who wanted to sell books was Alexander Pedachenko. Pedachenko was first brought to the attention of many by writer of tales William Le Queux; it's believed that Le Queux claims that he saw a manuscript in French by Rasputin claiming that Jack the Ripper was a Russian Doctor named Alexander Pedachenko, an agent of the Okhrana secret police of Imperial Russia.

It is claimed that Pedachenko was sent to commit murder to discredit Scotland Yard; he was supposedly to have had two accomplices working with him 'Levitski' and a Tailoress named Winberg. There is no evidence that Pedachenko existed and he was just placed on the suspect list by Donald McCormick who may have developed the story by adding his own inventions.

I believe that Pedachenko did not exist as there is no documentation or evidence that such a person travelled from Russia to England and there is no logic into Russia wanting to discredit Scotland Yard, if Russia wanted to discredit any part of England, it would have to be to discredit members of Parliament as that would have more of an impact on the British people.

Suspect number nine would be Walter Sickert. Walter Richard Sickert born 31 May 1860, Sickert was a German born artist of British and Danish ancestry and he was first named as a suspect in Donald McCormick's book the identity of Jack the Ripper (1959). Sickert went to University College School in 1870-1871 before transferring to Kings College School until he was 18.

Although he was the son and grandson of painters his first sought was acting, he appeared in small parts for Sir Henry Irving's company, before taking up the study of art in 1881, after less than a year at Slade School he left to become a pupil and etching assistant to James Abbott McNeill Whistler. Sickert's early paintings were small tonal studies painted alla prima from nature after Whistler's example.

In 1883, he travelled to Paris and met Edgar Degas the French artist, whose work had a big influence on his work. He was a cosmopolitan and eccentric who often favoured ordinary people and urban scenes as his subjects, in 1888 he joined the New English Art Club (NEAC), a group of French influenced realist artists, Sickert displayed a couple of his works at the NEAC in April 1888. In the late 1880s, Sickert spent most of his time in Dieppe, France.

Where he first visited in mid-1885, where his mistress and possibly illegitimate son lived. It is said that he had a fascination with the Ripper murders and he even depicted some scenes of the murders in his paintings. It is also said that he stayed in a room rumoured to have had Jack the Ripper himself as a lodger. Sickert's first major works dating late 1880's were portrayals of scenes in London.

Well, as far as I am concerned Sickert may have had a fascination for the Ripper murders but he was not the Ripper nor did he stay in a room that was once stayed in by Jack the Ripper himself; this would have been an impossible situation to have happened because no one knows who Jack the Ripper was, so how can you stay in a room of a murderer if you don't know the name of the murderer? Walter Sickert died in Bath on 22 January 1942.

We are down to the last four suspects from authors who in my opinion pose no connection with the murders at all. Next in line is James Kenneth Stephen. Stephen was born in London on 25 January 1859; he was the son of Mr Justice Stephen the man who was biased in the Florie Maybrick court case. In 1886, James went to School in South Borough near Tunbridge Wells.

The school was kept by Rev W.C. Wheeler, a year later he went to school kept by Rev W.T. Browning at Thorpe Mandeville, Banbury, which had a great reputation as a preparatory school for college at Eton. In1871, he was elected a Colleger at Eton, being placed second on the list; he remained at Eton until Easter 1878. James was a heavy set man strong and excelled in sport, he was a natural at the 'Wall game' of Football, a game played at Eton, occupying the position of 'Wall' he got his College Wall colours around 1874 and was captain of keeper of the Wall in 1876 and 1877.

In October 1878, James went into residence at King's. And became one of the best undergraduates of his time, in 1881 he was bracketed first class in the History Tripos. In the summer of 1883, he was selected to read History with Prince Edward of Wales, later the Duke of Clarence, when the Prince returned from his cruise in the Bacchante and was going to Trinity the following October.

For this reason, he lived at Sandringham for three months where his task was profoundly interesting. In 1885, he was called to the Bar, having been a pupil in the chambers of Mr Fletcher Moulton and Mr R.B. Haldane and the late Mr Northmore Lawrence.

His intention was to practice at the chancery Bar. After completing his term of pupillage with Mr Lawrence, he took chambers in stone buildings, during this time he adopted the practice journalism and in the latter part of 1886, he continued for a year and became a constant contributor to the St James's Gazette, which was edited by his father's old friend Mr Frederick Greenwood, who founded it in the summer of the preceding year.

In the Winter of 1886-87, he was paying a visit at Felixstowe, while there he received a severe blow to the head, he did not lose consciousness but did receive a very bad cut, the wound healed but his health was never the same. At the beginning of 1888, he found a newspaper called the Reflector. James had abandoned all his professional work but in the summer of 1888, his father appointed him clerk of Assize for the South Wales circuit, in the hope that in the intervals between circuits when the work became light, he would be able to resume his contributions to the newspapers or acquire some practice at the bar.

However, his health did not permit this and after vicissitudes of illness and one period of leave of absence from his official duties, he resigned his clerkship of Assize in 1890 and returned to Cambridge in the spring of 1891. During the Ripper murders, Stephen was living and working in Wales as clerk of Assize south Wales circuit. Stephen was not nor could be the Ripper, he had not spent time in Whitechapel and was in poor health to carry out the tasks, he never studied medicine, he was a poet and practicing barrister and journalist.

The next in line for the Ripper suspect from authors was Francis Thompson. Thompson was born on 16 December 1859 in Winckley Street Preston, Lancashire. Thompson was an English poet and mystic, at the behest of his father who was a doctor Thompson entered medical school at the age of eighteen, he went to Owen's college now known as university of Manchester for eight years but had no interest in medicine, his love was poetry and watching cricket.

Thompson never practiced as a doctor and to escape the approaches of his father he tried to enlist as a soldier but was rejected due to his slightness of statue, so he fled to London penniless in 1885, where he tried to make a living as a writer, meanwhile taking odd jobs working for a booksellers and bootmakers, selling matches, during this time he became an Opium addict, which he first took as medicine for his ill health, having experienced a nervous breakdown while in Manchester, he lived on the streets in Charing cross and slept by the Thames with other homeless people and addicts.

He was turned down by Oxford University because of his addiction and not because he was unqualified. Thompson thought of suicide in his nadir of despair but was saved from completing the action through a vision he had of a youthful poet Thomas Chatterton who committed suicide over a century earlier. A prostitute who Thompson never gave a name to befriended him and gave him lodgings.

Thompson later described her as his saviour in his poems. In 1888 after three years on the streets, he was discovered after sending his poetry to the magazine Merrie England. He was sought out by the magazine's editors Wilfred and Alice Maynell, who recognised the value of his work. They took him into their home and concerned about his addiction due to years on the streets sent him to Our Lady of England Priory, Storrington; for a couple of years, he continued to take Opium but only in small doses and at irregular intervals to relieve the nerve pain.

Thompson wrote most of his work during 1888 and 1897, after which he started writing prose. Thompson died of TB on 13 November 1907. Thompson although lived on the streets of London and studied medicine for eight years, he had no interest in medicine and was befriended by a prostitute who helped him find his feet gave him a roof over his head, why would a man who was saved by a prostitute start killing them, his love was poetry and writing he had no history of violence and was an addict on Opium.

Thompson was never really in the running as a Ripper suspect, it was just another author writing about a talented poet whose theories were all wrong and just to sell books.

We are now getting to the end of our author suspects, our all but one suspect now is the Duke of Clarence and Avondale. But we have already written that the Prince Albert was not the Ripper due to his commitments and his whereabouts at the time of the murders. So we are now down to the last suspect on the author's list, the last person is Sir John Williams.

Sir John Williams was born 6 November 1840. He was court physician to Queen Victoria and made 1st Baronet. He became court physician in 1886. He would have been 48–years-old at the time of the killings and his health was not good which is why it is said he only sought to treat his private clients and royal family as his workload lessened.

He was not the Ripper as said in a Ripper book, written by one of his later relatives. No evidence is given to his findings and they are just written to sell a story. So far we have been through 29 suspects and there is no hard evidence to prove that either one of them is Jack the Ripper.

All the writings about who Jack the Ripper was point to everyone who was on the lists as being Jack because when they moved from London, the murders stopped and with that in mind, then all the suspects in all the lists I have just spoke of were Jack the Ripper, so in theory there is that there are 29 Jack the Rippers. What rubbish. Let's concentrate on the officials who were around at the time and had some kind of input into the Whitechapel murders or the Ripper case.

Chapter Six
Officials Involved in the Murders

The following people are the officials involved in the death of eleven prostitutes in the Whitechapel area of the East End of London. Frederick Abberline, Edmund Reid, Robert Anderson, Thomas Arnold, Walter Dew, George Godley, Donald Swanson, Henry Moore, John Spratling, Henry Helson, Henry Smith, Robert Sagar, Adolphus Frederick Williamson, Stephen White, William Thick, James Harvey, Melville Macnaghten, James Munro, John Neil, William Smith, Ernest Thompson, Edward Watkins and Charles Warren.

We will start with Frederick Abberline. Born 8 January 1843 in Blandford Dorset. At the age of 20, Abberline joined the metropolitan police constable 43519, he was appointed to N division Islington. On 19 August 1865, Abberline was promoted to sergeant and moved to Y division Highgate. Abberline was promoted to Inspector on 10 March 1873. On 8 April 1878, he was moved to H division Whitechapel and promoted to local Inspector and on 26 February 1887, he was moved to a division Whitehall and on 19th November that same year, he moved to CO division Scotland Yard.

8 February 1888, he was promoted to First Class Inspector. In interviews with the Pall Mall Gazette in 1903, Abberline put forward the idea that George Chapman was Jack the Ripper stating that he cannot help feeling that Chapman was the man they struggled so hard to capture 15 years earlier. However, he said that Scotland Yard were no wiser on the subject than it was 15 years ago.

Abberline died on 10 December 1929 aged 86 at 'Estcourt', 195 Holdenhurst Road Bournemouth. He was buried at the Wimborne Cemetery, grave number Z259N. He is buried in the same cemetery as Ripper suspect Montague Druitt.

The next Inspector involved is Sir Robert Anderson. Anderson was born in 1841 in Dublin Ireland. He received a BA from Trinity College Dublin in 1862 and in 1963, he was called to the Bar. Anderson married in 1873 and in 1876 came to London as part of an intelligence branch to combat Fenianism but it soon closed. However but Anderson stayed on in London as an Home Office advisor in matters relating to Political crime.

He was also controller for the spy Thomas Miller Beach who had penetrated the Fenian movement. But in 1886, Anderson was relieved of all his duties except for controlling Beach after getting into trouble with Home Secretary Hugh Childers. In 1887-1888, he became secretary of the Prison Commissioners. In August 1888, he replaced James Munro as Assistant Commissioner of the CID. Anderson retired in 1901 and was knighted in the same year, on 15 November 1918 Anderson died.

The third police official on the list is Walter Simon Andrews. Andrews was born on 27 April 1847 in Boulge, Suffolk. He was one of three inspectors sent from Scotland Yard to strengthen the investigation into the Whitechapel murders; Andrews joined the metropolitan police service on 15 November 1869, he rose through the ranks and he was promoted to Detective Sergeant on 18 November 1875 and then to inspector on 6 July 1878. Andrews retired in 1889 aged 52 on 26 August 1899. Andrews committed suicide by hanging himself at Horndean, Hampshire.

Superintendent Thomas Arnold was another official to help in the investigation into the Whitechapel murders. Thomas Arnold was born 7 April 1835 in Weald, Essex. Arnold joined the metropolitan police B Division Chelsea on 19 March 1855 and on 20 September 1855, he resigned to fight in the Crimean war. At the end of hostilities, he re-joined the police on 29 September 1856.

He was attached to K division west Ham warrant number 35059. He served most of his career in the East End and was promoted to inspector on 14 March 1866 and transferred to B division. In 1887, Arnold was involved in the Lipski case another murder and in 1888, he was made police superintendent of H division Whitechapel at the same time of the Whitechapel murders. On 3 February 1893, Arnold retired from the force and in January 1907, he died in Leytonstone.

Walter Dew was born on 17 April 1863, at Far Cotton, Northampton. He was one of seven children, the family moved to London when he was ten years old. As a boy, he was not a natural scholar and left school when he was just 13 years old; as a youth, Dew found employment working in a solicitor's office off Chancery Lane but not liking the work he left and became a clerk for a seed merchant in Holborn. In 1882, he joined the metropolitan police aged 19 and his warrant number was 66711.

Dew was posted to the metropolitan police X division in Paddington green in June. In early 1887, Dew was transferred to H division Whitechapel where he was a Detective Constable, in the Criminal Investigation Department during the Jack the Ripper murders of 1888. Dew claims to being personally involved in the Ripper murders and he claimed to have known Mary Jane Kelly by sight.

In 1898, Dew was promoted to inspector and moved to Scotland yard T division in Hammersmith in 1900; in 1903, he was promoted to inspector 1st class and moved to E division in Bow Street. In 1906 he was promoted again, to Chief Inspector and returned to Scotland Yard; in 1910, Dew retired from the police his record shows he had received 130 recommendations from the commissioner of the Metropolitan police, Judges and Magistrates. Dew died on 16 December 1947 aged 84.

Next on the list is detective sergeant George Godley. George Godley was born on 31 October 1857 in East Grinstead Sussex. Godley like his father worked as a lawyer but in 1877, Godley joined the metropolitan police and assigned warrant number 61230, at the time of the Ripper murders Godley was sergeant in London's J division Bethnal Green, he was transferred to H division Whitechapel where he assisted inspector Abberline in the hunt for Jack the Ripper.

Godley captured poisoner George Chapman in 1903 and the then retired inspector Frederick Abberline is supposedly to have said:

"You have caught Jack the Ripper at last," or something like it. Godley died on 20 July 1941 aged 83.

Inspector Joseph Henry Helson was next on the list of police officials. Helson was born on 11 April 1845 in Buckland, Monachorum Devon. He joined the Metropolitan police on 4 January 1869. He was assigned to a division Whitehall and given warrant number 51389. He was promoted to Sergeant and transferred to L division Lambeth in May 1872, he was promoted to local Inspector of J division Bethnal Green on 24 October 1887.

In 1888, he headed the Bethnal Green C.I.D and therefore was responsible for investigating the Mary Ann Nichols murder and also assisted Inspector Abberline into the murder of Annie Chapman. He was also involved in the investigation of John Pizer and other Ripper suspects. Helson retired from the Metropolitan police on 14 January 1895 and settled in Tavistock, Devon. He was recalled back to duty in the Metropolitan police in 1902 for the Coronation parade through London. Helson was assigned to M division Southwark and had a temporary warrant number 1869. Helson died in 1920.

Chief Inspector John George Littlechild is another official assigned to the murders. Littlechild was born on 21 December 1848 in Royston, Hertfordshire. On 18 February 1867, he joined the Metropolitan police, on 11 January 1871 he was transferred to Scotland Yard and on 23rd March the same year, he was promoted to Detective Sergeant. In 1876, he was involved in investigating the turf fraud scandal and arrested the ringleader William Kurr.

On 8 April 1878, he was promoted to Detective Inspector, on 3 February 1882 he was promoted to chief Inspector and he was involved in the Phoenix Park murders. In 1883, he was made head of the newly formed Special Irish Branch renamed in 1888 to Special Branch. In 1893, he resigned from the Metropolitan police and worked as a private investigator. On 23 September 1913, Littlechild wrote a letter to Journalist G.R. Sims in which he identified a Doctor T, whom he described as an American Quack named Tumblety, as a likely suspect for the Ripper murders. Littlechild died on 2 January 1923.

One of the more famous officials investigating the Ripper murders was Detective Inspector Edmund Reid. If you watched the TV series Ripper Street, you would see that the Inspector was Edmund Reid. Reid was born on 21 March 1846, in Canterbury, Kent. Before he joined the Metropolitan police, Reid worked as a grocer's delivery boy in London and a Pastry cook and a ships steward, Reid joined the police in 1872, his warrant number was 56100 PC P478, Reid was small for a police officer standing at 5'6" tall.

In 1874, he was transferred to the CID as a Detective in P division and was promoted to Third Class Sergeant in 1878 and detective Sergeant in 1880. In 1885, Reid was promoted to Detective Inspector and based at Scotland Yard. In 1886, he organised the newly formed J division's CID in Bethnal Green. By the time the Ripper murders started in 1888, Reid was the Local Inspector and head of CID H division Whitechapel having been appointed in 1887 he succeeded Francis Abberline.

In 1895, he transferred to L division Lambeth, Reid was the officer in charge of enquiries into the murders of Emma Elizabeth Smith in April 1888 and Martha Tabram in August 1888, before Frederick Abberline was sent from Scotland Yard to co-ordinate the hunt for the killer. Reid retired from the Metropolitan police in 1896 from ill health in March and became land lord of the lower red lion public house in Herne in Kent. Reid died on 5 December 1917 aged 71 years old and was buried at Herne Bay Cemetery in plot J62.

PC James Harvey, the Constable on beat at time of Katherine Eddowes murder. PC James Harvey was born on 4 February 1855 in Ashburnham, Sussex. Harvey joined the city of London police in 1876, arrant number 5045. Harvey was dismissed from the police on 1 July 1889 for reasons unknown. Harvey took up a position as a warehouseman and later it was recorded that he was a Fireman Dustman, Harvey died in West Ham in 1903.

Melville Macnaghten, a well-known figure in police circles and the best decorated during the late Victorian and early Edwardian times. Macnaghten was born on 16 June 1853 in Woodford, Essex. He was the youngest of fifteen children, his father was the last chairman of the British India Tea Company in Bengal, Macnaghten went to Eton and left at seventeen in 1872 where he left for India to run his father's tea estates and remained there until 1888, with occasional visits home.

In 1881, he was assaulted by Indian land rioters and as a result, he became friends with James Munro, who was District Judge and Inspector-General in Bombay presidency at the time. On 3rd October Macnaghten married a daughter of a Canon in Chichester; they had four children, two boys and two girls. On his return to England, he was offered the post of first Assistant Chief Constable (CID) in the Metropolitan police by Munro, who had then been first assistant commissioner of crime; the appointment was opposed by commissioner of police of the Metropolis Charles Warren.

This is said to be because of 'the Hindus' in Bengal that gave him a beating. Even though he was not on the police force when the Ripper murders commenced in 1888, he was actively involved in the murders of Whitechapel prostitutes in 1989 and 1891. In 1913, Macnaghten retired from the Metropolitan police through ill health. Macnaghten died on 12 May 1921 at Queen Anne's Mansions Westminster.

James Munro CB was another official attached to the Whitechapel murders. Munro was born in Edinburgh in 1838. Munro was educated at the Edinburgh High School, the University of Edinburgh and the University of Berlin. In 1857, he joined the legal branch of the Indian civil service, before becoming the first assistant commissioner of crime of the London Metropolitan Police and also served as commissioner of police of the Metropolis from 188-1890.

Munro successfully served as an Assistant Magistrate, Collector and District Judge in the Bombay Presidency. He then became Inspector general of police in the Presidency. In 1884, Munro resigned from the Indian Civil Service and returned to Britain, being appointed first Assistant Commissioner of crime in London, in August 1888 he resigned after a struggle with Commissioner Charles Warren over the independence of the CID and Warren's blocking of the appointment of Melville Macnaghten.

Munro is appointed 'Head of the Detective Service' by the Home secretary Henry Matthews. In November 1888, Warren resigns as Commissioner and Munro takes his place. In June 1889, he appoints Melville Macnaghten Assistant Chief Constable (CID). Munro died on 28 January 1920 aged 81.

Henry Moore Chief Inspector, born 2 June 1848 in Northamptonshire, Moore joined the Metropolitan Police Service on 26 April 1886, he was promoted to Sergeant on 29 August 1872; on 25 August 1878, he was promoted to Inspector. He joined the Criminal Investigation Department at Scotland Yard on 30 April 1888. In September 1888, he was sent to Whitechapel to strengthen the Investigation into the Whitechapel murders, shortly after the Mary Ann Nichols case, by 1889 he had taken over from Inspector Frederick Abberline as lead Investigative Officer in the case.

He remained lead Detective until 1896 when the murderer was now inactive. He was promoted to First Class Inspector on 22 December 1890 and to Chief Inspector on 27 September 1895, after his retirement on 9 October 1899, he worked for the Great Eastern Railway Police with the rank of Superintendent until his second retirement in 1913, Moore died five years later in 1918 aged 70.

PC John Neil Born in 1850 County Cork, Ireland, Cork joined the Metropolitan Police in 1875 warrant number 59168, he served in J division Bethnal Green throughout his career. PC Neil found the body of Mary Ann Nichols while on his beat at 3.45am on 31 August 1888; in 1889, PC Neil was a reserve Police Officer and in 1897, he retired from the Police when he got injured while on duty.

Robert Sagar was also involved into the Whitechapel murders. Sagar was born in 1852, in 1880 he gave up studying medicine at St Bartholomew's Hospital and joined the Police force. In 1884, he was made a Detective Constable. He was promoted to Sergeant in 1888, a year later he was made a Detective Sergeant and in 1890, he was promoted to Detective Sergeant and retired in 1905. Commissioner of the City Police Henry Smith wrote:

"A better or more intelligent officer Robert Sagar, I never had under my control." Sagar died in 1924 aged 72.

Major Henry Smith was born in Penpoint Dumfriesshire, Scotland in 1835; he was educated at Edinburgh Academy and Edinburgh University, he commissioned at the Suffolk Artillery Militia 1869, in 1870 he became a constable in the Scottish county police force and later transferred to Newcastle. In 1879, he moved down to London; on 30 January 1885, he was appointed Chief Superintendent of the City of London Police. Then in 1890-1901, he became Commissioner of the City of London Police. In 1910, he was knighted and also wrote his memoirs from Constable to Commissioner. He died on 2 March 1921 in Edinburgh.

PC William Smith, 452H. Born on 14 September 1862 at Milton, (under Wychwood) in Oxfordshire; Smith joined the Metropolitan Police on 19 March 1883. His warrant number 67565; he was posted to H division Whitechapel in 1886 after serving initially in P division then C division on 30 July 1883, on 29 March 1886 he was with A division then on 25th June transferred to H division that same year.

PC Smith's beat took him from the corner of Gowers Walk and Commercial road to Christian Street; he went down Christian Street and Fairclough Street as far as Grove Street, along Fairclough Street then up Backchurch Lane to Commercial Road. He took in other streets along the way including Batty Street and Berner Street his beat took him around 25-30 minutes to walk. After 27 years in the force, Smith retired on 25 April 1910. On 4 May 1914, Smith died from aortic aneurism at home in Tottenham, he was only 52 years old.

Inspector John Thomas Spratling was born in St Pancras, London 1840; he joined the Metropolitan Police in 1870 warrant number 53457 after working as a clerk. Spratling was rapidly promoted to Inspector of J division Bethnal Green in 1887. Spratling retired in 1897 and moved to Berkshire, then moved to Reading where he died in 1935 aged 90. It is said that Spratling bragged that he drank blacker tea and smoked blacker tobacco than anyone else in the force.

Donald Swanson is next to read about some of his career. Donald Swanson was born in Thurso, Caithness, Scotland in 1848. His father was a brewer and distiller; on 17 April 1868 he joined the Metropolitan Police warrant number 50282. He started at a division and moved to Y division on 9 September 1870 and then on to K division on 12 December 1871, then he was back to a division on 15 September 1876.

In 1878, he achieved the rank of Chief Inspector CID Scotland Yard. In 1896, he was promoted to Superintendent. Swanson retired on 1 July 1903, having been awarded a pension of £280 a year is today's equivalent would be £23800. A healthy sum for a pension in the early 20th century, by the end of 1912 Swanson moved to New Malden Surrey, Swanson died on 25 November 1924 at the same address.

William Thick was a Police officer accused of being Jack the Ripper by Mr H.T. Haslewood of Tottenham, after he sent a letter to the Home Office on 14 October 1889. Thick was born 20 November 1845 in Salisbury, Wiltshire; on 6 March 1868, Thick joined the Metropolitan Police with a warrant number 49889. He was posted to H division Whitechapel, then to B division Chelsea, the P division Camberwell and back to H division where he spent the remainder of his career.

Thick was one of the more colourful members of the investigating team, Thick was nicknamed Johnny Upright, either because of his character or posture is not quite certain. Thick retired from the force on 23 April 1893. Thick died in 1930 aged 85. Frederick Wensley who would become Chief Constable CID said:

"Thick was the finest Policeman he had ever known."

In the 1880s, beat officers were on foot taking up to 30 minutes to walk their beat, they were walking up and down back street of the East end in near dark roads, it would be easy for a murder to know how long it would take a beat officer to arrive a certain locations so for them to catch criminals or murderers in the act of a crime would be almost impossible, while walking down one street, a criminal could be walking up an adjacent street out of sight.

Jack the Ripper was not in my opinion a person to just walk down the street and kill a prostitute, it would have had to be planned knowing when and where beat officers were at what time and when prostitutes were also alone and not within calling range of a beat Constable. This could be the reason why the canonical five were killed at weekends only during the week observation would be taking place to know the route of his victim and beat Constable.

I believe that the rest of the Whitechapel murders that took place were the result of muggings gone wrong or pimps putting other prostitutes in fear to gain them for their own gains, the more prostitutes they own, the more money they would earn. The murder of Mary Kelly, I do not believe that she was the victim of the Ripper, as this would not be the same pattern of the rest of the murders.

Jack the Ripper killed prostitutes in the streets of Whitechapel as a serial killer, the thrill of being caught and outsmarting the police would have to be greater than a temptation not to kill the way he did, to kill someone in their own home where was the thrill of being caught, there would not be one, serial killers follow a pattern; it is just in their mental state not to change that pattern, ask any psychiatrist or Police officer who ever tried to capture a serial killer. The Mary Kelly murder would, I believe, have been done by either a pimp or a mugger trying to copycat Jack the Ripper.

Chapter Seven
The Mary Ann Nichols Inquest

Day 1, Saturday, 1 September 1888.
The Daily Telegraph, Monday, 3 September 1888.

On Saturday, 1 September 1888 the Coroner for South East Middlesex, Mr Wynne E Baxter, opened the Inquest at the Working Lads Institute in Whitechapel Road, into the circumstances attending the death of a woman lying on the pavement in Buck's Row, Baker's Row, Whitechapel, believed to be that of Mary 'Polly' Ann Nichols in the early hours of Friday morning with her throat cut and other terrible injuries.

Inspector Helson who has the case in hand, attended along with other officers from the Criminal Investigation Department. The first witness was Edward Walker. Walker testified that he lived in Camberwell, with no occupation. He stated that he was a Smith when he was at work. He stated that he had seen the body in the Mortuary and that the woman was indeed his daughter but he has not seen her for three years.

He also said that he had recognised the body through her general appearance and by a tiny mark on her forehead that she has had since she was a small child. She also had one or two teeth out like the woman I have seen. He stated his daughters name and said that she was married but has been apart from her husband for seven or eight years. She was also 42 years old.

Walker said that she had written to him, the coroner showed him a letter and he confirmed that it was her letter. The letter was dated 7 April 1888 and the coroner read it out, the letter referred to a place she went to in Wandsworth. The coroner asked Walker when he last saw his daughter. He replied that he had not seen her for two years last June as they were not on speaking terms.

Coroner asked Walker if he had any reasonable doubt that she was his daughter, Walker replied no. PC John Neil was the next witness. He started his statement explaining that the he was on his beat walking down Buck's Row towards Brady Street and he had been there about half an hour previous and there was no one about. He said that he was on the right hand side of the street and he noticed a figure lying in the street, he said it was dark at the time but there was a street light shining at the end of the Row.

He said that the deceased was laying length ways with her head towards the East beside a gateway, her left hand was touching the gate and with the aid of his lamp, he saw that her throat had been cut and blood was pouring from it, she was lying on her back with her clothes disarranged. She was still warm and her eyes were wide open, she had a bonnet by her left hand, then he heard another constable passing Brady Street, he called out and did not use his whistle, he told the Constable to go and fetch Dr Llewellyn.

Seeing another Constable in Baker's Row, he told him to fetch an ambulance. The Doctor had arrived and confirmed that the woman was dead and he will make further examinations of the body in the Mortuary. Inspector Spratley arrived at the Mortuary and while taking a description of the body, turned up her clothes and found that she had been disembowelled. This had not been noticed at the scene.

Dr Llewellyn continued with his statement saying that the victim had a circular bruise on the left side of her face, it was done by either a fist or thumb. On the right side of her face, there is a bruise running along the lower part of her jaw indicating she was held by the right hand. On the left side of her neck about an inch below the jaw was an incision about four inches long running from a point immediately below the ear.

An inch below the same side and commencing about an inch in front of it, was a circular incision terminating at a point about three inches below the right jaw. The incision severed all the tissues down to the vertebrae. The cuts were caused by a long bladed knife, moderately sharp and used with great violence. No blood at all was found on the body or clothes.

There were no injuries about the body till the lower part of the abdomen, two or three inches from the left side was a wound running in a jagged manner, it was a very deep wound and the tissues were cut through. There were also several incisions running across the abdomen. On the right side, there were three or four similar cuts running downwards, all the wounds were from left to right indicating a left-handed person.

The trouble I am having at this point of the inquest. And it is that PC Neil stated that blood was pouring from the wound, so unless the victim was lying with her legs in the air there would have to be blood on her clothes. As Dr

Llewellyn stated, no blood on her clothes. Unless I am mistaken, if someone was lying on their back, blood pouring from a wound, would it not run down the back of the neck and onto the ground, build up on the floor in a puddle ending up on clothes as it spreads, especially as women in Victoria times wore high neck dresses with thrilled necks.

Mary Ann Nichols Inquest (Day 2)

It is Monday, 3 September 1888 and the second day of the inquest has started, Wynne E Baxter continues with the Inquiry at the Working Lads Institute, Whitechapel. At the second day hearing, Inspectors Helston and Abberline attend for the Police and Detective Sergeant Enright is attending for Scotland Yard. Inspector John Spratling of J division spoke that he first heard of the murder about four thirty on Friday morning, while he was in Hackney Road.

He headed straight to Buck's Row; there he met Constable Thain who showed him where the body was lying, Spratling noticed a blood stain on the footpath. The body was at the mortuary in old Montague Street, this is where Spratling had time to prepare a description of the dead woman; the body had been stripped. The skin had the appearance for not having been washed for some time prior to the murder.

Dr Llewellyn examined the body for about ten minutes. On the stand being questioned was Detective Sergeant Enright, when asked about the body being stripped; he said that the body had been stripped by two workhouse officials, did they have permission? No, I never gave them permission, in fact I told them to leave it as it was.

I have no objection to the stripping but we ought to have evidence about the clothes. Sergeant Enright continued. The clothes were lying in a heap in the yard; they consisted of a reddish-brown ulster, with seven large brass buttons and a brown dress, which looked new. There was also a woollen and flannel petticoat, belonging to the workhouse. Inspector Helston had cut out pieces P.R. Princess Road, to try and trace the body, who it was and where it had come from.

There was also a pair of stays, in fairly good condition but witness did not notice how they were adjusted, the Coroner stated that it was important to know the exact state stays were found. Inspector Abberline suggested that the clothes be sent for. The Jury foreman asked whether the stays were fastened to the body. Inspector Spratling replied that he could not say for certain.

There was blood on the upper part of the dress and the ulster but only a little in the under linen, this may have been when the body was moved from Buck's row. Around six o'clock, he made an examination of Buck's row and Brady Street which ran across Baker's Row but found no traces of blood. With the aid of Sergeant Godley, they examined the East London District Railway Lines and the embankment, they also examined the Great Eastern Railway Yard but still found no traces of blood.

The signalman for the Great Eastern Railway whose box was only fifty to sixty yards from where the body was found heard nothing that night. Spratling also made visits to the neighbourhood residences, they also did not notice anything suspicious that night. Replying to a jury Spratling said that Constable Neil was the only one whose duty it was to pass down Buck's Row but another Constable passing along Broad Street time to time would have been in hearing distance. In reply to a Juryman, Spratling said that he believed that the woman was dressed at the time of the murder.

Witness Henry Tomkins, a Horse slaughterer of Coventry Street Bethnal Green stated that he was employee of Messrs. Barber and working in the slaughterhouse, Winthrop Street, from between eight and nine o'clock Thursday evening to twenty past four Friday morning. Ask whether his work was noisy, he replied it was not. Was it quiet on Friday morning? Yes, the gates were open, we heard no cry. Did anyone pass the slaughterhouse that night? No, was the reply, only the Policeman.

Are there any women about there? I did not see any. The Coroner asked not even in Whitechapel Road? Oh yes, there all sorts of shapes and sizes; it's a rough neighbourhood. The Witness stated. Henry Tomkins continued his answers during the inquest by saying that no one passed the slaughterhouse, it was quite quiet and would have heard any noise outside he also said that the slaughterhouse was too far away from where the murder took place to hear any cry for help.

He also said he cannot say if he read anything in the newspapers. Does this mean he cannot read or he does not what to say if he had read something in the newspapers? He claimed that he did not see a soul from between one and four fifteen in the morning. When asked questions by the Jury, his answers were as follows. He did not hear a cart go by and he would have done if one had, between twelve twenty and one o'clock, he and a mate went to the front road, depending on what they have to do during the night the times they leave varies and the constable told of the murder because he called for his cape.

Inspector Helson was now in the witness box to answer questions from the coroner. Inspector Helson statement was as follows. He first knew of the murder at quarter to seven on Friday morning, later he went to the mortuary to see the body, which was clothed; there was no cuts on the clothes and no sign of a struggle. He also believed that the murder took place at the scene of the body and placed there from somewhere else.

Police Constable Mizen was the next witness; his statement was that at quarter to four Friday morning he was at the crossing of Hanbury Street and Bakers Row, when a Carman and another man informed him that he was wanted by another policeman in Bucks Row. When I arrived, Constable Neil sent me to fetch an ambulance. There was no one else with the body but PC Neil. Mizen had made a small detailed account of events that he was involved in.

Andrew Cross was now giving his statement to the events of that morning. Cross worked for Pickford & Co as a Carman for over 20 years. At around three thirty on Friday morning, Cross left home for work his route would take him down Buck's Row, where he saw what looked like a sheet lying against a gateway, on further inspection he saw a woman lying there.

He then heard footsteps of a man coming up Buck's Row about forty yards away, in the direction he had just come from, he told the other man to see what he has found a woman lying by the gateway, he said he believed she was dead, the other man put his hand to feel her heart and said she may be breathing but very little, then they heard a policeman coming because it was so dark they did not notice her throat had been cut.

They left the woman and met the policeman in Baker's Row and informed him of their find in Buck's Row. The witness said she looked either drunk or dead and he also denied meeting Constable Neil in Buck's Row. The other man never gave his name only mentioned that he was behind time the same as me. Answer to a Juryman, he did not tell Constable Mizen that another Constable wanted him in Buck's Row because he did not see a Constable in Buck's row. Cross and the other man saw a Constable in Baker's Row not Buck's row that needs to remembered and not get them both confused with each other.

The next witness was a Mr William Nichols the deceased woman's husband, he was said to be a printers machinist, Coburg Road, Old Kent Road. He collaborated what the father of the deceased said on day one of inquest and that it was his wife and they have been apart for 8 years and he last saw her 3 years previous, they had no contact since then. He had no idea of what she was doing in the meantime, answer to a Juryman question it was not a blacksmith she was living with but another man, I had her watched.

He said that he did not leave his wife, she had left him; it was her choice. Emily Holland, a married woman on the stand as a witness said that the deceased stayed at her lodgings for about six weeks, at 18 Thrawl Street. She had not been there for at least 10 days or so, I last saw the deceased walking down Osborne Street, Whitechapel Road at about two thirty Friday morning. The deceased was on her own and much the worse for drink, she informed me that she was unable to return to where she was living because she could not pay for her room.

She said she had earned her lodging money three times that day and went off along Whitechapel Road. The witness said she did not know how the deceased obtained a living, she always seemed to be a quiet woman and kept much to herself, she never seen her quarrel with anybody, she seemed to be weighed down by some sort of trouble. When she left me, she said she would be back soon.

The last witness of the day was Mary Ann Monk; she claimed to have seen the deceased seven o'clock entering a public house in the New Kent Road, she had seen her before in the workhouse but did not know of her means of livelihood. The inquiry was adjourned until 17th September.

Day three of the Mary Ann Nichols inquiry.

First to be asked questions was Dr Llewellyn. He said that he re-examined the body and no part of the viscera was missing.

Emma Green lives in a cottage next to the scene of the murder in Buck's Row. She said that she heard no unusual sounds during the night. And she knew of no disorderly house in Buck's Row, they are all hard-working people. Thomas Eades signalman for the East London railway Company said he saw a man with a knife on the 8th.

The Coroner was of the opinion that this was irrelevant to the present inquest but he would however accept the evidence. Ede stated that he was walking down Cambridge Heath road when he noticed a man on the other side of the street near the Foresters Arms; he had a peculiar appearance which is why I took notice of him, he seemed to have a wooden arm, I watched him until level with the Foresters Arms, then he put his hand in his pocket and I saw about four inches of a knife. I followed him but he quickened his pace and I lost sight of him.

Inspector Helson said that the man had not been found. The witness described the man as about five feet eight inches tall and about 35 years of age. He had a dark moustache and whiskers; he wore a double peaked cap and a short dark brown jacket. He wore a pair of clean white overalls over dark trousers.

The man walked as if he had a stiff knee, he had a fearful look about his eyes and he seemed to be a mechanic. He was not a muscular man. Walter Purkess manager residing at Essex wharf; said that his house fronted Buck's Row opposite to the gateway where the body was found. He said that he slept in the front room on the second floor and heard no noise, neither did his wife.

Alfred Malshaw, a night watchman in Winthorpe Street; he also heard no noise or cries but he did admit that sometimes he dozed. Coroner said that his watching was not up to much, his reply was he doesn't know it is 13 hours long for three shillings and in a straight line he was about thirty yards from the spot where the deceased was found.

Police Constable John Thail was the next officer on the stand, he stated that on his beat, the nearest place to Buck's Row was Brady Street. He passed by every 30 minutes on Thursday evening and nothing attracted his attention until 3.45 a.m. When he was flashed by Constable Neil's lantern, I went to Constable Neil and he was standing by the body of a woman. We sent a witness to fetch the doctor.

Robert Baul was now on the stand. Baul was a Carman of 30 Forster Street, Whitechapel, he claims that he was going to work at Cobbetts Court, Spitalfields, said that he saw in Buck's Row a man standing in the middle of the road, as I got closer I stepped in the road to pass him, the man tapped me on the shoulder and asked me to look at the deceased woman lying by the gateway. Her clothes were disarranged and he helped me re-arrange them.

We walked to Montague Street where we met a constable. No more than four minutes had elapsed from the time I first saw the woman, before reaching Buck's Row I saw no one running away. Robert Mann is keeper of the Mortuary. He said that the police came to the workhouse, of which he was an inmate; he went to the mortuary at 5 am. Saw the body placed there and then locked up and kept the keys.

After breakfast, Mann and Hatfield, another inmate of the workhouse undressed the body. James Hatfield said he did accompany Mann to the mortuary and undressed the deceased, Inspector Helson was not there. Coroner continued to ask question to Hatfield, who was there? Just me and my mate, Mann, what did you take off first? An Ulster, I put it aside on the ground.

We then took off the jacket and placed it in the same place. The outer dress was loose, we did not cut it. The bands on the petticoat were cut, so I tore them down with my hands. I also tore the chemise down the front, there were no stays. No one told us to undress the body, we did it to have it ready for the doctor, I heard someone say a doctor was coming, no one else was there when we undressed the body, then the police came, we did not do a post-mortem examination, the police examined the clothes and found the words Lambeth Workhouse on the petticoat bands.

I cut the lettering out because Inspector Helson told me to do it that was the first time I saw the Inspector, as I arrived at 6.30. The coroner then spoke to the police who were present. There was a man in Buck's Row when the doctor was examining the body. Have you heard anything from him? Inspector Abberline stated that they have not been able to find him. Inspector Spratley of J division stated that he made inquiries in Buck's Row but not all the houses.

The coroner told Spratley that the houses that were not made inquiries to will have to be done. Spratley said that he made inquiries in Green's, the Wharf, Snider's factory and Great Eastern Wharf but no one heard anything unusual on the morning of the murder. Spratley added that when he was at the mortuary, he gave instructions that the body was not to be touched. Coroner asked if there was any more evidence. Inspector Helston said that there was no more at present.

Inspector Helson answered a question by the foreman of the jury and the coroner, that all rewards had been discontinued for years. The Inquiry was adjourned again until Saturday, 22nd September.

Day four of the Polly Ann Nichols inquiry:

Again, the inquiry was opened by Mr Wynne E Baxter. Signalman Eades was recalled to the stand, to supplement his first evidence that he saw a man now known as John James carrying a knife near the scene of the murder, turns out to be a harmless lunatic who was well-known in the neighbourhood.

The Coroner then summed up. Having received the career of the deceased woman from the time she left her husband, reminded the jury of her irregular life style for the past 2 years. Mr E Baxter proceeded to point out that the deceased woman was last seen alive at two thirty on Saturday morning, 1st September by Mrs Holland, who knew her well. The deceased at that time was much the worse for drink and trying to walk east down Whitechapel.

What her movements were after this are impossible to say. But in less than an hour and a quarter later, she was found dead not far from where we are now. The condition of the body appeared to prove that the murder took place when the deceased was found, as there was no blood around except for where her neck was lying. The injury to her throat suggests it was inflicted while she was on the ground, the injuries to her abdomen due to the state of her clothes and no blood suggests she was still in the same position.

The Coroner statement was that he seemed to not understand how the culprit had easily escaped from the scene undetected and unnoticed in the morning market traffic. There must have been blood on him somewhere, his hands or clothes. Then he said that because of the slaughter-houses around the area to see someone with blood on them they would not stand out as it would be a normal appearance for some men.

So in fact the Coroner actually answered his own question. We cannot leave unnoticed that the death being investigated is only one of four in the last in the space of 5 months and all have a similarity about them. And all in the same area, all four murders were women of middle age, all were married but not with their husbands anymore and living in lodging houses. In each case, there were abdominal as well as other injuries, in each case the attacks were after midnight and in place of public resort and in each case the inhuman criminals are in our society undetected.

Emma Elizabeth Smith survived her injuries in the London Hospital 24 hours after being attacked in Osborn Street on the early Easter Tuesday, 3rd April and was able to give a statement, she was followed by some men, robbed, mutilated and managed to give an imperfect description of one of them. On Tuesday, 7th April at 3 am, Martha Tabram was found on the first floor landing of George Yard buildings, Wentworth Street with thirty nine puncture wounds on her body.

In addition to these and the case being considered by you the jury is Annie Chapman, still in the hands of another jury. After a short consultation, the jury returned a verdict of wilful murder against a person or persons unknown. The inquest was conducted with character witnesses as there were no witnesses to the actual murder or no person accused of the murder, the jury had to come back with their verdict as wilful murder because that is what it was, it was a premeditated murder by a person who for some reason walked away from the crime undetected and unnoticed by passers-by; the police and the neighbourhood.

It really is astounding that a murder can be committed in East London, where there is much poverty and high prostitution run by criminals and gangs, yet with such a small area patrolled at night by policemen within walking distance of each other because their beats cross each other and yet no sound was heard, no cries for help were heard and nothing unusual seemed to be occurring that had the locals out of their homes or lodgings, wondering what is happening.

What has to be remembered is that the streets were poorly lit by low light lamps, there were no automobiles, nor were there aeroplanes flying over, so in 1888 the streets were extremely quiet except where there were public houses and drunks.

It should not have been difficult to hear footsteps, yet none were heard, so did the murderer actually live in Buck's Row or did he go down an alleyway that led into Whitechapel Road, these would seem the only logical answers as no one was seen in the area after the murder. And it was in the same area to where all the other murders took place.

Chapter Eight
The Annie Chapman Inquest

Day 1, Monday, 10 September 1888.
The Daily Telegraph, Tuesday, 11 September 1888.

At the Working Lads' Institute, Whitechapel Road, yesterday morning, 10th September, Mr Wynne Baxter opened an inquiry into the circumstances attending the death of Annie Chapman, a widow whose body was found horribly mutilated in the back yard of 29, Hanbury-street, Spitalfields, early Saturday morning. The jury viewed the corpse at the mortuary in Montague Street but all evidences of the outrage to which the deceased had been subjected were concealed. The clothing was also inspected and subsequently, the following evidence was taken.

John Davies [Davis] deposed:

I am a Car man employed at Leadenhall Market. I have lodged at 29, Hanbury Street for a fortnight and I occupied the top front room on the third floor with my wife and three sons, who live with me. On Friday night, I went to bed at eight o'clock and my wife followed about half an hour later. My sons came to bed at different times, the last one at about a quarter to eleven. There is a weaving shed window or light across the room. It was not open during the night.

I was awake from 3 am to 5 am on Saturday and then fell asleep until a quarter to six, when the clock at Spitalfields Church struck. I had a cup of tea and went downstairs to the back yard. The house faces Hanbury Street, with one window on the ground floor and a front door at the side leading into a passage which runs through into the yard. There is a back door at the end of this passage opening into the yard. Neither of the doors was able to be locked and I have never seen them locked. Anyone who knows where the latch of the front door is could open it and go along the passage into the back yard.

[Coroner] When you went into the yard on Saturday morning, was the yard door open or shut? I found it shut. I cannot say whether it was latched, I cannot remember. I have been too much upset. The front street door was wide open and thrown against the wall. I was not surprised to find the front door open, as it was not unusual. I opened the back door and stood in the entrance.

[Coroner] Will you describe the yard? It is a large yard. Facing the door, on the opposite side, on my left as I was standing, there is a shed, in which Mrs Richardson keeps her wood. In the right hand corner, there is a closet. The yard is separated from the next premises on both sides by close wooden fencing, about 5 ft. 6 in. high.

The Coroner: I hope the police will supply me with a plan. In the country, in cases of importance, I always have one.

Inspector Helson: We shall have one at the adjourned hearing.

The Coroner: Yes, by that time we shall hardly require it.

Examination resumed: There was a little recess on the left. From the steps to the fence is about 3 ft. There are three stone steps, unprotected, leading from the door to the yard, which is at a lower level than that of the passage. Directly I opened the door, I saw a woman lying down in the left-hand recess, between the stone steps and the fence. She was on her back, with her head towards the house and her legs towards the wood shed. The clothes were up to her groins.

I did not go into the yard but left the house by the front door and called the attention of two men to the circumstances. They work at Mr Bailey's, a packing-case maker of Hanbury Street. I do not know their names but I know them by sight.

The Coroner: Have the names of these men been ascertained?

Inspector Chandler: I have made inquiries but I cannot find the men.

The Coroner: They must be found.

Davies: They work at Bailey's but I could not find them on Saturday, as I had my work to do.

The Coroner: Your work is of no consequence compared with this inquiry.

Davies: I am giving all the information I can.

The Coroner (to witness): You must find these men out, either with the assistance of the police or of my officer.

Examination resumed: Mr Bailey's is three doors off 29, Hanbury Street, on the same side of the road. The two men were waiting outside the workshop. They came into the passage and saw the sight. They did not go into the yard but ran to find a policeman. We all came out of the house together. I went to the Commercial Street Police station to report the case. No one in the house was informed by me of what I had discovered. I told the inspector at the police station and after a while I returned to Hanbury Street but did not re-enter the house. As I passed, I saw constables there.

[Coroner] Have you ever seen the deceased before? No.

[Coroner] Were you the first down in the house that morning? No; there was a lodger named Thompson, who was called at half-past three.

[Coroner] Have you ever seen women in the passage? Mrs Richardson has said there have been. I have not seen them myself. I have only been in the house a fortnight.

[Coroner] Did you hear any noise that Saturday morning? No sir.

Amelia Palmer, examined, stated: I live at 35, Dorset Street, Spitalfields, a common lodging house. Off and on, I have stayed there 3 years. I am married to Henry Palmer, a dock labourer. He was foreman but met with an accident at the beginning of the year. I go out charing. My husband gets a pension, having been in the Army Reserve.

I knew the deceased very well, for quite 5 years. I saw the body on Saturday at the mortuary and am quite sure that it is that of Annie Chapman. She was a widow and her husband, Frederick Chapman, was a veterinary surgeon in Windsor. He died about eighteen months ago. Deceased had lived apart from him for about 4 years or more. She lived in various places, principally in common lodging houses in Spitalfields. I never knew her to have a settled home.

[Coroner] Has she lived at 30, Dorset Street? Yes, about two years ago, with a man who made wire sieves and at that time she was receiving 10s a week from her husband by post-office order, payable to her at the Commercial Road. This payment stopped about 18 months ago and she then found, on inquiry of some relative, that her husband was dead. I am under the impression that she ascertained this fact either from a brother or sister of her husband in Oxford Street, Whitechapel.

She was nick named, 'Mrs Sivvy' because she lived with the sieve maker. I know the man perfectly well but don't know his name. I saw him last about 18 months ago in the City and he told me that he was living at Notting Hill. I saw deceased two or three times last week. On Monday, she was standing in the road opposite 35, Dorset Street. She had been staying there and had no bonnet on. She had a bruise on one of her temples, I think the right. I said:

"How did you get that?"

She said, "Yes, look at my chest." Opening her dress, she showed me a bruise. She said, "Do you know the woman?" and gave some name which I do not remember. She made me understand that it was a woman who goes about selling books. Both this woman and the deceased were acquainted with a man called 'Harry the Hawker'.

Chapman told me that she was with some other man, Ted Stanley, on Saturday, 1st September. Stanley is a very respectable man. Deceased said she was with him at a beer shop, 87, Commercial Street, at the corner of Dorset Street, where 'Harry the Hawker' was with the woman. This man put down a two shilling piece and the woman picked it up and put down a penny. There was some feeling in consequence and the same evening, the book-selling woman met the deceased and injured her in the face and chest.

When deceased told me this, she said she was living at 35, Dorset Street. On the Tuesday afternoon, I saw Chapman again near to Spitalfields Church. She said she felt no better and she should go into the casual ward for a day or two. I remarked that she looked very pale and asked her if she had had anything to eat.

She replied, "No, I have not had a cup of tea today." I gave her two pence to get some and told her not to get any rum, of which she was fond. I have seen her, the worse for drink.

[Coroner] What did she do for a living? She used to do crochet work, make antimacassars and sell flowers. She was out late at night at times. On Fridays, she used to go to Stratford to sell anything she had. I did not see her from the Tuesday to the Friday afternoon, 7th inst when I met her about five o'clock in Dorset Street. She appeared to be perfectly sober. I said:

"Are you going to Stratford today?"

She answered, "I feel too ill to do anything." I left her immediately afterwards and returned about ten minutes later and found her in the same spot.

She said, "It is of no use my going away. I shall have to go somewhere to get some money to pay my lodgings." She said no more and that was the last time that I saw her. Deceased stated that she had been in the casual ward but did not say which one. She did not say she had been refused admission. Deceased was a very industrious woman when she was sober. I have seen her often the worse for drink. She could not take much without making her drunk.

She had been living a very irregular life during the whole time that I have known her. Since the death of her husband, she has seemed to give way altogether. I understood that she had a sister and mother living at Brompton but

I do not think they were on friendly terms. I have never known her to stay with her relatives even for a night. On the Monday she observed:

"If my sister will send me the boots, I shall go hopping." She had two children, a boy and a girl. They were at Windsor until her husband's death and since then they have been in a school. Deceased was a very respectable woman and never used bad language. She has stayed out in the streets all night.

[Coroner] Do you know of any one that would be likely to have injured her? No.

The Coroner (having read a communication handed to him by the police): It seems to be very doubtful whether the husband was a veterinary surgeon. He may have been a coachman.

Timothy Donovan, 35, Dorset Street, Spitalfields, said: I am the deputy of a common lodging house. I have seen the body of the deceased and have identified it as that of a woman who stayed at my house for the last 4 months. She was not there last week until Friday afternoon, between two and three o'clock. I was coming out of the office after getting up and she asked me if she could go down in the kitchen and I said:

"Yes," and asked her where she had been all the week. She replied that she had been in the infirmary but did not say which. A police officer stated that the deceased had been in the casual ward.

Witness resumed: Deceased went down in the kitchen and I did not see her again until half past one or a quarter to two on Saturday morning. At that time, I was sitting in the office, which faces the front door. She went into the kitchen. I sent the watchman's wife, who was in the office with me, downstairs to ask her husband about the bed. Deceased came upstairs to the office and said:

"I have not sufficient money for my bed. Don't let it. I shan't be long before I am in."

[Coroner] How much was it? Eight pence for the night. The bed she occupied, No 29, was the one that she usually occupied. Deceased was then eating potatoes and went out. She stood in the door two or three minutes and then repeated.

"Never mind, Tim; I shall soon be back. Don't let the bed." It was then about ten minutes to two a.m. She left the house, going in the direction of Brushfield Street. John Evans, the watchman, saw her leave the house. I did not see her again.

[Coroner] Was she the worse for drink when you saw her last? She had had enough; of that I am certain. She walked straight. Generally on Saturdays, she was the worse for drink. She was very sociable in the kitchen. I said to her:

"You can find money for your beer and you can't find money for your bed." She said she had been only to the top of the street where there is a public house.

[Coroner] Did you see her with any man that night? No sir.

[Coroner] Where did you think she was going to get the money from? I did not know. She used to come and stay at the lodging house on Saturdays with a man, a pensioner of soldierly appearance, whose name I do not know.

[Coroner] Have you seen her with other men? At other times, she has come with other men and I have refused her.

[Coroner] You only allow the women at your place one husband? The pensioner told me not to let her a bed if she came with any other man. She did not come with a man that night. I never saw her with any man that week. In answer to the jury, witness said the beds were double at 8d per night and as a rule, deceased occupied one of them by herself.

The Coroner: When was the pensioner last with deceased at the lodging house? On Sunday, 2nd September I cannot say whether they left together. I have heard the deceased say:

"Tim, wait a minute. I am just going up the street to see if I can see him." She added that he was going to draw his pension. This occurred on Saturday, 25th August, at 3 a.m. In reply to the Coroner, the police said nothing was known of the pensioner.

Examination continued: I never heard deceased call the man by any name. He was between 40 and 45 years of age, about 5 ft. 6 in. or 5 ft. 8 in. in height. Sometimes he would come dressed as a dock labourer; at other times, he had a gentlemanly appearance. His hair was rather dark. I believe she always used to find him at the top of the street. Deceased was on good terms with the lodgers. About Tuesday, 28th August, she and another woman had a row in the kitchen. I saw them both outside.

As far as I know, she was not injured at that time. I heard from the watchman that she had had a clout. I noticed a day or two afterwards, on the Thursday, that she had a slight touch of a black eye. She said:

"Tim, this is lovely," but did not explain how she got it. The bruise was to be seen on Friday last. I know the other woman but not her name. Her husband hawks laces and other things.

John Evans testified: I am night watchman at 35, Dorset Street and have identified the deceased as having lived at the lodging house. I last saw her there on Saturday morning and she left at about a quarter to two o'clock. I was sent down in the kitchen to see her and she said she had not sufficient money. When she went upstairs I followed her and as she left the house, I watched her go through a court called Paternoster Street, into Brushfield Street and then turn towards Spitalfields Church.

Deceased was the worse for drink but not badly so. She came in soon after twelve (midnight), when she said she had been over to her sister's in Vauxhall. She sent one of the lodgers for a pint of beer and then went out again, returning shortly before a quarter to two. I knew she had been living a rough night life. She associated with a man, a pensioner, every Saturday and this individual called on Saturday at 2.30 p.m. and inquired for the deceased. He had heard something about her death and came to see if it was true. I do not know his name or address.

When I told him what had occurred he went straight out, without saying a word, towards Spitalfields Church. I did not see the deceased and this man leave the house last Sunday week.

[Coroner] Did you see the deceased and another woman have a row in the kitchen? Yes, on Thursday, 30th August. Deceased and a woman known as 'Eliza' at 11.30 am, quarrelled about a piece of soap and Chapman received a blow in the chest. I noticed that she had a slight black eye. There are marks on the body in a similar position. By the Jury: I have never heard any one threaten her, nor express any fear of any one. I have never heard any one of the women in the lodging house say that they had been threatened.

At this stage, the inquiry was adjourned.

Day 2, Wednesday, 12 September 1888.
The Daily Telegraph, Thursday, 13 September 1888.

Mr Wynne Baxter yesterday [12th Sep] resumed the inquiry into the circumstances attending the death of Annie Chapman, whose body was found brutally mutilated in the back yard of 29, Hanbury Street, Spitalfields, at six o'clock on the morning of Saturday last.

The Police were represented by Inspector Abberline, of the Criminal Investigation Department and Inspector Helson, J Division.

Fontain Smith, printer's warehouseman, stated: I have seen the body in the mortuary and recognise it as that of my eldest sister, Annie, the widow of John Chapman, who lived at Windsor, a coachman. She had been separated from her husband for about 3 years. Her age was 47. I last saw her alive a fortnight ago, in Commercial-street, where I met her promiscuously.

Her husband died at Christmas, 1886. I gave her 2s; she did not say where she was living nor what she was doing. She said she wanted the money for lodgings.

[Coroner] Did you know anything about her associates? No.

James Kent, 20, Drew's Blocks, Shadwell, a packing-case maker, said: I work for Mr Bayley, 23A, Hanbury Street and go there at 6 am. On Saturday, I arrived about ten minutes past that hour. Our employer's gate was open and there I waited for some other men. Davis, who lives two or three doors away, ran from his house into the road and cried:

"Men, come here." James Green and I went together to 29, Hanbury Street and ongoing through the passage, standing on the top of the back door steps, I saw a woman lying in the yard between the steps and the partition between the yard and the next. Her head was near the house but no part of the body was against the wall. The feet were lying towards the back of Bayley's premises.

(Witness indicated the precise position upon a plan produced by the police officers). Deceased's clothes were disarranged and her apron was thrown over them. I did not go down the steps but went outside and returned after Inspector Chandler had arrived. I could see that the woman was dead. She had some kind of handkerchief around her throat which seemed soaked in blood. The face and hands were besmeared with blood, as if she had struggled.

She appeared to have been on her back and fought with her hands to free herself. The hands were turned towards her throat. The legs were wide apart and there were marks of blood upon them. The entrails were protruding and were lying across her left side. I got a piece of canvass from the shop to throw over the body and by that time a mob had assembled and Inspector Chandler was in possession of the yard. The foreman gets to the shop at ten minutes to six every morning and he was there before us.

James Green, of Ackland Street, Burdett Road, a packing case maker, in the same employ as last witness, said: I arrived in Hanbury Street at ten minutes past six on Saturday morning and accompanied Kent to the back door of No 29. I left the premises with him. I saw no one touch the body.

Amelia Richardson, 29, Hanbury Street, deposed: I am a widow and occupy half of the house i.e. the first floor, ground floor and workshops in the cellar. I carry on the business of a packing case maker there and the shops are used by my son John, aged 37 and a man Francis Tyler, who have worked for me 18 years. The latter ought to have come at 6 am but he did not arrive until eight o'clock, when I sent for him.

He is often late when we are slack. My son lives in John Street, Spitalfields and he works also in the market on market mornings. At 6 am my grandson, Thomas Richardson, aged 14, who lives with me, got up. I sent him down to see what was the matter, as there was so much noise in the passage. He came back and said:

"Oh, grandmother, there is a woman murdered." I went down immediately and saw the body of the deceased lying in the yard. There was no one there at the time but there were people in the passage. Soon afterwards, a constable came and took possession of the place. As far as I know, the officer was the first to enter the yard.

[Coroner] Which room do you occupy? The first floor front and my grandson slept in the same room on Friday night. I went to bed about half past nine and was very wakeful half the night. I was awake at 3 am and only dozed after that.

[Coroner] Did you hear any noise during the night? No.

[Coroner] Who occupies the first floor back? Mr Walker, a maker of lawn tennis boots. He is an old gentleman and he sleeps there with his son, 27 years of age. The son is weak minded and inoffensive. On the ground floor, there are two rooms. Mrs Hardman occupies them with her son, aged 16. She uses the front room as a cats' meat shop. In the front room on the first floor on Friday night, I had a prayer meeting and before I went to bed, I locked the door of this room and took the key with me. It was still locked in the morning.

John Davies and his family tenant the third floor front and Mrs Sarah Cox has the back room on the same floor. She is an old lady I keep out of charity. Mr Thompson and his wife, with an adopted little girl, have the front room on the second floor. On Saturday morning, I called to Thompson at ten minutes to four o'clock. I heard him leave the house. He did not go into the back yard. Two unmarried sisters reside in the second floor back. They work at a cigar factory. When I went down, all the tenants were in the house except Mr Thompson and Mr Davies. I am not the owner of the house.

[Coroner] Were the front and back doors always left open? Yes, you can open the front and back doors of any of the houses about there. They are all let out in rooms. People are coming in or going out all the night.

[Coroner] Did you ever see anyone in the passage? Yes, about a month ago I heard a man on the stairs. I called Thompson and the man said he was waiting for market.

[Coroner] At what time was this? Between half past three and four o'clock. I could not hear anyone going through the passage. I did not hear anyone going through on Saturday morning.

[Coroner] You heard no cries? None. Supposing a person had gone through at half past three, would that have attracted your attention yes.

[Coroner] You always hear people going to the backyard? Yes; people frequently do go through.

[Coroner] People go there who have no business to do so? Yes; I daresay they do.

[Coroner] On Saturday morning you feel confident no one did go through? Yes; I should have heard the sound. They must have walked purposely quietly? Yes or I should have heard them.

By the Jury: I should not allow any stranger to go through for an immoral purpose if I knew it.

Harriett Hardiman [Hardyman, Hardman], living at 29, Hanbury Street, cats meat saleswoman, the occupier of the ground floor front room, stated: I went to bed on Friday night at half past ten. My son sleeps in the same room. I did not wake during the night. I was awakened by the trampling through the passage at about six o'clock. My son was asleep and I told him to go to the back as I thought there was a fire. He returned and said that a woman had been killed in the yard. I did not go out of my room. I have often heard people going through the passage into the yard but never got up to look who they were.

John Richardson, of John Street, Spitalfields Market porter, said: I assist my mother in her business. I went to 29, Hanbury Street, between 4.45 am and 4.50 am on Saturday last. I went to see if the cellar was all secure, as some while ago there was a robbery there of some tools. I have been accustomed to go on market mornings since the time when the cellar was broken in.

[Coroner] as the front door open? No, it was closed. I lifted the latch and went through the passage to the yard door.

[Coroner] Did you go into the yard? No, the yard door was shut. I opened it and sat on the doorstep, and cut a piece of leather off my boot with an old table knife, about five inches long. I kept the knife upstairs at John Street. I had been feeding a rabbit with a carrot that I had cut up and I put the knife in my pocket. I do not usually carry it there. After cutting the leather off my boot I tied my boot up, and went out of the house into the market. I did not close the back door. It closed itself. I shut the front door.

[Coroner] How long were you there? About two minutes at most.

[Coroner] Was it light? It was getting light but I could see all over the place.

[Coroner] Did you notice whether there was any object outside? I could not have failed to notice the deceased had she been lying there then. I saw the body two or three minutes before the doctor came. I was then in the adjoining yard. Thomas Pierman had told me about the murder in the market. When I was on the doorstep, I saw that the padlock on the cellar door was in its proper place.

[Coroner] Did you sit on the top step? No, on the middle step; my feet were on the flags of the yard.

[Coroner] You must have been quite close to where the deceased was found? Yes, I must have seen her.

[Coroner] You have been there at all hours of the night? Yes.

[Coroner] Have you ever seen any strangers there? Yes, plenty, at all hours both men and women. I have often turned them out. We have had them on our first floor as well, on the landing.

[Coroner] Do you mean to say that they go there for an immoral purpose? Yes, they do. At this stage, witness was dispatched by the coroner to fetch his knife. Mrs Richardson, recalled, said she had never missed anything and had such confidence in her neighbours that she had left the doors of some rooms unlocked. A saw and a hammer had been taken from the cellar a long time ago. The padlock was broken open.

[Coroner] Had you an idea at any time that a part of the house or yard was used for an immoral purpose?

Witness (emphatically): No, sir.

[Coroner] Did you say anything about a leather apron? Yes, my son wears one when he works in the cellar.

The Coroner: It is rather a dangerous thing to wear, is it not?

Witness: Yes. On Thursday, 6th September I found my son's leather apron in the cellar mildewed. He had not used it for a month. I took it and put it under the tap in the yard and left it there. It was found there on Saturday morning by the police, who took charge of it. The apron had remained there from Thursday to Saturday.

[Coroner] Was this tap used? Yes, by all of us in the house. The apron was on the stones. The police took away an empty box, used for nails and the steel out of a boy's gaiter. There was a pan of clean water near to the tap when I went in the yard at six o'clock on Saturday. It was there on Friday night at eight o'clock and it looked as if it had not been disturbed.

[Coroner] Did you ever know of strange women being found on the first floor landing? No.

[Coroner] Your son had never spoken to you about it? No.

John Piser [Pizer] was then called. He said: I live at 22, Mulberry Street, Commercial Road East. I am a shoemaker.

[Coroner] Are you known by the nickname of 'Leather Apron?' Yes, sir.

[Coroner] Where you were on Friday night last? I was at 22, Mulberry Street. On Thursday the 6th I arrived there.

[Coroner] From where? From the west end of town.

The Coroner: I am afraid we shall have to have a better address than that presently.

[Coroner] What time did you reach 22, Mulberry Street? Shortly before eleven p.m.

[Coroner] who lives at 22, Mulberry Street? My brother and sister-in-law and my stepmother. I remained indoors there.

[Coroner] Until when? Until I was arrested by Sergeant Thick, on Monday last at 9 am.

[Coroner] you say you never left the house during that time? I never left the house.

[Coroner] Why were you remaining indoors? Because my brother advised me.

[Coroner] You were the subject of suspicion? I was the object of a false suspicion.

[Coroner] You remained on the advice of your friends? Yes; I am telling you what I did.

[The Coroner]: It was not the best advice that you could have had. You have been released and are not now in custody? I am not.

Piser: I wish to vindicate my character to the world at large.

The Coroner: I have called you in your own interests, partly with the object of giving you an opportunity of doing so.

[Coroner] Can you tell us where you were on Thursday, 30th August?

Witness (after considering): In the Holloway Road.

[Coroner] You had better say exactly where you were. It is important to account for your time from that Thursday to the Friday morning.

[Pizer] What time, may I ask?

The Coroner: It was the week before you came to Mulberry Street.

Witness: I was staying at a common lodging house called the Round House, in the Holloway Road.

[Coroner] Did you sleep the night there? Yes. At what time did you go in? On the night of the London Dock fire, I went in about two or a quarter past. It was on the Friday morning.

[Coroner] When did you leave the lodging house? At 11 am on the same day. I saw on the placards, 'Another Horrible Murder'. Where were you before two o'clock on Friday morning? At 11 pm on Thursday, I had my supper at the Round House.

[Coroner] Did you go out? Yes, as far as the Seven Sisters Road and then returned towards Highgate Way, down the Holloway Road. Turning, I saw the reflection of a fire. Coming as far as the church in the Holloway Road, I saw two constables and the lodging housekeeper talking together. There might have been one or two constables, I cannot say which. I asked a constable where the fire was and he said it was a long way off. I asked him where he thought it was and he replied:

"Down by the Albert Docks." It was then about half past one, to the best of my recollection. I went as far as Highbury Railway Station on the same side of the way, returned and then went into the lodging house.

[Coroner] Did anyone speak to you about being so late? No, I paid the night watchman. I asked him if my bed was let and he said:

"They are let by eleven o'clock. You don't think they are to let to this hour." I paid him 4d for another bed. I stayed up smoking on the form of the kitchen, on the right hand side near the fireplace and then went to bed.

[Coroner] You got up at eleven o'clock? Yes. The day man came and told us to get up, as he wanted to make the bed. I got up and dressed and went down into the kitchen.

[Coroner] Is there anything else you want to say? Nothing.

[Coroner] When you said the West-end of town, did you mean Holloway? No; another lodging house in Peter Street, Westminster.

The Coroner: It is only fair to say that the witness's statements can be corroborated.

William Thick [Thick], detective sergeant, deposed: Knowing that 'Leather Apron' was suspected of being concerned in the murder, on Monday morning I arrested Piser at 22, Mulberry Street. I have known him by the name of 'Leather Apron' for many years.

[Coroner] When people in the neighbourhood speak of the 'Leather Apron' do they mean Piser? They do.

[Coroner] He has been released from custody? He was released last night at 9.30. John Richardson (recalled) produced the knife a much-worn dessert knife with which he had cut his boot. He added that as it was not sharp enough, he had borrowed another one at the market.

By the Jury: My mother has heard me speak of people having been in the house. She has heard them herself.

The Coroner: I think we will detain this knife for the present.

Henry John Holland, a box maker, stated: As I was passing 29, Hanbury Street, on my way to work in Chiswell Street, at about eight minutes past six on Saturday. I spoke to two of Bayley's men. An elderly man came out of the house and asked us to have a look in his back yard. I went through the passage and saw the deceased lying in the yard by the back door. I did not touch the body. I then went for a policeman in Spitalfields Market.

The officer told me he could not come. I went outside and could find no constable. Going back to the house, I saw an inspector run up with a young man, at about twenty minutes past six o'clock. I had told the first policeman that it was a similar case to Buck's Row and he referred me to two policemen outside the market but I could not find them. I afterwards complained of the policeman's conduct at the Commercial Street police station the same afternoon.

The Coroner: There does not seem to have been much delay. The inspector says there are certain spots where constables are stationed with instructions not to leave them. Their duty is to send someone else.

The Foreman of the Jury: That is the explanation.

The Coroner: The doctor will be here first thing tomorrow. This afternoon the inquiry will be resumed.

Day 3, Thursday, 13 September 1888.
The Daily Telegraph, Friday, 14 September 1888.

Yesterday [13th Sep] Mr Wynne Baxter, coroner, resumed, at the Working Lads' Institute, Whitechapel Road, his adjourned inquiry relative to the death of Annie Chapman, who was murdered in the back yard of 29, Hanbury Street, on Saturday morning last.

The police were represented by Inspectors Abberline, Helson and Chandler.

Joseph Chandler, Inspector H Division Metropolitan Police, deposed: On Saturday morning, at ten minutes past six, I was on duty in Commercial Street. At the corner of Hanbury Street, I saw several men running. I beckoned to them. One of them said:

"Another woman has been murdered." I at once went with him to 29, Hanbury Street and through the passage into the yard. There was no one in the yard. I saw the body of a woman lying on the ground on her back. Her head was towards the back wall of the house, nearly two feet from the wall, at the bottom of the steps but six or nine inches away from them. The face was turned to the right side and the left arm was resting on the left breast.

The right hand was lying down the right side. Deceased's legs were drawn up and the clothing was above the knees. A portion of the intestines, still connected with the body, were lying above the right shoulder, with some pieces of skin. There were also some pieces of skin on the left shoulder. The body was lying parallel with the fencing dividing the two yards. I remained there and sent for the divisional surgeon, Mr Phillips and to the police station for the ambulance and for further assistance.

When the constables arrived, I cleared the passage of people and saw that no one touched the body until the doctor arrived. I obtained some sacking to cover it before the arrival of the surgeon, who came at about half past six o'clock and he, having examined the body, directed that it should be removed to the mortuary. After the body had been taken away, I examined the yard and found a piece of coarse muslin, a small tooth comb and a pocket hair comb in a case. They were lying near the feet of the woman. A portion of an envelope was found near her head, which contained two pills.

[Coroner] What was on the envelope? On the back there was a seal with the words, embossed in blue, 'Sussex Regiment'. The other part was torn away. On the other side, there was a letter 'M' in writing.

[Coroner] A man's handwriting? I should imagine so.

[Coroner] Any postage stamp? No. There was a postal stamp 'London, 3 August 1888.' That was in red. There was another black stamp, which was indistinct.

[Coroner] Any other marks on the envelope? There were also the letters 'Sp' lower down, as if someone had written 'Spitalfields'. The other part was gone. There were no other marks.

[Coroner] Did you find anything else in the yard? There was a leather apron, lying in the yard, saturated with water. It was about two feet from the water tap.

[Coroner] Was it shown to the doctor? Yes. There was also a box, such as is commonly used by case makers for holding nails. It was empty. There was also a piece of steel, flat, which has since been identified by Mrs Richardson as the spring of her son's leggings.

[Coroner] Where was that found? It was close to where the body had been. The apron and nail box have also been identified by her as her property. The yard was paved roughly with stones in parts; in other places it was earth.

[Coroner] Was there any appearance of a struggle there? No.

[Coroner] Are the palings strongly erected? No; to the contrary.

[Coroner] Could they support the weight of a man getting over them? No doubt they might.

[Coroner] Is there any evidence of anybody having got over them? No. Some of them in the adjoining yard have been broken since. They were not broken then.

[Coroner] You have examined the adjoining yard? Yes.

[Coroner] Was there any staining as of blood on any of the palings? Yes, near the body.

[Coroner] Was it on any of the other yards? No.

[Coroner] Were there no other marks? There were marks discovered on the wall of No. 25. They were noticed on Tuesday afternoon. They have been seen by Dr Phillips.

[Coroner] Were there any drops of blood outside the yard of No 29? No; every possible examination has been made but we could find no trace of them. The blood stains at No. 29 were in the immediate neighbourhood of the body only. There were also a few spots of blood on the back wall, near the head of the deceased, 2ft from the ground. The largest spot was of the size of a sixpence. They were all close together. I assisted in the preparation of the plan produced, which is correct.

[Coroner] Did you search the body? I searched the clothing at the mortuary. The outside jacket a long black one, which came down to the knees had bloodstains round the neck, both upon the inside and out and two or three spots on the left arm. The jacket was hooked at the top and buttoned down the front. By the appearance of the garment, there did not seem to have been any struggle.

A large pocket was worn under the skirt (attached by strings), which I produce. It was torn down the front and also at the side and it was empty. Deceased wore a black skirt. There was a little blood on the outside. The two petticoats were stained very little; the two bodices were stained with blood round the neck but they had not been damaged. There was no cut in the clothing at all. The boots were on the feet of deceased. They were old. No part of the clothing was torn. The stockings were not bloodstained.

[Coroner] Did you see John Richardson? I saw him about a quarter to seven o'clock. He told me he had been to the house that morning about a quarter to five. He said he came to the back door and looked down to the cellar, to see if all was right and then went away to his work.

[Coroner] Did he say anything about cutting his boot? No.

[Coroner] Did he say that he was sure the woman was not there at that time? Yes.

By the Jury: The back door opens outwards into the yard, and swung on the left hand to the palings where the body was. If Richardson were on the top of the steps, he might not have seen the body. He told me he did not go down the steps.

The Foreman of the Jury: Reference has been made to the Sussex Regiment and the pensioner. Are you going to produce the man Stanley?

Witness: We have not been able to find him as yet.

The Foreman: He is a very important witness. There is evidence that he has associated with the woman week after week. It is important that he should be found.

Witness: There is nobody that can give us the least idea where he is. The parties were requested to communicate with the police if he came back. Every inquiry has been made but nobody seems to know anything about him.

The Coroner: I should think if that pensioner knows his own business, he will come forward himself. Sergeant Baugham [Badham], 31 H, stated that he conveyed the body of the deceased to the mortuary on the ambulance.

[Coroner] Are you sure that you took every portion of the body away with you? Yes.

[Coroner] Where did you deposit the body? In the shed, still on the ambulance. I remained with it until Inspector Chandler arrived. Detective Sergeant Thick viewed the body and I took down the description. There were present two women, who came to identify the body and they described the clothing. They came from 35, Dorset Street.

[Coroner] Who touched the clothing? Sergeant Thick. I did not see the women touch the clothing nor the body. I did not see Sergeant Thick touch the body.

Inspector Chandler, recalled, said he reached the mortuary a few minutes after seven. The body did not appear to have been disturbed. He did not stay until the doctor arrived. Police constable 376 H was left in charge, with the mortuary keeper. Robert Marne, the mortuary keeper and an inmate of the Whitechapel Union Workhouse, said he received the body at seven o'clock on Saturday morning. He remained at the mortuary until Dr Phillips came.

The door of the mortuary was locked except when two nurses from an infirmary came and undressed the body. No one else touched the corpse. He gave the key into the hands of the police.

The Coroner: The fact is that Whitechapel does not possess a mortuary. The place is not a mortuary at all. We have no right to take a body there. It is simply a shed belonging to the workhouse officials. Juries have over and over again reported the matter to the District Board of Works. The East End, which requires mortuaries, more than anywhere else, is most deficient. Bodies drawn out of the river have to be put in boxes and very often they are brought to this workhouse arrangement all the way from Wapping.

A workhouse inmate is not the proper man to take care of a body in such an important matter as this. The foreman of the jury called attention to the fact that a fund to provide a reward had been opened by residents in the neighbourhood and that Mr Montagu, MP had offered a reward of £100. If the Government also offered a reward, some information might be forthcoming.

The Coroner: I do not speak with any real knowledge but I am told that the Government have determined not to give any rewards in future, not with the idea to economise but because the money does not get into right channels.

To Witness: Were you present when the doctor was making his post mortem? Yes.

[Coroner] Did you see the doctor find the handkerchief produced? It was taken off the body. I picked it up from off the clothing, which was in the corner of the room. I gave it to Dr Phillips and he asked me to put it in some water, which I did.

[Coroner] Did you see the handkerchief taken off the body? I did not. The nurses must have taken it off the throat.

[Coroner] How do you know? I don't know.

[Coroner] Then you are guessing? I am guessing.

The Coroner: That is all wrong, you know.

(To the jury). He is really not the proper man to have been left in charge.

Timothy Donovan, the deputy of the lodging house, 35, Dorset Street, was recalled.

[Coroner] You have seen that handkerchief? I recognised it as one which the deceased used to wear. She bought it off a lodger and she was wearing it when she left the lodging house. She was wearing it three corner ways, placed round her neck, with a black woollen scarf underneath. It was tied in front with one knot.

The Foreman of the Jury: Would you recognise Ted Stanley, the pensioner?

A Juryman: Stanley is not the pensioner.

The Coroner (to witness): Do you know the name of Stanley?

Witness: No.

The Foreman: He has been mentioned and also 'Harry the Hawker'.

Witness: I know 'Harry the Hawker'.

The Coroner, having referred to the evidence, said: It may be an inference there is no actual evidence that the pensioner was called Ted Stanley.

The Foreman said he referred to the man who came to see the deceased regularly. The man ought to be produced.

The Coroner (to witness): Would you recognise the pensioner? Yes.

[Coroner] When did you see him last? On Saturday.

[Coroner] Why did you not then send him to the police? Because he would not stop.

The Foreman: What was he like? He had a soldierly appearance. He dressed differently at times sometimes gentlemanly.

A Juror: He is not Ted Stanley.

Mr George Baxter Phillips, divisional surgeon of police, said: On Saturday last, I was called by the police at 6.20 a.m. to 29, Hanbury Street and arrived at half past six. I found the body of the deceased lying in the yard on her back, on the left hand of the steps that lead from the passage. The head was about 6in in front of the level of the bottom step and the feet were towards a shed at the end of the yard.

The left arm was across the left breast and the legs were drawn up, the feet resting on the ground and the knees turned outwards. The face was swollen and turned on the right side and the tongue protruded between the front teeth but not beyond the lips; it was much swollen. The small intestines and other portions were lying on the right side of the body on the ground above the right shoulder but attached.

There was a large quantity of blood, with a part of the stomach above the left shoulder. I searched the yard and found a small piece of coarse muslin, a small tooth comb and a pocket comb, in a paper case, near the railing. They had apparently been arranged there. I also discovered various other articles, which I handed to the police. The body was cold, except that there was a certain remaining heat, under the intestines, in the body.

Stiffness of the limbs was not marked but it was commencing. The throat was dissevered deeply. I noticed that the incision of the skin was jagged and reached right round the neck. On the back wall of the house, between the steps and the palings, on the left side, about 18in from the ground, there were about six patches of blood, varying in size from a sixpenny piece to a small point and on the wooden fence, there were smears of blood, corresponding to where the head of the deceased laid and immediately above the part where the blood had mainly flowed from the neck, which was well clotted.

Having received instructions soon after two o'clock on Saturday afternoon, I went to the labour yard of the Whitechapel Union for the purpose of further examining the body and making the usual post-mortem investigation. I was surprised to find that the body had been stripped and was lying ready on the table.

It was under great disadvantage I made my examination. As on many occasions I have met with the same difficulty, I now raise my protest, as I have before, that members of my profession should be called upon to perform their duties under these inadequate circumstances.

The Coroner: The mortuary is not fitted for a post-mortem examination. It is only a shed. There is no adequate convenience and nothing fit and at certain seasons of the year, it is dangerous to the operator.

The Foreman: I think we can all endorse the doctor's view of it.

The Coroner: As a matter of fact, there is no public mortuary from the City of London up to Bow. There is one at Mile End but it belongs to the workhouse and is not used for general purposes.

Examination resumed: The body had been attended to since its removal to the mortuary and probably partially washed. I noticed a bruise over the right temple. There was a bruise under the clavicle and there were two distinct bruises, each the size of a man's thumb, on the fore part of the chest. The stiffness of the limbs was then well marked. The finger nails were turgid. There was an old scar of long standing on the left of the frontal bone.

On the left side, the stiffness was more noticeable and especially in the fingers, which were partly closed. There was an abrasion over the bend of the first joint of the ring finger and there were distinct markings of a ring or rings- probably the latter. There were small sores on the fingers. The head being opened showed that the membranes of the brain were opaque and the veins loaded with blood of a dark character.

There was a large quantity of fluid between the membranes and the substance of the brain. The brain substance was unusually firm and its cavities also contained a large amount of fluid. The throat had been severed. The incisions of the skin indicated that they had been made from the left side of the neck on a line with the angle of the jaw, carried entirely round and again in front of the neck and ending at a point about midway between the jaw and the sternum or breast bone on the right hand.

There were two distinct clean cuts on the body of the vertebrae on the left side of the spine. They were parallel to each other and separated by about half an inch. The muscular structures between the side processes of bone of the vertebrae had an appearance as if an attempt had been made to separate the bones of the neck.

There are various other mutilations of the body but I am of opinion that they occurred subsequently to the death of the woman and to the large escape of blood from the neck.

The witness, pausing, said: I am entirely in your hands, sir but is it necessary that I should describe the further mutilations. From what I have said, I can state the cause of death.

The Coroner: The object of the inquiry is not only to ascertain the cause of death but the means by which it occurred. Any mutilation which took place afterwards may suggest the character of the man who did it. Possibly you can give us the conclusions to which you have come respecting the instrument used.

The Witness: You don't wish for details. I think if it is possible to escape the details, it would be advisable. The cause of death is visible from injuries I have described.

The Coroner: You have kept a record of them?

Witness: I have.

The Coroner: Supposing any one is charged with the offence, they would have to come out then and it might be a matter of comment that the same evidence was not given at the inquest.

Witness: I am entirely in your hands.

The Coroner: We will postpone that for the present. You can give your opinion as to how the death was caused.

Witness: From these appearances, I am of opinion that the breathing was interfered with previous to death and that death arose from syncope or failure of the heart's action, in consequence of the loss of blood caused by the severance of the throat.

[Coroner] Was the instrument used at the throat the same as that used at the abdomen? Very probably. It must have been a very sharp knife, probably with a thin, narrow blade and at least six to eight inches in length and perhaps longer.

[Coroner] Is it possible that any instrument used by a military man, such as a bayonet, would have done it? No; it would not be a bayonet.

[Coroner] Would it have been such an instrument as a medical man uses for post-mortem examinations? The ordinary post-mortem case perhaps does not contain such a weapon.

[Coroner] Would any instrument that slaughterers employ have caused the injuries? Yes; well ground down.

[Coroner] Would the knife of a cobbler or of any person in the leather trades have done? I think the knife used in those trades would not be long enough in the blade.

[Coroner] Was there any anatomical knowledge displayed? I think there was. There were indications of it. My own impression is that that anatomical knowledge was only less displayed or indicated in consequence of haste. The person evidently was hindered from making a more complete dissection in consequence of the haste.

[Coroner] Was the whole of the body there? No; the absent portions being from the abdomen.

[Coroner] Are those portions such as would require anatomical knowledge to extract? I think the mode in which they were extracted did show some anatomical knowledge.

[Coroner] You do not think they could have been lost accidentally in the transit of the body to the mortuary? I was not present at the transit. I carefully closed up the clothes of the woman. Some portions had been excised.

[Coroner] How long had the deceased been dead when you saw her? I should say at least two hours and probably more but it is right to say that it was a fairly cold morning and that the body would be more apt to cool rapidly from its having lost the greater portion of its blood.

[Coroner] Was there any evidence of any struggle? No; not about the body of the woman. You do not forget the smearing of blood about the palings.

[Coroner] In your opinion did she enter the yard alive? I am positive of it. I made a thorough search of the passage and I saw no trace of blood, which must have been visible had she been taken into the yard.

[Coroner] You were shown the apron? I saw it myself. There was no blood upon it. It had the appearance of not having been unfolded recently.

[Coroner] You were shown some staining on the wall of No 25, Hanbury Street? Yes; that was yesterday morning. To the eye of a novice, I have no doubt it looks like blood. I have not been able to trace any signs of it. I have not been able to finish my investigation. I am almost convinced I shall not find any blood. We have not had any result of your examination of the internal organs.

[Coroner] Was there any disease? Yes. It was not important as regards the cause of death. Disease of the lungs was of long standing and there was disease of the membranes of the brain. The stomach contained a little food.

[Coroner] Was there any appearance of the deceased having taken much alcohol? No. There were probably signs of great privation. I am convinced she had not taken any strong alcohol for some hours before her death.

[Coroner] Were any of these injuries self-inflicted? The injuries which were the immediate cause of death were not self-inflicted.

[Coroner] Was the bruising you mentioned recent? Marks on the face were recent, especially about the chin and sides of the jaw. The bruise upon the temple and the bruises in front of the chest were of longer standing, probably of days. I am of opinion that the person who cut the deceased's throat took hold of her by the chin and then commenced the incision from left to right.

[Coroner] Could that be done so instantaneously that a person could not cry out?

Witness: By pressure on the throat, no doubt it would be possible.

The Forman: There would probably be suffocation.

The Coroner: The thickening of the tongue would be one of the signs of suffocation? Yes. My impression is that she was partially strangled.

Witness added that the handkerchief produced was, when found amongst the clothing, saturated with blood. A similar article was around the throat of the deceased when he saw her early in the morning at Hanbury Street.

[Coroner] It had not the appearance of having been tied on afterwards? No.

Sarah Simonds, a resident nurse at the Whitechapel Infirmary, stated that, in company of the senior nurse, she went to the mortuary on Saturday and found the body of the deceased on the ambulance in the yard. It was afterwards taken into the shed and placed on the table. She was directed by Inspector Chandler to undress it and she placed the clothes in a corner.

She left the handkerchief around the neck. She was sure of this. They washed stains of blood from the body. It seemed to have run down from the throat. She found the pocket tied round the waist. The strings were not torn. There were no tears or cuts in the clothes.

Inspector Chandler: I did not instruct the nurses to undress the body and to wash it.

The inquiry was adjourned.

Day 4, Wednesday, 19 September 1888
The Daily Telegraph, Thursday, 20 September 1888.

In the Whitechapel Working Lads' Institute, yesterday [19th Sep] afternoon, Mr Wynne Baxter, Coroner for East Middlesex, resumed his inquiry respecting the death of Mrs Annie Chapman, who was found dead in the yard of the house 29, Hanbury Street, Whitechapel, her body dreadfully cut and mutilated, early on the morning of Saturday, the 8th inst. The following evidence was called:

Eliza Cooper: I am a hawker and lodge in Dorset Street, Spitalfields. Have done so for the last 5 months. I knew the deceased and had a quarrel with her on the Tuesday before she was murdered. The quarrel arose in this way; on the previous Saturday, she brought Mr Stanley into the house where I lodged in

Dorset Street and coming into the kitchen asked the people to give her some soap. They told her to ask 'Liza' meaning me. She came to me and I opened the locker and gave her some.

She gave it to Stanley, who went outside and washed himself in the lavatory. When she came back, I asked for the soap but she did not return it. She said:

"I will see you by and bye." Mr Stanley gave her two shillings and paid for her bed for two nights. I saw no more of her that night. On the following Tuesday, I saw her in the kitchen of the lodging house. I said:

"Perhaps you will return my soap." She threw a halfpenny on the table and said:

"Go and get a halfpenny worth of soap." We got quarrelling over this piece of soap and we went out to the Ringers Public-house and continued the quarrel. She slapped my face and said:

"Think yourself lucky I don't do more." I struck her in the left eye, I believe and then in the chest. I afterwards saw that the blow I gave her had marked her face.

[Coroner] When was the last time you saw her alive? On the Thursday night in the Ringers.

[Coroner] Was she wearing rings? Yes, she was wearing three rings on the middle finger of the left hand. They were all brass.

[Coroner] Had she ever a gold wedding ring to your knowledge? No, not since I have known her. I have known her about fifteen months. I know she associated with Stanley, 'Harry the Hawker' and several others.

The Foreman: Are there any of those with whom she associated missing? I could not tell.

A Juryman: Was she on the same relations with them as she was with Stanley? No, sir. She used to bring them casually into the lodging house.

Dr Phillips, divisional surgeon of the metropolitan police, was then recalled.

The Coroner, before asking him to give evidence, said: Whatever may be your opinion and objections, it appears to me necessary that all the evidence that you ascertained from the post-mortem examination should be on the records of the Court for various reasons, which I need not enumerate. However painful it may be, it is necessary in the interests of justice.

Dr Phillips: I have not had any notice of that. I should have been glad if notice had been given me, because I should have been better prepared to give the evidence; however, I will do my best.

The Coroner: Would you like to postpone it?

Dr Phillips: Oh, no. I will do my best. I still think that it is a very great pity to make this evidence public. Of course, I bow to your decision but there are matters which have come to light now which show the wisdom of the course pursued on the last occasion and I cannot help reiterating my regret that you have come to a different conclusion.

On the last occasion, just before I left the court, I mentioned to you that there were reasons why I thought the perpetrator of the act upon the woman's throat had caught hold of her chin. These reasons were that just below the lobe of the left ear were three scratches and there was also a bruise on the right cheek.

When I come to speak of the wounds on the lower part of the body I must again repeat my opinion that it is highly injudicious to make the results of my examination public. These details are fit only for yourself sir, and the jury but to make them public would simply be disgusting.

The Coroner: We are here in the interests of justice and must have all the evidence before us. I see, however, that there are several ladies and boys in the room and I think they might retire. (Two ladies and a number of newspaper messenger boys accordingly left the court.)

Dr Phillips again raised an objection to the evidence, remarking: In giving these details to the public, I believe you are thwarting the ends of justice.

The Coroner: We are bound to take all the evidence in the case and whether it be made public or not is a matter for the responsibility of the press.

The Foreman: We are of opinion that the evidence the doctor on the last occasion wished to keep back should be heard. (Several Jurymen: Hear, hear.)

The Coroner: I have carefully considered the matter and have never before heard of any evidence requested being kept back.

Dr Phillips: I have not kept it back; I have only suggested whether it should be given or not.

The Coroner: We have delayed taking this evidence as long as possible, because you said the interests of justice might be served by keeping it back but it is now a fortnight since this occurred and I do not see why it should be kept back from the jury any longer.

Dr Phillips: I am of opinion that what I am about to describe took place after death, so that it could not affect the cause of death, which you are inquiring into.

The Coroner: That is only your opinion and might be repudiated by other medical opinion.

Dr Phillips: Very well. I will give you the results of my post-mortem examination. Witness then detailed the terrible wounds which had been inflicted upon the woman and described the parts of the body which the perpetrator of the murder had carried away with him.

He added: I am of opinion that the length of the weapon with which the incisions were inflicted was at least five to six inches in length probably more and must have been very sharp. The manner in which they had been done indicated a certain amount of anatomical knowledge.

The Coroner: Can you give any idea how long it would take to perform the incisions found on the body?

Dr Phillips: I think I can guide you by saying that I myself could not have performed all the injuries I saw on that woman and affect them, even without a struggle, under a quarter of an hour. If I had done it in a deliberate way, such as would fall to the duties of a surgeon, it would probably have taken me the best part of an hour. The whole inference seems to me that the operation was performed to enable the perpetrator to obtain possession of these parts of the body.

The Coroner: Have you anything further to add with reference to the stains on the wall?

Dr Phillips: I have not been able to obtain any further traces of blood on the wall.

The Foreman: Is there anything to indicate that the crime in the case of the woman Nicholls was perpetrated with the same object as this?

The Coroner: There is a difference in this respect, at all events that the medical expert is of opinion that, in the case of Nichols, the mutilations were made first.

The Foreman: Was any photograph of the eyes of the deceased taken, in case they should retain any impression of the murderer.

Dr Phillips: I have no particular opinion upon that point myself. I was asked about it very early in the inquiry and I gave my opinion that the operation would be useless, especially in this case. The use of a bloodhound was also suggested. It may be my ignorance but the blood around was that of the murdered woman and it would be more likely to be traced than the murderer. These questions were submitted to me by the police very early. I think within twenty four hours of the murder of the woman.

The Coroner: Were the injuries to the face and neck such as might have produced insensibility?

The witness: Yes; they were consistent with partial suffocation.

Mrs Elizabeth Long said: I live in Church Row, Whitechapel and my husband, James Long, is a cart minder. On Saturday, 8th Sept, about half past five o'clock in the morning, I was passing down Hanbury-street, from home, on my way to Spitalfields Market. I knew the time because I heard the brewer's clock strike half past five just before I got to the street. I passed 29, Hanbury Street. On the right-hand side, the same side as the house, I saw a man and a woman standing on the pavement talking.

The man's back was turned towards Brick Lane and the woman's was towards the market. They were standing only a few yards nearer Brick Lane from 29, Hanbury Street. I saw the woman's face. Have seen the deceased in the mortuary and I am sure the woman that I saw in Hanbury Street was the deceased. I did not see the man's face but I noticed that he was dark. He was wearing a brown low crowned felt hat.

I think he had on a dark coat, though I am not certain. By the look of him, he seemed to me a man over 40 years of age. He appeared to me to be a little taller than the deceased.

[Coroner] Did he look like a working man or what? He looked like a foreigner.

[Coroner] Did he look like a dock labourer or a workman or what? I should say he looked like what I should call shabby genteel.

[Coroner] Were they talking loudly? They were talking pretty loudly. I overheard him say to her 'Will you?' and she replied, 'Yes.' That is all I heard and I heard this as I passed. I left them standing there and I did not look back, so I cannot say where they went to.

[Coroner] Did they appear to be sober? I saw nothing to indicate that either of them was the worse for drink. Was it not an unusual thing to see a man and a woman standing there talking? Oh no. I see lots of them standing there in the morning.

[Coroner] At that hour of the day? Yes; that is why I did not take much notice of them.

[Coroner] You are certain about the time? Quite.

[Coroner] What time did you leave home? I got out about five o'clock, and I reached the Spitalfields Market a few minutes after half past five.

The Foreman of the jury: What brewer's clock did you hear strike half-past five? The brewer's in Brick Lane.

Edward Stanley, Osborn Place, Osborn Street, Spitalfields, deposed: I am a bricklayer's labourer.

The Coroner: Are you known by the name of the Pensioner? Yes.

[Coroner] Did you know the deceased? I did.

[Coroner] And you sometimes visited her? Yes.

[Coroner] At 35, Dorset Street? About once there, or twice, something like that. Other times, I have met her elsewhere.

[Coroner] When did you last see her alive? On Sunday, 2nd Sept, between one and three o'clock in the afternoon.

[Coroner] Was she wearing rings when you saw her? Yes, I believe two. I could not say on which finger but they were on one of her fingers.

[Coroner] What sort of rings were they, what was the metal? Brass, I should think by the look of them.

[Coroner] Do you know any one she was on bad terms with? No one, so far as I know. The last time I saw her she had some bruises on her face a slight black eye, which some other woman had given her. I did not take much notice of it. She told me something about having had a quarrel. It is possible that I may have seen deceased after 2nd Sept as I was doing nothing all that week. If I did see her, I only casually met her and we might have had a glass of beer together. My memory is rather confused about it.

The Coroner: The deputy of the lodging house said he was told not to let the bed to the deceased with any other man but you? It was not from me he received those orders. I have seen it described that the man used to come on the Saturday night and remain until the Monday morning. I have never done so.

The Foreman: You were supposed to be the pensioner.

The Coroner: It must be some other man?

Witness: I cannot say; I am only speaking for myself.

[Coroner] Are you a pensioner? Can I object to answer that question, sir? It does not touch on anything here.

Coroner: It was said the man was with her on one occasion when going to receive his pension?

Witness: Then it could not have been me. It has been stated all over Europe that it was me but it was not.

The Coroner: It will affect your financial position all over Europe when it is known that you are not a pensioner? It will affect my financial position in this way, sir, in that I am a loser by having to come here for nothing and may get discharged for not being at my work.

[Coroner] Were you ever in the Royal Sussex Regiment? Never sir. I am a law-abiding man, sir and interfere with no person who does not interfere with me.

The Coroner: Call the deputy.

Timothy Donovan, deputy of the lodging house, who gave evidence on a previous occasion, was then recalled.

The Coroner: Did ever you see that man (pointing to Stanley) before? Yes.

[Coroner] Is he the man you call 'the pensioner'? Yes.

[Coroner] Was it he who used to come with the deceased on Saturday and stay till Monday? Yes.

[Coroner] Was it he who told you not to let the bed to the deceased with any other man? Yes; on the second Saturday he told me.

[Coroner] How many times have you seen him there? I should think five or six Saturdays.

[Coroner] When was he last there? On the Saturday before the woman's death. He stayed until Monday. He paid for one night, and the woman afterwards came down and paid for the other.

The Coroner: What have you got to say to that, Mr Stanley?

Stanley: You can cross it all out, sir.

[Coroner] Cross your evidence out, you mean? Oh, no; not mine but his. It is all wrong. I went to Gosport on 6th Aug and remained there until 1st Sept.

The Coroner: Probably the deputy has made a mistake.

A Juror (to Stanley): Had that she once lived there.

[Juror] You did not know her there? No; I have only known her about two years. I have never been to Windsor.

[Juror] Did you call at Dorset Street on Saturday, the 8th, after the murder? Yes; I was told by a shoe black it was she who was murdered and I went to the lodging-house to ask if it was the fact. I was surprised and went away.

[Juror Did you not give any information to the police that you knew her? You might have volunteered evidence, you know? I did volunteer evidence. I went voluntarily to Commercial Street Police station and told them what I knew.

The Coroner: They did not tell you that the police wanted you? Not on the 8th but afterwards. They told me the police wanted to see me after I had been to the police.

Albert Cadosch [Cadoche] deposed: I live at 27, Hanbury-street and am a carpenter. 27 is next door to 29, Hanbury Street. On Saturday, 8th Sept I got up about a quarter past five in the morning and went into the yard. It was then about twenty minutes past five, I should think. As I returned towards the back door, I heard a voice say no just as I was going through the door.

It was not in our yard but I should think it came from the yard of No 29. I, however, cannot say on which side it came from. I went indoors but returned to the yard about three or four minutes afterwards. While coming back, I heard a sort of a fall against the fence which divides my yard from that of 29. It seemed as if something touched the fence suddenly.

The Coroner: Did you look to see what it was? No.

[Coroner] Had you heard any noise while you were at the end of your yard? No.

[Coroner] Any rustling of clothes? No. I then went into the house and from there into the street to go to my work. It was about two minutes after half-past five as I passed Spitalfields Church.

[Coroner] Do you ever hear people in these yards? Now and then but not often.

By a Juryman: I informed the police the same night after I returned from my work.

The Foreman: What height are the palings? About 5 ft. 6 in. to 6 ft. high.

[Coroner] And you had not the curiosity to look over? No, I had not.

[Coroner] It is not usual to hear thumps against the palings? They are packing-case makers and now and then there is a great case goes up against the palings. I was thinking about my work and not that there was anything the matter, otherwise most likely I would have been curious enough to look over.

The Foreman of the Jury: It's a pity you did not.

By the Coroner. I did not see any man and woman in the street when I went out.

William Stevens, 35, Dorset-street, stated: I am a painter. I knew the deceased. I last saw her alive at twenty minutes past twelve on the morning of Saturday, 8th Sept. She was in the kitchen. She was not the worse for drink.

[Coroner] Had she got any rings on her fingers? Yes.

[Witness was] Shown a piece of an envelope, witness said he believed it was the same as she picked up near the fireplace. Did not notice a crest but it was about that size and it had a red postmark on it. She left the kitchen and witness thought she was going to bed. Never saw her again. Did not know any one that she was on bad terms with. This was all the evidence obtainable.

A Juryman: Is there any chance of a reward being offered by the Home Secretary?

The Foreman: There is already a reward of £100 offered by Mr Samuel Montagu, M.P. There is a committee getting up subscriptions and they expect to get about £200. The coroner has already said that the Government are not prepared to offer a reward.

A Juror: There is more dignity about a Government reward and I think one ought to be offered.

The Foreman of the Jury: There are several ideas of rewards and it is supposed that about £300 will be got up. It will all be done by private individuals.

The Coroner: As far as we know, the case is complete.

The Foreman of the Jury: It seems to be a case of murder against some person or persons unknown. It was then agreed to adjourn the inquiry until next Wednesday before deciding upon the terms of the verdict.

Day 5, Wednesday, 26 September 1888.
(*The Daily Telegraph*, Thursday, 27 September 1888)

Yesterday 26th Sep afternoon Mr Wynne Baxter, coroner for East Middlesex, concluded his inquiry, at the Whitechapel Working Lads' Institute, relative to the death of Mrs Annie Chapman, whose body was found dreadfully cut and mutilated in the yard of 29, Hanbury Street, Whitechapel, early on the morning of Saturday, the 8th.

The Coroner inquired if there was any further evidence to be adduced. Inspector Chandler replied in the negative. The Coroner then addressed the jury.

He said: I congratulate you that your labours are now nearly completed. Although up to the present they have not resulted in the detection of any criminal, I have no doubt that if the perpetrator of this foul murder is eventually discovered, our efforts will not have been useless.

The evidence is now on the records of this court and could be used even if the witnesses were not forthcoming; while the publicity given has already elicited further information, which I shall presently have to mention and which, I hope I am not sanguine in believing, may perhaps be of the utmost importance.

We shall do well to recall the important facts. The deceased was a widow, forty seven years of age, named Annie Chapman. Her husband was a coachman living at Windsor. For three or four years before his death she had lived apart from her husband, who allowed her 10s a week until his death at Christmas, 1886. Evidently she had lived an immoral life for some time and her habits and surroundings had become worse since her means had failed.

Her relations were no longer visited by her and her brother had not seen her for five months, when she borrowed a small sum from him. She lived principally in the common lodging houses in the neighbourhood of Spitalfields, where such as she herd like cattle and she showed signs of great deprivation, as if she had been badly fed.

The glimpses of life in these dens which the evidence in this case discloses is sufficient to make us feel that there is much in the nineteenth century civilisation of which we have small reason to be proud but you who are constantly called together to hear the sad tale of starvation or semi-starvation, of misery, immorality and wickedness which some of the occupants of the 5,000 beds in this district have every week to relate to coroner's inquests, do not require to be reminded of what life in a Spitalfields lodging house means.

It was in one of these that the older bruises found on the temple and in front of the chest of the deceased were received, in a trumpery quarrel, a week before her death. It was in one of these that she was seen a few hours before her mangled remains were discovered.

On the afternoon and evening of Friday, 7th Sept she divided her time partly in such a place at 35, Dorset Street and partly in the Ringers public house, where she spent whatever money she had; so that between one and two on the morning of Saturday, when the money for her bed is demanded, she is obliged to admit that she is without means and at once turns out into the street to find it.

She leaves there at 1.45 a.m. is seen off the premises by the night watchman, and is observed to turn down Little Paternoster Row into Brushfield Street and not in the more direct route to Hanbury Street. On her wedding finger, she was wearing two or three rings, which appear to have been palpably of base metal, as the witnesses are all clear about their material and value.

We now lose sight of her for about four hours but at half past five, Mrs Long is in Hanbury Street on her way from home in Church Street, Whitechapel, to

Spitalfields Market. She walked on the northern side of the road going westward and remembers having seen a man and woman standing a few yards from the place where the deceased is afterwards found. And, although she did not know Annie Chapman, she is positive that that woman was deceased.

The two were talking loudly but not sufficiently so to arouse her suspicions that there was anything wrong. Such words as she overheard were not calculated to do so. The laconic inquiry of the man, 'Will you?' and the simple assent of the woman, viewed in the light of subsequent events, can be easily translated and explained.

Mrs Long passed on her way and neither saw nor heard anything more of her and this is the last time she is known to have been alive. There is some conflict in the evidence about the time at which the deceased was dispatched it is not unusual to find inaccuracy in such details but this variation is not very great or very important.

She was found dead about six o'clock. She was not in the yard when Richardson was there at 4.50 a.m. She was talking outside the house at half past five when Mrs Long passed them. Cadosh says it was about 5.20 when he was in the backyard of the adjoining house and heard a voice say no and three or four minutes afterwards a fall against the fence but if he is out of his reckoning but a quarter of an hour, the discrepancy in the evidence of fact vanishes and he may be mistaken, for he admits that he did not get up till a quarter past five and that it was after the half hour when he passed Spitalfields clock.

It is true that Dr Phillips thinks that when he saw the body at 6.30 the deceased had been dead at least two hours but he admits that the coldness of the morning and the great loss of blood may affect his opinion and if the evidence of the other witnesses be correct, Dr Phillips has miscalculated the effect of those forces.

But many minutes after Mrs Long passed the man and woman cannot have elapsed before the deceased became a mutilated corpse in the yard of 29, Hanbury Street, close by where she was last seen by any witness. This place is a fair sample of a large number of houses in the neighbourhood. It was built, like hundreds of others, for the Spitalfields weavers and when hand looms were driven out by steam and power, these were converted into dwellings for the poor.

Its size is about such as a superior artisan would occupy in the country but its condition is such as would to a certainty leave it without a tenant. In this place, seventeen persons were living, from a woman and her son sleeping in a cat's meat shop on the ground floor to Davis and his wife and their three grown up sons, all sleeping together in an attic.

The street door and the yard door were never locked and the passage and yard appear to have been constantly used by people who had no legitimate business there. There is little doubt that the deceased knew the place, for it was only 300 or 400 yards from where she lodged. If so, it is quite unnecessary to assume that her companion had any knowledge in fact, it is easier to believe that he was ignorant both of the nest of living beings by whom he was surrounded and of their occupations and habits.

Some were on the move late at night some were up long before the sun. A Carman, named Thompson, left the house for his work as early as 3.50 a.m.; an hour later John Richardson was paying the house a visit of inspection. Shortly after 5.15 Cadosh, who lived in the next house, was in the adjoining yard twice.

Davis, the carman, who occupied the third floor front, heard the church clock strike a quarter to six, got up, had a cup of tea and went into the back yard and was horrified to find the mangled body of deceased. It was then a little after six a.m. a very little, for at ten minutes past the hour Inspector Chandler had been informed of the discovery while on duty in Commercial Street.

There is nothing to suggest that the deceased was not fully conscious of what she was doing. It is true that she had passed through some stages of intoxication, for although she appeared perfectly sober to her friend who met her in Dorset Street at five o'clock the previous evening, she had been drinking afterwards and when she left the lodging house shortly before two o'clock, the night watchman noticed that she was the worse for drink but not badly so, while the deputy asserts that, though she had evidently been drinking, she could walk straight and it was probably only malt liquor that she had taken and its effects would pass off quicker than if she had taken spirits.

Consequently it is not surprising to find that Mrs Long saw nothing to make her think that the deceased was the worse for drink. Moreover, it is unlikely that she could have had the opportunity of getting intoxicants. Again the post-mortem examination shows that while the stomach contained a meal of food there was no sign of fluid and no appearance of her having taken alcohol and Dr Phillips is convinced that she had not taken any alcohol for some time.

The deceased, therefore, entered the yard in full possession of her faculties; although with a very different object from her companion. From the evidence which the condition of the yard affords and the medical examination discloses, it appears that after the two had passed through the passage and opened the swing door at the end, they descended the three steps into the yard.

On their left hand side, there was a recess between those steps and the palings. Here a few feet from the house and a less distance from the paling they must have stood. The wretch must have then seized the deceased, perhaps with Judas like approaches. He seized her by the chin. He pressed her throat and while thus preventing the slightest cry, he at the same time produced insensibility and suffocation.

There is no evidence of any struggle. The clothes are not torn. Even in these preliminaries, the wretch seems to have known how to carry out efficiently his nefarious work. The deceased was then lowered to the ground and laid on her back and although in doing so, she may have fallen slightly against the fence, this movement was probably effected with care.

Her throat was then cut in two places with savage determination and the injuries to the abdomen commenced. All was done with cool impudence and reckless daring but perhaps, nothing is more noticeable than the emptying of her pockets and the arrangement of their contents with business like precision in order near her feet.

The murder seems, like the Buck's Row case, to have been carried out without any cry. Sixteen people were in the house. The partitions of the different rooms are of wood. Davis was not asleep after three a.m. except for three quarters of an hour, or less, between five and 5.45. Mrs Richardson only dosed after three a.m. and heard no noise during the night.

Mrs Hardman, who occupies the front ground floor room, did not awake until the noise succeeding the finding of the body had commenced and none of the occupants of the houses by which the yard is surrounded heard anything suspicious. The brute who committed the offence did not even take the trouble to cover up his ghastly work but left the body exposed to the view of the first comer.

This accords but little with the trouble taken with the rings and suggests either that he had at length been disturbed or that as the daylight broke a sudden fear suggested the danger of detection that he was running. There are two things missing. Her rings had been wrenched from her fingers and have not been found and the uterus has been removed.

The body has not been dissected but the injuries have been made by someone who had considerable anatomical skill and knowledge. There are no meaningless cuts. It was done by one who knew where to find what he wanted, what difficulties he would have to contend against and how he should use his knife, so as to abstract the organ without injury to it.

No unskilled person could have known where to find it or have recognised it when it was found. For instance, no mere slaughterer of animals could have carried out these operations. It must have been some one accustomed to the post-mortem room. The conclusion that the desire was to possess the missing part seems overwhelming.

If the object were robbery, these injuries were meaningless, for death had previously resulted from the loss of blood at the neck. Moreover, when we find an easily accomplished theft of some paltry brass rings and such an operation, after, at least, a quarter of an hour's work and by a skilled person, we are driven to the deduction that the mutilation was the object and the theft of the rings was only a thin veiled blind, an attempt to prevent the real intention being discovered.

Had not the medical examination been of a thorough and searching character, it might easily have been left unnoticed. The difficulty in believing that this was the real purport of the murderer is natural. It is abhorrent to our feelings to conclude that a life should be taken for so slight an object but when rightly considered, the reasons for most murders are altogether out of proportion to the guilt.

It has been suggested that the criminal is a lunatic with morbid feelings. This may or may not be the case but the object of the murderer appears palpably shown by the facts and it is not necessary to assume lunacy, for it is clear that there is a market for the object of the murder. To show you this, I must mention a fact which at the same time proves the assistance which publicity and the newspaper press afford in the detection of crime.

Within a few hours of the issue of the morning papers containing a report of the medical evidence given at the last sitting of the Court, I received a communication from an officer of one of our great medical schools that they had information which might or might not have a distinct bearing on our inquiry. I attended at the first opportunity and was told by the sub-curator of the Pathological Museum that some months ago an American had called on him and asked him to procure a number of specimens of the organ that was missing in the deceased.

He stated his willingness to give œ20 for each and explained that his object was to issue an actual specimen with each copy of a publication on which he was then engaged. Although he was told that his wish was impossible to be complied with, he still urged his request. He desired them preserved, not in spirits of wine, the usual medium but in glycerine, in order to preserve them in a flaccid condition and he wished them sent to America direct.

It is known that this request was repeated to another institution of a similar character. Now, is it not possible that the knowledge of this demand may have incited some abandoned wretch to possess himself of a specimen. It seems beyond belief that such inhuman wickedness could enter into the mind of any man but unfortunately our criminal annals prove that every crime is possible.

I need hardly say that I at once communicated my information to the Detective Department at Scotland Yard. Of course I do not know what use has been made of it but I believe that publicity may possibly further elucidate this fact, and, therefore, I have not withheld from you my knowledge. By means of the press, some further explanation may be forthcoming from America if not from here.

I have endeavoured to suggest to you the object with which this offence was committed, and the class of person who must have perpetrated it. The greatest deterrent from crime is the conviction that detection and punishment will follow with rapidity and certainty and it may be that the impunity with which Mary Ann Smith and Anne Tabram were murdered suggested the possibility of such horrid crimes as those which you and another jury have been recently considering.

It is, therefore, a great misfortune that nearly three weeks have elapsed without the chief actor in this awful tragedy having been discovered. Surely, it is not too much even yet to hope that the ingenuity of our detective force will succeed in unearthing this monster. It is not as if there were no clue to the character of the criminal or the cause of his crime. His object is clearly divulged.

His anatomical skill carries him out of the category of a common criminal, for his knowledge could only have been obtained by assisting at post-mortems or by frequenting the post-mortem room. Thus the class in which search must be made, although a large one, is limited. Moreover it must have been a man who was from home, if not all night, at least during the early hours of 8th Sept.

His hands were undoubtedly blood stained, for he did not stop to use the tap in the yard as the pan of clean water under it shows. If the theory of lunacy be correct, which I very much doubt the class is still further limited; while, if Mrs Long's memory does not fail and the assumption be correct that the man who was talking to the deceased at half past five was the culprit, he is even more clearly defined.

In addition to his former description, we should know that he was a foreigner of dark complexion, over 40 years of age, a little taller than the deceased, of shabby genteel appearance, with a brown dear stalker hat on his head and a dark coat on his back. If your views accord with mine, you will be of opinion that we are confronted with a murder of no ordinary character, committed not from jealousy, revenge or robbery but from motives less adequate than the many which still disgrace our civilisation, mar our progress and blot the pages of our Christianity.

I cannot conclude my remarks without thanking you for the attention you have given to the case and the assistance you have rendered me in our efforts to elucidate the truth of this horrible tragedy.

The Foreman: We can only find one verdict; that of wilful murder against some person or persons unknown. We were about to add a rider with respect to the condition of the mortuary but that having been done by a previous jury, it is unnecessary.

A verdict of wilful murder against a person or persons unknown was then entered.

Chapter Nine
The Elizabeth Stride Inquest

Day 1, Monday, 1 October 1888.
(The Daily telegraph, Tuesday, 2 October 1888.)

Yesterday [1 Oct 1888], at the Vestry Hall in Cable Street, St George-in-the-East, Mr Wynne E. Baxter, coroner for East Middlesex, opened an inquest on the body of the woman who was found dead, with her throat cut, at one o'clock on Sunday morning, in Berner Street, Commercial Road East.

At the outset of the inquiry, the deceased was described as Elizabeth Stride but it subsequently transpired that she had not yet been really identified. A jury of 24 having been empanelled, they proceeded to view the body at the St George's Mortuary.

Detective Inspector Reid, H Division, watched the case on behalf of the police.

William Wess [West], who affirmed instead of being sworn, was the first witness examined and, in reply to the coroner, he said: I reside at No 2, William Street, Cannon Street Road and am overseer in the printing office attached to No 40, Berner Street, Commercial Road, which premises are in the occupation of the International Working Men's Education Society, whose club is carried on there.

On the ground floor of the club there is a room, the door and window of which face the street. At the rear of this is the kitchen, whilst the first floor consists of a large room which is used for our meetings and entertainments, I being a member of the club. At the south side of the premises is a courtyard, to which entrance can be obtained through a double door, in one section of which is a smaller one, which is used when the larger barriers are closed.

The large doors are generally closed at night but sometimes remain open. On the left side of the yard is a house, which is divided into three tenements and occupied, I believe, by that number of families. At the end is a store or workshop belonging to Messrs. Hindley and Co, sack manufacturers. I do not know that a way out exists there.

The club premises and the printing office occupy the entire length of the yard on the right side. Returning to the clubhouse, the front room on the ground floor is used for meals. In the kitchen is a window which faces the door opening into the yard. The intervening passage is illuminated by means of a fanlight over the door. The printing office, which does not communicate with the club, consists of two rooms, one for compositors and the other for the editor.

On Saturday the compositors finished their labours at two o'clock in the afternoon. The editor concluded earlier but remained at the place until the discovery of the murder.

[Coroner] How many members are there in the club? From seventy five to eighty. Working men of any nationality can join.

[Coroner] Is any political qualification required of members? It is a political a Socialist club.

[Coroner] Do the members have to agree with any particular principles? A candidate is proposed by one member and seconded by another and a member would not nominate a candidate unless he knew that he was a supporter of Socialist principles. On Saturday last, I was in the printing office during the day and in the club during the evening.

From nine to half past ten at night, I was away seeing an English friend home but I was in the club again till a quarter past midnight. A discussion was proceeding in the lecture room, which has three windows overlooking the courtyard. From ninety to 100 persons attended the discussion, which terminated soon after half past eleven, when the bulk of the members left, using the street door, the most convenient exit.

From twenty to thirty members remained, some staying in the lecture-room and the others going downstairs. Of those upstairs a few continued the discussion, while the rest were singing. The windows of the lecture room were partly open.

[Coroner] How do you know that you finally left at a quarter past twelve o'clock? Because of the time when I reached my lodgings. Before leaving, I went into the yard and thence to the printing office, in order to leave some literature there and on returning to the yard I observed that the double door at the entrance was open.

There is no lamp in the yard and none of the street lamps light it, so that the yard is only lit by the lights through the windows at the side of the club and of the tenements opposite. As to the tenements, I only observed lights in two first floor windows. There was also a light in the printing office, the editor being in his room reading.

[Coroner] Was there much noise in the club? Not exactly much noise but I could hear the singing when I was in the yard.

[Coroner] Did you look towards the yard gates? Not so much to the gates as to the ground but nothing unusual attracted my attention.

[Coroner] Can you say that there was no object on the ground? I could not say that.

[Coroner] Do you think it possible that anything can have been there without your observing it? It was dark and I am a little short sighted, so that it is possible. The distance from the gates to the kitchen door is 18 ft.

[Coroner]. What made you look towards the gates at all? Simply because they were open. I went into the club and called my brother and we left together by the front door.

[Coroner] On leaving did you see anybody as you passed the yard? No.

[Coroner] Or did you meet any one in the street? Not that I recollect. I generally go home between twelve and one o'clock.

[Coroner] Do low women frequent Berner Street? I have seen men and women standing about and talking to each other in Fairclough Street.

[Coroner] But have you observed them nearer the club? No.

[Coroner] Or in the club yard? I did once, at eleven o'clock at night, about a year ago. They were chatting near the gates. That is the only time I have noticed such a thing, nor have I heard of it.

Morris Eagle, who also affirmed, said: I live at No 4, New Road, Commercial Road and travel in jewellery. I am a member of the International Workmen's Club, which meets at 40, Berner Street. I was there on Saturday, several times during the day and was in the chair during the discussion in the evening. After the discussion, between half past eleven and a quarter to twelve o'clock, I left the club to take my young lady home, going out through the front door. I returned about twenty minutes to one. I tried the front door but finding it closed, I went through the gateway into the yard, reaching the club in that way.

[Coroner] Did you notice anything lying on the ground near the gates? I did not.

[Coroner] Did you pass in the middle of the gateway? I think so. The gateway is 9 ft. 2 in. wide. I naturally walked on the right side, that being the side on which the club door was.

[Coroner] Do you think you are able to say that the deceased was not lying there then? I do not know, I am sure, because it was rather dark. There was a light from the upper part of the club but that would not throw any illumination upon the ground. It was dark near the gates.

[Coroner] You have formed no opinion, I take it. Then as to whether there was anything there? No.

[Coroner] Did you see anyone about in Berner Street? I dare say I did but I do not remember them.

[Coroner] Did you observe anyone in the yard? I do not remember that I did.

[Coroner] If there had been a man and woman there you would have remembered the circumstance? Yes; I am sure of that.

[Coroner] Did you notice whether there were any lights in the tenements opposite the club? I do not recollect.

[Coroner] Are you often at the club late at night? Yes, very often.

[Coroner] In the yard too? No, not in the yard.

[Coroner] And you have never seen a man and woman there? No, not in the yard but I have close by, outside the beer shop, at the corner of Fairclough Street. As soon as I entered the gateway on Saturday night, I could hear a friend of mine singing in the upstairs room of the club. I went up to him. He was singing in the Russian language and we sang together. I had been there twenty minutes when a member named Gidleman came upstairs and said, 'there is a woman dead in the yard.'

I went down in a second and struck a match, when I saw a woman lying on the ground in a pool of blood, near the gates. Her feet were towards the gates, about six or seven feet from them. She was lying by the side of and facing the club wall. When I reached the body and struck the match, another member was present.

[Coroner] Did you touch the body? No. As soon as I struck the match I perceived a lot of blood and I ran away and called the police.

[Coroner] Were the clothes of the deceased disturbed? I cannot say. I ran towards the Commercial Road, Dienishitz, the club steward and another member going in the opposite direction down Fairclough Street. In Commercial Road, I found two constables at the corner of Grove Street. I told them that a woman had been murdered in Berner Street and they returned with me.

[Coroner] Was any one in the yard then? Yes, a few persons some members of the club and some strangers. One of the policemen turned his lamp on the deceased and sent me to the station for the inspector, at the same time telling his comrade to fetch a doctor. The onlookers seemed afraid to go near and touch the body. The constable, however, felt it.

[Coroner] Can you fix the time when the discovery was first made? It must have been about one o'clock. On Saturday nights, there is free discussion at the club and among those present last Saturday were about half a dozen women but they were those we knew not strangers. It was not a dancing night but a few members may have danced after the discussion.

[Coroner] If there was dancing and singing in the club, you would not hear the cry of a woman in the yard? It would depend upon the cry.

[Coroner] The cry of a woman in great distress, a cry of 'Murder'? Yes, I should have heard that.

Lewis Dienishitz [Diemschutz], having affirmed, deposed: I reside at No 40 Berner Street and am steward of the International Workmen's Club. I am married and my wife lives at the club too and assists in the management. On Saturday I left home about half past eleven in the morning and returned exactly at one o'clock on Sunday morning. I noticed the time at the baker's shop at the corner of Berner Street.

I had been to the market near the Crystal Palace and had a barrow like a costermonger's, drawn by a pony, which I keep in George Yard Cable Street. I drove home to leave my goods. I drove into the yard, both gates being wide open. It was rather dark there. All at once my pony shied at some object on the right. I looked to see what the object was and observed that there was something unusual but could not tell what.

It was a dark object. I put my whip handle to it and tried to lift it up but as I did not succeed I jumped down from my barrow and struck a match. It was rather windy and I could only get sufficient light to see that there was some figure there. I could tell from the dress that it was the figure of a woman.

[Coroner] You did not disturb it? No. I went into the club and asked where my wife was. I found her in the front room on the ground floor.

[Coroner] What did you do with the pony? I left it in the yard by itself, just outside the club door. There were several members in the front room of the club and I told them all that there was a woman lying in the yard, though I could not say whether she was drunk or dead. I then got a candle and went into the yard, where I could see blood before I reached the body.

[Coroner] Did you touch the body? No, I ran off at once for the police. I could not find a constable in the direction which I took, so I shouted out 'Police!' as loudly as I could. A man whom I met in Grove Street returned with me and when we reached the yard he took hold of the head of the deceased. As he lifted it up, I saw the wound in the throat.

[Coroner] Had the constables arrived then? At the very same moment, Eagle and the constables arrived.

[Coroner] Did you notice anything unusual when you were approaching the club? No.

[Coroner] You saw nothing suspicious? Not at all.

[Coroner] How soon afterwards did a doctor arrive? About 20 minutes after the constables came up. No one was allowed by the police to leave the club until they were searched and then they had to give their names and addresses.

[Coroner] Did you notice whether the clothes of the deceased were in order? They were in perfect order.

[Coroner] How was she lying? On her left side, with her face towards the club wall.

[Coroner] Was the whole of the body resting on the side? No, I should say only her face. I cannot say how much of the body was sideways. I did not notice what position her hands were in but when the police came I observed that her bodice was unbuttoned near the neck. The doctor said the body was quite warm.

[Coroner] What quantity of blood should you think had flowed from the body? I should say quite two quarts.

[Coroner] In what direction had it run? Up the yard from the street. The body was about one foot from the club wall. The gutter of the yard is paved with large stones and the centre with smaller irregular stones.

[Coroner] Have you ever seen men and women together in the yard? Never.

[Coroner] Nor heard of such a thing? No.

A Juror: Could you in going up the yard have passed the body without touching it? Oh, yes.

[Coroner] Any person going up the centre of the yard might have passed without noticing it? I, perhaps, should not have noticed it if my pony had not shied. I had passed it when I got down from my barrow.

[Coroner] How far did the blood run? As far as the kitchen door of the club.

[Coroner] Was any person left with the body while you ran for the police? Some members of the club remained; at all events, when I came back they were there. I cannot say whether any of them touched the body.

Inspector Reid (interposing): When the murder was discovered, the members of the club were detained on the premises and I searched them, whilst Dr Phillips examined them.

A Juror; was it possible for anybody to leave the yard between the discovery of the body and the arrival of the police?

Witness: Oh, yes or rather, it would have been possible before I informed the members of the club, not afterwards.

[Coroner] When you entered the yard, if any person had run out you would have seen them in the dark? Oh, yes, it was light enough for that. It was dark in the gateway but not so dark further in the yard.

The Coroner: The body has not yet been identified? Not yet.

The Foreman: I do not quite understand that. I thought the inquest had been opened on the body of one Elizabeth Stride.

The Coroner: That was a mistake. Something is known of the deceased but she has not been fully identified. It would be better at present to describe her as a woman unknown. She has been partially identified. It is known where she lived. It was thought at the beginning of the inquest that she had been identified by a relative but that turns out to have been a mistake.

The inquiry was then adjourned.

Day 2, Tuesday, 2 October 1888.
The Daily Telegraph, Wednesday, 3 October 1888.

Yesterday afternoon 2nd Oct, in the Vestry Hall of St George-in-the-East, Cable Street, Mr Wynne E. Baxter, coroner for East Middlesex, resumed the inquiry into the circumstances attending the death of the woman who was found with her throat cut in a yard adjoining the clubhouse of the International Working Men's Education Society, No. 40, Berner Street, Commercial Road East, at one o'clock on Sunday morning last.

Constable Henry Lamb, 252 H division, examined by the coroner, said: Last Sunday morning, shortly before one o'clock, I was on duty in Commercial Road, between Christian Street and Batty Street, when two men came running towards me and shouting. I went to meet them and they called out, 'Come on, there has been another murder.'

I asked where and as they got to the corner of Berner Street, they pointed down and said, 'There.' I saw people moving some distance down the street. I ran, followed by another constable 426 H. Arriving at the gateway of No 40, I observed something dark lying on the ground on the right hand side. I turned my light on, when I found that the object was a woman, with her throat cut and apparently dead.

I sent the other constable for the nearest doctor and a young man who was standing by, I dispatched to the police station to inform the inspector what had occurred. On my arrival, there were about thirty people in the yard and others followed me in. No one was nearer than a yard to the body. As I was examining the deceased, the crowd gathered round but I begged them to keep back, otherwise they might have their clothes soiled with blood and thus get into trouble.

[Coroner] Up to this time had you touched the body? I had put my hand on the face.

[Coroner] Was it warm? Slightly. I felt the wrist but could not discern any movement of the pulse. I then blew my whistle for assistance.

[Coroner] Did you observe how the deceased was lying? She was lying on her left side, with her left hand on the ground.

[Coroner] Was there anything in that hand? I did not notice anything. The right arm was across the breast. Her face was not more than five or six inches away from the club wall.

[Coroner] Were her clothes disturbed? No.

[Coroner] Only her boots visible? Yes and only the soles of them. There were no signs of a struggle. Some of the blood was in a liquid state and had run towards the kitchen door of the club. A little that nearest to her on the ground was slightly congealed. I can hardly say whether any was still flowing from the throat. Dr Blackwell was the first doctor to arrive; he came ten or twelve minutes after myself but I had no watch with me.

[Coroner] Did any one of the crowd say whether the body had been touched before your arrival? No. Dr Blackwell examined the body and its surroundings. Dr Phillips came ten minutes later. Inspector Pinhorn arrived directly after Dr Blackwell. When I blew my whistle other constables came and I had the entrance of the yard closed. This was while Dr Blackwell was looking at the body. Before that the doors were wide open.

The feet of the deceased extended just to the swing of the gate, so that the barrier could be closed without disturbing the body. I entered the club and left a constable at the gate to prevent any one passing in or out. I examined the hands and clothes of all the members of the club. There were from fifteen to twenty present and they were on the ground floor.

[Coroner] Did you discover traces of blood anywhere in the club? No.

[Coroner] Was the steward present? Yes.

[Coroner] Did you ask him to lock the front door? I did not. There was a great deal of commotion. That was done afterwards.

The Coroner: But time is the essence of the thing.

Witness: I did not see any person leave. I did not try the front door of the club to see if it was locked. I afterwards went over the cottages, the occupants of which were in bed. I was admitted by men, who came down partly dressed; all the other people were undressed. As to the water closets in the yard, one was locked and the other unlocked but no one was there. There is a recess near the dustbin.

[Coroner] Did you go there? Yes, afterwards, with Dr Phillips.

The Coroner: But I am speaking of at the time.

Witness: I did it subsequently. I do not recollect looking over the wooden partition. I, however, examined the store belonging to Messrs. Hindley, sack manufacturers but I saw nothing there.

[Coroner] How long were the cottagers in opening their doors? Only a few minutes and they seemed frightened. When I returned, Dr Phillips and Chief Inspector West had arrived.

[Coroner] Was there anything to prevent a man escaping while you were examining the body? Several people were inside and outside the gates and I should think that they would be sure to observe a man who had marks of blood.

[Coroner] But supposing he had no marks of blood? It was quite possible, of course, for a person to escape while I was examining the corpse. Everyone was more or less looking towards the body. There was much confusion.

[Coroner] Do you think that a person might have got away before you arrived? I think he is more likely to have escaped before than after.

Detective Inspector Reid: How long before had you passed this place?

Witness: I am not on the Berner Street beat but I passed the end of the street in Commercial Road six or seven minutes before.

[Coroner] When you were found what direction were you going in? I was coming towards Berner Street. A constable named Smith was on the Berner Street beat. He did not accompany me but the constable who was on fixed point duty between Grove Street and Christian Street in Commercial Road. Constables at fixed-points leave duty at one in the morning. I believe that is the practice nearly all over London.

The Coroner: I think this is important. The Hanbury Street murder was discovered just as the night police were going off duty.

(To witness): Did you see anything suspicious? I did not at any time. There were squabbles and rows in the streets but nothing more.

The Foreman: Was there light sufficient to enable you to see, as you were going down Berner Street, whether any person was running away from No 40? It was rather dark but I think there was light enough for that, though the person would be somewhat indistinct from Commercial Road.

The Foreman: Some of the papers state that Berner Street is badly lighted; but there are six lamps within 700 feet and I do not think that is very bad.

The Coroner: The parish plan shows that there are four lamps within 350 feet, from Commercial Road to Fairclough Street. Witness: There are three, if not four, lamps in Berner Street between Commercial Road and Fairclough Street. Berner Street is about as well lighted as other side streets. Most of them are rather dark but more lamps have been erected lately.

The Coroner: I do not think that London altogether is as well lighted as some capitals are.

Witness: There are no public house lights in Berner Street. I was engaged in the yard and at the mortuary all the night afterwards.

Edward Spooner, in reply to the coroner, said: I live at No 26, Fairclough Street and am a horse keeper with Messrs. Meredith, biscuit bakers. On Sunday morning, between half past twelve and one o'clock, I was standing outside the Beehive Public house, at the corner of Christian Street, with my young woman. We had left a public house in Commercial Road at closing time, midnight and walked quietly to the point named.

We stood outside the Beehive about twenty five minutes, when two Jews came running along, calling out 'Murder' and 'Police.' They ran as far as Grove Street and then turned back. I stopped them and asked what the matter was and they replied that a woman had been murdered. I thereupon proceeded down Berner Street and into Dutfields Yard, adjoining the International Workmen's Clubhouse and there saw a woman lying just inside the gate.

[Coroner] Was any one with her? There were about fifteen people in the yard.

[Coroner] Was any one near her? They were all standing round.

[Coroner] Were they touching her? No. One man struck a match but I could see the woman before the match was struck. I put my hand under her chin when the match was alight.

[Coroner] Was the chin warm? Slightly.

[Coroner] Was any blood coming from the throat? Yes; it was still flowing. I noticed that she had a piece of paper doubled up in her right hand and some red and white flowers pinned on her breast. I did not feel the body, nor did I alter the position of the head. I am sure of that. Her face was turned towards the club wall.

[Coroner] Did you notice whether the blood was still moving on the ground? It was running down the gutter. I stood by the side of the body for four or five minutes, until the last witness arrived.

[Coroner] Did you notice any one leave the yard while you were there? No.

[Coroner] Could anyone have left without your observing it? I cannot say but I think there were too many people about. I believe it was twenty five minutes to one o'clock when I arrived in the yard.

[Coroner] Have you formed any opinion as to whether the people had moved the body before you came? No.

The Foreman: As a rule, Jews do not care to touch dead bodies.

Witness: The legs of the deceased were drawn up but her clothes were not disturbed. When Police constable Lamb came I helped him to close the gates of the yard and I left through the club.

Inspector Reid: I believe that was after you had given your name and address to the police? Yes. And had been searched? Yes. And examined by Dr Phillips? Yes.

The Coroner: Was there no blood on your hands? No.

[Coroner] Then there was no blood on the chin of the deceased? No.

By the Jury: I did not meet any one as I was hastening through Berner Street.

Mary Malcolm was the next witness and she was deeply affected while giving her evidence. In answer to the coroner, she said: I live at No. 50, Eagle Street, Red Lion square, Holborn and am married. My husband Andrew

Malcolm, is a tailor. I have seen the body at the mortuary. I saw it once on Sunday and twice yesterday.

[Coroner] Who is it? It is the body of my sister, Elizabeth Watts.

[Coroner] You have no doubt about that? Not the slightest.

[Coroner] You did have some doubts about it at one time? I had at first.

[Coroner] When did you last see your sister alive? Last Thursday, about a quarter to seven in the evening.

[Coroner] Where? She came to see me at No 59, Red Lion Street, where I work as a trouser maker.

[Coroner] What did she come to you for? To ask me for a little assistance. I have been in the habit of assisting her for five years.

[Coroner] Did you give her anything? I gave her a shilling and a short jacket not the jacket which is now on the body.

[Coroner] How long was she with you? Only a few moments.

[Coroner] Did she say where she was going? No.

[Coroner] Where was she living? I do not know. I know it was somewhere in the neighbourhood of the tailoring Jews Commercial Road or Commercial Street or somewhere at the East End.

[Coroner] Did you understand that she was living in lodging houses? Yes.

[Coroner] Did you know what she was doing for a livelihood? I had my doubts.

[Coroner] Was she the worse for drink when she came to you on Thursday? No, sober.

[Coroner] But she was sometimes the worse for drink, was she not? That was, unfortunately, a failing with her. She was thirty seven years of age last March.

[Coroner] Had she ever been married? Yes.

[Coroner] Is her husband alive? Yes, so far as I know. She married the son of Mr Watts, wine and spirit merchant, of Walcot Street, Bath. I think her husband's Christian name was Edward. I believe he is now in America.

[Coroner] Did he get into trouble? No.

[Coroner] Why did he go away? Because my sister brought trouble upon him.

[Coroner] When did she leave him? About eight years ago but I cannot be quite certain as to the time. She had two children. Her husband caught her with a porter and there was a quarrel.

[Coroner] Did the husband turn her out of doors? No, he sent her to my poor mother, with the two children.

[Coroner] Where does your mother live? She is dead. She died in the year 1883.

[Coroner] Where are the children now? The girl is dead but the boy is at a boarding school kept by his aunt.

[Coroner] Was the deceased subject to epileptic fits?

Witness (sobbing bitterly): No, she only had drunken fits.

[Coroner] Was she ever before the Thames police magistrate? I believe so.

[Coroner] Charged with drunkenness? Yes.

[Coroner] Are you aware that she has been let off on the supposition that she was subject to epileptic fits? I believe that is so but she was not subject to epileptic fits.

[Coroner] Has she ever told you of troubles she was in with any man? Oh yes; she lived with a man.

[Coroner] Do you know his name? I do not remember now but I shall be able to tell you tomorrow. I believe she lived with a man who kept a coffee house at Poplar.

Inspector Reid: Was his name Stride? No; I think it was Dent but I can find out for certain by tomorrow.

The Coroner: How long had she ceased to live with that man? Oh, some time. He went away to sea and was wrecked on the Isle of St Paul, I believe.

[Coroner] How long ago should you think that was? It must be three years and a half; but I could tell you all about it by tomorrow, even the name of the vessel that was wrecked.

[Coroner] Had the deceased lived with any man since then? Not to my knowledge but there is some man who says that he has lived with her.

[Coroner] Have you ever heard of her getting into trouble with this man? No but at times she got locked up for drunkenness. She always brought her trouble to me.

[Coroner] You never heard of any one threatening her? No; she was too good for that.

[Coroner] Did you ever hear her say that she was afraid of any one? No.

[Coroner] Did you know of no man with whom she had relations? No.

Inspector Reid: Did you ever visit her in Flower and Dean Street? No.

[Coroner] Did you ever hear her called 'Long Liz'? That was generally her nickname, I believe.

[Coroner] Have you ever heard of the name of Stride? She never mentioned such a name to me. I think that if she had lived with any one of that name she would have told me. I have heard what the man Stride has said but I think he is mistaken.

The Coroner: How often did your sister come to you? Every Saturday and I always gave her 2s. That was for her lodgings.

[Coroner] Did she come to you at all last Saturday? No, I did not see her on that day.

[Coroner] The Thursday visit was an unusual one, I suppose? Yes.

[Coroner] Did you think it strange that she did not come on the Saturday? I did.

[Coroner] Had she ever missed a Saturday before? Not for nearly three years.

[Coroner] What time in the day did she usually come to you? At four o'clock in the afternoon.

[Coroner] Where? At the corner of Chancery Lane. I was there last Saturday afternoon from half past three till five but she did not turn up.

[Coroner] Did you think there was something the matter with her? On the Sunday morning when I read the accounts in the newspapers I thought it might be my sister who had been murdered. I had a presentiment that that was so. I came down to Whitechapel and was directed to the mortuary but when I saw the body I did not recognise it as that of my sister.

[Coroner] How was that? Why did you not recognise it in the first instance? I do not know, except that I saw it in the gaslight, between nine and ten at night. But I recognised her the next day.

[Coroner] Did you not have some special presentiment that this was your sister? Yes.

[Coroner] Tell the jury what it was? I was in bed and about twenty minutes past one on Sunday morning I felt a pressure on my breast and heard three distinct kisses. It was that which made me afterwards suspect that the woman who had been murdered was my sister.

The Coroner (to the jury): The only reason why I allow this evidence is that the witness has been doubtful about her identification.

(To witness) Did your sister ever break a limb? No. Never? Not to my knowledge.

The Foreman: Had she any special marks upon her? Yes, on her right leg there was a small black mark.

The Coroner: Have you seen that mark on the deceased? Yes.

[Coroner] When did you see it? Yesterday morning.

[Coroner] But when, before death, did you see it on your sister? Oh not for years. It was the size of a pea. I have not seen it for 20 years.

[Coroner] Did you mention the mark before you saw the body? I said that I could recognise my sister by this particular mark.

[Coroner] What was the mark? It was from the bite of an Adder. One day, when children, we were rolling down a hill together and we came across an Adder. The thing bit me first and my sister afterwards. I have still the mark of the bite on my left hand.

The Coroner (examining the mark): Oh, that is only a scar. Are you sure that your sister, in her youth, never broke a limb? Not to my knowledge.

[Coroner] Has your husband seen your sister? Yes.

[Coroner] Has he been to the mortuary? No; he will not go.

[Coroner] Have you any brothers and sisters alive? Yes, a brother and a sister but they have not seen her for years. My brother might recognise her. He lives near Bath. My sister resides at Folkestone. My sister (the deceased) had a hollowness in her right foot, caused by some sort of accident. It was the absence of this hollowness that made me doubt whether the deceased was really my sister. Perhaps it passed away in death. But the adder mark removed all doubt.

[Coroner] Did you recognise the clothes of the deceased at all? No.

(Bursting into tears). Indeed, I have had trouble with her. On one occasion she left a naked baby outside my door.

[Coroner] One of her babies? One of her own.

[Coroner] One of the two children by her husband? No, another one; one she had by a policeman, I believe. She left it with me and I had to keep it until she fetched it away.

Inspector Reid: Is that child alive, do you know? I believe it died in Bath.

The Coroner: It is important that the evidence of identification should be unmistakable and I think that the witness should go to the same spot in Chancery Lane on Saturday next, in order to see if her sister comes.

Witness: I have no doubt.

The Coroner: Still, it is better that the matter should be tested.

Witness (in reply to the jury): I did not think it strange that my sister came to me last Thursday instead of the Saturday, because she has done it before. But on previous occasions she has come on the Saturday as well. When she came last Thursday she asked me for money, stating that she had not enough to pay for her lodgings and I said, 'Elizabeth, you are a pest to me.'

The Coroner: Has your sister been in prison?

Witness: Yes.

[Coroner] Has she never been in prison on a Saturday? No; she has only been locked up for the night.

[Coroner] Never more? No, she has been fined.

A Juror: You say that before when she has come on the Thursday she has also come on the Saturday as well? Always.

The Coroner: So that the Thursday was an extra. You are quite confident now about the identity? I have not a shadow of doubt.

Mr Frederick William Blackwell deposed: I reside at No 100, Commercial Road and am a physician and surgeon. On Sunday morning last, at ten minutes past one o'clock, I was called to Berner Street by a policeman. My assistant, Mr Johnston, went back with the constable and I followed immediately I was dressed. I consulted my watch on my arrival and it was 1.16 a.m.

The deceased was lying on her left side obliquely across the passage, her face looking towards the right wall. Her legs were drawn up, her feet close against the wall of the right side of the passage. Her head was resting beyond the carriage wheel rut, the neck lying over the rut. Her feet were three yards from the gateway. Her dress was unfastened at the neck.

The neck and chest were quite warm, as were also the legs and the face was slightly warm. The hands were cold. The right hand was open and on the chest and was smeared with blood. The left hand, lying on the ground, was partially closed and contained a small packet of cachous wrapped in tissue paper.

There were no rings, nor marks of rings, on her hands. The appearance of the face was quite placid. The mouth was slightly open. The deceased had round her neck a check silk scarf, the bow of which was turned to the left and pulled very tight. In the neck, there was a long incision which exactly corresponded with the lower border of the scarf.

The border was slightly frayed, as if by a sharp knife. The incision in the neck commenced on the left side, 2 inches below the angle of the jaw and almost in a direct line with it, nearly severing the vessels on that side, cutting the windpipe completely in two and terminating on the opposite side 1 inch below the angle of the right jaw but without severing the vessels on that side.

I could not ascertain whether the bloody hand had been moved. The blood was running down the gutter into the drain in the opposite direction from the feet. There was about 1lb of clotted blood close by the body and a stream all the way from there to the back door of the club.

[Coroner] Were there no spots of blood about? No; only some marks of blood which had been trodden in.

[Coroner]. Was there any blood on the soles of the deceased's boots? No.

[Coroner] No splashing of blood on the wall? No, it was very dark and what I saw was by the aid of a policeman's lantern. I have not examined the place since. I examined the clothes but found no blood on any part of them. The bonnet of the deceased was lying on the ground a few inches from the head. Her dress was unbuttoned at the top.

[Coroner] Can you say whether the injuries could have been self-inflicted? It is impossible that they could have been.

[Coroner] Did you form any opinion as to how long the deceased had been dead? From twenty minutes to half an hour when I arrived. The clothes were not wet with rain. She would have bled to death comparatively slowly on account of vessels on one side only of the neck being cut and the artery not completely severed.

[Coroner] After the infliction of the injuries was there any possibility of any cry being uttered by the deceased? None whatever. Dr Phillips came about twenty minutes to half an hour after my arrival. The double doors of the yard were closed when I arrived, so that the previous witness must have made a mistake on that point.

A Juror: Can you say whether the throat was cut before or after the deceased fell to the ground? I formed the opinion that the murderer probably caught hold of the silk scarf, which was tight and knotted and pulled the deceased backwards, cutting her throat in that way. The throat might have been cut as she was falling or when she was on the ground. The blood would have spurted about if the act had been committed while she was standing up.

The Coroner: Was the silk scarf tight enough to prevent her calling out? I could not say that.

[Coroner] A hand might have been put on her nose and mouth? Yes and the cut on the throat was probably instantaneous.

The inquest was then adjourned.

Day 3, Monday, 3 October 1888.
The Daily Telegraph, Thursday, 4 October 1888.

Yesterday [3rd Oct], at St George's Vestry Hall, Cable-street, Mr Wynne E. Baxter, coroner for East Middlesex, again resumed the inquiry into the circumstances attending the death of the woman who was found with her throat cut at one o'clock on Sunday morning last in a yard adjoining the International Working Men's Club, Berner-street, Commercial Road East.

Elizabeth Tanner, examined by the Coroner, said: I am deputy of the common lodging house, No 32, Flower and Dean Street and am a widow. I have seen the body of the deceased at St George's Mortuary and recognise it as that of a woman who has lodged in our house, on and off, for the last six years.

[Coroner] Who is she? She was known by the nick-name of 'Long Liz.'

[Coroner] Do you know her right name? No.

[Coroner] Was she an English woman? She used to say that she was a Swedish woman. She never told me where she was born. She said that she was married and that her husband and children were drowned in the Princess Alice.

[Coroner] When did you last see her alive? Last Saturday evening, at half past six o'clock.

[Coroner] Where was she then? With me in a public house, called the Queen's Head, in Commercial Street.

[Coroner] Did she leave you there? She went back with me to the lodging house. At that time, she had no bonnet or cloak on. She never told me what her husband was.

[Coroner] Where did you actually leave her? She went into the kitchen and I went to another part of the building.

[Coroner] Did you see her again? No, until I saw the body in the mortuary today.

[Coroner] You are quite certain it is the body of the same woman? Quite sure. I recognise, beside the features, that the roof of her mouth is missing. Deceased accounted for this by stating that she was in the Princess Alice when it went down and that her mouth was injured.

[Coroner] How long had she been staying at the lodging house? She was there last week only on Thursday and Friday nights.

[Coroner] Had she paid for her bed on Saturday night? No.

[Coroner] Do you know any of her male acquaintances? Only of one.

[Coroner] Who is he? She was living with him. She left him on Thursday to come and stay at our house, so she told me.

[Coroner] Have you seen this man? I saw him last Sunday.

Detective Inspector Reid: He is present today.

Witness: I do not know that she was ever up at the Thames Police court, or that she suffered from epileptic fits. I am aware that she lived in Fashion Street but not that she has ever resided at Poplar. I never heard of a sister at Red Lion square. I never heard of any relative except her late husband and children.

[Coroner] What sort of a woman was she? Very quiet.

[Coroner] A sober woman? Yes.

[Coroner] Did she use to stop out late at night? Sometimes.

[Coroner] Do you know if she had any money? She cleaned two rooms for me on Saturday and I paid her 6d for doing it. I do not know whether she had any other money.

[Coroner] Are you able to say whether the two handkerchiefs now at the mortuary belonged to the deceased? No.

[Coroner] Do you recognise her clothes? Yes. I recognise the long cloak which is hanging up in the mortuary. The other clothes she had on last Saturday.

[Coroner] Did she ever tell you that she was afraid of any one? No.

[Coroner] Or that any one had ever threatened to injure her? No.

[Coroner] The fact of her not coming back on Saturday did not surprise you, I suppose? We took no notice of it.

[Coroner] What made you go to the mortuary, then? Because I was sent for. I do not recollect at what hour she came to the lodging house last Thursday. She was wearing the long cloak then. She did not bring any parcel with her. By the jury: I do not know of anyone else of the name of Long Liz. I never heard of her sister allowing her any money, nor have I heard the name of Stride mentioned in connection with her. Before last Thursday, she had been away from my house about three months.

The Coroner: Did you see her during that three months? Yes, frequently; sometimes once a week and at other times almost every other day.

[Coroner] Did you understand what she was doing? She told me that she was at work among the Jews and was living with a man in Fashion Street.

[Coroner] Could she speak English well? Yes but she spoke Swedish also.

[Coroner] When she spoke English could you detect that she was a foreigner?-She spoke English as well as an English woman. She did not associate much with Swedish people. I never heard of her having hurt her foot, nor of her having broken a limb in childhood. I had no doubt that she was what she represented herself to be a Swede.

Catherine Lane: I live in Flower and Dean Street and am a charwoman and married. My husband is a dock labourer and is living with me at the lodging house of which the last witness is deputy. I have been there since last February. I have seen the body of the deceased at the mortuary.

The Coroner: Did you recognise it? Yes, as the body of Long Liz, who lived occasionally in the lodging house. She came there last Thursday.

[Coroner]. Had you ever seen her before? I have known her for six or seven months. I used to see her frequently in Fashion Street, where she lived and I have seen her at our lodging house.

[Coroner] Did you speak to her last week? On Thursday and Saturday.

[Coroner] At what time did you see her first on Thursday? Between ten and eleven o'clock.

[Coroner] Did she explain why she was coming back? She said she had had a few words with the man she was living with.

[Coroner] When did you see her on Saturday? When she was cleaning the deputy's room.

[Coroner] And after that? I last saw her in the kitchen, between six and seven in the evening. She then had on a long cloak and a black bonnet.

[Coroner] Did she say where she was going? No. I first saw the body in the mortuary on Sunday afternoon and I recognised it then.

[Coroner] Did you see her leave the lodging-house? Yes; she gave me a piece of velvet as she left and asked me to mind it until she came back. (The velvet was produced and proved to be a large piece, green in colour.)

[Coroner] Had she no place to leave it? I do not know why she asked me, as the deputy would take charge of anything. I know deceased had sixpence when she left; she showed it to me, stating that the deputy had given it to her.

[Coroner] Had she been drinking then? Not that I am aware of.

[Coroner] Do you know of anyone who was likely to have injured her? No one.

[Coroner] Have you heard her mention any person but this man she was living with? No. I have heard her say she was a Swede and that at one time she lived in Devonshire Street, Commercial Road never in Poplar.

[Coroner] Did you ever hear her speak of her husband? She said he was dead. She never said that she was afraid or that anyone had threatened her life. I am satisfied the deceased is the same woman.

By the jury: I could tell by her accent that she was a foreigner. She did not bring all her words out plainly.

[Coroner] Have you ever heard of her speaking to any one in her own language? Yes; with women for whom she worked. I never heard of her having a sister, or of her having left a child at her sister's door.

Charles Preston deposed: I live at No 32, Flower and Dean Street and I am a barber. I have been lodging at my present address for eighteen months and have seen the deceased there. I saw the body on Sunday last and am quite sure it is that of Long Liz.

The Coroner: When did you last see her alive? On Saturday morning between six and seven o'clock.

[Coroner] Where was she then? In the kitchen of the lodging-house.

[Coroner] Was she dressed to go out? Yes and asked me for a brush to brush her clothes with but I did not let her have one.

[Coroner] What was she wearing? The jacket I have seen at the mortuary but no flowers in the breast. She had the striped silk handkerchief round her neck.

[Coroner] Do you happen to have seen her pocket handkerchiefs? No.

[Coroner] You cannot say whether she had two? No.

[Coroner] Do you know anything about her? I always understood that she was born at Stockholm and came to England in the service of a gentleman.

[Coroner] Did she ever tell you her age? She said once that she was thirty five.

[Coroner] Did she ever tell you that she was married? Yes; and that her husband and children went down in the Princess Alice that she had been saved while they were lost.

[Coroner] Did she ever state what her husband was? I have some recollection that she said he was a seafaring man and that he had kept a coffee house in Chrisp Street, Poplar.

[Coroner] Did she ever tell you that she was taken to the Thames Police court? I only remember her having been taken into custody for being drunk and disorderly at the Ten Bells public house, Commercial Street, one Sunday morning from four to five months ago.

[Coroner] Do you know of anyone who was likely to have injured her? No.

[Coroner] Did she ever state that she was afraid of any one? Never.

[Coroner] Did she say where she was going on Saturday? No.

[Coroner] Or when she was coming back? No.

[Coroner] Did she say whether she was coming back? She never said anything about it. She always gave me to understand that her name was Elizabeth Stride. She never mentioned any sister. She stated that her mother was still alive in Sweden. She apparently spoke Swedish fluently to people who came into the lodging house.

Michael Kidney said: I live at No 38, Dorset Street, Spitalfields and am a waterside labourer. I have seen the body of the deceased at the mortuary.

The Coroner: Is it the woman you have been living with? Yes.

[Coroner] You have no doubt about it? No doubt whatever.

[Coroner] What was her name? Elizabeth Stride.

[Coroner] How long have you known her? About three years.

[Coroner] How long has she been living with you? Nearly all that time.

[Coroner] What was her age? Between thirty six and thirty eight years.

[Coroner] Was she a Swede? She told me that she was a Swede and I have no doubt she was. She said she was born three miles from Stockholm that her father was a farmer and that she first came to England for the purpose of seeing the country but I have grave doubts about that. She afterwards told me that she came to England in a situation with a family.

[Coroner] Had she got any relatives in England? When I met her she told me she was a widow and that her husband had been a ship's carpenter at Sheerness.

[Coroner] Did he ever keep a coffee house? She told me that he had.

[Coroner] Where? In Chrisp Street, Poplar.

[Coroner] Did she say when he died? She informed me that he was drowned in the Princess Alice disaster.

[Coroner] Was the roof of her mouth defective? Yes.

[Coroner] You had a quarrel with her on Thursday? I did not see her on Thursday.

[Coroner] When did you last see her? On the Tuesday and I then left her on friendly terms in Commercial Street. That was between nine and ten o'clock at night, as I was coming from work.

[Coroner] Did you expect her home? I expected her home half an hour afterwards. I subsequently ascertained that she had been in and had gone out again and I did not see her again alive.

[Coroner] Can you account for her sudden disappearance? Was she the worse for drink when you last saw her? She was perfectly sober.

[Coroner] You can assign no reason whatever for her going away so suddenly? She would occasionally go away.

[Coroner] Oh, she has left you before? During the three years I have known her she has been away from me about five months altogether.

[Coroner] Without any reason? Not to my knowledge. I treated her the same as I would a wife.

[Coroner] Do you know whether she had picked up with any one? I have seen the address of the brother of the gentleman with whom she lived as a servant, somewhere near Hyde Park but I cannot find it now.

[Coroner] Did she have any reason for going away? It was drink that made her go on previous occasions. She always came back again. I think she liked me better than any other man. I do not believe she left me on Tuesday to take up with any other man.

[Coroner] Had she any money? I do not think she was without a shilling when she left me. From what I used to give her, I fancy she must either have had money or spent it in drink.

[Coroner] You know of nobody whom she was likely to have complications with or fall foul of? No but I think the police authorities are very much to blame or they would have got the man who murdered her. At Leman Street Police station, on Monday night, I asked for a detective to give information to get the man.

[Coroner] What information had you? I could give information that would enable the detectives to discover the man at any time.

[Coroner] Then will you give us your information now? I told the inspector on duty at the police station that I could give information provided he would let me have a young, strange detective to act on it and he would not give me one.

[Coroner] What do you think should be inquired into? I might have given information that would have led to a great deal if I had been provided with a strange young detective.

Inspector Reid: When you went to Leman Street and saw the inspector on duty, were you intoxicated? Yes; I asked for a young detective and he would not let me have one and I told him that he was uncivil. (Laughter.)

[Coroner] You have been in the army and I believe have a good pension? Only the reserve.

A Juror: Have you got any information for a detective? I am a great lover of discipline, sir. (Laughter.)

The Coroner: Had you any information that required the service of a detective? Yes. I thought that if I had one, privately, he could get more information than I could myself. The parties I obtained my information from knew me and I thought someone else would be able to derive more from them.

Inspector Reid: Will you give me the information directly, if you will not give it to the coroner? I believe I could catch the man if I had a detective under my command.

The Coroner: You cannot expect that. I have had over a hundred letters making suggestions and I dare say all the writers would like to have a detective at their service. (Laughter)

Witness: I have information which I think might be of use to the police.

The Coroner: You had better give it, then.

Witness: I believe that, if I could place the policeman myself, the man would be captured.

The Coroner: You must know that the police would not be placed at the disposal of a man the worse for drink.

Witness: If I were at liberty to place 100 men about this city the murderer would be caught in the act.

Inspector Reid: But you have no information to give to the police?

Witness: No, I will keep it to myself.

A Juror: Do you know of any sister who gave money to the deceased? No. On Monday, I saw Mrs Malcolm, who said the deceased was her sister. She is very like the deceased.

[Coroner] Did the deceased have a child by you? No.

[Coroner] Or by a policeman? She told me that a policeman used to court her when she was at Hyde Park, before she was married to Stride. Stride and the policeman courted her at the same time but I never heard of her having a child by the policeman.

She said she was the mother of nine children, two of whom were drowned with her husband in the Princess Alice and the remainders were either in a school belonging to the Swedish Church on the other side of London Bridge or with the husband's friends. I thought she was telling the truth when she spoke of Swedish people. I understood that the deceased and her husband were employed on the Princess Alice.

Mr Edward Johnson: I live at 100, Commercial Road and an assistant to Drs Kaye and Blackwell. On Sunday morning last, at a few minutes past one o'clock, I received a call from Constable 436 H. After informing Dr Blackwell, who was in bed, of the case, I accompanied the officer to Berner Street and in a courtyard adjoining No 40, I was shown the figure of a woman lying on her left side.

The Coroner: Were there many people about? There was a crowd in the yard.

[Coroner] And police? Yes.

[Coroner] Was any one touching the deceased? No.

[Coroner] Was there much light? Very little.

[Coroner] What light there was, where did it come from? From the policeman's lantern. I examined the woman and found an incision in the throat.

[Coroner] Was blood coming from the wound? No, it had stopped bleeding. I felt the body and found all warm except the hands, which were quite cold.

[Coroner] Did you undo the dress? The dress was not undone when I came. I undid it to see if the chest was warm.

[Coroner] Did you move the head at all? I left the body precisely as I found it. There was a stream of blood down to the gutter; it was all clotted. There was very little blood near the neck; it had all run away. I did not notice at the time that one of the hands was smeared with blood. The left arm was bent, away from the body. The right arm was also bent and across the body.

[Coroner] Can you say whether anyone had stepped into the stream of blood? There was no mark of it.

[Coroner] Did you look for any? Yes. I had no watch with me but Dr Blackwell looked at his when he arrived and the time was 1.16 a.m. I preceded him by three or four minutes. The bonnet of the deceased was lying three or four inches beyond the head on the ground. The outer gates were closed shortly after I came.

Thomas Coram: I live at No 67, Plummer's Road and work for a cocoanut dealer. On Monday shortly after midnight, I left a friend's house in Bath gardens, Brady Street. I walked straight down Brady Street and into Whitechapel Road towards Aldgate. I first walked on the right side of Whitechapel Road and afterwards crossed over to the left and when opposite No 253 I saw a knife lying on the doorstep.

[Coroner] What is No 253? A laundry. There were two steps to the front door and the knife was on the bottom step. The production of the knife created some sensation, its discovery not having been generally known. It was a knife such as would be used by a baker in his trade, it being flat at the top instead of pointed, as a butcher's knife would be. The blade, which was discoloured with something resembling blood, was quite a foot long and an inch broad, whilst the black handle was six inches in length and strongly riveted in three places.

Witness (continuing): There was a handkerchief round the handle of the knife, the handkerchief having been first folded and then twisted round the blade. A policeman coming towards me, I called his attention to the knife, which I did not touch.

[Coroner] Did the policeman take the knife away? Yes, to the Leman Street station, I was accompanying him.

[Coroner] Were there many people passing at the time? Very few. I do not think I passed more than a dozen from Brady Street to where I found the knife. The weapon could easily be seen; it was light there.

[Coroner] Did you pass any policeman between Brady Street and where the knife was? I passed three policemen.

Constable Joseph Drage, 282 H Division: On Monday morning at half past twelve o'clock I was on fixed point duty opposite Brady Street, Whitechapel Road, when I saw the last witness stooping down to pick up something about twenty yards from me. As I went towards him he beckoned with his finger and said, 'Policeman, there is a knife lying here.' I then saw a long bladed knife on the doorstep. I picked up the knife and found it was smothered with blood.

[Coroner] Was it wet? Dry. A handkerchief, which was also blood stained, was bound round the handle and tied with a string. I asked the lad how he came to see it and he said, 'I was just looking around and I saw something white.' I asked him what he did out so late and he replied, 'I have been to a friend's in Bath Gardens.' I took down his name and address and he went to the police station with me. The knife and handkerchief are those produced.

The boy was sober and his manner natural. He said that the knife made his blood run cold, adding, 'We hear of such funny things nowadays.' I had passed the step a quarter of an hour before. I could not be positive but I do not think the knife was there then. About an hour earlier, I stood near the door and saw the landlady let out a woman. The knife was not there then. I handed the knife and handkerchief to Dr Phillips on Monday afternoon.

Mr George Baxter Phillips: I live at No 2, Spital Square and am surgeon of the H Division of police. I was called on Sunday morning last at twenty past one to Leman Street Police station and was sent on to Berner Street, to a yard at the side of what proved to be a clubhouse. I found Inspector Pinhorn and Acting Superintendent West in possession of a body, which had already been seen by Dr Blackwell, who had arrived some time before me.

The body was lying on its left side, the face being turned towards the wall, the head towards the yard and the feet towards the street. The left arm was extended from elbow and a packet of cachous was in the hand. Similar ones were in the gutter. I took them from the hand and gave them to Dr Blackwell.

The right arm was lying over the body and the back of the hand and wrist had on them clotted blood. The legs were drawn up, feet close to wall, body still warm, face warm, hands cold, legs quite warm, silk handkerchief round throat, slightly torn (so is my note but I since find it is cut).

I produce the handkerchief. This corresponded to the right angle of the jaw. The throat was deeply gashed and there was an abrasion of the skin, about an inch and a quarter in diameter, under the right clavicle. On 1st Oct, at three p.m. at St George's Mortuary, present Dr Blackwell and for part of the time Dr Reigate and Dr Blackwell's assistant; temperature being about 55 degrees, Dr Blackwell and I made a post-mortem examination, Dr Blackwell kindly consenting to make the dissection and I took the following note:

"Rigor mortis still firmly marked. Mud on face and left side of the head. Matted on the hair and left side. We removed the clothes. We found the body fairly nourished. Over both shoulders, especially the right, from the front aspect under collar bones and in front of chest there is a bluish discolouration which I have watched and seen on two occasions since.

"On neck, from left to right, there is a clean cut incision six inches in length; incision commencing two and a half inches in a straight line below the angle of the jaw. Three quarters of an inch over undivided muscle, then becoming deeper, about an inch dividing sheath and the vessels, ascending a little and then grazing the muscle outside the cartilages on the left side of the neck.

"The carotid artery on the left side and the other vessels contained in the sheath were all cut through, save the posterior portion of the carotid, to a line about 1/12th of an inch in extent, which prevented the separation of the upper and lower portion of the artery.

"The cut through the tissues on the right side of the cartilages is more superficial and tails off to about two inches below the right angle of the jaw. It is evident that the haemorrhage which produced death was caused through the partial severance of the left carotid artery. There is a deformity in the lower fifth of the bones of the right leg, which are not straight but bow forward; there is a thickening above the left ankle.

"The bones are straighter here. No recent external injury to neck. The lower lobe of the ear was torn, as if by the forcible removing or wearing through of an earring but it was thoroughly healed. The right ear was pierced for an earring but had not been so injured and the earring was wanting. On removing the scalp there was no sign of bruising or extravasation of blood between it and the skullcap.

"The skull was about one sixth of an inch in thickness and dense in texture. The brain was fairly normal. Both lungs were unusually pale. The heart was small; left ventricle firmly contracted, right less so. Right ventricle full of dark clot; left absolutely empty. Partly digested food, apparently consisting of cheese, potato and farinaceous edibles. Teeth on left lower jaw absent."

On Tuesday, at the mortuary, I found the total circumference of the neck 12 inches. I found in the pocket of the underskirt of the deceased a key, as of a padlock, a small piece of lead pencil, a comb, a broken piece of comb, a metal spoon, half a dozen large and one small button, a hook, as if off a dress, a piece of muslin and one or two small pieces of paper. Examining her jacket I found that although there was a slight amount of mud on the right side, the left was well plastered with mud.

A Juror: You have not mentioned anything about the roof of the mouth. One witness said part of the roof of the mouth was gone.

Witness: That was not noticed.

The Coroner: What was the cause of death? Undoubtedly, the loss of blood from the left carotid artery and the division of the windpipe.

[Coroner] Did you examine the blood at Berner-street carefully, as to its direction and so forth? Yes.

[Coroner] The blood near to the neck and a few inches to the left side was well clotted and it had run down the waterway to within a few inches of the side entrance to the clubhouse.

[Coroner] Were there any spots of blood anywhere else? I could trace none except that which I considered had been transplanted if I may use the term from the original flow from the neck. Roughly estimating it, I should say there was an unusual flow of blood, considering the stature and the nourishment of the body.

By a Juror: I did notice a black mark on one of the legs of the deceased but could not say that it was due to an adder bite. Before the witness had concluded his evidence, the inquiry was adjourned.

Day 4, Monday, 5 October 1888.
The Daily Telegraph, Saturday, 6 October 1888.

Yesterday [5th Oct] afternoon at the Vestry Hall of St George-in-the-East, Cable Street, Mr Wynne E. Baxter, coroner for East Middlesex, resumed the inquiry concerning the death of the woman who was found early on Sunday last with her throat cut, in a yard adjoining the International Working Men's Club, Berner Street, Commercial Road East.

Dr Phillips, surgeon of the H Division of police, being recalled, said: On the last occasion I was requested to make a re-examination of the body of the deceased, especially with regard to the palate and I have since done so at the mortuary, along with Dr Blackwell and Dr Gordon Brown. I did not find any injury to or absence of any part of either the hard or the soft palate.

The Coroner also desired me to examine the two handkerchiefs which were found on the deceased. I did not discover any blood on them and I believe that the stains on the larger handkerchief are those of fruit. Neither on the hands nor about the body of the deceased did I find grapes, or connection with them. I am convinced that the deceased had not swallowed either the skin or seed of a grape within many hours of her death.

I have stated that the neckerchief which she had on was not torn but cut. The abrasion which I spoke of on the right side of the neck was only apparently an abrasion, for on washing it. It was removed and the skin found to be uninjured. The knife produced on the last occasion was delivered to me, properly secured, by a constable and on examination I found it to be such a knife as is used in a chandler's shop and is called a slicing knife.

It has blood upon it, which has characteristics similar to the blood of a human being. It has been recently blunted and its edge apparently turned by rubbing on a stone such as a kerbstone. It evidently was before a very sharp knife.

The Coroner: Is it such as knife as could have caused the injuries which were inflicted upon the deceased? Such a knife could have produced the incision and injuries to the neck but it is not such a weapon as I should have fixed upon as having caused the injuries in this case; and if my opinion as regards the position of the body is correct, the knife in question would become an improbable instrument as having caused the incision.

[Coroner] What is your idea as to the position the body was in when the crime was committed? I have come to a conclusion as to the position of both the murderer and the victim and I opine that the latter was seized by the shoulders and placed on the ground and that the murderer was on her right side when he inflicted the cut. I am of opinion that the cut was made from the left to the right side of the deceased and taking into account the position of the incision it is unlikely that such a long knife inflicted the wound in the neck.

[Coroner] The knife produced on the last occasion was not sharp pointed, was it? No, it was rounded at the tip, which was about an inch across. The blade was wider at the base.

[Coroner] Was there anything to indicate that the cut on the neck of the deceased was made with a pointed knife? Nothing.

[Coroner] Have you formed any opinion as to the manner in which the deceased's right hand became stained with blood? It is a mystery. There were small oblong clots on the back of the hand. I may say that I am taking it as a fact that after death the hand always remained in the position in which I found it across the body.

[Coroner] How long had the woman been dead when you arrived at the scene of the murder, do you think? Within an hour she had been alive.

[Coroner] Would the injury take long to inflict? Only a few seconds it might be done in two seconds.

[Coroner] Does the presence of the cachous in the left hand indicate that the murder was committed very suddenly and without any struggle? Some of the cachous were scattered about the yard.

The Foreman: Do you not think that the woman would have dropped the packet of cachous altogether if she had been thrown to the ground before the injuries were inflicted? That is an inference which the jury would be perfectly entitled to draw.

The Coroner: I assume that the injuries were not self-inflicted? I have seen several self-inflicted wounds more extensive than this one but then they have not usually involved the carotid artery. In this case, as in some others, there seems to have been some knowledge where to cut the throat to cause a fatal result.

[Coroner] Is there any similarity between this case and Annie Chapman's case? There is very great dissimilarity between the two. In Chapman's case the neck was severed all round down to the vertebral column, the vertebral bones being marked with two sharp cuts and there had been an evident attempt to separate the bones.

[Coroner] From the position you assume the perpetrator to have been in, would he have been likely to get bloodstained? Not necessarily, for the commencement of the wound and the injury to the vessels would be away from him and the stream of blood would be directed away from him and towards the gutter in the yard.

[Coroner] Was there any appearance of an opiate or any smell of chloroform? There was no perceptible trace of any anaesthetic or narcotic. The absence of noise is a difficult question under the circumstances of this case to account for but it must not be taken for granted that there was not any noise. If there was an absence of noise, I cannot account for it.

The Foreman: That means that the woman might cry out after the cut? Not after the cut.

[Coroner] But why did she not cry out while she was being put on the ground? She was in a yard and in a locality where she might cry out very loudly and no notice be taken of her. It was possible for the woman to draw up her legs after the wound but she could not have turned over. The wound was inflicted by drawing the knife across the throat.

A short knife, such as a shoemaker's well-ground knife, would do the same thing. My reason for believing that deceased was injured when on the ground was partly on account of the absence of blood anywhere on the left side of the body and between it and the wall.

A Juror: Was there any trace of malt liquor in the stomach? There was no trace.

Dr Blackwell [recalled] (who assisted in making the post-mortem examination) said: I can confirm Dr Phillips as to the appearances at the mortuary. I may add that I removed the cachous from the left hand of the deceased, which was nearly open. The packet was lodged between the thumb and the first finger and was partially hidden from view. It was I who spilt them in removing them from the hand.

My impression is that the hand gradually relaxed while the woman was dying, she dying in a fainting condition from the loss of blood. I do not think that I made myself quite clear as to whether it was possible for this to have been a case of suicide. What I meant to say was that, taking all the facts into consideration, more especially the absence of any instrument in the hand, it was impossible to have been a suicide.

I have myself seen many equally severe wounds self-inflicted. With respect to the knife which was found, I should like to say that I concur with Dr Phillips in his opinion that, although it might possibly have inflicted the injury, it is an extremely unlikely instrument to have been used.

It appears to me that a murderer, in using a round pointed instrument, would seriously handicap himself, as he would be only able to use it in one particular way. I am told that slaughterers always use a sharp pointed instrument.

The Coroner: No one has suggested that this crime was committed by a slaughterer.

Witness: I simply intended to point out the inconvenience that might arise from using a blunt-pointed weapon.

The Foreman: Did you notice any marks or bruises about the shoulders? They were what we call pressure marks. At first they were very obscure but subsequently they became very evident. They were not what are ordinarily called bruises; neither is there any abrasion. Each shoulder was about equally marked.

A Juror: How recently might the marks have been caused? That is rather difficult to say.

[Coroner] Did you perceive any grapes near the body in the yard? No.

[Coroner] Did you hear any person say that they had seen grapes there? I did not.

Mr Sven Ollsen deposed: I live at No 23, Prince's Square, St George's-in-the-East and am clerk of the Swedish Church there. I have examined the body of the deceased at the mortuary. I have seen her before.

The Coroner: Often? Yes. For how many years? Seventeen.

[Coroner] Was she a Swede? Yes.

[Coroner] What was her name? Her name was Elizabeth Stride and she was the wife of John Thomas Stride, carpenter. Her maiden name was Elizabeth Gustafdotter. She was born at Torlands, near Gothenburg, on 27 Nov 1843. How do you get these facts? From the register at our church. Do you keep a register of all the members of your church?

[Coroner] Of course. We register those who come into this country bringing a certificate and desiring to be registered.

[Coroner] When was she registered? Her registry is dated 10 July 1866 and she was then registered as an unmarried woman.

[Coroner] Was she married at your church? No.

[Coroner] Then how do you know she was the wife of John Thomas Stride? In the registry, I find a memorandum, undated, in the handwriting of the Rev. Mr Palmayer, in Swedish, that she was married to an Englishman named John Thos. Stride. This registry is a new one and copied from an older book. I have seen the original and it was written by Mr Frost, our pastor, until two years ago. I know the Swedish hymn book produced, dated 1821. I gave it to the deceased.

[Coroner] When? Last winter, I think. Do you know when she was married to Stride? I think it was in 1869.

[Coroner] Do you know when he died? No. She told me about the time the Princess Alice went down that her husband was drowned in that vessel.

[Coroner] Was she in good circumstances then? She was very poor.

[Coroner] Then she would have been glad of any assistance? Yes.

[Coroner] Did you give her some? I did about that time.

[Coroner] Do you remember that there was a subscription raised for the relatives of the sufferers by the Princess Alice? No.

[Coroner] I can tell you that there was and I can tell you another thing that no person of the name of Stride made any application. If her story had been true, don't you think she would have applied? I do not know.

[Coroner] Have you any schools connected with the Swedish Church? No, not in London.

[Coroner] Did not ever hear that this woman had any children? I do not remember.

[Coroner] Did you ever see her husband? No.

[Coroner] Did your church ever assist her before her husband died? Yes, I think so; just before he died.

[Coroner] Where has she been living lately? I have nothing to show. Two years ago she gave her address as Devonshire Street, Commercial Road.

[Coroner] Did she then explain what she was doing? She stated that she was doing a little work in sewing.

[Coroner] Could she speak English well? Pretty well.

[Coroner] Do you know when she came to England? I believe a little before the register was made, in 1866.

William Marshall, examined by the Coroner, said: I reside at No 64, Berner Street and am a labourer at an indigo warehouse. I have seen the body at the mortuary. I saw the deceased on Saturday night last.

[Coroner] Where? In our street, three doors from my house, about a quarter to twelve o'clock. She was on the pavement, opposite No 58, between Fairclough Street and Boyd Street.

[Coroner] What was she doing? She was standing talking to a man.

[Coroner] How do you know this was the same woman? I recognise her both by her face and dress. She did not then have a flower in her breast.

[Coroner] Were the man and woman whom you saw talking quietly? They were talking together.

[Coroner] Can you describe the man at all? There was no gas lamp near. The nearest was at the corner, about twenty feet off. I did not see the face of the man distinctly.

[Coroner] Did you notice how he was dressed? In a black cut-away coat and dark trousers.

[Coroner] Was he young or old? Middle-aged he seemed to be.

[Coroner] Was he wearing a hat? No, a cap.

[Coroner] What sort of a cap? A round cap, with a small peak. It was something like what a sailor would wear.

[Coroner] What height was he? About 5ft. 6in.

[Coroner] Was he thin or stout? Rather stout.

[Coroner] Did he look well dressed? Decently dressed.

[Coroner] What class of man did he appear to be? I should say he was in business and did nothing like hard work.

[Coroner] Not like a dock labourer? No.

[Coroner] Nor a sailor? No.

[Coroner] Nor a butcher? No.

[Coroner] A clerk? He had more the appearance of a clerk.

[Coroner] Is that the best suggestion you can make? It is.

[Coroner] You did not see his face. Had he any whiskers? I cannot say. I do not think he had.

[Coroner] Was he wearing gloves? No.

[Coroner] Was he carrying a stick or umbrella in his hands? He had nothing in his hands that I am aware of.

[Coroner] You are quite sure that the deceased is the woman you saw? Quite. I did not take much notice whether she was carrying anything in her hands.

[Coroner] What first attracted your attention to the couple? By their standing there for some time and he was kissing her.

[Coroner] Did you overhear anything they said? I heard him say, 'You would say anything but your prayers.'

[Coroner] Different people talk in a different tone and in a different way. Did his voice give you the idea of a clerk? Yes, he was mild speaking.

[Coroner] Did he speak like an educated man? I thought so. I did not hear them say anything more. They went away after that. I did not hear the woman say anything but after the man made that observation, she laughed. They went away down the street, towards Ellen Street. They would not then pass No 40, (the club).

[Coroner] How was the woman dressed? In a black jacket and skirt.

[Coroner] Was either the worse for drink? No, I thought not.

[Coroner] When did you go indoors? About twelve o'clock.

[Coroner] Did you hear anything more that night? Not till I heard that the murder had taken place, just after one o'clock. While I was standing at my door, from half past eleven to twelve, there was no rain at all. The deceased had on a small black bonnet. The couple were standing between my house and the club for about ten minutes.

Detective Inspector Reid: Then they passed you? Yes.

A Juror: Did you not see the man's face as he passed? No; he was looking towards the woman and had his arm round her neck. There is a gas lamp at the corner of Boyd Street. It was not closing time when they passed me.

James Brown: I live in Fairclough Street and am a dock labourer. I have seen the body in the mortuary. I did not know deceased but I saw her about a quarter to one on Sunday morning last.

The Coroner: Where were you? I was going from my house to the chandler's shop at the corner of the Berner Street and Fairclough Street, to get some supper. I stayed there three or four minutes and then went back home, when I saw a man and woman standing at the corner of the Board School. I was in the road just by the kerb and they were near the wall.

[Coroner] Did you see enough to make you certain that the deceased was the woman? I am almost certain.

[Coroner] Did you notice any flower in her dress? No.

[Coroner] What were they doing? He was standing with his arm against the wall; she was inclined towards his arm, facing him and with her back to the wall.

[Coroner] Did you notice the man? I saw that he had a long dark coat on.

[Coroner] An overcoat? Yes; it seemed so.

[Coroner] Had he a hat or a cap on? I cannot say.

[Coroner] You are sure it was not her dress that you chiefly noticed? Yes. I saw nothing light in colour about either of them.

[Coroner] Was it raining at the time? No. I went on.

[Coroner] Did you hear anything more? When I had nearly finished my supper, I heard screams of 'Murder' and 'Police'. This was a quarter of an hour after I had got home. I did not look at any clock at the chandler's shop. I arrived home first at ten minutes past twelve o'clock and I believe it was not raining then.

[Coroner] Did you notice the height of the man? I should think he was 5ft. 7in.

[Coroner] Was he thin or stout? He was of average build.

[Coroner] Did either of them seem the worse for drink? No.

[Coroner] Did you notice whether either spoke with a foreign accent? I did not notice any. When I heard screams, I opened my window but could not see anybody. The cries were of moving people going in the direction of Grove Street. Shortly afterwards, I saw a policeman standing at the corner of Christian Street and a man called him to Berner Street.

William Smith, 452 H Division: On Saturday last, I went on duty at ten p.m. My beat was past Berner Street and would take me 25 minutes or half an hour to go round. I was in Berner Street about half past twelve or twenty five minutes to one o'clock and having gone round my beat, was at the Commercial Road corner of Berner Street again at one o'clock.

I was not called. I saw a crowd outside the gates of No 40, Berner Street. I heard no cries of 'Police'. When I came to the spot two constables had already arrived. The gates at the side of the club were not then closed. I do not remember that I passed any person on my way down. I saw that the woman was dead and I went to the police station for the ambulance, leaving the other constables in charge of the body. Dr Blackwell's assistant arrived just as I was going away.

The Coroner: Had you noticed any man or woman in Berner Street when you were there before? Yes, talking together.

[Coroner] Was the woman anything like the deceased? Yes. I saw her face and I think the body at the mortuary is that of the same woman.

[Coroner] Are you certain? I feel certain. She stood on the pavement a few yards from where the body was found but on the opposite side of the street.

[Coroner] Did you look at the man at all? Yes.

[Coroner] What did you notice about him? He had a parcel wrapped in a newspaper in his hand. The parcel was about 18in. long and 6in. to 8in. broad.

[Coroner] Did you notice his height? He was about 5ft. 7in.

[Coroner] His hat? He wore a dark felt deerstalker's hat.

[Coroner] Clothes? His clothes were dark. The coat was a cutaway coat.

[Coroner] Did you overhear any conversation? No.

[Coroner] Did they seem to be sober? Yes, both.

[Coroner] Did you see the man's face? He had no whiskers but I did not notice him much. I should say he was twenty-eight years of age. He was of respectable appearance but I could not state what he was. The woman had a flower in her breast. It rained very little after eleven o'clock. There were but few about in the by streets. When I saw the body at the mortuary I recognised it at once.

Michael Kidney, the man with whom the deceased last lived, being recalled, stated: I recognise the Swedish hymn-book produced as one belonging to the deceased. She used to have it at my place. I found it in the next room to the one I occupy in Mrs Smith's room. Mrs Smith said deceased gave it to her when she left last Tuesday not as a gift but to take care of.

When deceased and I lived together I put a padlock on the door when we left the house. I had the key but deceased has got in and out when I have been away. I found she had been there during my absence on Wednesday of last week, the day after she left and taken some things.

The Coroner: What made you think there was anything the matter with the roof of her mouth? She told me so.

[Coroner] Have you ever examined it? No.

[Coroner] Well, the doctors say there is nothing the matter with it? Well, I only know what she told me.

Philip Krantz (who affirmed) deposed: I live at 40, Berner Street and an editor of the Hebrew paper called 'The Worker's Friend'. I work in a room forming part of the printing office at the back of the International Working Men's Club. Last Saturday night, I was in my room from nine o'clock until one of the members of the club came and told me that there was a woman lying in the yard.

[Coroner] Had you heard any sound up to that time? No.

[Coroner] Any cry? No. Or scream? No.

[Coroner] Or anything unusual? No.

[Coroner] Was your window or door open? No.

[Coroner] Supposing a woman had screamed, would you have heard it? They were singing in the club, so I might not have heard. When I heard the alarm, I went out and saw the deceased but did not observe any stranger there.

[Coroner] Did you look to see if anybody was about anybody who might have committed the murder? I did look. I went out to the gates and found that some members of the club had gone for the police.

[Coroner] Do you think it possible that any stranger escaped from the yard while you were there? No but he might have done so before I came. I was afterwards searched and examined at the club.

Constable Albert Collins, 12 H. R. stated that by order of the doctors, he, at half past five o'clock on Sunday morning, washed away the blood caused by the murder.

Detective Inspector Reid said: I received a telegram at 1.25 on Sunday morning last at Commercial Street Police office. I at once proceeded to No 40, Berner Street, where I saw several police officers, Drs Phillips and Blackwell and a number of residents in the yard and persons who had come there and been shut in by the police.

At that time Drs Phillips and Blackwell were examining the throat of the deceased. A thorough search was made by the police of the yard and the houses in it but no trace could be found of any person who might have committed the murder. As soon as the search was over, the whole of the persons who had come into the yard and the members of the club were interrogated, their names and addresses taken, their pockets searched by the police and their clothes and hands examined by the doctors.

The people were twenty eight in number. Each was dealt with separately and they properly accounted for themselves. The houses were inspected a second time and the occupants examined and their rooms searched. A loft close by was searched but no trace could be found of the murderer. A description was taken of the body and circulated by wire around the stations.

Inquiries were made at the different houses in the street but no person could be found who had heard screams or disturbance during the night. I examined the wall near where the body was found but could detect no spots of blood. About half past four, the body was removed to the mortuary. Having given information of the murder to the coroner, I returned to the yard and made another examination and found that the blood had been removed.

It being daylight I searched the walls thoroughly but could discover no marks of their having been scaled. I then went to the mortuary and took a description of the deceased and her clothing as follows:

Aged 42; length 5ft. 2in; complexion pale; hair dark brown and curly; eyes light grey; front upper teeth gone. The deceased had on an old black skirt, dark-brown velvet body, a long black jacket trimmed with black fur, fastened on the right side, with a red rose backed by a maidenhair fern. She had two light serge petticoats, white stockings and white chemise with insertion, side spring boots and black crape bonnet.

In her jacket pocket were two handkerchiefs, a thimble and a piece of wool on a card. That description was circulated. Since then, the police have made a house-to-house inquiry in the immediate neighbourhood, with the result that we have been able to produce the witnesses who have appeared before the Court. The investigation is still going on. Every endeavour is being made to arrest the assassin but up to the present without success. The inquiry was adjourned.

Day 5, Tuesday, 23 October 1888.
The Times, 24 October 1888.

Yesterday afternoon 23rd Oct, Mr Wynne E. Baxter, Coroner for the South-Eastern Division of Middlesex, resumed his adjourned inquiry at the Vestry-hall, Cable-street, St George's-in-the-East, respecting the death of Elizabeth Stride, who was found murdered in Berner Street, St George's, on the 30th.

Detective-Inspector Reid, H Division, watched the case on behalf of the Criminal Investigation Department.

Detective-Inspector Edmund Reid, recalled, said: I have examined the books of the Poplar and Stepney Sick Asylum and find therein the entry of the death of John Thomas William Stride, a carpenter, of Poplar. His death took place on 24 October 1884.

Witness then said that he had found Mrs Watts, who would give evidence.

Constable Walter Stride stated that he recognised the deceased by the photograph as the person who married his uncle, John Thomas Stride, in 1872 or 1873. His uncle was a carpenter and the last time witness saw him he was living in the East India Dock Road, Poplar.

Elizabeth Stokes, 5, Charles Street, Tottenham, said: my husband's name is Joseph Stokes and he is a brick maker. My first husband's name was Watts, a wine merchant of Bath. Mrs Mary Malcolm, of 15, Eagle Street, Red Lion Square, Holborn, is my sister. I have received an anonymous letter from Shepton Mallet, saying my first husband is alive. I want to clear my character.

My sister I have not seen for years. She has given me a dreadful character. Her evidence is all false. I have five brothers and sisters. A juryman. Perhaps she refers to another sister.

Inspector Reid: she identified the deceased person as her sister and said she had a crippled foot. This witness has a crippled foot.

Witness: This has put me to a dreadful trouble and trial. I have only a poor crippled husband, who is now outside. It is a shame my sister should say what she has said about me and that the innocent should suffer for the guilty.

The Coroner: Is Mrs Malcolm here?

Inspector Reid: No, Sir.

The Coroner, in summing up, said the jury would probably agree with him that it would be unreasonable to adjourn this inquiry again on the chance of something further being ascertained to elucidate the mysterious case on which they had devoted so much time. The first difficulty which presented itself was the identification of the deceased. That was not an unimportant matter.

Their trouble was principally occasioned by Mrs Malcolm, who, after some hesitation and after having had two further opportunities of viewing again the body, positively swore that the deceased was her sister Mrs Elizabeth Watts, of Bath. It had since been clearly proved that she was mistaken, notwithstanding the visions which were simultaneously vouchsafed at the hour of the death to her and her husband.

If her evidence was correct, there were points of resemblance between the deceased and Elizabeth Watts which almost reminded one of the Comedy of Errors. Both had been courted by policemen; they both bore the same Christian name and were of the same age; both lived with sailors; both at one time kept coffee houses at Poplar; both were nick-named 'Long Liz'.

Both were said to have had children in charge of their husbands' friends; both were given to drink; both lived in East End common lodging houses; both had been charged at the Thames Police court; both had escaped punishment on the ground that they were subject to epileptic fits, although the friends of both were certain that this was a fraud; both had lost their front teeth and both had been leading very questionable lives.

Whatever might be the true explanation of this marvellous similarity, it appeared to be pretty satisfactorily proved that the deceased was Elizabeth Stride and that about the year 1869 she was married to a carpenter named John Thomas Stride. Unlike the other victims in the series of crimes in this neighbourhood a district teeming with representatives of all nations, she was not an Englishwoman.

She was born in Sweden in the year 1843 but, having resided in this country for upwards of 22 years, she could speak English fluently and without much foreign accent. At one time, the deceased and her husband kept a coffee house in Poplar. At another time, she was staying in Devonshire Street, Commercial Road, supporting herself, it was said, by sewing and charing.

On and off for the last six years, she lived in a common lodging house in the notorious lane called Flower and Dean Street. She was there known only by the nick-name of 'Long Liz' and often told a tale, which might have been apocryphal, of her husband and children having gone down with the Princess Alice.

The deputy of the lodging-house stated that while with her she was a quiet and sober woman, although she used at times to stay out late at night an offence very venial, he suspected, among those who frequented the establishment. For the last two years, the deceased had been living at a common lodging house in Dorset Street, Spitalfields, with Michael Kidney, a waterside labourer, belonging to the Army Reserve.

But at intervals during that period, amounting altogether too about five months, she left him without any apparent reason, except a desire to be free from the restraint even of that connection and to obtain greater opportunity of indulging her drinking habits. She was last seen alive by Kidney in Commercial Street on the evening of Tuesday, 25th September.

She was sober but never returned home that night. She alleged that she had some words with her paramour but this he denied. The next day she called during his absence and took away some things but, with this exception, they did not know what became of her until the following Thursday, when she made her appearance at her old quarters in Flower and Dean Street.

Here she remained until Saturday, 29th September. On that day, she cleaned the deputy's rooms and received a small remuneration for her trouble. Between 6 and 7 o'clock on that evening, she was in the kitchen wearing the jacket, bonnet and striped silk neckerchief which were afterwards found on her. She had at least 6d.

In her possession, which was possibly spent during the evening. Before leaving she gave a piece of velvet to a friend to take care of until her return but she said neither where she was going nor when she would return. She had not paid for her lodgings, although she was in a position to do so. They knew nothing of her movements during the next four or five hours at least possibly not till the finding of her lifeless body.

But three witnesses spoke to having seen a woman that they identified as the deceased with more or less certainty and at times within an hour and a quarter of the period when and at places within 100 yards of the spot where she was ultimately found.

William Marshall, who lived at 64, Berner Street, was standing at his doorway from half-past 11 till midnight. About a quarter to 12 o'clock, he saw the deceased talking to a man between Fairclough Street and Boyd Street. There was every demonstration of affection by the man during the ten minutes they stood together and when last seen, strolling down the road towards Ellen Street, his arms were round her neck.

At 12 30 pm the constable on the beat (William Smith) saw the deceased in Berner Street standing on the pavement a few yards from Commercial Street and he observed she was wearing a flower in her dress. A quarter of an hour afterwards James Brown, of Fairclough Street, passed the deceased close to the Board school.

A man was at her side leaning against the wall and the deceased was heard to say, 'Not tonight but some other night.' Now, if this evidence was to be relied on, it would appear that the deceased was in the company of a man for upwards of an hour immediately before her death and that within a quarter of an hour of her being found a corpse, she was refusing her companion something in the immediate neighbourhood of where she met her death.

But was this the deceased? And even if it were, was it one and the same man who was seen in her company on three different occasions? With regard to the identity of the woman, Marshall had the opportunity of watching her for ten minutes while standing talking in the street at a short distance from him and she afterwards passed close to him.

The constable feels certain that the woman he observed was the deceased and when he afterwards was called to the scene of the crime he at once recognised her and made a statement; while Brown was almost certain that the deceased was the woman to whom his attention was attracted.

It might be thought that the frequency of the occurrence of men and women being seen together under similar circumstances might have led to mistaken identity but the police stated and several of the witnesses corroborated the statement that although many couples are to be seen at night in the Commercial Road, it was exceptional to meet them in Berner Street.

With regard to the man seen, there were many points of similarity but some of dissimilarity, in the descriptions of the three witnesses but these discrepancies did not conclusively prove that there was more than one man in the company of the deceased, for every day's experience showed how facts were differently observed and differently described by honest and intelligent witnesses.

Brown, who saw least in consequence of the darkness of the spot at which the two were standing, agreed with Smith that his clothes were dark and that his height was about 5ft 7in but he appeared to him to be wearing an overcoat nearly down to his heels; while the description of Marshall accorded with that of Smith in every respect but two. They agreed that he was respectably dressed in a black cut away coat and dark trousers and that he was of middle age and without whiskers.

On the other hand, they differed with regard to what he was wearing on his head. Smith stated he wore a hard felt deer stalker of dark colour; Marshall that he was wearing a round cap with a small peak, like a sailor's. They also differed as to whether he had anything in his hand. Marshall stated that he observed nothing.

Smith was very precise and stated that he was carrying a parcel, done up in a newspaper, about 18in. in length and 6in. to 8in. in width. These differences suggested either that the woman was, during the evening, in the company of more than one man a not very improbable supposition or that the witness had been mistaken in detail.

If they were correct in assuming that the man seen in the company of deceased by the three was one and the same person it followed that he must have spent much time and trouble to induce her to place herself in his diabolical clutches. They last saw her alive at the corner of Fairclough Street and Berner Street, saying 'Not tonight but some other night.'

Within a quarter of an hour, her lifeless body was found at a spot only a few yards from where she was last seen alive. It was late and there were few people about but the place to which the two repaired could not have been selected on account of its being quiet or unfrequented. It had only the merit of darkness. It was the passage-way leading into a court in which several families resided.

Adjoining the passage and court there was a club of Socialists, who, having finished their debate, were singing and making merry. The deceased and her companion must have seen the lights of the clubroom and the kitchen and of the printing office. They must have heard the music and dancing, for the windows were open. There were persons in the yard but a short time previous to their arrival.

At 40 minutes past 12, one of the members of the club, named Morris Eagle, passed the spot where the deceased drew her last breath, passing through the gateway to the back door, which opened into the yard. At 1 o'clock, the body was found by the manager of the club. He had been out all day and returned at the time. He was in a two-wheeled barrow drawn by a pony and as he entered the gateway his pony shied at some object on his right.

There was no lamp in the yard and having just come out of the street it was too dark to see what the object was and he passed on further down the yard. He returned on foot and on searching, found the body of deceased with her throat cut. If he had not actually disturbed the wretch in the very act, at least he must have been close on his heels; possibly the man was alarmed by the sound of the approaching cart, for the death had only just taken place.

He did not inspect the body himself with any care but blood was flowing from the throat, even when Spooner reached the spot some few minutes afterwards and although the bleeding had stopped when Dr Blackwell's assistant arrived, the whole of her body and the limbs, except her hands, were warm and even at 16 minutes past 1 a.m. Dr Blackwell found her face slightly warm and her chest and legs quite warm.

In this case, as in other similar cases which had occurred in this neighbourhood, no call for assistance was noticed. Although there might have been some noise in the club, it seemed very unlikely that any cry could have been raised without its being heard by some one of those near. The editor of a Socialist paper was quietly at work in a shed down the yard, which was used as a printing office.

There were several families in the cottages in the court only a few yards distant and there were 20 persons in the different rooms of the club. But if there was no cry, how did the deceased meet with her death? The appearance of the injury to her throat was not in itself inconsistent with that of a self-inflicted wound. Both Dr Phillips and Dr Blackwell have seen self-inflicted wounds more extensive and severe but those have not usually involved the carotid artery.

Had some sharp instrument been found near the right hand of the deceased this case might have had very much the appearance of a determined suicide. But no such instrument was found and its absence made suicide an impossibility. The death was, therefore, one by homicide and it seemed impossible to imagine circumstances which would fit in with the known facts of the case and which would reduce the crime to manslaughter.

There were no signs of any struggle; the clothes were neither torn nor disturbed. It was true that there were marks over both shoulders, produced by pressure of two hands but the position of the body suggested either that she was willingly placed or placed herself where she was found. Only the soles of her boots were visible.

She was still holding in her left hand a packet of cachous and there was a bunch of flowers still pinned to her dress front. If she had been forcibly placed on the ground, as Dr Phillips opines, it was difficult to understand how she failed to attract attention, as it was clear from the appearance of the blood on the ground that the throat was not cut until after she was actually on her back.

There were no marks of gagging, no bruises on the face and no trace of any anaesthetic or narcotic in the stomach; while the presence of the cachous in her hand showed that she did not make use of it in self-defence. Possibly the pressure marks may have had a less tragical origin, as Dr Blackwell says it was difficult to say how recently they were produced.

There was one particular which was not easy to explain. When seen by Dr Blackwell, her right hand was lying on the chest, smeared inside and out with blood. Dr Phillips was unable to make any suggestion how the hand became soiled. There was no injury to the hand, such as they would expect if it had been raised in self-defence while her throat was being cut.

Was it done intentionally by her assassin, or accidentally by those who were early on the spot? The evidence afforded no clue. Unfortunately the murderer had disappeared without leaving the slightest trace. Even the cachous were wrapped up in unmarked paper, so that there was nothing to show where they were bought.

The cut in the throat might have been affected in such a manner that bloodstains on the hands and clothes of the operator were avoided, while the domestic history of the deed suggested the strong probability that her destroyer was a stranger to her. There was no one among her associates to whom any suspicion had attached.

They had not heard that she had had a quarrel with any one unless they magnified the fact that she had recently left the man with whom she generally cohabited; but this diversion was of so frequent an occurrence that neither a breach of the peace ensued, nor, so far as they knew, even hard words. There was therefore in the evidence no clue to the murderer and no suggested motive for the murder.

The deceased was not in possession of any valuables. She was only known to have had a few pence in her pocket at the beginning of the evening. Those who knew her best were unaware of any one likely to injure her. She never accused any one of having threatened her. She never expressed any fear of anyone and, although she had outbursts of drunkenness, she was generally a quiet woman.

The ordinary motives of murder revenge, jealousy, theft and passion appeared, therefore, to be absent from this case; while it was clear from the accounts of all who saw her that night, as well as from the post-mortem examination, that she was not otherwise than sober at the time of her death. In the absence of motive, the age and class of woman selected as victim and the place and time of the crime, there was a similarity between this case and those mysteries which had recently occurred in that neighbourhood.

There had been no skilful mutilation as in the cases of Nichols and Chapman and no unskilful injuries as in the case in Mitre square possibly the work of an imitator but there had been the same skill exhibited in the way in which the victim had been entrapped and the injuries inflicted, so as to cause instant death and prevent blood from soiling the operator and the same daring defiance of immediate detection, which unfortunately for the peace of the inhabitants and trade of the neighbourhood, had hitherto been only too successful.

He himself was sorry that the time and attention which the jury had given to the case had not produced a result that would be a perceptible relief to the metropolis the detection of the criminal but he was sure that all had used their utmost effort to accomplish this object and while he desired to thank the gentlemen of the jury for their kind assistance, he was bound to acknowledge the great attention which Inspector Reid and the police had given to the case. He left it to the jury to say, how, when and by what means the deceased came by her death.

The jury, after a short deliberation, returned a verdict of 'Wilful murder against some person or persons unknown'.

Chapter Ten
The Mary Jane Kelly Inquest

Monday, 12 November 1888.
The Daily Telegraph, Tuesday, 13 November 1888.

Yesterday 12th Nov at the Shoreditch Town Hall, Dr Macdonald, M.P. the coroner for the North Eastern District of Middlesex, opened his inquiry relative to the death of Marie Jeanette Kelly, the woman whose body was discovered on Friday morning, terribly mutilated, in a room on the ground floor of 26, Dorset Street, entrance to which was by a side door in Miller's Court.

Superintendent T Arnold, H Division; Inspector Abberline, of the Criminal Investigation.

Department and Inspector Nairn represented the police. The deputy coroner, Mr Hodgkinson, was present during the proceedings. The jury having answered to their names, one of them said:

"I do not see why we should have the inquest thrown upon our shoulders, when the murder did not happen in our district but in Whitechapel."

The Coroner's Officer (Mr Hammond): It did not happen in Whitechapel.

The Coroner (to the juror, severely): Do you think that we do not know what we are doing here and that we do not know our own district? The jury are summoned in the ordinary way and they have no business to object. If they persist in their objection, I shall know how to deal with them. Does any juror persist in objecting?

The Juror: We are summoned for the Shoreditch district. This affair happened in Spitalfields.

The Coroner: It happened within my district.

Another Juryman: This is not my district. I come from Whitechapel and Mr Baxter is my coroner.

The Coroner: I am not going to discuss the subject with jurymen at all. If any juryman says he distinctly objects, let him say so.

(After a pause): I may tell the jurymen that jurisdiction lies where the body lies, not where it was found, if there was doubt as to the district where the body was found.

The jury having made no further objection, they were duly sworn and were conducted by Inspector Abberline to view the body which, decently coffined, was at the mortuary adjoining Shoreditch Church and subsequently the jury inspected the room, in Miller's Court, Dorset Street, where the murder was committed.

The apartment, a plan of which was given in yesterday's Daily Telegraph, is poorly furnished and uncarpeted. The position of the two tables was not altered. One of them was placed near the bed, behind the door and the other next to the larger of the two windows which look upon the yard in which the dustbin and water tap are situated.

The Coroner (addressing the reporters) said a great fuss had been made in some papers about the jurisdiction of the coroner and who should hold the inquest. He had not had any communication with Dr Baxter upon the subject. The body was in his jurisdiction; it had been taken to his mortuary and there was an end of it.

There was no foundation for the reports that had appeared. In a previous case of murder which occurred in his district the body was carried to the nearest mortuary, which was in another district. The inquest was held by Mr Baxter and he made no objection. The jurisdiction was where the body lay.

Joseph Barnett deposed: I was a fish porter and I work as a labourer and fruit porter. Until Saturday last I lived at 24, New Street, Bishopsgate and have since stayed at my sister's, 21, Portpool Lane, Gray's Inn Road. I have lived with the deceased one year and eight months. Her name was Marie Jeanette Kelly with the French spelling as described to me. Kelly was her maiden name.

I have seen the body and I identify it by the ear and eyes, which are all that I can recognise; but I am positive it is the same woman I knew. I lived with her in No 13 room, at Miller's Court for eight months. I separated from her on 30th Oct.

[Coroner] Why did you leave her? Because she had a woman of bad character there, whom she took in out of compassion and I objected to it. That was the only reason. I left her on the Tuesday between five and six p.m. I last saw her alive between half past seven and a quarter to eight on Thursday night last, when I called upon her. I stayed there for a quarter of an hour.

[Coroner] Were you on good terms? Yes, on friendly terms but when we parted, I told her I had no work and had nothing to give her, for which I was very sorry.

[Coroner] Did you drink together? No, sir. She was quite sober.

[Coroner] Was she, generally speaking, of sober habits? When she was with me I found her of sober habits but she has been drunk several times in my presence.

[Coroner] Was there any one else there on the Thursday evening? Yes, a woman who lives in the court. She left first and I followed shortly afterwards.

[Coroner] Have you had conversation with deceased about her parents? Yes, frequently. She said she was born in Limerick and went when very young to Wales. She did not say how long she lived there but that she came to London about four years ago. Her father's name was John Kelly, a 'gaffer' or foreman in an iron works in Carnarvonshire, or Carmarthen.

She said she had one sister, who was respectable, who travelled from market place to market place. This sister was very fond of her. There were six brothers living in London and one was in the army. One of them was named Henry. I never saw the brothers to my knowledge. She said she was married when very young in Wales to a collier.

I think the name was Davis or Davies. She said she had lived with him until he was killed in an explosion but I cannot say how many years since that was. Her age was, I believe, 16 when she married. After her husband's death, deceased went to Cardiff to a cousin.

[Coroner] Did she live there long? Yes, she was in an infirmary there for eight or nine months. She was following a bad life with her cousin, who as I reckon and as I often told her, was the cause of her downfall.

[Coroner] After she left Cardiff, did she come direct to London? Yes. She was in a gay house in the West End but in what part she did not say. A gentleman came there to her and asked her if she would like to go to France.

[Coroner] Did she go to France? Yes; but she did not remain long. She said she did not like the part but whether it was the part or purpose I cannot say. She was not there more than a fortnight and she returned to England and went to Ratcliffe Highway. She must have lived there for some time. Afterwards, she lived with a man opposite the Commercial Gas Works, Stepney. The man's name was Morganstone.

[Coroner] Have you seen that man? Never. I don't know how long she lived with him.

[Coroner] Was Morganstone the last man she lived with? I cannot answer that question but she described a man named Joseph Fleming, who came to Pennington Street, a bad house, where she stayed. I don't know when this was. She was very fond of him. He was a mason's plasterer and lodged in the Bethnal Green Road.

[Coroner] Was that all you knew of her history when you lived with her? Yes. After she lived with Morganstone or Fleming I don't know which one was the last she lived with me.

[Coroner] Where did you pick up with her first? In Commercial Street. We then had a drink together and I made arrangements to see her on the following day a Saturday. On that day, we both of us agreed that we should remain together. I took lodgings in George Street, Commercial Street, where I was known. I lived with her, until I left her, on very friendly terms.

[Coroner] Have you heard her speak of being afraid of any one? Yes; several times. I bought newspapers and I read to her everything about the murders, which she asked me about.

[Coroner] Did she express fear of any particular individual? No, sir. Our own quarrels were very soon over.

The Coroner: You have given your evidence very well indeed.

(To the Jury): The doctor has sent a note asking whether we shall want his attendance here today. I take it that it would be convenient that he should tell us roughly what the cause of death was, so as to enable the body to be buried. It will not be necessary to go into the details of the doctor's evidence but he suggested that he might come to state roughly the cause of death.

The jury acquiesced in the proposed course.

Thomas Bowyer stated: I live at 37, Dorset Street and am employed by Mr McCarthy. I serve in his chandler's shop, 27, Dorset Street. At a quarter to eleven a.m. on Friday morning, I was ordered by McCarthy to go to Mary Jane's room, No 13. I did not know the deceased by the name of Kelly. I went for rent, which was in arrears.

Knocking at the door, I got no answer and I knocked again and again. Receiving no reply, I passed round the corner by the gutter spout where there is a broken window it is the smallest window.

Charles Ledger, an inspector of police, G Division, produced a plan of the premises. Bowyer pointed out the window, which was the one nearest the entrance.

He [Bowyer] continued: There was a curtain. I put my hand through the broken pane and lifted the curtain. I saw two pieces of flesh lying on the table.

[Coroner] Where was this table? In front of the bed, close to it. The second time I looked, I saw a body on this bed and blood on the floor. I at once went very quietly to Mr McCarthy. We then stood in the shop and I told him what I had seen. We both went to the police station but first of all we went to the window and McCarthy looked in to satisfy himself. We told the inspector at the police station of what we had seen. Nobody else knew of the matter. The inspector returned with us.

[Coroner] Did you see the deceased constantly? I have often seen her. I knew the last witness, Barnett. I have seen the deceased drunk once.

By the Jury: When did you see her last alive? On Wednesday afternoon, in the court, when I spoke to her. McCarthy's shop is at the corner of Miller's Court.

John McCarthy, grocer and lodging house keeper, testified: I live at 27, Dorset Street. On Friday morning, about a quarter to eleven, I sent my man Bowyer to Room 13 to call for rent. He came back in five minutes, saying, 'Guv'nor, I knocked at the door and could not make any one answer; I looked through the window and saw a lot of blood.'

I accompanied him and looked through the window myself, saw the blood and the woman. For a moment I could not say anything and I then said, 'You had better fetch the police.' I knew the deceased as Mary Jane Kelly and had no doubt at all about her identity. I followed Bowyer to Commercial Street Police station, where I saw Inspector Beck. I inquired at first for Inspector Reid. Inspector Beck returned with me at once.

[Coroner] How long had the deceased lived in the room? Ten months. She lived with Barnett. I did not know whether they were married or not; they lived comfortably together but they had a row when the window was broken. The bedstead, bedclothes, table and every article of furniture belonged to me.

[Coroner] What rent was paid for this room? It was supposed to be 4s 6d a week. Deceased was in arrears 29s. I was to be paid the rent weekly. Arrears are got as best you can. I frequently saw the deceased the worse for drink. When sober she was an exceptionally quiet woman but when in drink she had more to say. She was able to walk about and was not helpless.

Mary Ann Cox stated: I live at No 5 Room, Miller's Court. It is the last house on the left hand side of the court. I am a widow and get my living on the streets. I have known the deceased for eight or nine months as the occupant of No 13 Room. She was called Mary Jane. I last saw her alive on Thursday night, at a quarter to twelve, very much intoxicated.

[Coroner] Where was this? In Dorset Street, she went up the court, a few steps in front of me.

[Coroner] Was anybody with her? A short, stout man, shabbily dressed. He had on a longish coat, very shabby and carried a pot of ale in his hand.

[Coroner] What was the colour of the coat? A dark coat.

[Coroner] What hat had he? A round hard billycock.

[Coroner] Long or short hair? I did not notice. He had a blotchy face and full carroty moustache.

[Coroner] The chin was shaven? Yes. A lamp faced the door.

[Coroner] Did you see them go into her room? Yes; I said 'Good night, Mary' and she turned round and banged the door.

[Coroner] Had he anything in his hands but the can? No.

[Coroner] Did she say anything? She said 'Good night, I am going to have a song.' As I went in, she sang 'A violet I plucked from my mother's grave when a boy.' I remained a quarter of an hour in my room and went out. Deceased was still singing at one o'clock when I returned. I remained in the room for a minute to warm my hands as it was raining and went out again. She was singing still and I returned to my room at three o'clock. The light was then out and there was no noise.

[Coroner] Did you go to sleep? No; I was upset. I did not undress at all. I did not sleep at all. I must have heard what went on in the court. I heard no noise or cry of 'Murder' but men went out to work in the market.

[Coroner] How many men live in the court who work in Spitalfields Market? One. At a quarter past six I heard a man go down the court. That was too late for the market.

[Coroner] From what house did he go? I don't know.

[Coroner] Did you hear the door bang after him? No.

[Coroner] Then he must have walked up the court and back again? Yes.

[Coroner] It might have been a policeman? It might have been.

[Coroner] What would you take the stout man's age to be? Six-and-thirty.

[Coroner] Did you notice the colour of his trousers? All his clothes were dark.

[Coroner] Did his boots sound as if the heels were heavy? There was no sound as he went up the court.

[Coroner] Then you think that his boots were down at heels? He made no noise.

[Coroner] What clothes had Mary Jane on? She had no hat; a red pelerine and a shabby skirt.

[Coroner] You say she was drunk? I did not notice she was drunk until she said good night. The man closed the door.

By the Jury: There was a light in the window but I saw nothing, as the blinds were down. I should know the man again, if I saw him.

By the Coroner: I feel certain if there had been the cry of 'Murder' in the place, I should have heard it; there was not the least noise. I have often seen the woman the worse for drink.

Elizabeth Prater, a married woman, said: My husband, William Prater, was a boot machinist and he has deserted me. I live at 20 Room, in Miller's Court, above the shed. Deceased occupied a room below. I left the room on the Thursday at five p.m. and returned to it at about one a.m. on Friday morning. I stood at the corner until about twenty minutes past one. No one spoke to me.

McCarthy's shop was open and I called in and then went to my room. I should have seen a glimmer of light in going up the stairs if there had been a light in deceased's room but I noticed none. The partition was so thin I could have heard Kelly walk about in the room. I went to bed at half past one and barricaded the door with two tables. I fell asleep directly and slept soundly.

A kitten disturbed me about half past three o'clock or a quarter to four. As I was turning round, I heard a suppressed cry of 'Oh murder!' in a faint voice. It seemed to proceed from the court.

[Coroner] Do you often hear cries of 'Murder'? It is nothing unusual in the street. I did not take particular notice.

[Coroner] Did you hear it a second time? No.

[Coroner] Did you hear beds or tables being pulled about? None what so ever. I went asleep and was awake again at five a.m. I passed down the stairs and saw some men harnessing horses. At a quarter to six, I was in the Ten Bells.

[Coroner] Could the witness, Mary Ann Cox, have come down the entry between one and half past one o'clock without your knowledge? Yes, she could have done so.

[Coroner] Did you see any strangers at the Ten Bells? No. I went back to bed and slept until eleven.

[Coroner] You heard no singing downstairs? None what so ever. I should have heard the singing distinctly. It was quite quiet at half past one o'clock.

Caroline Maxewell, 14, Dorset Street, said: My husband is a lodging house deputy. I knew the deceased for about four months. I believe she was an unfortunate. On two occasions, I spoke to her.

The Coroner: You must be very careful about your evidence, because it is different to other people. You say you saw her standing at the corner of the entry to the court? Yes, on Friday morning, from eight to half past eight. I fix the time by my husband's finishing work. When I came out of the lodging house, she was opposite.

[Coroner] Did you speak to her? Yes; it was an unusual thing to see her up. She was a young woman who never associated with any one. I spoke across the street, 'What, Mary, brings you up so early?'

She said, 'Oh, Carrie, I do feel so bad.'

[Coroner] And yet you say you had only spoken to her twice previously; you knew her name and she knew yours? Oh, yes; by being about in the lodging house.

[Coroner] What did she say? She said, 'I've had a glass of beer and I've brought it up again'; and it was in the road. I imagined she had been in the Britannia beer shop at the corner of the street. I left her, saying that I could pity her feelings. I went to Bishopsgate Street to get my husband's breakfast. Returning I saw her outside the Britannia public house, talking to a man.

[Coroner] This would be about what time? Between eight and nine o'clock. I was absent about half-an-hour. It was about a quarter to nine.

[Coroner] What description can you give of this man? I could not give you any, as they were at some distance.

Inspector Abberline: The distance is about sixteen yards.

Witness: I am sure it was the deceased. I am willing to swear it.

The Coroner: You are sworn now. Was he a tall man? No; he was a little taller than me and stout.

Inspector Abberline: On consideration, I should say the distance was twenty five yards.

The Coroner: What clothes had the man?

Witness: Dark clothes; he seemed to have a plaid coat on. I could not say what sort of hat he had.

[Coroner] What sort of dress had the deceased? A dark skirt, a velvet body, a maroon shawl and no hat.

[Coroner] Have you ever seen her the worse for drink? I have seen her in drink but she was not a notorious character.

By the Jury: I should have noticed if the man had had a tall silk hat but we are accustomed to see men of all sorts with women. I should not like to pledge myself to the kind of hat.

Sarah Lewis deposed: I live at 24, Great Pearl Street and am a laundress. I know Mrs Keyler, in Miller's Court and went to her house at 2, Miller's Court, at 2.30a.m, on Friday. It is the first house. I noticed the time by the Spitalfields' Church clock. When I went into the court, opposite the lodging house I saw a man with a wide awake.

There was no one talking to him. He was a stout looking man and not very tall. The hat was black. I did not take any notice of his clothes. The man was looking up the court; he seemed to be waiting or looking for someone. Further on there was a man and woman the latter being in drink. There was nobody in the court. I dozed in a chair at Mrs Keyler's and woke at about half past three. I heard the clock strike.

[Coroner] What woke you up? I could not sleep. I sat awake until nearly four, when I heard a female's voice shouting 'Murder' loudly. It seemed like the voice of a young woman. It sounded at our door. There was only one scream.

[Coroner] Were you afraid? Did you wake anybody up? No, I took no notice, as I only heard the one scream.

[Coroner] You stayed at Keyler's house until what time? Half past five p.m. on Friday. The police would not let us out of the court.

[Coroner] Have you seen any suspicious persons in the district? On Wednesday night, I was going along the Bethnal Green Road with a woman, about eight o'clock, when a gentleman passed us. He followed us and spoke to us and wanted us to follow him into an entry. He had a shiny leather bag with him.

[Coroner] Did he want both of you? No; only one. I refused. He went away and came back again, saying he would treat us. He put down his bag and picked it up again, saying, 'What are you frightened about? Do you think I've got anything in the bag?' We then ran away, as we were frightened.

[Coroner] Was he a tall man? He was short, pale faced, with a black moustache, rather small. His age was about 40.

[Coroner] Was it a large bag? No. His hat was a high round hat. He had a brownish overcoat, with a black short coat underneath. His trousers were a dark pepper and salt.

[Coroner] After he left you what did you do? We ran away.

[Coroner] Have you seen him since? On Friday morning, about half past two a.m. when I was going to Miller's Court, I met the same man with a woman in Commercial Street, near Mr Ringer's public house (the Britannia). He had no overcoat on.

[Coroner] Had he the black bag? Yes.

[Coroner] Were the man and woman quarrelling? No; they were talking. As I passed he looked at me. I don't know whether he recognised me. There was no policeman about.

Mr George Bagster Phillips, divisional surgeon of police, said: I was called by the police on Friday morning at eleven o'clock and on proceeding to Miller's Court, which I entered at 11.15, I found a room, the door of which led out of the passage at the side of 26, Dorset-street, photographs of which I produce. It had two windows in the court.

Two panes in the lesser window were broken and as the door was locked I looked through the lower of the broken panes and satisfied myself that the mutilated corpse lying on the bed was not in need of any immediate attention from me and I also came to the conclusion that there was nobody else upon the bed, or within view, to whom I could render any professional assistance.

Having ascertained that probably it was advisable that no entrance should be made into the room at that time, I remained until about 1.30p.m. when the door was broken open by McCarthy, under the direction of Superintendent Arnold. On the door being opened it knocked against a table which was close to the left hand side of the bedstead and the bedstead was close against the wooden partition.

The mutilated remains of a woman were lying two thirds over, towards the edge of the bedstead, nearest the door. Deceased had only an under linen garment upon her and by subsequent examination I am sure the body had been removed, after the injury which caused death, from that side of the bedstead which was nearest to the wooden partition previously mentioned.

The large quantity of blood under the bedstead, the saturated condition of the paillasse, pillow and sheet at the top corner of the bedstead nearest to the partition leads me to the conclusion that the severance of the right carotid artery, which was the immediate cause of death, was inflicted while the deceased was lying at the right side of the bedstead and her head and neck in the top right hand corner.

The jury had no questions to ask at this stage and it was understood that more detailed evidence of the medical examination would be given at a future hearing.

An adjournment for a few minutes then took place and on the return of the jury the coroner said: It has come to my ears that somebody has been making a statement to some of the jury as to their right and duty of being here. Has anyone during the interval spoken to the jury, saying that they should not be here today? Some jurymen replied in the negative.

The Coroner: Then I must have been misinformed. I should have taken good care that he would have had a quiet life for the rest of the week if anybody had interfered with my jury.

Julia Vanturney [Van Turney], 1, Miller's Court, a charwoman, living with Harry Owen, said: I knew the deceased for some time as Kelly and I knew Joe Barnett, who lived with her. He would not allow her to go on the streets. Deceased often got drunk. She said she was fond of another man, also named Joe. I never saw this man. I believe he was a costermonger.

[Coroner] When did you last see the deceased alive? On Thursday morning at about ten o'clock. I slept in the court on Thursday night and went to bed about eight. I could not rest at all during the night.

[Coroner] Did you hear any noises in the court? I did not. I heard no screams of 'Murder', nor any one singing.

[Coroner] You must have heard deceased singing? Yes; I knew her songs. They were generally Irish.

Maria Harvey, 3, New Court, Dorset Street, stated: I knew the deceased as Mary Jane Kelly. I slept at her house on Monday night and on Tuesday night. All the afternoon of Thursday we were together.

[Coroner] Were you in the house when Joe Barnett called? Yes. I said, 'Well, Mary Jane, I shall not see you this evening again' and I left with her two men's dirty shirts, a little boy's shirt, a black overcoat, a black crepe bonnet with black satin strings, a pawn-ticket for a grey shawl, upon which 2s had been lent and a little girl's white petticoat.

[Coroner] Have you seen any of these articles since? Yes; I saw the black overcoat in a room in the court on Friday afternoon.

[Coroner] Did the deceased ever speak to you about being afraid of any man? She did not.

Inspector Beck, H Division, deposed that, having sent for the doctor, he gave orders to prevent any persons leaving the court and he directed officers to make a search. He had not been aware that the deceased was known to the police.

Inspector Frederick G. Abberline, inspector of police, Criminal Investigation Department, Scotland Yard, stated: I am in charge of this case. I arrived at Miller's Court about 11.30 on Friday morning.

[Coroner] Was it by your orders that the door was forced? No; I had an intimation from Inspector Beck that the bloodhounds had been sent for and the reply had been received that they were on the way. Dr Phillips was unwilling to force the door, as it would be very much better to test the dogs, if they were coming.

We remained until about 1.30 p.m. when Superintendent Arnold arrived and he informed me that the order in regard to the dogs had been countermanded and he gave orders for the door to be forced. I agree with the medical evidence as to the condition of the room. I subsequently took an inventory of the contents of the room.

There were traces of a large fire having been kept up in the grate, so much so that it had melted the spout of a kettle off. We have since gone through the ashes in the fireplace; there were remnants of clothing, a portion of a brim of a hat and a skirt and it appeared as if a large quantity of women's clothing had been burnt.

[Coroner] Can you give any reason why they were burnt? I can only imagine that it was to make a light for the man to see what he was doing. There was only one small candle in the room, on the top of a broken wine glass. An impression has gone abroad that the murderer took away the key of the room.

Barnett informs me that it has been missing some time and since it has been lost they have put their hand through the broken window and moved back the catch. It is quite easy. There was a man's clay pipe in the room and Barnett informed me that he smoked it.

[Coroner] Is there anything further the jury ought to know? No; if there should be I can communicate with you, sir.

The Coroner (to the jury): The question is whether you will adjourn for further evidence. My own opinion is that it is very unnecessary for two courts to deal with these cases and go through the same evidence time after time, which only causes expense and trouble. If the coroner's jury can come to a decision as to the cause of death, then that is all that they have to do.

They have nothing to do with prosecuting a man and saying what amount of penalty he is to get. It is quite sufficient if they find out what the cause of death was. It is for the police authorities to deal with the case and satisfy themselves as to any person who may be suspected later on. I do not want to take it out of your hands.

It is for you to say whether at an adjournment you will hear minutiae of the evidence, or whether you will think it is a matter to be dealt with in the police courts later on and that, this woman having met with her death by the carotid artery having been cut, you will be satisfied to return a verdict to that effect. From what I learn the police are content to take the future conduct of the case.

It is for you to say whether you will close the inquiry today; if not, we shall adjourn for a week or fortnight, to hear the evidence that you may desire. The Foreman, having consulted with his colleagues, considered that the jury had had quite sufficient evidence before them upon which to give a verdict.

The Coroner: What is the verdict?

The Foreman: Wilful murder against some person or persons unknown.

Chapter Eleven
The Martha Tabram Inquest

Day 1, Thursday, 9 August 1888.
The Times 10 August 1888.

Yesterday afternoon [9th Aug] Mr G. Collier, Deputy Coroner for the South Eastern Division of Middlesex, opened an inquiry at the Working Lads' Institute, Whitechapel Road, respecting the death of the woman who was found on Tuesday last, with 39 stabs on her body, at George Yard Buildings, Whitechapel.

Detective Inspector Reid, H Division, watched the case on behalf of the Criminal Investigation Department.

Alfred George Crow, cabdriver, 35, George Yard Buildings, deposed that he got home at half past 3 on Tuesday morning. As he was passing the first floor landing, he saw a body lying on the ground. He took no notice, as he was accustomed to seeing people lying about there. He did not then know whether the person was alive or dead. He got up at half past 9 and when he went down the staircase the body was not there. Witness heard no noise while he was in bed.

John S. Reeves, of 37, George Yard Buildings, a waterside labourer, said that on Tuesday morning he left home at a quarter to 5 to seek for work. When he reached the first floor landing, he found the deceased lying on her back in a pool of blood. He was frightened and did not examine her but at once gave information to the police. He did not know the deceased. The deceased's clothes were disarranged, as though she had had a struggle with someone. Witness saw no footmarks on the staircase, nor did he find a knife or other weapon.

Police constable Thomas Barrett, 226 H, said that the last witness called his attention to the body of the deceased. He sent for a doctor, who pronounced life extinct.

Dr T. R. Killeen, of 68, Brick Lane, said that he was called to the deceased and found her dead. She had 39 stabs on the body. She had been dead some three hours. Her age was about 36 and the body was very well nourished. Witness had since made a post-mortem examination of the body. The left lung was penetrated in five places and the right lung was penetrated in two places.

The heart, which was rather fatty, was penetrated in one place and that would be sufficient to cause death. The liver was healthy but was penetrated in five places, the spleen was penetrated in two places and the stomach, which was perfectly healthy, was penetrated in six places.

The witness did not think all the wounds were inflicted with the same instrument. The wounds generally might have been inflicted by a knife but such an instrument could not have inflicted one of the wounds, which went through the chest bone. His opinion was that one of the wounds was inflicted by some kind of dagger and that all of them were caused during life.

The Coroner said he was in hopes that the body would be identified but three women had identified it under three different names. He therefore proposed to leave that question open until the next occasion.

The case would be left in the hands of Detective Inspector Reid, who would endeavour to discover the perpetrator of this dreadful murder. It was one of the most dreadful murders any one could imagine. The man must have been a perfect savage to inflict such a number of wounds on a defenceless woman in such a way. The case was then adjourned.

Day 2, Thursday, 23 August 1888.
The Times, 24 August 1888.

Yesterday afternoon 23rd August, Mr George Collier, the Deputy Coroner for the South Eastern Division of Middlesex, resumed his inquiry at the Working Lads' Institute, Whitechapel Road, respecting the death of the woman who was found dead at George Yard Buildings, on the early morning of Tuesday, the 7th inst. with no less than 39 wounds on various parts of her body. The body has been identified as that of Martha Tabram, aged 39 or 40 years, the wife of a foreman packer at a furniture warehouse.

Henry Samuel Tabram, 6, River Terrace, East Greenwich, husband of the deceased woman, said he last saw her alive about 18 months ago, in the Whitechapel Road. They had been separated for 13 years, owing to her drinking habits. She obtained a warrant against him. For some part of the time witness allowed her 12s. a week but in consequence of her annoyance, he stopped this allowance ten years ago, since which time he had made it half a crown a week, as he found she was living with a man.

Henry Turner, a carpenter, staying at the Working Men's Home, Commercial Street, Spitalfields, stated that he had been living with the woman Tabram as his wife for about nine years. Two or three weeks previously to this occurrence he ceased to do so. He had left her on two or three occasions in consequence of her drinking habits but they had come together again.

He last saw her alive on Saturday, the 4th inst. in Leadenhall Street. He then gave her 1s. 6d. to get some stock. When she had money she spent it in drink. While living with witness deceased's usual time for coming home was about 11 o'clock. As far as he knew she had no regular companion and he did not know that she walked the streets. As a rule he was, he said, a man of sober habits and when the deceased was sober they usually got on well together.

By Inspector Reid. At times the deceased had stopped out all night. After those occasions, she told him she had been taken in a fit and was removed to the police station or somewhere else.

By the Coroner. He knew she suffered from fits but they were brought on by drink.

Mrs Mary Bousfield, wife of a wood cutter, residing at 4, Star-place, Commercial Road, knew the deceased by the name of Turner. She was formerly a lodger in her house with the man Turner. Deceased would rather have a glass of ale than a cup of tea but she was not a woman who got continually drunk and she never brought home any companions with her. She left without giving notice and owed two weeks' rent.

Mrs Ann Morris, a widow, of 23, Lisbon Street, E. said she last saw the deceased, who was her sister-in-law, at about 11 o'clock on Bank Holiday night in the Whitechapel Road. She was then about to enter a public house. Mary Ann Connolly ('Pearly Poll'), who at the suggestion of Inspector Reid was cautioned in the usual manner before being sworn, stated she had been for the last two nights living at a lodging house in Dorset Street, Spitalfields. Witness was a single woman.

She had known the woman Tabram for about four or five months. She knew her by the name of Emma. She last saw her alive on Bank Holiday night, when witness was with her about three quarters of an hour and they separated at a quarter to 12. Witness was with Tabram and two soldiers one private and one corporal. She did not know what regiment they belonged to but they had white bands round their caps.

After they separated, Tabram went away with the private and witness accompanied the corporal up Angel Alley. There was no quarrelling between any of them. Witness had been to the barracks to identify the soldiers and the two men she picked out were, to the best of her belief, the men she and Tabram were with. The men at the Wellington Barracks were paraded before witness. One of the men picked out by witness turned out not to be a corporal but he had stripes on his arm.

By Inspector Reid. Witness heard of the murder on the Tuesday. Since the occurrence witness had threatened to drown herself but she only said it for a lark. She stayed away two days and two nights and she only said that when asked where she was going. She knew the police were looking after her but she did not let them know her whereabouts.

By a juryman. The woman Tabram was not drunk. They were, however, drinking at different houses for about an hour and three quarters. They had ale and rum.

Detective Inspector Reid made a statement of the efforts made by the police to discover the perpetrator of the murder. Several persons had stated that they saw the deceased woman on the previous Sunday with a corporal but when all the corporals and privates at the Tower and Wellington Barracks were paraded before them, they failed to identify the man.

The military authorities afforded every facility to the police. 'Pearly Poll' picked out two men belonging to the Coldstream Guards at the Wellington Barracks. One of those men had three good conduct stripes and he was proved beyond doubt to have been with his wife from 8 o'clock on the Monday night until 6 o'clock the following morning.

The other man was also proved to have been in barracks at five minutes past 10 on Bank Holiday night. The police would be pleased if anyone would give them information of having seen anyone with the deceased on the night of Bank Holiday. The Coroner having summed up, the jury returned a verdict to the effect that the deceased had been murdered by some person or persons unknown.

The Daily Telegraph
Last Day of inquest, Thursday, 23 August 1888.
Published Friday, 24 August 1888.

Yesterday afternoon 23rd August, Mr George Collier, the Deputy Coroner for South East Middlesex, resumed the inquiry at the Working Lads' Institute, Whitechapel, into the circumstances attending the death of Martha Turner or Tabram, a hawker, lately living at 4, Star Place, Star Street, Commercial Road E. who was discovered early on the morning of Tuesday, the 7th inst. lying dead on the first floor landing of some model dwellings known as George Yard Buildings, Commercial Street, Spitalfields. When found, the woman presented a shocking appearance, there being 39 stab wounds on the body, some of them apparently having been inflicted with a bayonet.

Henry Samuel Tabram, of 6, River Terrace, East Greenwich, stated that he was a foreman packer in a furniture warehouse. He identified the body as that of his wife. Her name was Martha Tabram and she was 39 years of age. He last saw her alive eighteen months ago in the Whitechapel Road. Witness had been separated from her thirteen years.

Henry Turner, who stated that he lived at the Working Men's Home, Commercial Street, deposed that he was a carpenter by trade but latterly he had got his living as a hawker. Up till three weeks previous to this affair, he was living with the deceased. They had lived together on and off for nine years. She used to get her living, like himself, as a street hawker.

He last saw her alive on the Saturday before her death, when they met accidentally in Leadenhall Street. She said she had got no money, so witness gave her some to buy stock with. Deceased was a woman who, when she had the money, would get drunk with it.

Mary Bousfiled, 4, Star Place, Commercial Road, deposed that Turner and the deceased lived at her house till three weeks before her death. Turner was very good to her and helped to support two children she had by her husband.

Ann Morris, 23, Lisburn Street, E. a widow, deposed that she was the sister-in-law of the deceased. Witness last saw her alive on Bank Holiday, as she was entering the White Swan public house in Whitechapel Road. Deceased then appeared to be sober. She was alone when she entered the bar. Mary Ann Connelly said she had known the deceased for four or five months under the name of Emma.

The last time she saw her alive was on Bank Holiday, at the corner of George Yard, Whitechapel. They went to a public house together and parted about 11.45. They were accompanied by two soldiers, one a private and the other a corporal. She did not know to what regiment they belonged but they had white bands round their caps. Witness did not know if the corporal had any side arms.

They picked up with the soldiers together and entered several public houses, where they drank. When they separated, the deceased went away with the private. They went up George Yard, while witness and the corporal went up Angel Alley. Before they parted witness and the corporal had a quarrel and he hit her with a stick. She did not hear deceased have any quarrel. Witness never saw the deceased again alive.

The Coroner, in summing up, said that the crime was one of the most brutal that had occurred for some years. For a poor defenceless woman to be outraged and stabbed in the manner which this woman had been was almost beyond belief. They could only come to one conclusion and that was that the deceased was brutally and cruelly murdered.

The jury returned a verdict of wilful murder against some person or persons unknown.

The Daily Telegraph did not turn up for day one of the inquest, they only covered the second day and only had a small report in the paper.

Chapter Twelve
The Alice McKenzie Inquest

Day 1, Wednesday, 17 July 1889.
The Times, Thursday, 18 July 1889.

Last evening, 17th July, Mr Wynne E. Baxter, coroner for the South Eastern Division of Middlesex, opened his inquiry at the Working Lad's Institute, High Street Whitechapel. Borated her evidence but stated that it was not raining when she passed and the rain did not come down until a quarter to 1.

Detective Inspector Reid: I am certain it was not raining at half past 12, as I was out at that time. The coroner said the Superintendent T Arnold and Detective Inspector E. Reid were present to watch the case on behalf of the Criminal Investigation Department.

The jury viewed the body.

John M'Cormack, [McCormack], was the first witness called. He said, I live at 54, Gun Street, Spitalfields. It is a common lodging house. I am a porter. I have seen the body in the mortuary and recognise it as that of Alice M'Kenzie [McKenzie]. I can't exactly tell her age but it was about 40.

The Coroner: Has she been living with you? Yes, for about six years. I recognise her by her thumb, which had been crushed at the top by a machine. The nail was half off.

[Coroner] Did you recognise her face? Yes, Sir; by the scars on her forehead. I also recognised her clothes she was wearing and also the boots. She told me she came from Peterborough. I did not know if she had any children. She worked very hard as a washerwoman and charwoman to the Jews.

[Coroner] When did you last see her alive? Between 3 and 4 o'clock yesterday afternoon. She left me in bed at that time. She went from me with the intention of paying a night's rent 8d.

[Coroner] Did you give her the money? Of course I did. I gave her 1s. 8d. altogether; to pay the rent and to do what she liked with the remainder.

[Coroner] You did not see her again? Not until I saw the body in the mortuary. The deputy told me that my old woman was lying dead in the mortuary and I went and recognised her.

[Coroner] Was she sober when she left you? Perfectly.

[Coroner] How come you in bed at 4 o'clock? As soon as I come home I lie down; and, having a little drop of drink, I go and lie down. When I came home yesterday, I went and lay down immediately.

[Coroner] Had the deceased been to work on Tuesday? No; she told me she went to work on Monday but I did not believe it. She came home about 7 o'clock on Monday evening and she then went to bed.

[Coroner] Why did you not believe she went to work? Because I know she did not.

[Coroner] How do you know? Because I was told by others she did not go to work.

[Coroner] Did she often come home late at night? Not to my knowledge. Deceased was usually at home at night.

[Coroner] Did you have any words with the deceased yesterday? I had a few words and that upset her.

[Coroner] Did she tell you she was going to walk the streets? She did not; she told me nothing.

[Coroner] Did you not go down to the deputy and ask if the deceased had paid the money? I did; that was between half past 10 and 11 o'clock.

[Coroner] What did the deputy say? She told me she had not paid the rent.

[Coroner] Did you say, 'What am I to do? Am I to go and walk the streets as well?' That's what I did say. The deputy said, 'No; don't you go.' I then went upstairs and went to bed. I got up at a quarter to 6 that morning and that was my usual time.

[Coroner] Did you think she had gone out looking for money? I can't say nothing about that.

[Coroner] Was the deceased a great smoker? Yes; she used to smoke but I can't tell what sort of pipe she smoked; all I can say is she smoked.

[Coroner] Was it a clay pipe or a wooden pipe? It was always a clay pipe.

[Coroner] In bed? Yes, of course.

Elizabeth Ryder said, I live at 52 and 54, Gun Street, Spitalfields. I am married and my husband's name is Richard John Ryder and he is a cooper. I act as deputy of a common lodging house. I have seen the body in the mortuary and recognise it as that of Alice M'Kenzie. She has been living there for about four months. She lived with John M'Cormack as his wife.

I have no doubt about the identity of the body. I knew she was wearing old stockings. I last saw her alive last night. She was then sober and was not wearing a bonnet or hat.

[Coroner] Did she speak to you? Yes. She had been at the lodging house all day. M'Cormack came home between 3 and 4 o'clock in the afternoon.

[Coroner] Do you know whether there had been any disagreement? I believe there had but I did not hear anything. When deceased came downstairs between 8 and 9 o'clock she passed through the kitchen and went out.

[Coroner] Did she usually wear a bonnet or hat? Never; but she wore a shawl and had one on when she left the lodging house. It was a light shawl and witness saw it in the mortuary.

[Coroner] Was she a woman who was in the habit of being out late at night? No. She was generally in bed by 10 o'clock. As far as I know, she got her living honestly and did not get money in the streets. Between 11 and 12 last night M'Cormack came down and asked me if I had seen the deceased since 8 or 9 o'clock. I told him I had not.

He then asked me if she had paid the lodging and I told him she had not. M'Cormack then asked what he was to do and I told him to go to bed. He then went upstairs. Before that, he told me he had a few words with the deceased and sent her down to pay the lodging. Witness told him deceased would soon be home.

Deceased had some drink during the day and when her husband came home from work she was drunk. I did not think it necessary to make any remark to deceased when she went out. I have seen her smoke in the kitchen. She used to borrow pipes, which were short clay ones, like the one produced.

[Coroner] What time is the lodging-house closed? At 2 o'clock in the morning. At 3:30 this morning I went into the kitchen for the deceased and another young woman but they had not come home.

[Coroner] Has the other young woman come home? No.

[Coroner] What is the name of this young woman? Mog Cheeks.

[Coroner] Do you know where deceased got the drink from? I do not but there is a public house about two doors away.

[Coroner] Had you seen deceased with any other man but M'Cormack that day? No. Between 3 and 4 in the afternoon she went to meet her husband and they came home together. When she went out at night she was alone. Deceased and M'Cormack had lodged on and off at the lodging house for the past 12 months.

When they were not there they occupied a room at Crossingham's in White's Row. The other woman referred to had lodged there for 18 months and she was on the streets.

The Foreman: It is important that that woman should be found.

The Coroner: I have no doubt that she will be.

Witness: She was in the habit of staying out all night if she had no money to pay for her lodging.

Police-constable Joseph Allen, 423 H, deposed: Last night, I was in Castle Alley. It was then 20 minutes past 12 when I passed through. I was through the alley several times. I remained there for five minutes. I entered the alley through the archway in Whitechapel Road. I had something to eat under the lamp where the deceased was found. Having remained in the alley for five minutes, I went into Wentworth Street. There was neither man nor woman there. There were wagons in the alley too right underneath the lamp.

[Coroner] Would you swear there was no one in the wagons? I would not swear to that, as I did not look into them; one of the wagons was an open one. Everything was very quiet at the time. The backs of some of the houses in Newcastle Street faced the alley and in some of the upper windows were lights.

That was not an unusual thing at that time. I cannot say if any of the windows were open. No sounds came from those houses. On leaving the alley, I met Constable Walter Andrews, 272 H, in Wentworth Street. It was about 100 yards from the alley where I met Andrews. I spoke to Andrews, who then went towards Goldston Street. [Goulston Street]

[Coroner] How did you fix the time? I looked at my watch. It was 12:30 when I left the alley. At the end is a public house the Three Crowns and as I passed, the landlord was shutting up the house. After leaving Andrews, I went towards Commercial Street and met Sergeant Badlam, [Badham] 31 H, who told me a woman had been found murdered in Castle Alley and he directed me to go to the station. When the sergeant spoke to me it was five minutes to 1 and 1 o'clock when I got to the station.

Police constable Walter Andrews, 272 H, said: about ten minutes to 1 this morning I saw Sergeant Badlam at the corner of Old Castle Street, leading into Castle Alley. That was on the opposite corner of the public house. The sergeant said, 'All right' and I said the same. I then proceeded up Castle Alley and tried the doors on the west side of the alley.

While doing so, I noticed a woman lying on the pavement. Her head was lying eastward and was on the edge of the kerbstone, with her feet towards the building, which was a wheelwright's shop and warehouse.

[Coroner] Was the body touched before the doctor arrived? Only by my touching the face to see if it was cold. It had not been disturbed.

[Coroner] How far was it from the lamp? Almost underneath. About 2 ft. from the lamp post.

[Coroner] Was any wagon there? Two; one was a scavenger's wagon and the other a brewer's dray. They were on the same side of the way. The wagons hid the body from persons in the cottages opposite. The head was almost underneath the scavenger's wagon.

[Coroner] Where [sic] her clothes up? Yes, almost level to the chin. Her legs and body were exposed. I noticed that blood was running from the left side of the neck.

[Coroner] You said you felt her? I touched the abdomen. It was quite warm. I then blew my whistle and between two and three minutes Sergeant Badlam came up. The sergeant gave me orders to stay by the body and not touch it until the doctor arrived. The body was not touched until Dr Phillips arrived about five or ten minutes past 1.

[Coroner] Had you seen any one? I had not. There was not a soul in the alley that I saw. After I saw the body lying on the pavement I heard a footstep coming from Old Castle Place and I saw a young man, named Isaac Lewis Jacobs. I said, 'Where are you going?' He said, 'I am going to Wentworth Street to fetch something for my supper.' At the time he was carrying a plate in his hand. Jacobs came back with me and stayed there until the sergeant arrived.

[Coroner] Had you been in the alley before? Yes. Between 20 and 25 minutes past 12. I went into the alley after Allen. After he came out I went in some two or three minutes later. No one was in the alley then. After I left Allen, I went into

Goldston Street, then into Whitechapel High Street, down Middlesex Street into Wentworth Street again. It was there I saw the sergeant, as I have already stated.

[Coroner] Did any one attract your attention? No, I saw no one in Goldston or Middlesex streets.

The Foreman: Do you think deceased had been drawn to where you found her or murdered there? I think she was killed there. I should think she had been standing up against the lamp post and then pulled or dragged down. There was no trail of blood away from the body and no splashes of blood.

[Coroner?] How long have you been on the beat? A fortnight.

[Coroner] Do people come there? People often come to sleep in the vans but when we find them we turn them out. I have not seen the alley used for immoral purposes and have not seen any women there at all.

[Coroner] How many vans are there at night in the alley? Six or eight, besides several costermongers' barrows.

[Coroner] Did you see any one the worse for drink about last night? I did not.

Isaac Lewis Jacobs said: I live at 12, Newcastle Place and am a bootmaker. About ten minutes to 1 this morning, I left home to buy some supper in M'Carthy's in Dorset Street. I had occasion to pass Newcastle Place into Old Castle Street. When I got to Cocoanut Place a constable ran up to me; I stopped. He said, 'Where have you been?' I replied, 'I have been nowhere, I am just going on an errand and have just left my home.' The constable then said, 'Come with me; there has been a murder committed.'

I went with him and when we got to Old Castle Street, he blew his whistle. I believe a sergeant then came up. We then hurried down to the lamp post in Castle Alley. I saw a woman lying there in a pool of blood, with a wound in the throat and another wound in the side. I waited there until another police constable came and afterwards saw the body removed. Then I went home.

[Coroner] Did you see any one before you saw the constable? No, sir.

[Coroner] Does your house look over Castle Alley? No. That is Castle Street. [Newcastle Street]. I had not been there during the night.

Police sergeant Badham, 31 H, stated: About 12 minutes to 1 this morning, I was in Old Castle Street and saw Constable Andrews. I went up to him and said, 'All right?' He replied, 'All right, sergeant.' I then left him and went to visit another man on the adjoining beat. I then went to Pell Lane, when I heard two blows from a whistle. I listened for the second blow to ascertain from where it came.

On hearing the second whistle, I rushed up Newcastle Street and met Andrews who shouted out, 'Come on, quick.' I threw my cape to the ground and rushed up after him. I saw a woman lying on the pavement on the near side with her throat cut and her head lying in a pool of blood. The legs and stomach were exposed.

I got the assistance of other constables and blocked up the ends of the alley and directed Constable 423 H to fetch the doctor and acquaint the doctor on duty. I also directed Constable 101 H to search the place and also the surrounding streets and Constable 272 H to remain with the body and not to let any one touch it until the doctor arrived. Sergeant 21 H and the local inspector came up and made search.

They were followed by Detective Inspector Reid. I also acquainted the Superintendent and directed other constables to make careful inquiry at the lodging houses, coffee houses and places where men were likely to go. In the meantime the doctor arrived. I also made search myself but failed to find trace of any person that was likely to have committed the murder.

[Coroner] Had you been in the alley at all that night? No.

Police constable George Neve, 101 H, stated, about five minutes to 1am I met the sergeant in Commercial Street. He said, 'Hurry up into Castle Alley. There has been a murder done; go and search all round.' I searched all round but did not find anything. It was all quiet. I then went into Castle Alley, to where the body was lying. I searched the conveyances in Castle Alley and looked over the hoarding but could see no trace of any one about. I saw no one move and heard no sound.

[Coroner] Did you know the deceased? I have known her about the place for 12 months and have seen her the worse for drink.

[Coroner] Have you ever seen her about at night? Between 10 and 11 o'clock. It was my opinion she was a prostitute. I have seen her talking to men. I have seen her in Gun Street, Brick Lane and Dorset Street. I did not know where she lived. I had not seen her before that evening. In fact, I had not seen her for about a fortnight.

Mrs Sarah Frances Smith stated: I live at the Whitechapel Baths and Washhouses. My husband is a retired police officer and is Superintendent of the baths. I am money taker there. The baths back on to Castle Alley and the window of my room looks into Castle Alley, close to where the body was found.

I went to bed this morning between 12:15 and 12:30. I did not go to sleep and had no idea that anything had happened, until I heard a knock at the door and also a whistle blown.

[Coroner] If there had been any call for help in the alley would you have heard it? Yes, certainly. My bedstead is up against the wall, next to Castle Alley.

At this stage, the inquiry was adjourned.

Day 2, Thursday, 18 July 1889.
The Times, Friday, 19 July 1889.

Yesterday morning [18th July] Mr Wynne E. Baxter, coroner for the South Eastern Division of Middlesex, resumed his adjourned inquiry at the Working Lad's Institute into the circumstances attending the death of Alice M'Kenzie, aged about 40 years, who was found murdered in Castle Alley, Whitechapel, early on Wednesday morning.

Sergeant [Superintendent] T. Arnold and Detective-Inspector E. Reid watched the case on behalf of the Commissions of Police and Criminal Investigation Department.

Detective Inspector Edmund Reid, H Division, said: I received a call to Castle Alley about five minutes past 1 on the morning of the murder. I dressed and ran down at once. On arriving at Castle Alley, I found the Wentworth Street end blocked by a policeman. On arriving at the back of the baths, I saw the deceased woman.

I saw she had a cut on the left side of the throat and there was a quantity of blood under the head which was running into the gutter. The clothes were up and her face was slightly turned towards the road. She was lying on her back. I felt the face and body and found they were warm. Dr Phillips arrived.

At the time I arrived, I ascertained the fact that the other end (Whitechapel) was blocked and search was being made through the alley and also in the immediate neighbourhood. The deputy superintendent and his wife at the baths were seen and stated they heard nothing unusual. After the body had been examined by the doctor, it was placed on the police ambulance and underneath the body of the deceased was found the short clay pipe produced.

The pipe was broken and there was blood on it and in the bowl was some unburnt tobacco. I also found a bronze farthing underneath the clothes of the deceased. There was also blood on the farthing. I produce a rough plan of Castle Alley; a correct copy of which will be sent by the draughtsman. During the whole time from the finding of the body only one private person was present, except Lewis Jacobs, who was examined yesterday.

Everything was done very quietly. The fence on the other side of the alley, to where the body was found, is about 10 ft. high. Along that were a row of barrows. Close to where the body was found were two barrows chained together. There was a lamp where the body was found; one outside the public house; one at the entrance to Old Castle Street and one at the entrance to the passage leading into the alley. I do not think any stranger would go down there unless he was taken there.

I did not go into the High Street Whitechapel, within a few minutes of my arrival in the alley. There are people in the High Street, Whitechapel all night. Two constables are continually passing through the alley all night. It is hardly ever left alone for more than five minutes. Although it is called an alley it is really a broad turning, with two narrow entrances.

Any person standing at the Wentworth Street end would look upon it as a blind street. No stranger would think he could pass through it and none but foot passengers can. It was raining when the body was removed. It was raining when I arrived but a very little. The spot under which the deceased was lying was dry except where there was blood.

I searched the body at the mortuary and found nothing. There is no doubt about the name of the deceased. I have since made inquiries at 54, Gun Street and have ascertained from the deputy, Ryder that Mog Cheeks, the woman that was mentioned yesterday, stayed with her sister all night. I saw the deputy this morning and she said she would try to get Mog Cheeks here.

I have no doubt the deed was committed on the spot where the body was found. I should say she was lying down on the pavement when she was murdered, as if she had been standing up there would have been blood on the wall. She was lying along the pavement, her head being towards Whitechapel. No person, unless he went along the pathway, could have seen the body on account of the shadow of the lamp and the vans which screened the body.

Any person going along the road would have seen it. If I wanted to watch any one I would stand under the lamp. The darkness was so great that it was necessary to use the constable's lamp to see that the throat was cut, although it was just under the lamp. I think the alley is sufficiently lighted; there are five lamps here.

In another instance of this kind, the Hanbury Street murder two similar farthings were found. The tobacco in the pipe had not been smoked. The pipe was a very old one and was what was termed in the lodging house 'a nose warmer.'

Dr George Baxter Phillips, divisional surgeon of the H Division, said that he was called and arrived at Castle Alley at 1:10 a.m. on Wednesday, when it was raining very hard. On his arrival in Castle Alley, at the back premises of the washhouses he found the body lying on the pavement in the position already described, as to which the witness gave full details. Having inspected the body, he had it removed to the shed used as a mortuary in the Pavilion Yard, Whitechapel.

There he re-examined the body and left it in charge of the police. Yesterday, he made a post-mortem examination at the same shed a most inconvenient and altogether ill-appointed place for such a purpose. It tended greatly to the thwarting of justice having such a place to perform such examinations in. With several colleagues he made the examination at 2 o'clock, when rigor mortis was well marked.

The witness then described the wounds, of which there were several and these were most of them superficial cuts on the lower part of the body. There were several old scars and there was the loss of the top of the right thumb, apparently caused by some former injury. The wound in the neck was 4 in. long, reaching from the back part of the muscles, which were almost entirely divided.

It reached to the fore part of the neck to a point 4 in. below the chin. There was a second incision, which must have commenced from behind and immediately below the first. The cause of death was syncope, arising from the loss of blood through the divided carotid vessels and such death probably was almost instantaneous.

The Coroner: There are various points that the doctor would rather reserve at this moment.

Margaret Cheeks said: I generally live at 52, Gun Street. I am married and my husband's name is Charles Cheeks, when he is with me. He is a bricklayer and has not been living with me for three years. I knew the deceased from living in the same house. I saw her on Tuesday morning getting her husband's breakfast. I have not seen her since.

Margaret Franklin stated: I live at 56, Flower and Dean Street and am a widow. I have known the deceased for 15 years. Between 11:30 and 12 o'clock on Tuesday night, I saw the deceased and was speaking to her. I was sitting with two others on the steps of a house at the top of Flower and Dean Street. Deceased was passing and going in the direction of Brick Lane and Whitechapel. We exchanged a few words. I do not think she was under the influence of drink.

I have often seen her out as late as that, as she did domestic work for the Jews. I did not see her speak to anyone in Brick Lane on Tuesday night. The only name I knew her by was Alice. I knew she was living in Gun Street with a man that I knew by the name of Bryant. It was the same one that gave evidence yesterday. I have never seen her talking with other men. She worked hard for the Jews and they do not give much. It had just begun to rain when deceased passed.

Catherine Hughes, who was sitting with the last witness, generally corroquiry would be adjourned until the 14th of August. In the meantime, he hoped there would not be another affair of this kind. People having the character of the victims had it entirely in their hands to prevent this kind of thing. If they could only be induced not to assist the man who did this sort of work it would be stopped but unfortunately it was hoping against hope, because they would lend themselves to it.

The inquiry was then adjourned.

Day 3, Wednesday, 14 August 1889.
(The Times, Thursday, 15 August 1889.)

Yesterday [14th August] Mr Wynne E Baxter, Coroner for the South Eastern Division of Middlesex, resumed his adjourned inquiry at the Working Lad's Institute, Whitechapel, respecting the death of Alice McKenzie, who was found brutally murdered in Castle Alley, Whitechapel, on the early morning of the 17th.

Detective Inspector Moore (Scotland Yard) and Detective Inspector E. Reid, H Division, watched the case on behalf of the Criminal Investigation Department.

Dr George Bagster Phillips, divisional surgeon of H Division, was recalled and deposed: On the occasion of my making the post-mortem examination, the attendants of the mortuary, on taking off the clothing of the deceased woman removed a short clay pipe, which one of them threw upon the ground, by which means it was broken.

I had the broken pieces placed upon a ledge at the end of the post-mortem table but it has disappeared and although inquiry has been made about it, up to the present time it has not been forthcoming. The pipe had been used. It came from the woman's clothing. The attendants, whom I have often seen there before, are old workhouse men.

There were five marks on the abdomen and, with the exception of one, were on the left side of the abdomen. The largest one was the lowest and the smallest one was the exceptional one mentioned and was typical of a finger nail mark. They were coloured and in my opinion were caused by the finger nails and thumb nail of a hand. I have on a subsequent examination assured myself of the correctness of this conclusion.

The Coroner: When you first saw the body, how long should you say she had been dead? Not more than half an hour and very possibly a much shorter time. It was a wet and cold night. The deceased met her death, in my opinion, while lying on the ground on her back. The injuries to the abdomen were caused after death.

[Coroner] In what position do you think the assailant was at the time? The great probability is that he was on the right side of the body at the time he killed her and that he cut her throat with a sharp instrument. I should think the latter had a shortish blade and was pointed. I cannot tell whether it was the first or second cut that terminated the woman's life.

The first cut, whether it was the important one or not, would probably prevent the woman from crying out on account of the shock. The whole of the air passages were uninjured, so that if she was first forced on to the ground, she might have called out. The bruises over the collar-bone may have been caused by finger pressure. There were no marks suggestive of pressure against the windpipe.

[Coroner] Did you detect any skill in the injuries? A knowledge of how effectually to deprive a person of life and that speedily.

[Coroner] Are the injuries to the abdomen similar to those you have seen in the other cases? No, Sir. I may volunteer the statement that the injuries to the throat are not similar to those in the other cases.

The Foreman: Do I understand this pipe you speak of was in addition to the one produced on the last occasion? Yes. I cannot tell from where it came but my impression is that it came from the bosom of the dress. The knife that was used could not have been as large as the ordinary butcher's slaughter knife.

[Coroner] Were the finger nail marks on the body those of the woman herself? My impression is that they were caused by another hand. These marks were caused after the throat was cut. Inspector Reid. That is all the evidence we have.

The Coroner: Then we have practically come to the end of this inquiry. Opportunity has now been given to ascertain whether any further light could be thrown upon this unfortunate case. The first point the jury have to consider is as to the identity of the deceased woman and, fortunately, in regard to that there is no question.

There is an interval of nearly five hours from when M'Cormack saw the deceased until she is seen between half past 11 and 12 by some women in Flower and Dean Street. This is the last that was seen of her. At a quarter past 12 a constable had his supper under the very lamp under which the deceased was afterwards found and at that time no one was near.

Another constable was there at 25 minutes past 12 and the place was then all right. The officer next entered the alley at 12:50 and it was between those times that the murder must have been done. When the body was discovered there was no one about and nothing suspicious had been seen. Had there been any noise, there were plenty of opportunities for it to have been heard.

There is great similarity between this and the other class of cases which have happened in this neighbourhood and if this crime has not been committed by the same person, it is clearly an imitation of the other cases. We have another similarity in the absence of motive. None of the evidence shows that the deceased was at enmity with any one.

There is nothing to show why the woman is murdered or by whom. I think you will agree with me that so far as the police are concerned every care was taken after the death to discover and capture the assailant. All the ability and discretion the police have shown in their investigations have been unavailing, as in the other cases. The evidence tends to show that the deceased was attacked, laid on the ground and murdered.

It is to be hoped that something will be done to prevent crimes of this sort and to make such crimes impossible. It must now be patent to the whole world that in Spitalfields there is a class of persons who, I think, cannot be found in such numbers, not only in any other part of this metropolis but in any other metropolis and the question arises, should this state of affairs continue to exist? I do not say it is for you to decide.

The matter is one for a higher power than ourselves to suggest a remedy. But it certainly appears to me there are two ways in which the matter ought to be attacked. In the first place, it ought to be attacked physically. Many of the houses in the neighbourhood are unfit for habitation. They want clearing away and fresh ones built.

Those are physical alterations which, I maintain, require to be carried out there. Beyond this there is the moral question. Here we get a population of the same character and not varied, as in a moderately sized town or village. Here there is a population of 20,000 of the same character, not one of whom is capable of elevating the other.

Of course there is an opinion among the police that it is a proper thing that this seething mass should be kept together rather than be distributed all over the metropolis. Every effort ought to be made to elevate this class. I am constantly struck by the fact that all the efforts of charitable and religious bodies here are comparatively unavailing.

It is true a great deal has been done of late years, especially to assist the moral development of the East End but it is perfectly inadequate to meet the necessities of the case. If no other advantage comes from these mysterious murders, they will probably wake up the Church and others to the fact that it is the duty of every parish in the West to have a mission and localise work in the East End.

Otherwise, it will be impossible to stop these awful cases of crime. Here is a parish of 21,000 persons with only one church in it. There are not only cases of murder here but many of starvation. I hope at least these cases will open the eyes of those who are charitable to the necessity of doing their duty by trying to elevate the lower classes.

The jury, after a short deliberation, returned a verdict of 'Wilful murder against some person or persons unknown' and added a rider endorsing the remarks of the Coroner and requesting him to forward a recommendation to the County Council and the Whitechapel District Board of Works to open up Castle Alley to the Whitechapel High Street as a thoroughfare.

Chapter Thirteen
The Catherine Eddowes Inquest

Day 1, Thursday, 4 October 1888.
The Daily Telegraph, Friday, 5 October 1888.

At the Coroner's Court, Golden Lane, yesterday [4th Oct], Mr S. F. Langham, coroner for the City of London, opened the inquest into the death of Catherine Eddowes or Conway, or Kelly, who was murdered in Mitre Court, Aldgate, about half past one o'clock on Sunday morning last.

The court was crowded and much interest was taken in the proceedings, many people standing outside the building during the whole of the day. Mr Crawford, City solicitor, appeared on behalf of the Corporation, as responsible for the police; Major Smith and Superintendent Forster represented the officers engaged in the inquiry.

After the jury had viewed the body, which was lying in the adjoining mortuary, Mr Crawford, addressing the coroner, said: I appear here as representing the City police in this matter, for the purpose of rendering you every possible assistance and if I should consider it desirable, in the course of the inquiry, to put any questions to witnesses, probably I shall have your permission when you have finished with them.

The Coroner: Oh, certainly. The following evidence was then called.

Eliza Gold deposed: I live at 6, Thrawl Street, Spitalfields. I have been married but my husband is dead. I recognise the deceased as my poor sister (witness here commenced to weep very much and for a few moments, she was unable to proceed with her story).

Her name was Catherine Eddowes. I cannot exactly tell where she was living. She was staying with a gentleman but she was not married to him. Her age last birthday was about 43 years, as far as I can remember. She has been living for some years with Mr Kelly. He is in court. I last saw her alive about four or five months ago.

She used to go out hawking for a living and was a woman of sober habits. Before she went to live with Kelly, she had lived with a man named Conway for several years and had two children by him. I cannot tell how many years she lived with Conway. I do not know whether Conway is still living. He was a pensioner from the army and used to go out hawking also.

I do not know on what terms he parted from my sister. I do not know whether she had ever seen him from the time they parted. I am quite certain that the body I have seen is my sister.

By Mr Crawford: I have not seen Conway for seven or eight years. I believe my sister was living with him then on friendly terms.

[Coroner] Was she living on friendly terms with Kelly? I cannot say. Three or four weeks ago I saw them together and they were then on happy terms. I cannot fix the time when I last saw them. They were living at 55, Flower and Dean Street a lodging house. My sister when staying there came to see me when I was very ill. From that time, until I saw her in the mortuary, I have not seen her.

A Juryman pointed out that witness previously said she had not seen her sister for three or four months, whilst later on she spoke of three or four weeks.

The Coroner: You said your sister came to see you when you were ill and that you had not seen her since. Was that three or four weeks ago?

Mrs Gold: Yes.

[Coroner] So, that you're saying three or four months was a mistake? Yes. I am so upset and confused.

Witness commenced to cry again. As she could not write she had to affix her mark to the deposition.

John Kelly, a strong-looking labourer, was then called and said: I live at a lodging house, 55, Flower and Dean Street. Have seen the deceased and recognise her as Catherine Conway. I have been living with her for seven years. She hawked a few things about the streets and lived with me at a common lodging house in Flower and Dean Street. The lodging house is known as Cooney's.

I last saw her alive about two o'clock in the afternoon of Saturday in Houndsditch. We parted on very good terms. She told me she was going over to Bermondsey to try and find her daughter Annie. Those were the last words she spoke to me. Annie was a daughter whom I believe she had had by Conway. She promised me before we parted that she would be back by four o'clock and no later. She did not return.

[Coroner] Did you make any inquiry after her? I heard she had been locked up at Bishopsgate Street on Saturday afternoon. An old woman who works in Then Lane told me she saw her in the hands of the police.

[Coroner] Did you make any inquiry into the truth of this? I made no further inquiries. I knew that she would be out on Sunday morning, being in the City.

[Coroner] Did you know why she was locked up? Yes, for drink; she had had a drop of drink, so I was told. I never knew she went out for any immoral purpose. She occasionally drank but not to excess. When I left her she had no money about her. She went to see and find her daughter to get a trifle, so that I shouldn't see her walk about the streets at night.

[Coroner] What do you mean by 'walking the streets'? I mean that if we had no money to pay for our lodgings we would have to walk about all night. I was without money to pay for our lodgings at the time. I do not know that she was at variance with anyone not in the least. She had not seen Conway recently not that I know of. I never saw him in my existence. I cannot say whether Conway is living. I know of no one who would be likely to injure her.

The Foreman of the Jury: You say you heard the deceased was taken into custody. Did you ascertain, as a matter of fact, when she was discharged? No. I do not know when she was discharged.

[Coroner] What time was she in the habit of returning to her lodgings? Early.

[Coroner] What do you call early? About eight or nine o'clock.

[Coroner] When she did not return on this particular evening, did it not occur to you that it would be right to inquire whether she had been discharged or not? No, I did not inquire. I expected she would turn up on the Sunday morning.

Mr Crawford: You say she had no money. Do you know with whom she had been drinking that afternoon? I cannot say.

[Coroner] Do you know anyone who paid for drink for her? No.

[Coroner] Had she on a recent occasion absented herself from you at night? No.

[Coroner] This was the only time? Yes.

[Coroner] But had not she left you previously? Yes, a long time ago some months ago.

[Coroner] for what purpose? We had a few words and she went away but came back in a few hours.

[Coroner] Had you had any angry conversation with her on Saturday afternoon? No not in the least.

[Coroner] No words about money? No.

[Coroner] Have you any idea where her daughter lives? She told me in King Street, Bermondsey and that her name was Annie.

[Coroner] Had she been previously there for money? Yes, once last year.

[Coroner] How long have you been living in this lodging house together? Seven years, in the self-same house.

[Coroner] Previous to this Saturday had you been sleeping there each evening during the week? No; I slept there on Friday night but she didn't.

[Coroner] Did she not sleep with you? No.

[Coroner] Was she walking the streets that night? She had the misfortune to go to Mile End.

[Coroner] What happened there? She went into the casual ward.

[Coroner] What was the evening you two slept at the lodging house during that week? Not one.

[Coroner] Where did you sleep? On Monday, Tuesday and Wednesday we were down at the hop picking and came back to London on Thursday. We had been unfortunate at the hop picking and had no money. On Thursday night, we both slept in the casual ward.

On the Friday, I earned 6d at a job and I said, 'Here, Kate, you take 4d and go to the lodging house and I will go to Mile End' but she said, 'No, you go and have a bed and I will go to the casual ward' and she went. I saw her again on Saturday morning early.

[Coroner] At what time did you quit one another on Friday? I cannot tell but I think it would be about three or four in the afternoon.

[Coroner] What did she leave you for? To go to Mile End.

[Coroner] What for? To get a night's shelter in the casual ward.

[Coroner] When did you see her next morning? About eight o'clock. I was surprised to see her so early. I know there was some tea and sugar found on her body. She bought that out of some boots we pawned at Jones's for 2s 6d. I think it was on Saturday morning that we pawned the boots. She was sober when she left me. We had been drinking together out of the 2s 6d. All of it was spent in drink and food.

She left me quite sober to go to her daughter's. We parted without an angry word. I do not know why she left Conway. In the past seven years she only lived with me. I did not know of her going out for immoral purposes at night. She never brought me money in the morning after being out at night.

A Juryman: Is not eight o'clock a very early hour to be discharged from a casual ward? I do not know.

[Juryman] There is some tasks picking oakum before you can be discharged. I know it was very early.

Mr Crawford: Is it not the fact that the pawning took place on the Friday night? I do not know. It was either Friday night or Saturday morning. I am all muddled up. (The tickets were produced and were dated the 28th, Friday.)

[Crawford] She pawned the boots, did she not? Yes and I stood at the door in my bare feet.

[Crawford] Seeing the date on the tickets, cannot you recollect when the pawning took place? I cannot say, I am so muddled up. It was either Friday or Saturday.

The Coroner: Had you been drinking when the pawning took place? Yes.

Frederick William Wilkinson deposed: I am deputy of the lodging house at Flower and Dean Street. I have known the deceased and Kelly during the last seven years. They passed as man and wife and lived on very good terms. They had a quarrel now and then but not violent. They sometimes had a few words when Kate was in drink but they were not serious.

I believe she got her living by hawking about the streets and cleaning amongst the Jews in Whitechapel. Kelly paid me pretty regularly. Kate was not often in drink. She was a very jolly woman, always singing. Kelly was not in the habit of drinking and I never saw him the worse for drink. During the week the first time I saw the deceased at the lodging house was on Friday afternoon.

Kelly was not with her then. She went out and did not return until Saturday morning, when I saw her and Kelly in the kitchen together having breakfast. I did not see her go out and I do not know whether Kelly went with her. I never saw her again.

[Coroner] Did you know she was in the habit of walking the streets at night? No; she generally used to return between nine and ten o'clock. I never knew her to be intimate with any particular individual except Kelly; and never heard of such a thing. She use to say she was married to Conway; that her name was bought and paid for meaning that she was married. She was not at variance with any one that I know of.

When I saw her last, on Saturday morning, between ten and eleven, she was quite sober. I first heard from Kelly on Saturday night that Kate was locked up and he said he wanted a single bed. That was about 7.30 in the evening. A single bed is 4d and a double 8d.

By a Juryman: I don't take the names of the lodgers but I know my 'regulars'. If a man comes and takes a bed, I put the number of the bed down in my book but not his name. Of course, I know the names of my regular customers.

Mr Crawford: When was the last time Kelly and the deceased had slept together in your house previous to last week? The last time the two slept at the lodging house was five or six weeks ago, before they went to the hop picking. Kelly slept there on Friday and Saturday but not Kate. I did not make any inquiry about her not being there on Friday.

I could not say whether Kate went out with Kelly on Saturday but I saw them having their breakfast together. I saw Kelly in the house about ten o'clock on Saturday night. I am positive he did not go out again. I cannot tell when he got up on Sunday. I saw him about dinner time. I believe on Saturday morning Kate was wearing an apron. Nothing unusual struck me about her dress. The distance between our place and the scene of the murder is about 500 yards.

Several Jurymen: Oh, more than that.

Mr Crawford: Did any one come into your lodging house and take a bed between one and two o'clock on the Sunday morning? No stranger came in then.

[Crawford] Did any one come into your lodging house about that hour? No; two detectives came about three and asked if I had any women out.

[Crawford] Did anyone come into your lodging house about two o'clock on Sunday morning whom you did not recognise? I cannot say; I could tell by my book, which can soon be produced.

By a Juryman: Kelly and the deceased were at breakfast together between ten and eleven on Saturday morning. If they had told me the previous day that they had no money I would have trusted them. I trust all lodgers I know. The body was found half a mile from my lodging house. The deputy was dispatched for his book, with which after an interval he returned.

It merely showed, however, that there were fifty two beds occupied in the house on Saturday night. There were only six strangers. He could not say whether any one took a bed about two o'clock on Sunday morning. He had sometimes over 100 persons sleeping in the house at once. They paid for their beds and were asked no questions.

Edward Watkin, No. 881 of the City Police, said: I was on duty at Mitre Square on Saturday night. I have been in the force seventeen years. I went on duty at 9.45 upon my regular beat. That extends from Duke Street, Aldgate, through Heneage Lane, a portion of Bury Street, through Cree Lane, into Leadenhall Street, along eastward into Mitre Street, then into Mitre Square, round the square again into Mitre Street, then into King Street to St James's Place, round the place, then into Duke Street, where I started from.

That beat takes twelve or fourteen minutes. I had been patrolling the beat continually from ten o'clock at night until one o'clock on Sunday morning.

[Coroner] Had anything excited your attention during those hours? No.

[Coroner] Or any person? No. I passed through Mitre Square at 1.30 on the Sunday morning. I had my lantern alight and on fixed to my belt. According to my usual practice, I looked at the different passages and corners.

[Coroner] At half past one did anything excite your attention? No.

[Coroner] Did you see anyone about? No.

[Coroner] Could any people have been about that portion of the square without your seeing them? No. I next came into Mitre Square at 1.44, when I discovered the body lying on the right as I entered the square. The woman was on her back, with her feet towards the square.

Her clothes were thrown up. I saw her throat was cut and the stomach ripped open. She was lying in a pool of blood. I did not touch the body. I ran across to Kearley and Long's warehouse. The door was ajar and I pushed it open and called on the watchman Morris, who was inside. He came out.

I remained with the body until the arrival of Police-constable Holland. No one else was there before that but myself. Holland was followed by Dr Sequeira. Inspector Collard arrived about two o'clock and also Dr Brown, surgeon to the police force.

[Coroner] When you first saw the body did you hear any footsteps as if anybody were running away? No. The door of the warehouse to which I went was ajar, because the watchman was working about. It was no unusual thing for the door to be ajar at that hour of the morning.

By Mr Crawford: I was continually patrolling my beat from ten o'clock up to half-past one. I noticed nothing unusual up till 1.44, when I saw the body.

By the Coroner: I did not sound an alarm. We do not carry whistles.

By a Juror: My beat is not a double but a single beat. No other policeman comes into Mitre Street.

Frederick William Foster, of 26, Old Jewry, architect and surveyor, produced a plan which he had made of the place where the body was found and the district. From Berner Street to Mitre Street is three quarters of a mile and a man could walk the distance in twelve minutes.

Inspector Collard, of the City Police, said: At five minutes before two o'clock on Sunday morning last, I received information at Bishopsgate Street Police station that a woman had been murdered in Mitre Square. Information was at once telegraphed to headquarters. I dispatched a constable to Dr Gordon Brown, informing him and proceeded myself to Mitre Square, arriving there about two or three minutes past two.

There I found Dr Sequeira, two or three police officers and the deceased person lying in the south west corner of the square, in the position described by Constable Watkins. The body was not touched until the arrival shortly afterwards of Dr Brown. The medical gentlemen examined the body and in my presence Sergeant Jones picked up from the foot way by the left side of the deceased three small black buttons, such as are generally used for boots, a small metal button, a common metal thimble and a small penny mustard tin containing two pawn tickets.

They were handed to me. The doctors remained until the arrival of the ambulance and saw the body placed in the conveyance. It was then taken to the mortuary and stripped by Mr Davis, the mortuary keeper, in presence of the two doctors and myself. I have a list of articles of clothing more or less stained with blood and cut.

[Coroner] Was there any money about her? No; no money whatever was found. A piece of cloth was found in Goulston Street, corresponding with the apron worn by the deceased. When I got to the square, I took immediate steps to have the neighbourhood searched for the person who committed the murder. Mr M Williams, chief of the Detective Department, on arriving shortly afterwards sent men to search in all directions in Spitalfields, both in streets and lodging houses.

Several men were stopped and searched in the streets, without any good result. I have had a house-to-house inquiry made in the vicinity of Mitre Square as to any noises or whether persons were seen in the place but I have not been able to find any beyond the witnesses who saw a man and woman talking together.

Mr Crawford: When you arrived was the deceased in a pool of blood? The head, neck and, I imagine, the shoulders were lying in a pool of blood when she was first found but there was no blood in front. I did not touch the body myself but the doctor said it was warm.

[Crawford] Was there any sign of a struggle having taken place? None whatever. I made a careful inspection of the ground all round. There was no trace whatever of any struggle. There was nothing in the appearance of the woman, or of the clothes, to lead to the idea that there had been any struggle.

From the fact that the blood was in a liquid state I conjectured that the murder had not been long previously committed. In my opinion the body had not been there more than a quarter of an hour. I endeavoured to trace footsteps but could find no trace whatever. The backs of the empty houses adjoining were searched but nothing was found.

Dr Frederick Gordon Brown was then called and deposed: I am surgeon to the City of London Police. I was called shortly after two o'clock on Sunday morning and reached the place of the murder about twenty minutes past two. My attention was directed to the body of the deceased.

It was lying in the position described by Watkins, on its back, the head turned to the left shoulder, the arms by the side of the body, as if they had fallen there. Both palms were upwards, the fingers slightly bent. A thimble was lying near. The clothes were thrown up. The bonnet was at the back of the head. There was great disfigurement of the face. The throat was cut across.

Below the cut was a neckerchief. The upper part of the dress had been torn open. The body had been mutilated and was quite warm no rigor mortis. The crime must have been committed within half an hour or certainly within forty minutes from the time when I saw the body. There were no stains of blood on the bricks or pavement around.

By Mr Crawford: There was no blood on the front of the clothes. There was not a speck of blood on the front of the jacket.

By the Coroner: Before we removed the body Dr Phillips was sent for, as I wished him to see the wounds, he having been engaged in a case of a similar kind previously. He saw the body at the mortuary. The clothes were removed from the deceased carefully. I made a post-mortem examination on Sunday afternoon.

There was a bruise on the back of the left hand and one on the right shin but this had nothing to do with the crime. There were no bruises on the elbows or the back of the head. The face was very much mutilated, the eyelids, the nose, the jaw, the cheeks, the lips and the mouth all bore cuts. There were abrasions under the left ear. The throat was cut across to the extent of six or seven inches.

[Coroner] Can you tell us what the cause of death was? The cause of death was haemorrhage from the throat. Death must have been immediate.

[Coroner] There were other wounds on the lower part of the body? Yes; deep wounds, which were inflicted after death.

(Witness here described in detail the terrible mutilation of the deceased's body.)

Mr Crawford: I understand that you found certain portions of the body removed? Yes. The uterus was cut away with the exception of a small portion and the left kidney was also cut out. Both these organs were absent and have not been found.

[Coroner] Have you any opinion as to what position the woman was in when the wounds were inflicted? In my opinion the woman must have been lying down. The way in which the kidney was cut out showed that it was done by somebody who knew what he was about.

[Coroner] Does the nature of the wounds lead you to any conclusion as to the instrument that was used? It must have been a sharp-pointed knife and I should say at least 6 in. long.

[Coroner] Would you consider that the person who inflicted the wounds possessed anatomical skill? He must have had a good deal of knowledge as to the position of the abdominal organs and the way to remove them.

[Coroner] Would the parts removed be of any use for professional purposes? None whatever.

[Coroner] Would the removal of the kidney, for example, require special knowledge? It would require a good deal of knowledge as to its position, because it is apt to be overlooked, being covered by a membrane.

[Coroner] Would such knowledge be likely to be possessed by someone accustomed to cutting up animals? Yes.

[Coroner] Have you been able to form any opinion as to whether the perpetrator of this act was disturbed? I think he had sufficient time but it was in all probability done in a hurry.

[Coroner] How long would it take to make the wounds? It might be done in five minutes. It might take him longer; but that is the least time it could be done in.

[Coroner] Can you, as a professional man, ascribe any reason for the taking away of the parts you have mentioned? I cannot give any reason whatever.

[Coroner] Have you any doubt in your own mind whether there was a struggle? I feel sure there was no struggle. I see no reason to doubt that it was the work of one man.

[Coroner] Would any noise be heard, do you think? I presume the throat was instantly severed, in which case there would not be time to emit any sound.

[Coroner] Does it surprise you that no sound was heard? No.

[Coroner] Would you expect to find much blood on the person inflicting these wounds? No, I should not. I should say that the abdominal wounds were inflicted by a person kneeling at the right side of the body. The wounds could not possibly have been self-inflicted.

[Coroner] Was your attention called to the portion of the apron that was found in Goulston Street? Yes. I fitted that portion which was spotted with blood to the remaining portion, which was still attached by the strings to the body.

[Coroner] Have you formed any opinion as to the motive for the mutilation of the face? It was to disfigure the corpse, I should imagine.

A Juror: Was there any evidence of a drug having been used? I have not examined the stomach as to that. The contents of the stomach have been preserved for analysis.

Mr Crawford said he was glad to announce that the Corporation had unanimously approved the offer by the Lord Mayor of a reward of £500 for the discovery of the murderer. Several jurymen expressed their satisfaction at the promptness with which the offer was made.

The inquest was then adjourned.

Day 2, Thursday, 11 October 1888.
The Daily Telegraph, 12 October 1888.

Yesterday [11th Oct], at the City Coroner's Court, Golden Lane, Mr S. F. Langham resumed the inquest respecting the death of Catherine Eddowes, who was found murdered and mutilated in Mitre Square, Aldgate, early on the morning of Sunday, 30th Sept.

Mr Crawford, City Solicitor, again watched the case on behalf of the police.

Dr G. W. Sequeira, surgeon, of No. 34, Jewry Street, Aldgate, deposed: On the morning of 30th Sept, I was called to Mitre Square and I arrived at five minutes to two o'clock, being the first medical man on the scene of the murder. I saw the position of the body and I entirely agree with the evidence of Dr Gordon Brown in that respect.

By Mr Crawford: I am well acquainted with the locality and the position of the lamps in the square. Where the murder was committed was probably the darkest part of the square but there was sufficient light to enable the miscreant to perpetrate the deed. I think that the murderer had no design on any particular organ of the body. He was not possessed of any great anatomical skill.

[Coroner] Can you account for the absence of noise? The death must have been instantaneous after the severance of the windpipe and the blood vessels.

[Coroner] Would you have expected the murderer to be bespattered with blood? Not necessarily.

[Coroner] How long do you believe life had been extinct when you arrived? Very few minutes probably not more than a quarter of an hour.

Mr William Sedgwick Saunders, medical officer of health for the City, said: I received the stomach of the deceased from Dr Gordon Brown, carefully sealed and I made an analysis of the contents, which had not been interfered with in any way. I looked more particularly for poisons of the narcotic class but with negative results, there being not the faintest trace of any of those or any other poisons.

Annie Phillips stated: I reside at No 12, Dilston Road, Southwark Park Road and am married, my husband being a lamp black packer. I am daughter of the deceased, who formerly lived with my father. She always told me that she was married to him but I have never seen the marriage lines. My father's name was Thomas Conway.

The Coroner: Have you seen him lately? Not for the last fifteen or eighteen months.

[Coroner] Where was he living then? He was living with me and my husband, at No 15, Acre Street Southwark Park Road.

[Coroner] What calling did he follow? That of a hawker.

[Coroner] What became of him? I do not know.

[Coroner] Did he leave on good terms with you? Not on very good terms.

[Coroner] Did he say that he would never see you again, or anything of that sort? No.

[Coroner] Was he a sober man? He was a teetotaller.

[Coroner] Did he live on bad terms with your mother? Yes, because she used to drink.

[Coroner] Have you any idea where Conway is now? Not the least. He ceased to live with Eddowes entirely on account of her drinking habits.

[Coroner] Your father was in the 18th Royal Irish Regiment? So I have been told. He had been a pensioner ever since I was eight years old. I am twenty three now. They parted about seven or eight years ago.

[Coroner] Did your mother ever apply to you for money? Yes.

[Coroner] When did you last see her? Two years and one month ago.

[Coroner] Where did you live when you last saw her? In King Street Bermondsey.

[Coroner] Have you any brothers or sisters by Conway? Two brothers.

[Coroner] Where are they living? In London.

[Coroner] Did your mother know where to find either of you? No.

[Coroner] Were your addresses purposely kept from her? Yes.

[Coroner] To prevent her applying for money.

The Foreman: Was your father aware when he left you that your mother was living with Kelly? Yes.

Mr Crawford: Are you quite certain that your father was a pensioner of the 18th Royal Irish? I was told so but I am not sure whether it was the 18th or the Connaught Rangers. It may have been the latter.

The Coroner: That is the 18th I do not know.

Mr Crawford: That is so. It so happens that there is a pensioner of the name of Conway belonging to the Royal Irish but that is not the man.

To witness: When did your mother last receive money from you?

Witness: Just over two years ago. She waited upon me in my confinement and I paid her for it.

[Coroner] Did you ever get a letter from her? No.

[Coroner] Do you know anything about Kelly? I have seen him two or three times at the lodging house in Flower and Dean Street, with my mother.

[Coroner] When did you last see them together? About three years and a half ago.

[Coroner] You knew they were living together as man and wife? Yes.

[Coroner] Is it the fact that your father is living with your two brothers? He was.

[Coroner] Where are your brothers residing now? I do not know.

[Coroner] He was always with them. One was fifteen and the other eighteen years of age.

[Coroner] When did you last see them? About eighteen months ago. I have not seen them since.

[Coroner] Are we to understand that you had lost all trace of your mother, father and two brothers for at least eighteen months? That is so.

Detective-Sergeant John Mitchell, of the City police, said: I have, under instructions and with other officers, made every endeavour to find the father and brothers of the last witness but without success up to the present.

The Coroner: Have you found a pensioner named Conway belonging to the 18th Royal Irish? I have. He has not been identified as the husband of the deceased.

Detective Baxter Hunt: Acting under instructions, I discovered the pensioner, Conway, of the Royal Irish and have confronted him with two sisters of the deceased, who, however, failed to recognise him as the man who used to live with the deceased. I have made every endeavour to trace the Thomas Conway in question and the brothers of Annie Phillips but without success.

A Juror: Why did you not confront this Conway with the daughter of the deceased, Annie Phillips? That witness had not been found then.

Mr Crawford: The theory has been put forward that it was possible for the deceased to have been murdered elsewhere and her body brought to where it was found. I should like to ask Dr Gordon Brown, who is present, what his opinion is about that.

Dr Gordon Brown: I do not think there is any foundation for such a theory. The blood on the left side was clotted and must have fallen at the time the throat was cut. I do not think that the deceased moved the least bit after that.

The Coroner: The body could not have been carried to where it was found?
Witness: Oh, no.

City constable Lewis Robinson, 931, deposed: At half past eight, on the night of Saturday, 29th Sept, while on duty in High Street, Aldgate, I saw a crowd of persons outside No 29, surrounding a woman whom I have since recognised as the deceased.

The Coroner: What state was she in? Drunk. Lying on the footway? Yes. I asked the crowd if any of them knew her or where she lived but got no answer. I then picked her up and sat her against the shutters but she fell down sideways.

With the aid of a fellow constable, I took her to Bishopsgate Police-station. There she was asked her name and she replied 'Nothing'. She was then put into a cell.

[Coroner] Did any one appear to be in her company when you found her? No one in particular.

Mr Crawford: Did any one appear to know her? No. The apron being produced, torn and discoloured with blood, the witness said that to the best of his knowledge it was the apron the deceased was wearing.

The Foreman: What guided you in determining whether the woman was drunk or not?

Witness: Her appearance.

The Foreman: I ask you because I know of a case in which a person was arrested for being drunk who had not tasted anything intoxicating for eight or nine hours.

[Coroner] You are quite sure this woman was drunk? She smelt very strongly of drink.

Sergeant James Byfield, of the City Police: I remember the deceased being brought to the Bishopsgate Station at a quarter to nine o'clock on the night of Saturday, 29th Sept.

[Coroner] In what condition was she? Very drunk. She was brought in supported by two constables and placed in a cell, where she remained until one o'clock the next morning, when she had got sober. I then discharged her, after she had given her name and address.

[Coroner] What name and address did she give? Mary Ann Kelly, No 6, Fashion Street, Spitalfields.

[Coroner] Did she say where she had been, or what she had been doing? She stated that she had been hopping.

Constable George Henry Hutt, 968, City Police: I am gaoler at Bishopsgate station. On the night of Saturday, 29th Sept, at a quarter to ten o'clock, I took over our prisoners, among them the deceased. I visited her several times until five minutes to one on Sunday morning. The inspector, being out visiting, I was directed by Sergeant Byfield to see if any of the prisoners were fit to be discharged.

I found the deceased sober and after she had given her name and address, she was allowed to leave. I pushed open the swing door leading to the passage and said, 'This way, missus.' She passed along the passage to the outer door. I said to her, 'Please, pull it to.' She replied, 'All right. Good night, old cock.'

(Laughter) She pulled the door to within a foot of being close and I saw her turn to the left.

The Coroner: That was leading towards Houndsditch? Yes.

The Foreman: Is it left to you to decide when a prisoner is sober enough to be released or not? Not to me but to the inspector or acting inspector on duty.

[Coroner] Is it usual to discharge prisoners who have been locked up for being drunk at all hours of the night? Certainly.

[Coroner] How often did you visit the prisoners? About every half hour. At first the deceased remained asleep; but at a quarter to twelve she was awake and singing a song to herself, as it were. I went to her again at half past twelve and she then asked when she would be able to get out. I replied: 'Shortly.' She said, 'I am capable of taking care of myself now.'

Mr Crawford: Did she tell you where she was going? No. About two minutes to one o'clock, when I was taking her out of the cell, she asked me what time it was. I answered, 'Too late for you to get any more drink.'

She said, 'Well, what time is it?'

I replied, 'Just on one.'

Thereupon she said, 'I shall get a fine hiding when I get home, then.'

[Coroner] Was that her parting remark? That was in the station yard. I said, 'Serve you right; you have no right to get drunk.'

[Coroner] You supposed she was going home? I did.

[Coroner] In your opinion is that the apron the deceased was wearing? To the best of my belief it is.

[Coroner] What is the distance from Mitre Square to your station? About 400 yards.

[Coroner] Do you know the direct route to Flower and Dean Street? No.

A Juror: Do you search persons who are brought in for drunkenness? No but we take from them anything that might be dangerous. I loosened the things round the deceased's neck and I then saw a white wrapper and a red silk handkerchief.

George James Morris, night watchman at Messrs. Kearley and Tonges tea warehouse, Mitre Square, deposed: On Saturday, 29th Sept, I went on duty at seven o'clock in the evening. I occupied most of my time in cleaning the offices and looking about the warehouse.

The Coroner: What happened about a quarter to two in the morning? Constable Watkins, who was on the Mitre Square beat, knocked at my door, which was slightly ajar at the time. I was then sweeping the steps down towards the door. The door was pushed when I was about two yards off. I turned round and opened the door wide.

The constable said, 'For God's sake mate, come to my assistance.'

I said, 'Stop till I get my lamp. What is the matter?'

"Oh, dear," he exclaimed, "here is another woman cut to pieces!"

I asked where and he replied, 'In the corner.' I went into the corner of the square and turned my light on the body. I agree with the previous witnesses as to the position of the body. I ran up Mitre Street into Aldgate, blowing my whistle all the while.

[Coroner] Did you see any suspicious persons about? No. Two constables came up and asked what the matter was. I told them to go down to Mitre Square, as there was another terrible murder. They went and I followed and took charge of my own premises again.

[Coroner] Before being called by Constable Watkins, had you heard any noise in the square? No.

[Coroner] If there had been any cry of distress, would you have heard it from where you were? Yes.

By the Jury: I was in the warehouse facing the corner of the square.

By Mr Crawford: Before being called I had no occasion to go into the square. I did not go there between one and two o'clock; of that I am certain. There was nothing unusual in my door being open and my being at work at so late an hour. I had not seen Watkins before during the night. I do not think my door had been ajar more than two or three minutes when he knocked.

James Harvey, City constable, 964: On the night of Saturday, 29th Sept, I was on duty in the neighbourhood of Houndsditch and Aldgate. I was there at the time of the murder but did not see any one nor hear any cry. When I got into Aldgate, returning towards Duke Street, I heard a whistle and saw the witness Morris with a lamp.

I asked him what was the matter and he told me that a woman had been ripped up in Mitre Square. Together with Constable Hollins I went to Mitre Square, where Watkins was by the side of the body of the deceased. Hollins went for Dr Sequeira and a private individual was dispatched for other constables, who arrived almost immediately, having heard the whistle. I waited with Watkins and information was sent to the inspector.

[Coroner] At what time previous to that were you in Aldgate? At twenty-eight minutes past one o'clock I passed the post-office clock.

George Clapp, caretaker at No 5, Mitre Street, deposed: The back part of the house looks into Mitre Square. On the night of Saturday week last, I retired to rest in the back room on the second floor about eleven o'clock.

The Coroner: During the night did you hear any disturbance in the square? No.

[Coroner] When did you first learn that a murder had been perpetrated? Between five and six o'clock in the morning.

By Mr Crawford: A nurse, who was in attendance upon my wife, was sleeping at the top of the house. No person slept either on the ground floor or the first floor.

Constable Richard Pearce, 922 City: I reside at No 3, Mitre Square. There are only two private houses in the square. I retired to rest at twenty minutes past twelve on the morning of last Sunday week.

[Coroner] Did you hear any noise in the square? None at all. When did you first hear of the murder? At twenty past two, when I was called by a constable.

[Coroner] From your bedroom window could you see the spot where the murder was committed? Yes, quite plainly.

By Mr Crawford: My wife and family were in no way disturbed during the night.

Joseph Lawende: I reside at No. 45, Norfolk Road Dalston and am a commercial traveller. On the night of 29th Sept, I was at the Imperial Club, Duke Street, together with Mr Joseph Levy and Mr Harry Harris. It was raining and we sat in the club till half past one o'clock, when we left. I observed a man and woman together at the corner of Church passage, Duke Street, leading to Mitre Square.

The Coroner: Were they talking? The woman was standing with her face towards the man and I only saw her back. She had one hand on his breast. He was the taller. She had on a black jacket and bonnet. I have seen the articles at the police station and believe them to be those the deceased was wearing.

[Coroner] What sort of man was this? He had on a cloth cap with a peak of the same.

Mr Crawford: Unless the jury wish it, I do not think further particulars should be given as to the appearance of this man.

The Foreman: The jury do not desire it.

Mr Crawford (to witness): You have given a description of the man to the police? Yes.

[Coroner] Would you know him again? I doubt it. The man and woman were about nine or ten feet away from me. I have no doubt it was half past one o'clock when we rose to leave the club, so that it would be twenty five minutes to two o'clock when we passed the man and woman.

[Coroner] Did you overhear anything that either said? No.

[Coroner] Did either appear in an angry mood? No.

[Coroner] Did anything about their movements attract your attention? No. The man looked rather rough and shabby.

[Coroner] When the woman placed her hand on the man's breast, did she do it as if to push him away? No; it was done very quietly.

[Coroner] You were not curious enough to look back and see where they went. No.

Mr Joseph Hyam Levy, the butcher in Hutcheson Street, Aldgate, stated: I was with the last witness at the Imperial Club on Saturday night, 29th Sept, We got up to leave at half past one on Sunday morning and came out three or four minutes later. I saw a man and woman standing at the corner of Church passage but I did not take any notice of them. I passed on, thinking they were up to no good at so late an hour.

[Coroner] What height was the man? I should think he was three inches taller than the woman, who was, perhaps, 5ft high. I cannot give any further description of them. I went down Duke Street into Aldgate, leaving them still talking together.

By the Jury: The point in the passage where the man and woman were standing was not well lighted. On the contrary, I think it was badly lighted then but the light is much better now.

By Mr Crawford: Nothing in what I saw excited my suspicion as to the intentions of the man. I did not hear a word that he uttered to the woman.

[Coroner] Your fear was rather about yourself? Not exactly. (Laughter)

Constable Alfred Long, 254 A, Metropolitan police: I was on duty in Goulston Street, Whitechapel, on Sunday morning, 30th Sept and about five minutes to three o'clock, I found a portion of a white apron (produced). There were recent stains of blood on it.

The apron was lying in the passage leading to the staircase of Nos. 106 to 119, a model dwelling house. Above on the wall was written in chalk, 'The Jews are the men that will not be blamed for nothing.'

I at once searched the staircase and areas of the building but did not find anything else. I took the apron to Commercial Road Police station and reported to the inspector on duty.

[Coroner] Had you been past that spot previously to your discovering the apron? I passed about twenty minutes past two o'clock.

[Coroner] Are you able to say whether the apron was there then?-It was not.

Mr Crawford: As to the writing on the wall, have you not put a 'not' in the wrong place? Were not the words, 'The Jews are not the men that will be blamed for nothing'? I believe the words were as I have stated.

[Coroner] Was not the word 'Jews' spelt 'Juwes'? It may have been.

[Coroner] Yet you did not tell us that in the first place. Did you make an entry of the words at the time? Yes, in my pocket-book. Is it possible that you have put the 'not' in the wrong place? It is possible but I do not think that I have.

[Coroner] Which did you notice first the piece of apron or the writing on the wall? The piece of apron, one corner of which was wet with blood.

[Coroner] How come you to observe the writing on the wall? I saw it while trying to discover whether there were any marks of blood about.

[Coroner] Did the writing appear to have been recently done? I could not form an opinion.

[Coroner] Do I understand that you made a search in the model dwelling-house? I went into the staircases.

[Coroner] Did you not make inquiries in the house itself? No.

The Foreman: Where is the pocket-book in which you made the entry of the writing? At Westminster.

[Coroner] Is it possible to get it at once? I dare say.

Mr Crawford: I will ask the coroner to direct that the book be fetched.

The Coroner: Let that be done.

Daniel Halse, detective officer, City police: On Saturday, 29th Sept, pursuant to instructions received at the central office in Old Jewry, I directed a number of police in plain clothes to patrol the streets of the City all night. At two minutes to two o'clock on the Sunday morning, when near Aldgate Church, in company with Detectives Outram and Marriott, I heard that a woman had been found murdered in Mitre Square.

We ran to the spot and I at once gave instructions for the neighbourhood to be searched and every man stopped and examined. I myself went by way of Middlesex Street into Wentworth Street, where I stopped two men, who, however, gave a satisfactory account of themselves. I came through Goulston Street about twenty minutes past two and then returned to Mitre Square, subsequently going to the mortuary.

I saw the deceased and noticed that a portion of her apron was missing. I accompanied Major Smith back to Mitre Square, when we heard that a piece of apron had been found in Goulston Street. After visiting Leman Street police station, I proceeded to Goulston Street, where I saw some chalk-writing on the black fascia of the wall.

Instructions were given to have the writing photographed but before it could be done the Metropolitan police stated that they thought the writing might cause a riot or outbreak against the Jews and it was decided to have it rubbed out, as the people were already bringing out their stalls into the street.

When Detective Hunt returned inquiry was made at every door of every tenement of the model dwelling house but we gained no tidings of any one who was likely to have been the murderer.

By Mr Crawford: At twenty minutes past two o'clock, I passed over the spot where the piece of apron was found but did not notice anything then. I should not necessarily have seen the piece of apron.

[Coroner] As to the writing on the wall, did you hear anybody suggest that the word 'Jews' should be rubbed out and the other words left? I did. The fear on the part of the Metropolitan police that the writing might cause riot was the sole reason why it was rubbed out. I took a copy of it and what I wrote down was as follows:

'The Juwes are not the men who will be blamed for nothing.'

[Coroner] Did the writing have the appearance of having been recently done? Yes. It was written with white chalk on a black fascia.

The Foreman: Why was the writing really rubbed out?

Witness: The Metropolitan police said it might create a riot and it was their ground.

Mr Crawford: I am obliged to ask this question. Did you protest against the writing being rubbed out?

Witness: I did. I asked that it might, at all events, be allowed to remain until Major Smith had seen it. Why do you say that it seemed to have been recently written? It looked fresh and if it had been done long before it would have been rubbed out by the people passing. I did not notice whether there was any powdered chalk on the ground, though I did look about to see if a knife could be found.

There were three lines of writing in a good schoolboy's round hand. The size of the capital letters would be about 3/4 in and the other letters were in proportion. The writing was on the black bricks, which formed a kind of dado, the bricks above being white.

Mr Crawford: With the exception of a few questions to Long, the Metropolitan constable, that is the whole of the evidence I have to offer at the present moment on the part of the City police. But if any point occurs to the coroner or the jury I shall be happy to endeavour to have it cleared up.

A Juror: It seems surprising that a policeman should have found the piece of apron in the passage of the buildings and yet made no inquiries in the buildings themselves. There was a clue up to that point and then it was altogether lost.

Mr Crawford: As to the premises being searched, I have in court members of the City police who did make diligent search in every part of the tenements the moment the matter came to their knowledge. But unfortunately it did not come to their knowledge until two hours after. There was thus delay and the man who discovered the piece of apron is a member of the Metropolitan police.

A Juror: It is the man belonging to the Metropolitan police that I am complaining of.

At this point Constable Long returned and produced the pocket-book containing the entry which he made at the time concerning the discovery of the writing on the wall.

Mr Crawford: What is the entry?

Witness: The words are, 'The Jews are the men that will not be blamed for nothing.'

[Coroner] Both here and in your inspector's report the word 'Jews' is spelt correctly? Yes; but the inspector remarked that the word was spelt 'Juwes'.

[Coroner] Why did you write 'Jews' then? I made my entry before the inspector made the remark.

[Coroner] But why did the inspector write 'Jews'? I cannot say.

[Coroner] At all events, there is a discrepancy? It would seem so.

[Coroner] What did you do when you found the piece of apron? I at once searched the staircases leading to the buildings.

[Coroner] Did you make inquiry in any of the tenements of the buildings? No.

[Coroner] How many staircases are there? Six or seven.

[Coroner] And you searched every staircase? Every staircase to the top.

[Coroner] You found no trace of blood or of recent footmarks? No.

[Coroner] About what time was that? Three o'clock.

[Coroner] Having examined the staircases, what did you next do? I proceeded to the station.

[Coroner] Before going did you hear that a murder had been committed? Yes. It is common knowledge that two murders have been perpetrated.

[Coroner] Which did you hear of? I heard of the murder in the City. There were rumours of another but not certain.

[Coroner] When you went away did you leave anybody in charge? Yes; the constable on the next beat 190, H Division but I do not know his name.

[Coroner] Did you give him instructions as to what he was to do? I told him to keep observation on the dwelling house and see if any one entered or left.

[Coroner] When did you return? About five o'clock.

[Coroner] Had the writing been rubbed out then? No; it was rubbed out in my presence at half past five.

[Coroner] Did you hear any one object to its being rubbed out? No. It was nearly daylight when it was rubbed out.

A Juror: Having examined the apron and the writing, did it not occur to you that it would be wise to search the dwelling? I did what I thought was right under the circumstances.

The Juror: I do not wish to say anything to reflect upon you, because I consider that altogether the evidence of the police redounds to their credit but it does seem strange that this clue was not followed up.

Witness: I thought the best thing to do was to proceed to the station and report to the inspector on duty.

The Juror: I am sure you did what you deemed best.

Mr Crawford: I suppose you thought it more likely to find the body there than the murderer?

Witness: Yes and I felt that the inspector would be better able to deal with the matter than I was.

The Foreman: Was there any possibility of a stranger escaping from the house? Not from the front.

[Coroner] Did you not know about the back? No, that was the first time I had been on duty there.

That being all the evidence forthcoming the coroner said he considered a further adjournment unnecessary and the better plan would be for the jury to return their verdict and then leave the matter in the hands of the police. In summing up, it would not be at all necessary for him to go through the testimony of the various witnesses but if the jury wanted their memories refreshed on any particular point he would assist them by referring to the evidence on that point.

That the crime was a most fiendish one could not for a moment be doubted, for the miscreant, not satisfied with taking a defenceless woman's life, endeavoured so to mutilate the body as to render it unrecognisable. He [Coroner] presumed that the jury would return a verdict of wilful murder against some person or persons unknown and then the police could freely pursue their inquiries and follow up any clue they might obtain.

A magnificent reward had been offered and that might be the means of setting people on the track and bringing to speedy justice the creature who had committed this atrocious crime. On reflection, perhaps it would be sufficient to return a verdict of wilful murder against some person unknown, in as much as the medical evidence conclusively demonstrated that only one person could be implicated.

The jury at once returned a verdict accordingly. The coroner, for himself and the jury, thanked Mr Crawford and the police for the assistance they had rendered in the inquiry.

Mr Crawford: The police have simply done their duty.

The Coroner: I am quite sure of that.

The jury having presented their fees to Annie Phillips, daughter of the deceased, the proceedings terminated.

Chapter Fourteen
The Emma Smith Inquest

Day of inquest, Saturday, 7 April 1888.
The Times, Monday, 9 April 1888.

Mr Wynne E. Baxter, the East Middlesex Coroner, held an inquiry on Saturday [7th Apr] at the London Hospital respecting the death of Emma Elizabeth Smith, aged 45, a widow, lately living at 18, George Street, Spitalfields, who, it was alleged, had been murdered.

Chief Inspector West, of the H Division of Police, attended for the Commissioners of Police.

Mrs Mary Russell, deputy keeper of a common lodging house, stated that she had known the deceased for about two years. On the evening of Bank Holiday 2nd April she left home at 7 o'clock and returned about 4 or 5 the next morning in a dreadful state. Her face and head were much injured, one of her ears being nearly torn off.

She told the witness that she had been set upon and robbed of all her money. She also complained of pains in the lower part of the body. Witness took her to the hospital and when passing along Osborne Street, the deceased pointed out the spot where she was assaulted. She said there were three men but she could not describe them.

Mr George Haslip, house surgeon, stated that when the deceased was admitted to the hospital she had been drinking but was not intoxicated. She was bleeding from the head and ear and had other injuries of a revolting nature. Witness found that she was suffering from rupture of the peritoneum, which had been perforated by some blunt instrument used with great force.

The deceased told him that at half past 1 that morning she was passing near Whitechapel Church when she noticed some men coming towards her. She crossed the road to avoid them but they followed, assaulted her, took all the money she had and then committed the outrage.

She was unable to say what kind of instrument was used, nor could she describe her assailants, except that she said that one was a youth of 19. Death ensued on Wednesday morning 4th April through peritonitis set up by the injuries. Margaret Hayes, living at the same address as the deceased, deposed to seeing Mrs Smith in company with a man at the corner of Farrant Street and Burdett Road.

The man was dressed in a dark suit and wore a white silk handkerchief round his neck. He was of medium height but witness did not think she could identify him. Chief Inspector West, H Division, stated that he had no official information on the subject and was only aware of the case through the daily papers.

He had questioned the constables on the beat but none of them appeared to know anything about the matter. The Coroner said The Coroner said that from the medical evidence, which must be true, it was clear that the woman had been barbarously murdered. It was impossible to imagine a more brutal and dastardly assault and he thought the ends of justice would be better met by the jury recording their verdict at once than by adjourning to some future date in the hope of having more evidence brought before them.

The jury returned a verdict of 'Wilful murder against some person or persons unknown.' The police are making every possible inquiry into the case but up to yesterday 8th April had not any clue to the persons who committed the outrage.

Only Day of inquest, Saturday, 7 April 1888.
Lloyd's Weekly Newspaper, Sunday, 8 April 1888.

Mr Wynne Baxter held an inquiry yesterday morning 7th April at the London hospital into the terrible circumstances attending the death of an unfortunate, named Emma E. Smith, who was assaulted in the most brutal manner early on Tuesday morning last, 3rd April in the neighbourhood of Osborn Street, Whitechapel, by several men.

Mary Russell, (the first witness), the deputy keeper of a lodging house in George Street, Spitalfields, deposed to the statement made by the deceased on the way to the London hospital, to which she was taken between four and five o'clock on Tuesday morning [3rd Apr].

The deceased told her she had been shockingly maltreated by a number of men and robbed of all the money she had. Her face was bleeding and her ear was cut. She did not describe the men but said one was a young man of about 19. She also pointed out where the outrage occurred, as they passed the spot, which was near the cocoa factory (Taylor's).

Dr Hellier [Haslip], (The house surgeon on duty), described the internal injuries which had been caused and which must have been inflicted by a blunt instrument. It had even penetrated the peritoneum, producing peritonitis, which was undoubtedly the cause of death, in his opinion. The woman appeared to know what she was about but she had probably had some drink.

Her statement to the surgeon as to the circumstances was similar to that already given in evidence. He had made a post-mortem examination and described the organs as generally normal. He had no doubt that death was caused by the injuries to the perineum, the abdomen and the peritoneum. Great force must have been used.

The injuries had set up peritonitis, which resulted in death on the following day after admission on the 4th April. Another woman [Hayes] gave evidence that she had last seen Emma Smith between midnight and 1am on Tuesday morning 3rd April she was seen talking to a man in a black dress, wearing a white neckerchief.

It was near Farrant Street, Burdett Road. She was hurrying away from the neighbourhood, as she had herself been struck in the mouth a few minutes before by some young men. She did not believe that the man talking to Smith was one of them. The quarter was a fearfully rough one. Just before Christmas last, she had been injured by men under circumstances of a similar nature and was a fortnight in the infirmary.

Mr Chief Inspector West, H division, said he had made inquiries of all the constables on duty on the night of the 2nd and 3rd April in the Whitechapel Road.

The jury returned a verdict of 'Wilful murder against some person or persons unknown.'

Only Day of inquest, Saturday, 7 April 1888.
East London Advertiser, Saturday, 14 April 1888.

On Saturday [7th Apr] the East Middlesex coroner [Baxter] held an inquiry at the London Hospital, Whitechapel, on the body of Emma Elizabeth Smith, aged 45, a widow, who was brutally assaulted when returning home along the Whitechapel Road on Bank Holiday night.

Mary Russell, the deputy of a common lodging house at which the deceased had been a lodger for some months, said that on Bank Holiday [2nd Apr] the deceased left the house in the evening, apparently in good health. She returned between 4 and 5 o'clock the next morning [3rd Apr] and she had been shockingly treated by some men.

Her face was bleeding and she said that she was also injured about the lower part of the body. The deceased had often come home with black eyes that men had given her. Mr George Haslip, house surgeon, deposed that the deceased was admitted suffering from severe injuries, which he thought had been caused by some blunt instrument.

She had been drinking but was not intoxicated. She had a ruptured perineum of very recent date and also some bruises on her head. Her right ear was torn and bleeding. She told witness that at 1.30am that morning she was going by Whitechapel Church when she saw some men coming and she crossed the road to get out of their way but they followed her.

They assaulted her and robbed her of all the money she had. She could not describe the men, except that one looked a youth of 19. After her admission, she gradually sank and died two days later on 5th April. The deceased stated that she had not seen any of her friends for 10 years.

The Coroner said from the medical evidence it was clear that the woman had been barbarously murdered. Such a dastardly assault he had never heard of and it was impossible to imagine a more brutal case.

The jury returned a verdict of wilful murder against some person unknown.

The following inquest was covered by three different newspapers. I have given you all three reports to compare how different papers reported news back in the 1800s.

The Conclusion

As you have read, all the inquests have returned a verdict of wilful murder by person or persons unknown. And it is believed by most that Alice Mackenzie was the sixth Ripper victim as her injuries were the same or as near as the other five victims. Having heard statements from witnesses in the inquests and reading about their upbringing for at least 5 of the 6 murdered women, finding out the life of the victims is very clear in most cases, we know how they lived their lives, through poverty and working on the streets.

It seems that the women came from fairly well-off families with working parents and siblings, they were women of at least some education able to read and write, the path they took in later life was strictly down to them only, it was their own decision to leave their husbands families and lead a life of drink and prostitution or can you judge what a person should do in a life of poor living conditions and poverty.

The murders were unprovoked and were well thought out for the following reason's, firstly the murderer would have to know how a police officer walked his beat and how long his beat would take, unless this was known the murderer could have easily been caught in the act of his or her crimes. Or was it that he or she got the adrenalin rush from the thought that they might get caught. Did he or she know that there would be no persons around at the time of the killings?

Probably, I very much doubt it was just a random act of savagery a spur of the moment thing. The victims would have been led to their final destination by the murderer. Was it done by a surgeon maybe, a butcher, could have but would a butcher know how to remove the organs of a human? Probably, maybe it was a butcher and he used the organs to sell in a butcher's shop, just as the fictional character Sweeny Todd the Demon barber of Fleet Street used human organs for pie fillings back in the late 1700s.

Sound's grotesque I know but it could have happened. Back to the Ripper mystery, if you have seen the Whitechapel murders on TV it is a spin off, of

Ripper Street, set in modern day London's East End all murders are based on the Ripper cases re-enacted. As I was watching it I got to thinking, as these are based on the Ripper, the murderer in the programme who was nearly caught but got away worked in the London Hospital, so I got to thinking was the murderer someone who worked in what was known then as the casual ward in the London Hospital, where prostitutes and other less fortunate persons would stay if they could not afford lodgings elsewhere.

This is one theory that has never been approached by researchers, doctors yes but a person who worked on a ward for the less fortunate people of the East End. The Ripper was and will be the most successful serial killer to ever live and not get caught and would never be named. Theories about who he was from modern day forensics are all hearsay. It will never be known as to the identity of the ripper, I think that Jack the Ripper is wrong to call a person that, when no one knows if it was a man, woman.

So the Whitechapel murderer from 1888 was a mystery beyond anyone's imagination. As to why these murders were committed in the first place is also a question to be answered, what was the reason behind the killings, why did they suddenly stop, there seems to be more questions than answers into these murders with no outcome as to the truth behind any of the questions that have been asked.

So a couple of theories, was the murderer scorned by a women he or she wanted to be with? Was the murderer given a sexual disease and then wanted to rant his anger on prostitutes? But then why did they suddenly stop in November? Was this person truly a sailor or traveller from overseas? We have had the best forensic experts and criminologists trying to work out who the murderer was but they can only come up with theories.

We have even had American's excavating a body of an ancestor trying to prove that they are descendants of the Whitechapel murderer. All have failed to given cast iron evidence that their findings are proof of the murderer's identity. After reading this book I leave it up to you the reader to come to your own conclusion as to who you think is the Whitechapel murderer.

But my own opinion is that coming from the East End myself, born and raised in Bethnal Green, the Whitechapel murders will never be solved as to the identity of the killer, this is what you might call the perfect murder in 1888 and yet it is thought that something like this could never happen the perfect murder. This person brutally murdered on the Streets of London at night never to be seen or caught and remember that it took less than 5 minutes to commit each murder and leave not only the scene but also the area.

There is only one question that confuses me. Why did the Ripper kill Mary Jane Kelly in her home and not in the street, like all the other victims? There would be no adrenalin rush for the murderer to kill inside a house where there would be no chance they could get caught. It also seems that a serial killer had changed the way to murder their victims.

Was she really killed by the Ripper or was she killed by a copycat killer? 5 women killed on the streets and one inside a house, it seems that a leopard can change its spots. And serial killers can change the way they murder, although it is said that serial killers never change the way they kill their victims, but this killer has, not in the sense of the way he killed them but where he killed them.

Do you have a theory? Share your thoughts and join the discussion on who was behind the crime. Visit the website below and see if you can solve the mystery.

theripperpuzzle.com